LIVING A LIE

"Carol . . ." He moved toward her, his eyes and arms supplicating, but she evaded his embrace.

"No, Jeffrey. I'm sorry, but you'll have to give me time to think about this. It's not just a slip you made, something that happened once or twice while you were drunk or despondent. I wish it were, there wouldn't be these human complications. But you had an affair, Jeff. A love affair, and a child, and you've been living a lie with me. Maybe our whole marriage was a lie, a masquerade."

Books by Patricia Gallagher
from Berkley and Jove

ON WINGS OF DREAMS
A PERFECT LOVE

PATRICIA GALLAGHER

A PERFECT LOVE

JOVE BOOKS, NEW YORK

A PERFECT LOVE

A Jove Book / published by arrangement with
the author

PRINTING HISTORY
Jove edition / September 1987

ISBN: 0-515-08842-0

Jove Books are published by The Berkley Publishing Group,
200 Madison Avenue, New York, NY 10016.
The words ''JOVE'' and the ''J'' logo
are trademarks belonging to Jove Publications, Inc.

PRINTED IN THE UNITED STATES OF AMERICA

10 9 8 7 6 5 4 3 2 1

*For every woman
who ever sent a man
off to war . . .*

Part One

Cross that rules the Southern Sky!
Stars that sweep, and turn, and fly,
Hear the Lovers' Litany:—
"Love like ours can never die!"

Rudyard Kipling (1865–1936)
The Lovers' Litany

1

Ordinarily Jeffrey Courtland would have been on his way to Washington at that hour of the morning. But a power failure during the night delayed the electric alarm clock some twenty minutes; he was just leaving his home in Virginia when the postman arrived and handed him a stack of mail with a small, blue airmail envelope on top marked *Private and Personal*.

"Lucky that little one didn't get lost," he said, "coming all the way from Britain."

"Lucky," Jeff agreed and went back into the house.

The return address was familiar, but the handwriting was not—an unsteady, labored hand that had scrawled in haste, scraping the pen, spattering ink.

An obituary was enclosed. Brief and simple, it told him nothing except that a girl he had once known was dead. Her name was Anne Bentley then, and it was the same at death. But her age had changed from twenty-three to

3

forty-one, and her residence from London to Tilbury. She was survived by a son and an aunt.

The aunt had written the letter, spending her words as frugally as she spent her money, confining them to necessities. Anne had died in an accident, but she did not say what kind of accident. She did not dwell on her niece's death at all. Obviously her concern now was for Anne's son. She explained that her own advanced age and frail health made it impossible for her to care for the boy much longer, and while he was not a child, he was not yet a man ready to face the future alone. He would need help, and she thought Mr. Courtland would want to know this; indeed, that it was her duty to inform him and urge his immediate attention. She signed herself, *"Yours in hope and trust, Agatha Linton."*

Jeff read the obituary again, trying to remember Anne Bentley. After seventeen years the memory was vague, nebulous as an image in a cloud. And more so the memory of the child, an infant image appearing so often in his dreams it was sometimes difficult to believe he existed beyond them. There had been no correspondence, no pictures, no record of his growth and progress. Jeff's letters were unanswered, his checks uncashed, his gifts unacknowledged, until finally they ceased altogether. Anne had wanted it that way—though not, he knew, because of petty motives of revenge or punishment. She had made that clear in the beginning, and he had understood her logic. Why pursue an emotional attachment which could not transcend sentiment or obligation? She was always so practical. So proud and adamant, too.

"It's my problem," she said when first they discovered there was a problem.

"Our problem, Anne."

"Mine," she insisted. "I knew this might happen, and

you couldn't do anything about it. I should have been more careful. A nurse should know better."

Her calm resignation had astonished Jeff. Most single women in her straits would have been hysterical. Then, remembering the horrors she had seen, the tragedies she had experienced, he realized that she did not regard her pregnancy as any sort of catastrophe.

"What will you do, Anne?"

"Oh, I'll manage."

"How?" he demanded, thinking the worst.

She smiled and touched his face, smoothing away the frown of remorse and dismay, and her smile was her most charming feature, illuminating an otherwise plain face with the beauty of faith and courage. "Not that way," she said softly and told him about a relative in the Cotswold Hills. "Aunt Agatha is a spinster. She lives alone and will be happy to have me and the baby. We'll be company for her and safer from the bombs in the country. Don't worry, Jeffrey, I'll be fine." At his continued skepticism, she cried, "My God! With innocent people dying everywhere now, do you think I could destroy my unborn child!"

There had not been time for either of them to worry much. Anne was busy at the hospital and Jeffrey, along with a million or so other men in the British Isles, was involved in the plans and preparations for the Allied invasion of Europe. They saw less and less of each other, their personal problem resolved by the common emergency. Except for the few bad times when her pregnancy manifested itself in sudden nausea or depression, they tried to ignore it, pretend it did not exist. Before the physical changes in her body became apparent, Jeff was gone, and only when he saw a pregnant woman in France or Germany did he think and wonder about the girl in England.

When finally he saw Anne Bentley again, she looked

much the same as when they had met. Willowy slender, her washed-blue eyes too prominent in her pale face and slightly shadowed, her fair hair a shade darker and straighter, for there were no beauty salons in the village. If there was a change, it was in her smile, a little less luminous and courageous, perhaps, although she tried valiantly to conceal this from him.

Actually, they were not supposed to meet again at all. They had agreed on that before D-day, and Anne was determined. One parting was enough, she decided. No sense repeating it. It would be easier on him to have no memory of the child when he returned to America.

"If I return, Anne."

"You will," she said confidently. "You love your wife too much to die, Jeffrey. You'll live and go home to her, and that's as it should be. So we'll say our little adieux now, and I don't want you to write or try to find me. I won't answer or see you if you do."

The agreement stood for over a year, until the war ended and Jeff himself broke it immediately upon notification of his passage back to the States. Time was short when he wrote Anne to come to Southampton and bring the child, threatening to go to Tilbury if she refused. She had no choice. In a hotel room overlooking the harbor Jeff met his son, a long, thin, pale infant named Christopher.

"Do you like the name?" she asked anxiously.

"Yes, I like it, Anne."

"I've always admired Christopher Wren's church architecture, and I got the idea one Sunday during services." She paused, apparently mistaking his bewilderment for disappointment, and added somewhat apologetically, "I really wanted to name him for you, Jeffrey. I wanted him to look like his father, too. Dark and handsome. But I'm afraid he resembles me. Too bad you had to see him."

"Don't be silly," he said brusquely, embarrassed. "He's cute, Anne. A cute kid."

She shook her head ruefully. "Not now, but maybe he'll grow up to be beautiful. Children change, you know. And I'll train him well, Jeffrey. Oh, he'll be a scholar and a fine gentleman, too! Lord Mayor, perhaps, or even Prime Minister." She said it proudly and hopefully, as American mothers predicted their sons might be future presidents.

In another part of the house the vacuum cleaner began to hum. Jeff had not heard the housekeeper come in. Nor had he realized the yardman was in the garden until he heard the lawn mower. The house ran like a piece of well-oiled machinery, so smoothly he was not aware of its operation unless it stopped—and that rarely happened. Even the nocturnal electrical failure, which had temporarily upset the household schedule, had been a blessing in disguise. A reprieve, allowing the evidence to fall into his hands first. For though his wife respected the privacy of his mail, there was an urgency about this letter that would surely have piqued her curiosity.

Jeff picked up the telephone, called his office, and told his secretary to cancel his appointments for the day. And not until he hung up did he remember why Carol went out so early this morning, leaving immediately after breakfast.

"Sorry I have to run, darling. I promised to pick Mother up at nine, and I'm late already. That stupid blackout! I still have loads of shopping to do for the party. Weather permitting, we'll have it in the garden. Music, soft light, champagne—the whole romantic bit! After all, twenty's a pretty special number, isn't it?"

"Very," he had agreed, smiling.

Dear Lord! What an anniversary gift!

2

His immediate reaction was resentment and even anger, as if he had been ambushed. A thing like this should not take a man by surprise! Yet he knew the possibility had been in the back of his mind for years, a lengthening shadow over his life and marriage, his Damocles' sword and Achilles' heel. At times it was like sitting on an active volcano, wondering when it would erupt and how much damage and destruction would follow.

He removed some stationery from the desk in the study, glanced at the calendar, and dated it. June 6, 1962. Suddenly he remembered another June sixth, another year, another eruption. Fate, irony, coincidence?

He wrote, *"Dear Miss Linton."* That sounded cold, stiff. He crumpled the sheet of paper, tossed it in the wastebasket, and began another. *"Dear Aunt Agatha."* But that was wrong, too. She was not his aunt. She was someone he did not know, had never even met, an old woman living, dying, in a part of England he had never seen.

It was a great shock to realize how little he actually knew of the circumstances under which his son had lived for seventeen years. Comfortable, he assumed, taking Anne's word for it because it was convenient and solacing to accept her assurance. But he should have made certain. He should have gone back to England at least once in all these years. He had the time and money, even the inclination, and he could have made the opportunity. But he could not go with his wife or without her, and so had to assuage his conscience when doubts assailed him. He tried to forget by concentrating on business, by making Carol happy, for she too had something to forget.

Unfortunately, they could not help each other. They were like lost souls wandering in a secret limbo, waiting for a mystic light to guide them. Yet neither was fully aware of the other's groping, and their friends not at all. Outwardly their marriage was good enough to inspire both admiration and envy. Inwardly they simply adjusted to emotional darkness and stumbled less in its familiarity.

This letter was his opportunity to light a candle in their relationship, if he had the courage to strike the match—to risk explosion, fire, disaster. He had possessed courage once, but was not sure he still did. He was uncertain about many things in his life now, including the happiness of his marriage and the financial wisdom of maintaining a historic Georgian mansion as a residence.

The prerevolutionary construction presented foundation and roofing problems, heating and cooling and other heavy expenses, without which his credit rating in *Dun & Bradstreet* would have been considerably more impressive. Nor would he have felt responsible to the Daughters of the

American Revolution and the Historical Society for preserving the place for future generations.

But Carol loved her burden like a mother loves a burdensome child. It was a nepenthe for her, taking her mind off other matters, and money able to achieve that was well spent. For her sake, Jeff shouldered his fiscal obligations and learned to cope with the battle of the beams, the leaking slates, the periodic termite invasions. The view of the Potomac River was not as expansive as the one which the British sea captain who originally built the house had enjoyed when watching the tall masts of his ships in the harbor of the then Port of Alexandria, yet it was still pleasant, and the landscaped grounds had their special appeal, too.

Some of the furnishings had come from his family's plantation in the Piedmont—prized possessions to which his grandmother had clung through several economic depressions. Indeed, his father's gross mismanagement of the estate had brought her to the brink of bankruptcy. Through it all, she remained matriarch of the county, its social and civic leader, patron of its arts and charities, godmother to its children. She was landed gentry, but more important in her mind, a First Family Virginian.

Jeff knew the letter from England would have distressed his late grandmother greatly, and that her sympathies would have been with his wife. She had been fond of Carol from the moment they had met at the Warrenton Horse Show and pleased to learn that she was a native Virginian, a graduate of Foxcroft School, and student at Sweet Briar College. It did not matter that the Wiltons, landowners in the Tidewater a century ago, were then selling real estate. Elizabeth Courtland distinguished between heritage and inheritance. She thought that Carol Wilton's heritage would enrich her grandson's and had encouraged a swift court-

ship and marriage. It was Carol's mother who had thought
they were rushing things and tried to delay the ceremony
until after the war.

No, his grandmother would not have understood, any
more than she had understood his father's character lapses,
although she had condoned them, believing they resulted
from the early loss of his lovely young wife and his
inability to truly love another woman. Elizabeth Courtland
was just grateful that her son was discreet in his indiscre-
tions, as a gentleman should be. Clarence, always gentle
with ladies, horses, and hounds, constantly abused his
bourbon. He died at forty-nine, his dark hair prematurely
gray, his once handsome face and fine body emaciated and
hideously bloated with cirrhotic edema. He was buried in
the family plot at Belle Manor Plantation, in the company
of Courtland heroes from Yorktown to Appomattox. Clarence, beloved husband of Miriam Taylor Courtland, slept
beside her under a marble slab, faithful in spirit if not in
flesh.

This was Jeff's memory of his father. Of his mother he
had only a vague recollection, for she had died when he
was seven. He had a portrait, some photographs, and a
diary. He also had a son who neither of his parents would
ever see.

Ella had moved her cleaning downstairs, singing spiritu-
als as she worked. Toby had progressed to the boxwood
hedge under the windows, whistling as he snipped and
shirred. The Negro servants were important cogs in the
perfectly aligned household wheel.

Jeff was seated at the Jeffersonian desk, the stationery
still blank before him, when Carol returned shortly after
noon. And suddenly he knew why he had been unable to

answer the letter. The words would have to come from her.

Packages filled her arms. A cluster of fresh violets, enhancing the vivid color of her eyes, was pinned to the lapel of her beige suit, and she wore a white hat and crisp white gloves. She was one of the few women Jeff knew who could look fresh and radiant after a shopping trip. But the radiance soon dimmed when she saw that he had not gone to the office.

"Darling, you're not ill?"

"No, baby, just goofing off today."

She frowned and dumped her burden on the leather sofa. "Goofing off" was not like him. In fact, she worried because she thought he worked too hard and was trying to persuade him to take a partner, or at least shift more responsibility onto his assistants.

"Are you sure?"

"I'm sure," he said. "Can't a man stay home for any other reason?"

"Of course, dear, and I wish you would more often. But I wouldn't have shopped if I'd known—or at least invited you to help spend your money."

He smiled mirthlessly, one hand covering the letter which was still his secret. "Did you go to Washington?"

"No, you know Mother's fierce community loyalty. She acts as if Alexandria were still a trading post, and economic survival depended on commerce with the local Indians. Actually, I think the District traffic unnerves her. The pace is just too hectic for her leisurely Southern blood."

"It's wild, all right," Jeff said, wishing that he did not have to battle it twice a day himself. "Where's Margaret now?"

"At a club meeting. Have you had lunch yet?"

"I'm not hungry."

"Oh, Jeffrey, you *are* ill!"

Immediately she began to fuss over him, loosening his tie, feeling his forehead—ministrations which she always performed with a frustrated maternal instinct, as if he were a helpless child. Usually he indulged her, but now he scowled impatiently and brushed her hands away.

"I'm not sick, I tell you!"

"Then it's business or something else," she insisted. "You're certainly not yourself. Is the stock market worse than Wall Street admits? Are your clients panicking?"

"Only a few panicky females. What makes women so goddamned hysterical?"

"Men," she murmured, gathering up her bundles. "I'll be upstairs if you need me."

He did not answer, but his expression was familiar. She had seen it before, often over the years, and it worried her. It was as if he were looking back into the past, or trying to see into the future. It would appear unexpectedly over the dinner table, while dancing at the club or driving in the country. She could even sense it at night, in the intimate darkness, and would wonder if it had anything to do with the war, like the nightmares he sometimes had. But she wished, whatever it was, he would confide in her. Why was it so hard for a man to understand a woman's need for his trust and confidence, her desire to share all of him, his hopes and dreams, the good and the bad?

In the master suite she imagined that she could hear him pacing the floor below and had to discipline herself not to interrupt. Poor man, he had his troubles, disappointments, frustrations. She had hers, too, and was always trying to compensate for them. The new white boudoir ensemble, reminiscent of the one in her bridal trousseau, was an attempt at compensation. The black chiffon nightgown in her dresser was another. The uplift bras and girdles, the clothes and cosmetics and perfumes—all bought with one thought, one hope, one prayer in mind. *Love me, need me, want me.*

Even the house was a form of compensation. Most of their friends lived in modern apartments, expensive and often elegant, but she did not envy them, not even the Cranshaws in their fabulous Washington penthouse. The Courtlands' historic home was a status symbol now that the Kennedys had made Americans aware of their heritage. Millionaires from all over the country were searching for antebellum mansions in Virginia. They could turn a neat profit on their investment, which proved that she was as wise as her father had been about real estate. And she ran the house efficiently, too. The meals on time, fresh flowers in the vases, fires on the hearths in season. But there had never been a tiny Christmas stocking on the decorated mantel, a toy on the floor, fingerprints on the immaculate woodwork. The cliff dwellers had planter boxes or a few potted plants on a cantilevered terrace. The Courtlands had a large, charming garden with magnificent old trees. But never a little red wagon on the paths, the sound of roller skates on the driveway, the thump of a rubber ball against the faded red brick walls.

When her inadequacy had become painfully evident, they had discussed adoption. But her husband had never encouraged it, perhaps because he still hoped in his heart. Hope vanished in her early thirties, and Jeff seemed relieved to abandon the idea of adoption. Carol had then devoted herself to him and their home, and it was only when he looked as he had a few minutes ago that she wondered if this was enough for him—if it had ever been enough for either of them.

She removed her suit, hung it in her closet. Then she slipped on the new negligee and stood before the mirror.

Would it remind him of their honeymoon? Could the memory still be important to him after twenty years? Of course she had changed in that time, but the changes were subtle. She liked to think that maturity added new dimensions to her physical beauty and charm. Her hair, though shorter than on her wedding day, was still silky and golden bright, her skin fair and smooth, her body as lithe and slender as the first time he had beheld it nude. *Love me, need me, want me*.

The door opened and Jeff entered and paused apologetically, sensing that he had interrupted a private reverie.

"Lovely," he said hoarsely.

"You weren't supposed to see it yet."

She smiled tremulously and waited for him to come to her, to take her in his arms and make love to her. He was still an incredibly handsome and virile man, and her jealousy was sometimes as immediate and intense as her passion and desire. But he still had that faraway look in his eyes, that haunting reflection of unshared emotions and experiences, which was beginning to alarm her. She eased herself down on the bench before the dressing table, feeling scorned and foolish, ready to cry.

"Carol. . . ."

His voice seemed to come from a distance, but he was on the floor at her knees, his head writhing in her lap. And he was holding something in his hand, which her rapidly blurring vision vaguely discerned as a letter.

3

For a long while Carol thought she had fainted and was slowly struggling back to consciousness. But she had not moved, and Jeff was still kneeling on the floor beside her, like a penitent sinner in confession.

There had been times during the war when long silences from him had led her to suspect the worst, and she had come perilously close to the breaking point. She had experienced a series of such crises on the emotional precipice, never knowing if she were keeping a vigil or wake, and the remembered suspense, agony, and despair were suddenly epitomized in this one letter—she saw it as the explanation of all the unexplained and tormenting silences. It was a terrible realization, a kind of physical death, leaving her cold and desolate.

"How did it happen?" she asked tearfully.

"Darling, I don't want to hurt you."

"Hurt me?"

"Any more than I have already," he said humbly.

"If I can bear to listen, surely you can bear to tell me. And you must, Jeffrey. You owe me that much."

He rose slowly and stood by the big double bed with its reeded mahogany posts and ruffled white canopy lined in blue, like a cradle of love cuddling its occupants in luxury. The other bed had been brass, too short and narrow, a utilitarian vehicle of ugliness and discomfort with a lumpy mattress, squeaky springs, worn sheets. It was difficult to remember if he had found pleasure there, or mere release.

"Well, as you can see from the obituary, her name was Anne Bentley. She was a nurse. I met her in an air raid shelter in London."

"When?"

"August of '43."

"Less than a year after you left me!"

"It had nothing to do with you, Carol. Or our marriage. Please believe me."

"Was she beautiful?"

"No, rather plain, actually."

"But terribly brave and British?"

"She had been through a lot. Her parents and a younger brother and sister were killed in the raid on Coventry in '40. Her entire family wiped out overnight. One old maiden aunt in the country was all she had left."

She glanced at the signature on the letter. "Agatha Linton?"

"Yes."

"Did you spend the night in the shelter?"

"No. The raid was mostly a nuisance attack, V-2 rockets and buzz bombs to keep the populace uneasy; it didn't last long. Anne had been on her way to work when the sirens sounded. She was in uniform, and I think I noticed her because she looked and smelled clean. Nothing else in that dim, dank hole did.

"When the attack was over, I offered to escort her to the hospital, and she accepted. It wasn't far. We walked. Homes and buildings had been hit, and people were fighting the fires, but there was little panic or terror. I couldn't help admiring the civilian attitude, and Anne said they had been conditioned by the blitz. The tears and hysteria were past, and there was just blood, sweat, and survival. British stoicism or not, it was a philosophy to live by in those days. The only one, in fact."

"How long before you saw her again?"

"A few days, when she went off night duty. I picked her up at the hospital. We went to . . . her flat."

Carol said nothing, but he saw the pain in her face, the shattered illusions in her eyes. She sat rigidly on the bench, her hands gripping the sides as if to leave their imprint in the wood. Doggedly, Jeff continued, "Anything I add now will sound sordid, Carol."

"Wasn't it, Jeff?"

"It didn't seem so at the time. It still doesn't. She was alone and lonely. So was I."

"And there was a war on, which is every man's license and dispensation from decency! Why should you have been any different?"

"I'm not blaming the war."

"Why not? Do you think you'd have met an Englishwoman in an air raid shelter and had a child by her under any other circumstances? Blame the war, Jeffrey! It's easier than blaming yourself or Anne Bentley. What did you do the first time in her flat? Jump into bed and comfort each other!"

"No!" he shouted, sweating, flexing his hands at his sides. "We talked over drinks. She had some hoarded

Scotch—a real treat because it was almost impossible to buy without a signed requisition from Churchill.''

"We had the same difficulty here, unless you had one from Roosevelt. I wrote you about it, but maybe you didn't get my letter, or were too busy to read it. I wonder now if you read my letters. You certainly didn't answer all of them.''

"I read them, Carol, and answered all that I received. The mail didn't always get through, you know.''

"I suppose not," she relented. "Go on, Jeff. The truth, please. That's all I ask.''

The truth?

He could tell her in a few words: I met a girl, one thing led to another, and finally to bed.

But it wasn't quite that simple or crude or impulsive. Nor was it romantic, even in retrospect . . .

London was quiet that evening and hot as a brick oven. They took the bottle of precious whiskey up on the roof of the tenement and sat on the dusty ventilators, gazing at the burned-out, blacked-out city.

She lived in Lambeth, convenient to St. Thomas Hospital, a Nazi target during the blitz. The building had caught its share of bombs and incendiaries and was scarred, gutted, windows shattered and missing, walls and chimneys crumbling. Some of the Lambeth flats had been too badly damaged for occupancy, and the tenants had vacated, leaving behind pitiful piles of charred and broken belongings.

Anne's three rooms were on the fourth floor, with a view of the Thames between Westminster and Lambeth bridges, miserably hot in summer, chillingly cold in winter owing to strict fuel rationing, and the plumbing was archaic and communal. But there was pleasant female companionship there, which made it preferable to his better-equipped billet.

The August night was clear, with a bombers' moon, and Jeff wondered if the Jerries would take advantage of it, or if it was true, as the newspapers and the BBC claimed, that Germany was gradually disintegrating and saving the Luftwaffe for a last desperate defense of the fatherland. Hitler might have been encouraged, he thought, if he could witness the London scene from the rooftop of any structure still standing. This view was especially awesome, with the omnipresent barrage balloons casting phantomlike shadows on the dark ruins. Pedestrians were picking their way with flashlights through the debris, skirting or stumbling over the firehoses curled and crawling like monstrous serpents in the cluttered streets.

"Weird, the torches," Anne said. "Like a Guy Fawkes parade in a stone jungle. I sit up here and watch and think how far back civilization has gone, how much progress has been impeded. It will take years to rebuild the city."

"If it's ever rebuilt," Jeff said somberly.

"That's defeatism, Leftenant. We've survived fires and plagues and wars before, you know."

"Nothing of this magnitude, though. Reconstruction will be a job for giants and geniuses, and the world had better hope some such men survive." He sighed, remembering his own college ambition to design and build.

"Some will," Anne was confident. "Some always do. London will rise again. Come back in ten, twenty years. You'll see."

"There'll always be an England, eh?"

"Always," she nodded firmly. "If I didn't believe that, Jeffrey, I'd jump in the river now."

The Thames flowed not far away, a dark undulating mirror reflecting the pale, eerie moonlight and the Gothic, bomb-ravaged houses of Parliament on its banks. Jeff thought of Washington on the Potomac, safe so far, fortunate. He thought of Belle Manor in the green, peaceful Piedmont of Virginia and his beautiful bride in Alexandria, and drank and brooded.

Anne Bentley was not beautiful. She was not even physically desirable. Her face was somewhat gaunt, and her thin body seemed all bones and sinew. He anticipated no pleasure in its touch, no passion, perhaps not even warmth. Moreover, the medicinal odor of her uniform, which had appealed to him in the fetid basement shelter, repelled him now, reminding him of sickness, wounds, death. Surveying the depressing ruins, everything reminded him of death and destruction. It was like sitting in an erupting cemetery on Doomsday. The somber chimes of Big Ben striking the hour sounded like the death knell.

"I'm married," he told Anne.

"Most men are," she said.

"I'm in love with my wife."

"Naturally. You wouldn't have married her otherwise. They say Americans never marry for any other reason."

"Not this American, anyway." He sipped from the bottle again. "Have you ever been in love?"

"Once," she nodded.

"Once. Then you still are?"

"He's dead. Dieppe."

"Is that his picture in your flat? The Commando?"

"Yes."

"Rugged outfit."

"He was a rugged man," she reflected wistfully.

"But mortal. That's the trouble with all men, Anne. They die. Don't be foolish enough to fall in love with another one before the war is over."

"I'm used to death, Jeffrey, no longer afraid of it.

We're almost friends, Death and I. I've seen so much of it.''

"I guess so, being a nurse. Sister Bentley. I can't get used to that. To me, a sister is a nun.''

"Let me assure you, Leftenant, I'm not a nun.''

"How old are you, Anne?''

"Twenty-three. Older than you?''

"No, the same age.''

"That's young for an officer.''

"Ninety-Day Wonder," he shrugged. "They're mass-producing officers in the States now, like everything else. A college degree, especially with some previous military training, is an automatic qualification for a commission. A course in electronics communications landed me in the Signal Corps. I was promptly promoted from shavetail second lieuy to first. I'm working on a captaincy now. Where's your home, Anne?''

"Three years ago it was Coventry," she said and told him about her personal tragedy, the search for the bodies in the wreckage and finding her own family's burnt almost beyond recognition. "Thousands died with them. The attack was so successful, according to Germany's Lord Haw-haw, the Nazis invented a word for it—Conventrated—and beamed it proudly to their people on the wireless." She paused. "This tenement is my home now and as good as any, at present.''

In no condition to cope with grief and nostalgia then, Jeff was relieved that she did not weep for her lost family. In the few hazy minutes before the Scotch blitzed him, he regarded Anne Bentley as a comrade, a pal, a buddy to drink with and perhaps confide his troubles. He woke in her flat, in her bed, with a big head and blank memory. Anne had already gone to market and was fixing breakfast in the kitchen. The coffee smelled good. Jeff went in sheepishly and asked, "What happened last night?"

"Nothing." She smiled. "You Yanks just can't drink."

"We haven't had as much practice as you British." Jeff laughed, and despite his monstrous hangover, he felt good again, human and decent and glad to be alive, as he had not been glad last night. "How did I get down here from the roof, Anne? All those stairs!"

"You walked."

"Alone?"

"No, Yank, not alone."

"Thanks, but you should have left me up there, Nurse. To dry out. I'd have been all right."

"It might have rained."

"My head needed soaking," he said. "You shouldn't have given me your bed, anyway."

"I didn't, Leftenant. It's not much of a bed, I know, but serviceable and big enough for two." His gaze embarrassed her. "Well, why not?" she demanded. "You didn't know the difference. Should I have slept on the floor?"

"No, of course not. But you were taking a chance, lady. I may not have been as drunk as you thought. What would you have done then?"

"Whatever you wanted," she replied honestly.

" 'Eat, drink, and be merry, for tomorrow we die'?"

"We might, you know."

"Yes, we might," he agreed. "May I borrow your bath? I'm afraid I'd be court-martialed if I reported to headquarters in this condition."

"Down the hall, third door on your left, and community property, so knock first. There may not be any hot water, and the other facilities may be on the blink. Just have to take your luck. My razor is on the dresser. I hope the blade isn't too dull. They're deucedly hard to get these days. I lifted that one from the hospital.''

"I'll send you some," Jeff promised.

While he shaved and showered in cold water, Anne pressed his uniform. Then she served him a fairly palatable meal of weak black coffee, toast with margarine, and mutton chops on which she had spent precious ration coupons. Jeff thanked her sincerely and left without so much as a comradely hug or kiss on the cheek.

He did not see her again for a month. Several Signal Corps officers were flown to Malta on special duty, and they agreed to celebrate if the mission was successful. They returned to London in jovial spirits and proceeded to find dates. Lieutenant Courtland called Anne Bentley. She was free that evening and apparently happy to hear from him.

Out of her uniform, in a formal feminine gown of some frothy pink stuff and smelling of lilac water, she was a different person, less a pal or chum, more a woman. They dined and danced at the Dorchester, and Jeff enjoyed the feel of her body in his arms, the scent of her hair in his nostrils, the wine on her breath. In the taxi on the way to Lambeth, they sang and laughed and kissed for the sheer joy of being alive. By the time they reached her flat, they were more than friends, they were lovers. Liquor, loneliness, lilacs—somehow it added up to love or lust, Jeff was never sure which. But he did not have to tell this to Carol.

"You weren't too drunk that night, were you?" Carol surmised. "You made love to her. Was she a virgin?"

He scowled. "I didn't ask."

"Couldn't you tell? You had some experience with me."

"Stop it, Carol."

But a force stronger than curiosity impelled her, and she could not spare him or herself. The inquisition had to be conducted, endured, however distasteful, if ever there was to be truth and honor and trust between them again. "Did you move in with her, keep her?"

"No, she paid her own bills, and I had my own billet. I visited her when I could, but it wasn't all fun and folly, Carol. All games and sport. She had long hours at the hospital, and I wasn't exactly on vacation myself. There was a little thing called Operation Overlord on the agenda. D-day. Thousands of ships were amassing in English ports, and hundreds of thousands of men were training on the beaches. I was away from London part of the time, on coastal maneuvers. Dover, mostly."

"I wouldn't know, you see. All I had was an APO address in New York and my work at the Red Cross Blood Bank. I donated my own as often as they would accept it believing that you might be wounded and need it. Evenings I listened to Mother's ration problems and to Dad fighting World War I all over again. I wouldn't even go to a movie or visit a friend, for fear a telegram might come in my absence. I wrote letters half the night and cried myself to sleep the rest of the time. And you—you were screwing Anne Bentley!"

"Don't talk that way, Carol."

"It's true, isn't it? And how do you know the child is yours, Jeff? You weren't with her every moment. She may have had other men."

"I don't think so."

"You mean she was in love with you?"

"Yes."

"And you?"

"I was in love with you, Carol."

"Thanks. That's a great comfort to me now," she said

wryly. "But I'm sorry for you, Jeff. All these years with a thing like that on your mind. How could you bear it?"

"It was hell sometimes," he admitted. "But I could endure it as long as the boy had his mother. I'm afraid I couldn't now, though, knowing my son needs me."

"And you need him," she sighed. "You've always needed him, Jeff. That's why you wouldn't adopt a child, isn't it? You wanted your own, not another man's. At last I understand. So many things."

Carol had remained seated because she feared instability. Now she stood, and the reflection in the dressing table mirror sickened her—the sentimental, seductive white lure in which she was going to tempt him, cater to her love and his lust, hoping for miracles after twenty years! Revulsion shook her. She wanted to rip the garment off, shred it to rags, stand as bare and bold as the other woman had probably done. How stupid she had been to imagine that because she had always been faithful he, too, had been; to believe that he was sinless because he did not confess; content because he did not complain; and happy because he did not say he was unhappy.

"Carol . . ." He moved toward her, his eyes and arms supplicating, but she evaded his embrace.

"No, Jeffrey. I'm sorry, but you'll have to give me time to think about all this. It's not just a slip you made, something that happened once or twice while you were drunk or despondent. I wish it were, there wouldn't be these human complications. But you had an affair, Jeff. A love affair, and a child, and you've been living a lie with me. Maybe our whole marriage was a lie, a masquerade."

"You're hysterical," he said gently.

"Yes, I am! You bet I am! I'm not your stoical British mistress, who could face bombs and death and an illegitimate child as calmly as a cup of tea. I'm your neurotic

American housewife, your naive, gullible spouse who thinks that infidelity is something that happens to other people. I'm Chicken Little, the sky has just fallen on my benighted head, and I don't know where to run!'' Her voice rose shrilly, quivering on the keen edge of hysteria, and she screamed at him, ''Get out of here, damn you! Leave me alone, let me think! Oh, God, I have to think . . .''

4

Doris Ledlow had come to Courtland Investments via Vassar and Wall Street and had been confidential secretary to Jeffrey Courtland for ten years. She wore a Phi Beta Kappa key on the lapel of her tailored suits, glasses with harlequin frames, subtle makeup, and had short auburn hair. She was thirty-four, single, and dedicated to her career.

Jeff knew Miss Ledlow could have filled any number of responsible government positions and that he was fortunate to keep her. In appreciation he gave her a handsome salary, attractive fringe benefits, and the privilege of arranging her own hours and holidays. She also made delicious coffee, of which he had already consumed four cups, black.

His head ached fiercely from lack of sleep and food. There was pain in his eyeballs and behind them, and a tightness in his chest which might have alarmed him under ordinary circumstances. A man his age had to watch such symptoms, along with his weight and blood pressure, and worry more about his paunch than his potency.

Although still in excellent health at forty-one, Jeff realized he had reached a definite physical plateau, and from here on nature would determine his life's course. The realization disturbed him enough to regret the things he had not done more than those he had, and to consider his accomplishments less important than his failures—the greatest of which was fatherhood. Perhaps it was presumptuous and foolhardy to imagine he could balance that ledger at this late date, but he had to try. This much he knew and thought that Carol must know it, too. He had heard her crying during the night and had wanted to go to her, needing her more now than ever, but she had pleaded for time and emotional asylum.

His desk was cluttered with financial reports, clients' portfolios, graphs and prospectuses, the *Wall Street Journal*, and several yards of ticker tape. The chaos disturbed his secretary, who was as neat and efficient in the office as his wife was at home. Doris emptied the tray of half-smoked cigarettes and pencils snapped in tension and brought him his fifth cup of coffee.

"Is anything wrong, sir?"

"No," he lied unconvincingly.

Doris had an uncanny intuition about his personal and professional lives, sensing his domestic difficulties as aptly as his housekeeper. Ella had given him a sympathetic look when he had emerged from the guest room this morning, and Jeff recognized the same "poor devil" sentiment in Doris's hazel eyes now. He seemed to be surrounded by perspicacious women—except for his wife who, blinded by love, had not seen through him in twenty years.

"Mrs. Buxton called again about that Yukon uranium mine," Doris said.

"I *told* her it doesn't exist. It's a swindle, and if she *wants* to be taken in it, she'll have to find another broker. Her husband should have appointed a guardian for her."

"Senator Toliver is interested in some solid fuel stocks."

"Must have inside information." John Glenn's successful orbital flight in February and President Kennedy's visions of a man on the moon during the decade had made commodities and securities dealing with space highly desirable.

"Mr. Rheams is having property settlement problems and wants to know if there's some way he can keep the lion's share of their community stocks."

"That's a question for his attorney," Jeff said. "And I have to consult mine, too. Get Kenneth Cranshaw on the phone and ask if he can meet me for lunch at Foster's, at one."

"Yes, sir."

Doris completed the call in seconds; Ken was free.

Foster's, on Second Street, specialized in beefsteaks, booze, and businessmen. Capitol Hill boys also patronized it when their appetites or tempers ran to rare meat expertly prepared and served on hickory boards with precision cutlery. The latter clientele were easily recognizable, seeming always in caucus, and occasionally carving up their steak as if it were a political opponent. They invariably drank during these dissections, and unscrupulous waiters could leak "top secret" information to newspaper and broadcast columnists.

Jeff was sipping bourbon on the rocks when his friend arrived. Ken, who had an avid interest in politics, paused to speak with the senior senator of his state. Watching him approach the table, Jeff thought Kenneth Cranshaw would certainly have the ladies' vote if ever he decided to change professions. He had the suave good looks and self-assurance, the personality and persuasion, to inspire feminine confidence. Small wonder so many women engaged him for their divorces. Maybe Carol would, too. The possibility sent a cold tremor along his spine.

They shook hands, and Ken saw his favorite Scotch already at his place. Without consulting the menu, they ordered rare sirloins, and when the waiter had gone Ken lifted his glass in a premature toast.

"To Saturday! Congratulations, Jeff."

"I'm not sure congratulations are in order, Ken."

"Come again?"

"This lunch invitation wasn't purely social, my friend." Removing the letter from inside his coat, Jeff handed it across the table and drank while Ken read it.

"Brief me," he said then.

"It's self-explanatory, isn't it?"

Ken considered the obituary. "On the surface, yes. But I'd like a few pertinent facts."

Jeff supplied them. His attorney listened, shaking his head, almost as surprised as his wife had been.

"Good Lord."

"I'll need some legal advice, Ken."

"No doubt of that, Jeff. But it's not an unusual case. I've handled similar ones. These things happen in war."

"I'm not looking for alibis, Ken. This wasn't in the line of duty. She was just there, a decent type basically, and we sort of shacked up."

"Who didn't?"

"Did you?"

"I was in the Aleutians, remember? Nothing but Eskimos and caribou. But I got back to Seattle once during a blizzard, met a lonely bimbo in a bar, and we stayed in bed three days. Funny, I can't remember her name now, nor much of anything else about her, except that she had big boobs and a hot box. I was drunk most of the time." He shrugged. "C'est la vie! I knew a colonel who took his mistress everywhere he was stationed. In this way, according to his theory, he reduced the VD risk with tramps, thereby doing his wife and himself a salubrious service."

"I guess you can rationalize just about anything, if you try hard enough," Jeff said. "But I don't think I was motivated by hygiene, and I'm not seeking excuses or vindication. Like you said, it happens and not only in war. The only incredible part about it now is that I was in love with Carol all along. That's some kind of paradox, I suppose. Infidelity is contrary to true love, isn't it?"

"Maybe, but not to biology," Ken said. "After all, you were physically separated from her a damned long time for a guy your age. But poor naive Carol—this must have exploded over her head like a delayed bombshell."

"It hit her hard, all right. Knocked her down, and she's still on the ground, emotionally."

"Speaking to you?"

"Just barely."

"You hurt her, Jeff. A deep wound, the kind that has to heal from within and often festers first with proud flesh. I know. I've dealt with numerous marital crises, and infidelity is always the most difficult offense for a wife to understand and forgive. Probably because society has conditioned women to equate marriage and fidelity, to believe love and sex are synonymous. Drinking, gambling, penury, even brutality, are more easily condoned and forgiven than adultery. Stray off the reservation sexually, and there's instant frost on the tepee. Are you persona non grata in the tent?"

"She hasn't locked the bedroom door yet, but there's not exactly a welcome sign hanging on it, either."

"Too bad. Locked doors are easy to breach. Locked minds and hearts are the tough barriers."

"Sex isn't the major issue between us now, Ken. It's what to do about the child."

"What do you want to do?"

"The right thing."

"Even at the risk of destroying your marriage? I know of nothing in American or English law that could compel you to acknowledge paternity at this late date, especially with the mother unable to make any claims. But that's a professional opinion, Jeff, not a personal one. This is primarily a moral issue."

"The kid is mine, Ken. I've no doubt of that and no intention of denying it. I've had a free dance for seventeen years, now it's time to pay the piper. And I want to pay, whatever the cost."

"Financially? You can afford plenty, Jeff. Put him in a good school, pay the bills, take a tax deduction." He paused. "Or do you have something else in mind?"

"He's my son," Jeff reiterated, pain in his face.

"And Carol can't give you a son," Ken said, increasing his pain. "I used to wonder why you didn't adopt, now I know." He indicated the letter. "This must seem like a stroke of good fortune to you. Shall I keep it?"

Jeff nodded. "Whatever it's to be—divorce, support, adoption—I'd like you to handle it, Ken."

"I'll do my best, Jeff. And about Carol . . . humor her. Allow her some whims and tantrums. She may be about to become a mother."

"That's not funny, Ken."

"I didn't intend it to be," the other said, signaling the waiter. "How about another drink before the steaks arrive? Alcohol is supposed to whet the appetite for blood. Wasn't that one of General Patton's battle theories?''

"Yeah," Jeff frowned. "Old Blood and Guts encouraged his troops to indulge their baser instincts. He thought it made mighty warriors and great victories. Not much is said about the innocent victims of some of these macho heroes' exploits, though.''

"The spoils of war," Ken said. "And at the time, people are only concerned with winning it.''

Jeff nodded gravely. "In Gibraltar I saw something rather profound scrawled on a sentry box, probably by a disillusioned serviceman:

> *God and the soldier all men adore,*
> *In time of danger and no more,*
> *For when the danger is past and all things righted,*
> *God is forgotten and the old soldier slighted.''*

"General MacArthur put it another way to Congress, when Truman relieved him of duty," Ken reflected.

"Unfortunately, he neglected to mention that men's deeds, good and evil, live after them, and the old soldiers' bastards don't just fade away!''

5

They stood in the garden, tense and wary as figures on a stage afraid of missing their cues.

The whole affair was beginning to seem like a play to Carol, a fantasy. The guests were characters in formal costume following rehearsed routines. Strange that she had never seen through their acts before. Was it because she had been engaged in a pretense of her own? Remote and detached now, she watched the scene with distaste, reluctant to believe that she had ever participated, even indirectly, herself. The unwholesome preoccupation with alcohol and sex; the cynicism and hypocrisy and subterfuge; the petty ambitions and jealousies; the excesses and extravagances and revolving debts.

The men who were not bald wore their graying hair in crew cuts and drove expensive sports cars. The women tinted their hair to suit their moods or donned fanciful wigs, followed fad diets, and spent fortunes they could not afford on clothes, cosmetics, entertainment, travel. They behaved like members of some crazy youth cult, but they were middle-aged, desperate, frantic people at the core, sick with the ancient ills of disillusionment and despair, and there were no miracle drugs to cure them.

"What happened to the orchestra?" Jeff asked Carol.

"Cancelled. I didn't think we'd feel much like dancing the 'Anniversary Waltz.' "

"Probably not," he agreed. "But thanks, anyway, for wearing my gift."

Carol touched the wide gold bracelet on her arm; it was exquisitely executed and tenderly inscribed, *For twenty wonderful years, with love and appreciation, Jeff.*

She had an impressive collection of sentimentally engraved jewelry, and the sentiments cluttered her mind now, jumbled, echoing the years. Lies? she wondered. Tokens of love or remorse? How could she know now, how could she ever be sure in the future?

As if sensing her doubts and bewilderment, Jeff said, "I mean the inscription, Carol."

"Of course, darling. You meant all of them, over the years. So many hearts and flowers. So many years."

"I hope there'll be many more."

True or not, she wanted desperately to believe him, and suddenly wished she had followed his suggestion to skip the celebration and go away somewhere alone together to study the problem and try to reach an intelligent solution. This was needless cruelty and torture for both of them and could easily degenerate into a debacle.

"Skeets is drunk already," she said, "and it's not yet ten o'clock. He'll be doing that silly pocket dance before long. I'm not sure I can endure it again."

The "pocket dance" was Skeets Martin's specialty. He performed it spontaneously at almost every party he attended. It consisted of a series of vulgar pelvic gyrations manipulated with his hands in his trouser pockets. It was obscene, suggestive, disgusting, but people laughed. Skeets loved laughter, although he seldom joined in it himself. An insurance broker, he called himself a bookie when drunk and said he was engaged in the biggest lottery in the world.

"The only way the customer can collect is to kick off early," he often said, "which doesn't happen often enough to upset the percentages because only the good die young, and they're the minority in this wicked world. The sinners live on and on, the insurance bookies insure them, and the companies make millions gambling on human lives. Double indemnity? Man, your beneficiary's chances of collecting the Irish Sweepstakes are better!" But Skeets talked this way only when drunk and among friends. Sober, he declared insurance a fine investment for a man's family, although he did not carry a cent on his own life. "Don't trust my wife," he winked, and his friends laughed, thinking he was joking.

"Skeets does that to embarrass Shirley," Jeff said.

"Because she was on the stage?"

"That, and because he knows about her affairs. He ends that jig by pulling out the empty linings of his pockets to show her that's all she's going to get from him. Some pelvic maneuvers and empty pockets."

"He must loathe her."

"On the contrary, I think he loves her."

"A strange manifestation."

"People in love often behave strangely."

"Yes, don't they?" Carol quipped with irony.

"Smile, darling, and relax. Here come the Martins."

Shirley was in a black sequin sheath, the skirt slit to the knee, bodice slashed to the navel. Her figure was statuesque, perfect for unveiling. A silver frost, the latest coiffure rage, sparkled on her sleek blond hair like ice crystals. She had unusual eyes, the color changing with her mood, from amber to topaz to gold, and she gave them an Oriental slant with mascara and luminous green shadow, tricks she had learned in her profession. She was a flamboyantly beautiful woman, and an exceptionally miserable one.

"How does it feel to be married twenty years?" she asked. "Me, I'd rather celebrate four five-year anniversaries with different mates."

"No doubt you will," drawled Skeets, her third. "Hey, don't Shirl look her part tonight? One zip and that gown would be off and 'Look, Mom, no undies!' Talk about the Common Market, this broad's been in it for years."

Shirley bit her tongue, but the profanity, as it sometimes did, slipped out, anyway. "Bastard."

Skeets grinned. "See what I mean?"

The Fighting Martins and Bickering Benedicts were standards in the cast, and no one was much surprised or embarrassed by their antics. They engaged in sarcasm and slander, bandying repartee as if their tongues were rapiers, smiling "touché" when one got the better of the other. It was this sort of tournament between the sexes that caused Mrs. Wilton to shun her daughter's entertainments, or escape early when attendance was required. She had appeared briefly this evening, congratulated the couple, and presented them with a set of Haviland demitasse cups, then pleaded a headache and left.

"The Dowager Queen departs early again," Beth Benedict muttered to her husband. "It's obvious she doesn't approve of some of the company her daughter keeps. But I'm glad the old crone is gone, now we can liven up the doings in this antebellum abode. Remember when we christened it with mint juleps and planter's punch? Canopied beds, candlelight, Strauss waltzes! I'm surprised they don't use monogrammed chamber pots and ride in a crested coach.''

Frank Benedict yawned, in a perpetual state of boredom around his wife. He was a tall thin man, worn gaunt by dissipation. An airline executive, Frank's absences from home needed no alibis, and he frequently went on "inspection tours" all over the world.

"It chafes you, doesn't it, to know that Carol and Jeff both have the backgrounds to make this house an appropriate setting for them?"

"Because their family trees have roots in England? So what? We all have roots in Eden. I can trace my ancestry to Adam and Eve."

"You can trace it to a Brooklyn bartender."

"And you can trace yours to a Boston bean-eater," his wife thrust, smiling her touché. She was in scarlet satin, vivid as a flame, and potentially as dangerous and destructive to her enemies, but Frank had no fear of her.

"My point, exactly. Most of our present company are just twentieth-century carpetbaggers, displaced Yankees who wandered south with the other opportunists. We come and go, like the birds and the politicians. We don't even have a nest to call our own. But the Courtlands . . ."

"I know, they're native Virginians, a special breed. They were all aristocrats before that 'dreadful ol' wah!' They all had plantations and slaves and gallant men who died for their glorious cause. Well, they can have their tombs and antiques and legends and ancestor-worship! I'll take my yoga and yogurt and modern pad in the District any time."

"God, how it bugs you, Beth, to think some other couple is happy. They should all be miserable, because we are."

"Not only us, Frankie Boy. We're in the midst of misery, a regular cornucopia of it, and I detect a discordant note in the harmony of the Perfect Courtlands, too. Maybe they're celebrating a wake this evening and don't know it. Then again, maybe they do. Twenty years! Sounds like a sentence, doesn't it?"

"It would be with you."

"Oh, shut up and drink!"

"That's the most sensible thing you've said today," Frank grinned and obliged, turning to the white-coated Negro behind the bar on the terrace. "Scotch on the rocks, Rochester."

The black man glared at him. "Name's Rothchild."

"Whatever," Frank shrugged. "Scotch, please."

Skeets staggered up to the rail. "Don't you know anything but bourbon is verboten in Virginny? Make mine straight, Mac, and to the brim."

"I'll stick to Yankee martinis," Beth giggled.

"I'm cultivating a taste for Brightons," Shirley said. "A friend of ours brought the recipe back from Brighton— that's Britain's Atlantic City, you know."

"Not when I saw it," Frank reflected grimly. "The beaches were lined with tanks and artillery and strung with barbed wire. Men were practicing amphibious landings for D-day. It was March and cold as Siberia, and no decent liquor available. The guys were trying to warm their frozen guts with some vicious poison called kümmel. 'Brewed temporarily in the British Commonwealth,' the label said, a kind of apology by the Crown. The food was lousy, too. They were breaking us in on K rations. Ever eat cold sawdust and seaweed? Great cure for jaded appetites. And that rotten weather! If it didn't rain or snow, the goddamn fog—" He paused, shuddered, then drank. "Ask Jeff. He was in England, too. His Walkie-Talkie boys did some training on the coast. Dover, wasn't it, Jeff? Hell, none of it was a resort then."

"Oh, forget that war!" Beth told him impatiently. "It's long over. We've had Korea since, and there won't be another full-fledged conflict until the new generation grows up to fight it."

"The war babies are maturing now."

Carol heard and grabbed a glass of champagne off a passing tray. Jeff reached for a bourbon. Frank continued, "Yep, the cannon fodder is about ready now, and a place will be found to slaughter 'em. Cuba, Vietnam, Berlin, the moon. They'll find a sacrificial altar, because every generation's got to be baptized in the blood of battle. It's an old human custom prophesied in the Bible. So spake the Prophet Frank."

"Amen," said Skeets.

"You can always tell when the Big War Vets are getting crocked," Shirley declared. "They won't discuss The Experience when they're sober, or much of anything else when they're drunk." Her eloquent eyes admonished Frank, afraid he might inadvertently betray them, for only yesterday they had been in bed together. "Knock it off, Frank. You're loaded."

He flashed her an intimate grin. "You too, baby."

Immediately Skeets moved to the center of the arena and went into his act with more violence and abandon than usual, garnering an amused audience who substituted clapping hands and tapping toes for music. Skeets danced like a puppet manipulated by invisible strings, his face a changeless mask, and Shirley watched him with a curious expression of mingled contempt and compassion.

The spectacle sickened Carol. She turned away, bumping blindly into the Cranshaws. Joan, a lithe brunette in swirls of ivory chiffon, smiled and caught her hand, but

Carol saw only knowledge in the warm smile and pity in the gentle gray-blue eyes. Jeff had told her that he had discussed the matter with Ken, and Carol had never believed that doctors and lawyers, oath or no oath, kept all their cases confidential when mutual acquaintances were concerned. Who was to know how many codes and ethics were violated in the privacy of the bedroom?

"Nice party," Joan said.

"Terrific," Ken agreed.

"I love your gown," Joan complimented, sincerely admiring the Balenciaga of pale-gold Chantilly lace.

The chitchat irritated and embarrassed Carol, who felt they were trying to protect her. She glanced at Ken. "I understand my husband has been consulting you professionally?"

"A little business matter," he nodded.

"Don't pretend for Joan's sake, Ken. I'm sure she knows all about it."

"All about what?" Joan asked interestedly.

"Go powder your nose," Ken told her. "It's gleaming like the Capitol dome at midnight."

"Must be that new foundation cream," Joan said, taking her cue. "I was afraid it was too oily."

When she had gone, Ken took Carol's arm and ushered her into a secluded corner of the garden, under a feathery mimosa in butterfly bloom. "How much bubbly have you had, baby?"

"Who's counting?"

"Behave, Carol, or you'll destroy two people tonight, and something fine and beautiful between them."

"Is adultery your idea of something fine and beautiful, Ken? Is lying and cheating and deceiving your idea of something wonderful? If so, we're surrounded by beauty and splendor this evening!"

"Carol, I know this thing is difficult for you to understand and accept, especially coming after all these years. You're deeply shocked and hurt, and it's only natural. But try to maintain your equilibrium and perspective and be rational and charitable. Try to remember there were reasons and extenuating circumstances."

"Don't sing me any sad war songs, Ken. I've heard them all, including the love ballads and lullabies."

"Whatever you may think now, Carol, Jeff loves you, and always has. There was never really anyone else."

"I believed that for twenty years, Ken. I lived on the belief—it was food and drink to me. I thought our love was genuine, permanent. Now I wonder if it wasn't just K rations and kümmel all along—an ersatz substitute for the love he really wanted."

"That's wine talking. Better lay off, Carol. Even vintage champagne is poison in large doses if you're not inured to it."

"Then I'll just have to develop an immunity."

"That's not the answer, my dear. If you think so, look around you."

"What is the answer, Ken? Jeff and I have one hell of a problem, and he always said you were the math ace in his class at Washington and Lee. How do you figure this triangle?"

"It's not a triangle anymore, Carol. Besides, there are some things you can't measure with calipers and scales, and life is one of them. The measure of life is living."

"Then I must have been in suspended animation most of mine. Hibernating from reality."

"Perhaps," Ken agreed. "But surely you can't be jealous of a dead woman?"

"No? She gave Jeff something I can't give him."

"You can give him something equally important, Carol.

Something he needs desperately now: forgiveness. And you can give his son something he needs, too. A home, and parents."

"I don't know, Ken. I've thought about it, but I don't know if I could live with a constant reminder of Jeff's infidelity and my . . . my sterility. I don't know if I have the strength, courage, compassion. It would be terrible to bring that poor boy over here and make a mess of his life, too. Unforgivable."

"Then consider it a while longer, until you're sure. Meanwhile, Christopher can be made comfortable in England."

"You have a daughter, Ken. Would you like to see her comfortable in another country?"

"It's different with Kay."

"Yes, she was born in wedlock, which makes her special."

"Not special, just legitimate."

"Suppose Kay wasn't legitimate, but you knew she was the only child you might ever have. Well, that's Jeff's case now. I'm sure he has wanted his son more with each passing year, and he doesn't want to wait any longer." She swallowed the remainder of her Dom Perignon, choking slightly. "I guess I could force a delay. I might even force a choice, the boy or me. But that would be malicious and vindictive, the vengeance of a barren bitch, and I hope I'm not. A bitch, I mean. So I won't do it, Ken. I can't do it!"

Joan returned in time to catch her last emphatic words. "What can't you do, sweetie?"

"Oh, I propositioned her," Ken hedged, "and she said she couldn't."

Carol conjured a smile. "Not tonight, anyway. It's my wedding anniversary."

"I smell a conspiracy," Joan mused. "Have you two cooked up a surprise for us this evening?"

"A regular potpourri," Carol murmured.

Skeets ambled up, leaning a heavy hand on Ken's shoulder. " 'Scuse, please . . . thought I heard a joke about a pot o' pee?"

Joan laughed. "Potpourri, you idiot. We're going to be treated to a delicious sur—"

Ken interrupted, "Go powder your nose again."

"Don't you dare, Joan," Carol said with sudden decision, "or you'll miss our surprise." Escaping the corner before Ken could stop her, she clapped her hands for silence. "Quiet, everybody! Listen! I have an announcement!"

The babble gradually subsided, and Carol saw Jeff emerge from the shadows of a magnolia, a look of horror and incredulity on his face. She would never be sure exactly what she said, nor what reactions the blur of faces registered, least of all her husband's, for she could no longer locate him. He seemed to have disappeared from her sight, vanished in a mist. She did not feel his arms around her, did not hear his voice in her ear.

"Say, that's great!" Skeets bellowed drunkenly. "A visitor from abroad."

"She said she wasn't sure, she only hoped they'd have a visitor from England," Shirley said. "A young man."

"Why England?" Beth Benedict wondered aloud.

"Exchange student, probably."

"But why British? Why not French, Italian, Greek?"

"Furthering British-American relations," her husband surmised. "Jeff always was a diplomat at heart."

"How long was he stationed in England?"

"Long enough to get to know the people."

"Some of them, anyway," Beth drawled suspiciously.

"What's that supposed to mean?"

She smiled and wagged a scarlet-tipped finger. "Guess?"

"Your hands look like claws dipped in blood."

"That's the shade of my nail polish."

"Blood?"

"Falcon."

"Should be vulture," Frank muttered.

Skeets proposed a round of toasts, and glasses touched.

"Darling," Jeff whispered, "are you all right?"

Carol was trembling violently. "No, I'm cold, and I feel sick. I'm going in, Jeff."

"I'll go with you."

"No, please. We can't both desert our guests. Make some excuse for me," she said, breaking his embrace, and hurrying across the terrace into the house.

Observing the hasty flight, Beth sidled next to Joan. "I must say she doesn't seem too goddamned happy about it."

"She's just excited, Beth."

"Maybe. But if you ask me . . ."

Joan caught her husband's eye. "Excuse me, Beth. I have to go powder my nose again."

6

The Martins' Mercedes-Benz was the last car to leave the Courtlands, roaring away at a little past two in the morning, the drunken occupants arguing violently.

Jeff switched off the outdoor lights and blew out the candles in the hurricane globes. The caterers had cleaned up the debris, and Toby would do his best to repair the damage of spike heels to the lawn and carelessly tossed cigarettes to the plants. The garden was quiet and peaceful again, lighted only by the moon. Jeff strolled in the shadows, smoking, thinking. God, how sick he sometimes got of parties! And tonight Carol had gotten sick, too. Did she realize what she had said and done?

The master bedroom was dark, but a lamp flashed on immediately as he opened the door. She sat up, looking small and lost and lonely in the big testered bed, wearing a pair of yellow silk pajamas Jeff had never seen before. He wondered what she had done with the fluffy white thing she had originally intended for this night. The gold bracelet had been removed and lay on the nightstand like a discarded trinket.

"I'm sorry I abandoned you to the lions," she said, "and I tried to force myself to go back out there. But I really was ill, Jeffrey, my head splitting and my stomach churning. Maybe I drank too much champagne. But I just couldn't take any more of Skeets's clowning and Beth giving tongue like a bitch hound scenting a fox in the field."

"I know, Carol. I wanted to escape with you. Sometimes I think I'm antisocial. How do you feel now?"

"Better, if a bit foolish. Did I provide a fillip, a grand finale for the party?"

"They were surprised, all right. So was I. But grateful, Carol. I can't tell you how grateful."

She did not want his gratitude. "Of course, there'll be lots to do now, and I hope there won't be too much red tape. I suppose you'll go to England?"

"Not if Ken can handle it alone."

"Oh, but you should go, Jeff! See the kind of home the boy has, meet the old lady who helped to raise him. It might help you to know and understand him. Help both of us."

"I'd go, Carol, if he were still a child, incapable of making his own decision about this. But I don't think it'd be either wise or fair at his age to try to coax or influence him in any way. Ken will point up the advantages without becoming personally involved as I would, and Christopher can decide for himself what he wants to do."

"You're afraid, aren't you?" Carol perceived. "Afraid of knowing and wanting Christopher, and being rejected. Yes, it would be easier if he were a small child. Innocent, helpless, trusting, dependent. But a boy of seventeen is a definite individual, with a strong personality and ingrained habits. He may know the truth about his birth and have been exposed to gossip and ridicule. I don't suppose English villages are much different from American small towns in that respect.''

Jeff stared at the carpet. ''Yes, I'm afraid of those things, Carol, and that's why I'm not going. If he knows the truth and wants no part of me, then it's better that we never meet, never know each other at all. There's no sense making this more difficult than necessary for any of us.''

''If only we had a picture of him, even a snapshot! You can tell about a person from a picture, sometimes.''

''His mother was fair and slight,'' Jeff reflected. ''He resembled her at birth.''

''I thought you weren't in England when he was born?''

''I wasn't, but I saw him before he was a year old. He had blue eyes and a little fuzz of blond hair.''

''All babies have blue eyes at birth—I know that much about them. But their eyes often change color. Their hair, too.'' She did not want Christopher to resemble Anne Bentley, to be a pale, frail boy arousing instincts of pity and protection. If he was to be Jeff's only son, then he should do his father justice, give him pride and joy.

''I don't expect to recognize him, Carol.''

''So you saw his mother after the war? You didn't tell me that, Jeffrey.''

''Didn't I? Yes, I saw her in Southampton, while I was awaiting transportation back to the States. I thought I could sail without seeing the baby, but in the end I couldn't. Finally, I asked Anne to bring him.''

''I see,'' she murmured.

''No, you don't see, Carol. It wasn't what you think. I paid her train fare and expenses at the hotel, but we had separate rooms. Whatever had been between us was over, and we both knew it.''

Actually, it was a time of extreme tension and embarrassment for him and possibly for Anne, too, for he could not be sure how much of her stoical poise was pretense. She seemed so valiantly resigned, so utterly without recriminations or demands. She refused even to discuss her future or the child's. Jeff knew she could always return to her profession; nurses were in dire need throughout the Kingdom.

"I'll give you my address, anyway," he insisted, writing it down for her. "If I move, I'll send you the new one. Promise you'll get in touch, Anne, if ever you need help. Write or cable me. I'll answer."

Her promise made him feel better. He took the baby into his arms, but it was hard to believe that he was the father. Hard to believe they had created a human being that had survived the exigencies of his birth—and would continue to need care long after they were over. Not even watching Anne cuddle their son to her breast and croon him to sleep made Jeffrey feel much filial attachment. His mind was too filled with thoughts of reuniting with his wife. Anne Bentley and her baby were a part of the war, and he could forget the war. *He must forget it!* So he told himself that day in Southampton while the SS *America* waited in the harbor.

"Don't lie to me, Jeff," Carol pleaded. "There can't be any more lies between us."

"I'm not lying, Carol. I wanted to see my child and try to make some arrangements for his care. But that was all." At her skeptical gaze, he cried, "Listen to me, Carol! I can't brainwash myself of Anne Bentley, pretend she never existed. She was real, but the only reality she can have for me now is the reality *you* give her, and the only importance she can have for me now is the amount *you* give her. If you refuse to let her die, then it's quite possible she will live forever. But I swear to God and to you, I didn't sleep with her in Southampton!''

She said quietly, "It doesn't matter," and told herself that it really didn't, not anymore, not the affair, only the result of it mattered now. "I imagine Christopher will want a room quite different from any we have now," she rushed on. "Different furniture, decoration. I don't know much about boys. What did you like at that age?"

"Football, cars, and girls."

"Especially girls?"

He shrugged. "Just an All-American Boy."

"But Christopher is only half-American," Carol said. "English ways are different."

"Not that different, Carol, and people are pretty much the same everywhere. He'll probably like cricket, cars, and girls. A boy is a boy is a boy."

And a bastard is a bastard is a bastard, she thought. How can you change that, my dear husband? How can you make *that* up to him?

She asked, "Will you adopt Christopher, legitimize him?"

"That'll depend on him, what he wants me to do. But it'd have to be adoption—I don't believe you can legitimize a child except by marrying the mother. And why advertise his status to the world?"

"This part of the world, anyway," Carol said ruefully, "although I don't imagine anyone will be much fooled."

"Perhaps not, Carol. And a few, like Beth, will stick pins in you."

"I'll try not to bleed."

Jeff had been standing during the conversation. Now he sat down beside her on the bed and took her hands in his. "Have you forgiven me?"

"I think so," she nodded.

"Only think?"

"What is forgiveness?"

"The act of forgiving."

"Words, Jeff. Are they magic, hypnotic? Can they blot out memory, stop pain? I'll say them, then. I forgive you."

It was a deep wound that would have to heal slowly, from within. Ken knew women, all right. This was something Jeff could not rush. Carol had taken a step toward reconciliation, but she was not yet ready to meet him running. She was offering her hand, no more, and a wise man would leave before she withdrew it.

"You're tired," he said. "I'd better let you rest."

"It's been a long evening."

"Yes. Happy anniversary, darling."

"That was yesterday, Jeffrey."

She never called him that unless she wanted to be left alone. "Well, good night, Carol. I'll talk to Ken in the morning. Try to get some sleep."

"You, too," she whispered, stifling the sob in her throat.

His arms ached for her. "Carol—"

"Don't linger, Jeffrey, please? Good night."

7

Mrs. Wilton had just returned from Sunday services when her daughter arrived unexpectedly, looking as if she had just lost Paradise, or discovered that it had never existed.

"You missed a fine sermon, Carol. But I didn't expect you and Jeffrey in church this morning. I suppose you got to bed terribly late last night. You don't look as if you've slept at all. Did I miss anything by leaving early?"

"Just the Martin and Benedict shows, which you've seen before."

Margaret sighed. "Those poor, wretched souls! My heart weeps for them. Where's Jeffrey?"

"On his way to Washington."

"Business on the Lord's Day?"

"A special kind of business, Mother. I want to talk with you. It's important."

"Come upstairs, dear."

Margaret's sitting room adjoined the bedroom she had shared with her late husband. Charles's lounge chair, reading lamp, and the table holding his tobacco pipes and humidor still sat companionably beside her rocker, sewing basket, and magazine rack. A picture of him, enlarged from a snapshot taken by the Eiffel Tower in his World War I uniform, suddenly made Carol wonder if the kind, generous, slightly bald and obese man she had known bore any resemblance to the trim, dashing young soldier who had known Paris; made her also wonder how well her mother had known him, and how worthy he was of her devotion to his memory.

Carol had often brought the problems of childhood and adolescence to her mother in this intimate little parlor. Here, when she was eighteen and a sophomore at Sweet Briar College, she had confided her love for Jeffrey Courtland and her intention to forgo graduation and a debut to marry him. Young, stubborn, eager for life, she would hear no counsel or dissuasion, crying rebelliously, "You and Daddy didn't wait in 1917! Why should Jeff and I wait now? Oh, Mother, can't you remember how you felt then? Weren't you afraid if you didn't marry him and he didn't come back—" Then the petulant and tearful accusation, which had weakened Margaret into reluctant consent: "You just don't like Jeffrey and don't want us to be happy together even for a little while!"

So the wedding was solemnized, as was many another in those crucial days, in haste, but as properly as Margaret could make it. A minister, a reception, the bride in traditional white costume and the groom in uniform walking beneath the crossed sabers of his fellow officers. They had a brief honeymoon and a few ardent weeks together before his orders to ship out. After a clinging farewell at the port of embarkation, Carol returned home again, disappointed because she was not pregnant, disappointed through the years for the same reason. There were trips to gynecologists in Baltimore, New York, Boston, an occasional bright flare of hope that inevitably dimmed in the darkness of despair, and finally resignation. And then the little blue letter!

Margaret read it without flinching, listened to the story without comment. Her eyes, faded to a lighter shade of blue than her daughter's, were contemplative. Whatever reaction Carol had expected, it was not this calm rationality. Her mother's physical delicacy was deceiving, she thought, as deceiving as the blue rinse on her gray hair and the rose tint on her pale lips. She was actually much stronger than she appeared.

"Well?" Carol cried, astonished. "Aren't you shocked!"

"Not especially, dear. The women of my family lived through many wars, from the Revolution to the Civil War and the Spanish American. And, of course, your father was with General Pershing in France. You heard him recount his experiences at Chateau-Thierry and Belleau Wood, Argonne Forest, and St. Mihiel often enough. His trophies are still in the attic."

"Oh, I know the men were all great adventurers, Mother, but don't tell me they were all great adulterers, too? That all marched into battle with a gun in one arm and a girl in the other, and even Daddy had a doll in France?"

Margaret glanced through the windows, at the tall, tiered steeple of Christ Church, where Generals Washington and Lee had worshipped, and Charles Wilton had given his daughter in marriage to Lt. Jeffrey Courtland. "When men go to war, Carol, there usually is a girl if one is near—and one usually is. When I urged you to be patient with Jeffrey, I was trying to spare you the miseries and anxieties of a wartime marriage. Your father and I were impetuous that way, you see, unable to wait for the topsy-turvy world of our day to right itself. Overriding our families' objections, we rushed to the altar. A few months later Charles was en route to France, and I was trying to occupy myself by rolling bandages for the Red Cross, selling Liberty Bonds at rallies, and writing reams of letters, some of which were never answered.''

"Like mine?"

"Yes, dear, like yours. Oh, we grew up afterwards! We had you, and Charles was a model husband and father. But there were two years between, two long lonely lost years of separation and uncertainty. I don't know how Charles spent his leisure time away from me. I never asked, primarily because I was afraid of learning something I'd be better off not knowing. But he had some furloughs in Paris, and he was sentimental about French ballads and French perfume. And once there was a scented letter . . .''

"Yes?" Carol prompted, moving to the edge of her chair. "What about the letter, Mother?"

"He said it was from a nurse who tended him after he caught that bullet at Argonne, just inquiring about his health. But he did not offer to let me read it. He must have destroyed it eventually because I never found it among his effects. Maybe it was a love letter, or contained information such as Jeffrey's from England, and Charles just handled it differently. I'll never know. Too bad you had to know.''

"It always seems to be a nurse," Carol mused ruefully. "The two uniforms must have a mutual attraction, a special affinity for each other in war.'' But it further saddened and disillusioned her to think that her father may have had a foreign mistress, too, and that she may even have a half-sibling somewhere in Europe. Carol was glad Charles had destroyed the letter, rather than risk destroying his wife, and she fervently wished Jeffrey had done likewise.

"I think it's mostly because they're there," Margaret said. "Angels of mercy, symbols of life and hope amid the death and despair. And a woman is extremely fortunate if her husband brings home only memories and souvenirs."

"Jeff didn't bring back anything tangible," Carol said. "No enemy helmets or weapons. Just memories, I guess."

"Some medals for bravery, too," Margaret reminded.

"And if decorations were given for infidelity, mendacity, and deceit, he'd have won those, too! That's the worst part, Mother. All these years he let me believe . . ."

"Maybe he was trying to spare you more than himself, Carol. Give him the benefit of the doubt, anyway."

"Whose side are you on?"

"I wasn't aware that we were choosing sides. But if so, I think I'd take the boy's. And if the situation were reversed, if this had happened to you during his absence, I would hope that Jeffrey would forgive you and accept the child as his own."

"That would be the marital millennium!" Carol scoffed. "Wives are not supposed to make such mistakes, are they? You were raised on morals and conventions, and you raised me on them, too."

"Are you sorry now? Do you wish you'd had a few serious affairs? Do you think it would help you to understand your husband's transgressions better?"

"Perhaps."

"Don't talk that way, Carol. If anything shocks me, it's to hear such an obscenity from you."

"Oh, don't worry, Mother! I'm not going to start bed-hopping to get even." She paused, biting her lip. "And I've already decided to accept Jeff's son. That's what the business in Washington is about now, and why I'm here.''

"You want reassurance, Carol? To be told that you're doing the right thing? Not just the only thing, but the right one?''

"I want to feel that I'm doing what's best for the boy,'' Carol replied, ''not merely what will please Jeffrey and save our marriage.'' But her mind sang its old refrain: *Love me, need me, want me.*

Yet she had, in effect, refused him last night. For the first time in their marital relationship, she had not wanted him physically, nor loved him enough to cater to his need of her. She had felt something akin to revulsion at his touch, an involuntary but nonetheless real repugnance, and it had surprised and frightened her. What if she never desired him that way again? What if her love for him was not as deep and strong as she imagined, and the rift between them not merely temporary? How could she cope with such doubts, much less the reason for them?

She knew nothing about adolescent boys, except what she had read in books and magazines. With a girl she could have drawn on her own experience. But a boy with recent memories of his mother, and perhaps a bitter knowledge of his father . . .

Her mother interrupted her thoughts. "There's no way to be certain of that now, Carol. It would be nice if we were clairvoyant, but life is just not that simple. Not even expectant parents know in advance how the coming of a child will affect their lives. It's something that has to be proved in reality.''

Ken had said essentially the same thing last night, Carol reflected: *The measure of life is living.* Was the measure of love giving and forgiving? How easy it was to be philosophical about someone else's problem!

"I suppose so," she agreed. "Will you help me fix a room for Christopher, Mother?"

"Of course, dear. Which one?"

Gazing down into the garden of the fine old Federal house on Cameron Street, Carol could see her childhood swing still hanging from a hoary oak, the seat and chains kept neatly painted. Had her mother preserved it out of sentiment, or expectation of grandchildren? "The one we had hoped to turn into a nursery," she said, her voice breaking.

Within a week the pale-blue walls of the "nursery" were painted a sunny yellow, and the delicate white furniture was replaced with sturdy Colonial maple. Margaret donated a captain's chair for the desk and a treasured pair of Currier & Ives prints, which she had just finished hanging.

"Maybe we should use some English scenes, too?" she suggested. "A landscape of his native Cotswold Hills would be nice, if we could find one."

Carol smiled wryly. "Or a reproduction of *Blue Boy*? Let's wait and see what Christopher thinks, shall we? He may not be here long enough to care, if he comes at all."

"Oh, don't say that!"

"It's a possibility we have to face, Mother. Lord, how desperately you want a grandchild! I've seen the way you look at the Cranshaws' daughter, the paper boy, and the kid who carries out your groceries at the market. You're in Granny Heaven dishing out treats to youngsters on Halloween. You remind me of an old movie I saw on late television the other night. This old man had a son who somehow got involved with a girl and a baby, and he thought the child was his son's and refused to believe otherwise. Then during a family argument, he shouted, 'I don't care *who* the father is, *I'm* the grandfather!' And you don't seem to care who Christopher's mother was, you just want to be his grandmother.''

"What's wrong with that?"

Carol spun the globe thoughtfully. "Nothing. Only he may not want an American grandmother. He may not want American parents, either, at this late date. He may be perfectly happy and content with that old lady in the Cotswold Hills. Ken hasn't cabled any definite news from England yet. You know, Jeff is worried."

"I feel sorry for him," Margaret said. "For you, too, Carol. You should be close together now, and instead you're apart. Physically, anyway."

"Have you been snooping in the guest room, Mother?"

"Just curious to know if what I suspected was true, and apparently it is, Carol. How long do you propose to keep this arrangement?"

"It's not an arrangement, Mother. I mean, we didn't plan it this way, it just developed. But maybe separation is good for couples, occasionally. Togetherness can be a habit after 'twenty years. The double bed makes for convenience and laziness. It doesn't take much effort to roll over, and a woman can prostitute herself to her husband as well as to any other man."

"You've been reading feminist tracts," Margaret surmised. "You'll have to guard against that attitude with Jeffrey, Carol. Guard your emotions in public, too, or your friends will find their answers by studying your face, rather than your husband's or the boy's."

Carol frowned. "They'll suspect the truth, anyway. We won't be able to bluff this, not after all these years."

"Perhaps not, though actually I think time is in your favor. It would have been infinitely more incriminating, I should imagine, if Jeffrey had brought home a bundle from

Britain while Americans were still sending them over there. Many servicemen did, you know. I used to see pictures in the papers and read stories about German, French, Italian children being adopted into American families. Are they all orphans brought to this country out of pity? I doubt it. Some of the wives in the pictures weren't smiling; they looked sad, bewildered, resigned.''

"Like me?''

"I'm afraid so, dear. And I'd wonder how the natural mother looked, if she were alive, and how she felt giving up her child. One thing about Anne Bentley, nothing but death could separate her from her child. There must have been a lot of good in a woman like that, don't you think?''

Carol nodded. "Apparently Jeff thought so, and I should hate to think he could have fathered a child with some cheap tramp, or worse.''

"Well, that—and the fact that he claims not to have been in love with her—should make your cross a little easier to bear, darling.''

Carol remained silent, adjusting a curtain.

Margaret stepped back for a better perspective of the cherished prints. "There now! All done. But that wall still seems a bit bare. What do you think it needs?''

"What it's always needed, Mother. Fingerprints.''

Part Two

Do ye hear the children weeping,
O my brothers,
Ere the sorrow comes with years?

Elizabeth Barrett Browning (1806–1861)
The Cry of the Children

8

There was frost in the hills the night before and fog in the morning. The sun burned away the mist by noon, but the thick stone walls of the Cotswold homes held the chill like an ice chest. Perishables could be adequately preserved without mechanical refrigeration in the uniformly cool pantries of the kitchen walls, and covers were necessary at night even in summer.

Agatha Linton sat before her fireplace now, a wool shawl over her thin shoulders. The dampness aggravated her arthritis and coronary cough, impairing both her movements and her speech. "I've discussed this with Mr. Tary," she said to Kenneth Cranshaw, "and he'll handle the details on this end, sir. I've also discussed it with Dr. Trumble and Vicar Tisdale."

Tary, Trumble, and Tisdale were known as The Three T's of Tilbury. They practiced law, medicine, and religion, respectively. An elderly trio by youth's standards, they were wise and influential patriarchs of the village, and Christopher knew Agatha Linton's generation put their faith and trust in them.

He was sure the old lady had acted on their combined counsel in writing that letter to Jeffrey Courtland immediately after his mother's death. She seemed greatly relieved now, conferring with the visitor from America, as if she had performed a duty, kept a promise, righted a wrong.

Although he listened attentively to proposed plans for him, Christopher was not at all happy. He had read much about the United States, primarily to please his mother, who had imagined they would go there someday. The more limited his horizons appeared in England, the more wistfully Anne spoke of America. The idea obsessed her as much as his education, especially after his failure to win a university scholarship against some of the stiffest competition in the Kingdom. "Education is too difficult and selective here," she had despaired. "Such scores would probably have qualified you to enter Harvard or Yale in America."

Christopher had been equally disappointed, aware that the trade school and factory were the alternatives, for there was not enough money in their savings to pay for college. After high school graduation he went to London to find a job—and that was an education in itself.

The city was a world apart from the country, and he learned more in one year there than he had in fifteen in Tilbury. He worked at some odd jobs, lived in some odd places, met some odd people. And each experience left its imprint, some indelible.

While cleaning chimneys in Chelsea, he met an artist who saw death as a nude angel and filled his studio with bizarre paintings of beautiful young women wearing only golden haloes. Upon seeing Christopher his conception of the grim reaper changed to that of a naked young man, and he tried to persuade the handsome youth to pose thus for him. Merely laughing at the proposition, Christopher moved on.

In Soho a bearded bard guzzled red wine from a greasy goatskin and composed a passionate ode to the Cotswold chap, while Christopher washed the dirty windows in his flat and ignored his more obvious advances. It remained for a pretty and precocious young girl in Bethnal Green, where he lived while employed by a scrap dealer, to seduce the virginal country lad. Christopher fancied himself in love with Sally Sawyer until he discovered her initiating another novice on the same filthy old mattress in the tenement basement.

Next came Covent Garden market, where he unpacked fruit and vegetables and met a boy his own age and in his same predicament. The chap knew several others like him, products of war, by-products of peace. They formed an ironic fraternity, The Brotherhood of Bastards of American Bastards. They drank ale and cheap liquor and talked about going to the States, finding their sires, and beating hell out of them. Already engaged in mischief and petty crime, Christopher feared the only place they would go was to gaol, which was not one of his ambitions. He returned to the wholesome atmosphere of the village, to the fresh air, green hills, clear streams—and his mother spoke more and more about America.

Dreams, delusions, sometimes babbling delirium. Then, for long spells, she was strangely silent, staring at the walls or ceiling, as if transfixed. In one of her peculiar moods Anne told her son about his father, and Christopher did not admit that he had long ago overheard a conversation between her and Aunt Agatha—and though she soon forgot what she had told him, Christopher never could or would. Containing his knowledge was exceedingly difficult, as he watched his mother's physical and mental decline.

No longer able to practice nursing, Anne became completely dependent upon her aunt. She grew thin, pale, haggard. Whatever her illness, Dr. Trumble was unable to cure or even alleviate it. Christopher feared she would die—but not in the manner she did. And he hated with all the passion and fury of youth the American man who, he felt, had contributed to her ultimate fate.

The bloody coward! he thought now. Why hadn't he come in person to fetch his bastard son? Could Courtland really do all the things for him that his solicitor was promising? Was he as rich and generous as all that!

Christopher gazed pensively into the hearth, petting the shaggy old collie beside him. "How long would the visit be, Mr. Cranshaw?" he asked.

"That would depend on you, Christopher," Ken answered. "You might like it well enough to stay forever."

"I doubt that, sir. And so Mr. Courtland was a friend of my mother during the war, was he?"

"Yes, he was, son. And he would like to repay her kindness to him through you."

Never had Ken seen so much cynicism in a youth's expression. He appeared older and far wiser than his years, as fatherless boys often did. This one might be hard to handle, and Jeff might regret his decision.

"I'll think about it," Christopher muttered.

Agatha Linton was very tired. She tried to steady her shaking hands by folding them in her lap and suppress the yawn that told Ken the discussion must be continued tomorrow. With apologies, he took his leave.

Accompanying him to the door, Christopher asked, "Would you like to see the hills, sir?"

"Yes, thank you. Very much."

Outside, Christopher picked up a crooked walking stick. "We don't get many American tourists here," he said.

"They don't know what they're missing. This is beautiful country."

"Full of history, too. Our village is over three hundred years old. Aunt Agatha's cottage was one of the first built in this valley."

"It belongs on a picture postcard," Ken said, admiring the yellowed limestone walls and chipped-stone roof. "Do you tend the garden, Chris?"

"The vegetables, mostly. She enjoys the flowers."

They passed the common, which still had its historic stocks and gibbet, although the green was used now only for bowling and other community entertainment. Mildew and lichen covered the ancient inn where Ken was staying and where the village men gathered in the evening to enjoy ale and darts.

"Where does Mr. Tary live?"

"Number nine Oliver Street." Christopher pointed to a tiered row of cottages, set into the hillside as naturally as if they had grown there. "The house with the yellow door and shutters. But we go this way, sir."

Soon they were on a lane edged with purple bay willows. Blue campion tinted the meadows, and scarlet poppies brightened the slopes. Sleek cattle and fat sheep grazed in the lush pastures, and here and there a big shaggy shire cropped the sweet grass. On a distant hilltop, Ken could see a medieval structure and inquired, "What's that building up there?"

"Watchtower used by the Roman legions, and the Saxon and Norman invaders after them. Some folks say their ghosts still roam the region, and old Mr. Farnsby claims to see headless horsemen in armor riding in the mists. I think his spirits come mostly out of bottles, but tourists like to hear such tales. They want to visit haunted castles, too. Spooks themselves, most of 'em.''

Ken smiled. "How long have you been in the guide business, Chris?"

"Since I was ten. Sometimes I wear a Robin Hood cap and Wellington boots, and folks snap my picture. I must be in a few family albums. You came by Foss Way from the station, didn't you? That's the Old Roman Road."

"So the driver said. He was friendly and informative until I gave him a pack of cigarettes. He smoked one after the other and never said another word."

"Americans do make good cigarettes, all right. I'll say that for them."

"You smoke, Chris?"

"Sometimes."

"Drink?"

"I've tasted the stuff."

"Got a girl friend?"

"No special one. I like 'em all."

Ken laughed. "That's a good healthy attitude."

"Do you have a son, sir?"

"No. A daughter. Kay is almost sixteen, and naturally, her mother and I adore her."

Christopher paused by a vigorous brook fringed with ferns and alive with rainbow trout. "Good angling here," he said. "Good rabbit hunting in the hills, too. This forest used to be a royal preserve, and 'tis said King John built a hunting lodge hereabouts. No trace of it now, though. No sign of the stags, wolves, or wild boars, either."

"You like to hunt and fish, Chris?"

"Well, sure."

"Mr. Courtland will be glad of that. He enjoys both sports himself. You'll have fun together."

The boy ignored that, quickly turning guide again. "The
Thames rises in the Cotswolds, from a tiny spring. You
can't even find it, unless you know where to look. 'TH,'
for Thames Head, is carved in the trunk of a big ash tree
beside it. My mother and I had a picnic there last summer," he reflected, his voice breaking.

"I'm sorry about your mother, Christopher. Terribly
sorry about her accident."

Accident. That was another thing they thought he didn't
know, because he'd been away at the time. They told him
Anne had tripped and fallen downstairs, breaking her neck,
but they lied. He had seen the popped eyes and the green-
black swell of her throat—and later he had found the
evidence they had tried to conceal from him: the hemp
rope with its noose cut, and the chair she had used to
attach it to a beam in the garret.

His mouth trembled, his eyes moistened. Embarrassed,
he slashed a bramble bush with his stick. And as they
mounted an arched stone bridge over a brook, Christopher
pounded the railing furiously.

"Easy, son."

Ken put a comforting hand on his shoulder. Immediately
the boy shrugged it off and took another whack at a
blooming hawthorn bush along their path, scattering blossoms, bees, butterflies. Abruptly, he asked, "What's Virginia like?"

"Parts of it are much like this, Chris. Hills and woods.
But the Courtlands live in Alexandria, an old town just
across the Potomac River from Washington. Of course,
you know that's the capital of the United States?"

"Yes, sir. What sort of chap is Courtland?"

"A nice sort, Chris. You'll like him. Mrs. Courtland,
too. They're fine people."

"Do they have children?"

"Unfortunately, no."

Christopher thought he knew then why they wanted him at this late date, but he said nothing.

They strolled awhile in silence, Ken taking in the lovely scenery and wondering what was on the boy's mind. Dusk was falling, along with the chilly evening dampness. Lights flickered in the cottages, smoke plumed from the chimneys. The brown and white collie came barking up the lane.

"Isn't that your dog, Chris?"

"Yes, sir. Aunt Agatha sent him to fetch me to supper. Good old Bounder. I'm going to miss him." And in saying this it was clear—he had decided to go to America.

Horace Tary, Esquire, was a magnificent old gentleman with gray hair and a clipped gray beard. After reading the paternity affidavit and other documents signed by Jeffrey Courtland, he said, "Everything seems to be in order, Mr. Cranshaw. I don't foresee any problems."

"I understand Christopher already has a passport?"

He nodded. "Anne Bentley applied for it six months ago. I wondered why, until her death. Agatha Linton has given me the pertinent facts."

"Miss Linton is seriously ill, isn't she? How will she manage now? Who'll look after her?"

"No cause for concern about her," Tary assured him. "We take care of our own here—it's an old Cotswold custom. Christopher will inherit her estate, a mere pittance now. As executor of her will, I'll contact you when the time comes. The good doctor will attend her, and the good vicar will bury her. Friends and neighbors won't let her be alone or lonely. She'll die easy, now she thinks the lad's future is secure. Courtland has a lot to redeem here, Cranshaw."

"He's aware of that, sir, and he'll do his best. Perhaps Miss Linton did not tell you that his help was always refused before. But you can depend on it now."

"The child will depend on it," Tary said gravely, rising from his desk. "And the old lady." He paused thoughtfully. "Virginia, eh? Isn't that the state of presidents?"

"It's been called that, sir."

"Well, who knows? Churchill's mother was American." He smiled, extending his hand. "Nice meeting you, Cranshaw. Have a safe trip back."

"Thank you, Mr. Tary. I'll be in touch."

Christopher's bags were packed. He took the dog for a last long romp in his beloved hills—and almost changed his mind about leaving them.

On the eve of his departure, he cut a large bouquet of flowers from the garden and visited the cemetery. It was drizzling lightly, and fog shrouded the village. He stood bareheaded beside the new raw mound of earth and fervently promised his mother a tombstone. "An angel, Mum. White marble. I'll make him buy it. I'll make him do a lot of things. Most of all, I'll make him sorry for what he did to you. You'll see."

When Cranshaw came for him early the next morning, Miss Linton was up and preparing tea, forcing an appearance of cheerful well-being. She embraced Christopher warmly, shook Ken's hand gently, and waved good-bye from the stoop. Bounder followed his master to the garden gate. Christopher could not look back as they drove away.

He had hoped the journey would be made on a great ocean liner, sailing from Southampton or Liverpool, and was disappointed to learn that they would fly from Gatwick Airport, near London. The train carried them there, whistling sadly past the stations. Christopher was quiet and uncomfortable in the new dark-blue suit Cranshaw had bought for him at the Tilbury haberdashery. His passport was in the jacket, and a wallet with more money than he had ever had at one time before: Aunt Agatha's bon voyage gift to him.

His last view of England was vague and distorted, as if seen through mist, although the sky was brilliantly clear, the sun glinting on the silver wings of the airplane. It was his eyes that were blurred. Below them, like a relief map studied in school, he saw forests, lakes and streams, fields and houses, towns and factories. Then there was nothing below but green water, and nothing above but billowy white clouds.

"We're over the Atlantic Ocean," Ken apprised.

"Three thousand miles of it," Christopher nodded.

"You won't think so on a jet, Chris. We'll land at New York's Idlewild Airport in record time."

"I can wait," he said, brooding.

9

Carol and Jeff arrived an hour ahead of the scheduled flight from New York. A few minutes later, Joan Cranshaw and her daughter drove up and parked beside them.

"Hi!" Joan waved from the white Cadillac convertible. "We're lucky to find an empty niche. There's a caravan from D.C. on the road. Official limousines. A VIP must be expected."

"One usually is around here," Jeff said.

"I think it's terribly thrilling!" Kay bubbled excitedly, her crystal-gray eyes sparkling, her dark ponytail bouncing. "Maybe I'll see a prince or movie star!"

Media reporters and cameramen were gathered at the various gates, and technical crews from radio and television networks were setting up equipment. Everyone who was anyone eventually came to Washington, and most of them arrived by way of Washington National Airport. But Carol was conscious only of the visitor they were expecting, afraid that she was not sufficiently prepared and may not be able to cope. When Joan suggested coffee, she quickly agreed.

"I'll wait out here," Jeff said.

"Me, too," Kay giggled. "Don't want to miss anything."

"I've never seen Kay so excited," Joan said on the way to the terminal restaurant. "I think it's more than just the possibility of seeing someone famous—that's almost an everyday occurrence since the Kennedy Administration, and she has a nice autograph collection. Right now, I think she's curious about Christopher."

"So am I," Carol admitted.

She tried to remain calm, but by the time they had managed a table and ordered, she was shaking so hard she had to take a tranquilizer. Would she soon be carrying them around in a chic container, like Shirley Martin and Beth Benedict, perhaps gulping them down as indiscriminately and even joking about her "habit" and "addiction"? Beth had learned to swallow her capsules without liquid, and Shirley could actually suck her Miltown tablets like Life Savers.

Joan frowned. "You never needed that stuff before, Carol. I used to admire your composure."

"That was ages ago, Joan. B.C. Before Christopher." She paused. "You know, don't you?"

"Yes, but don't blame Ken or anyone else. You betrayed yourself at the party."

Carol sighed. "I intended to be nonchalant, sophisticated with my announcement. I came across like a blithering idiot! So afraid those who weren't too drunk to add could figure the score. One and one can make three, if they're male and female. It's a serious situation, Joan, and a tremendous challenge. I only hope the Courtlands are equal to it."

"Jeff has aged ten years since that night," Joan said.

"I guess I've been hard on him, but not purposely. I just can't help myself, Joan. It's as if a part of me died with the revelation of his infidelity; my faith in him, or whatever, I can't seem to resurrect it. I keep wondering how many others there've been."

"Confession may be good for the soul, but it also breeds suspicion, doesn't it? If every woman he comes in contact with now is going to be suspect—"

"Oh, I know, Joan! I'm behaving like a jealous young bride more than a matron of twenty years. But it's like suddenly discovering a scar on his person and automatically searching for other imperfections."

" 'Seek and ye shall find,' " Joan warned. "You really shouldn't be here now, Carol. You should be at home, in bed. You are a prospective mother in labor—that's most of your trouble. The fact that another woman suffered the ordeal physically only makes it more painful for you mentally and emotionally. But try to bear up, dear. You're not the first or only woman to experience this kind of travail."

"Don't worry, Joan. I'll survive with the aid of my trusty tranquilizers."

"Enough of them will put you in a twilight sleep," Joan cautioned. "You won't feel a thing. But you want to be just a little conscious, don't you?"

Carol smiled wryly. "You sound like a midwife."

"I just don't want you to become dependent on drugs, Carol, and unable to function without them, like some of our friends. Beth is hooked on Librium, and most of the time only semiconscious. Which, of course, is a blessing to her victims, because she can be a devastating bitch when alert. Oh, Lord! Speak of the devil's wife—"

Beth was approaching in swirls of burnt-orange silk, fluttering like a bird in brilliant plumage. "Ah, there you are, darlings! I called your pad, Joanie Girl, and the maid said Mr. Cranshaw was returning from England today and you were meeting his plane. I knew the Courtlands would be with you and decided to join the Welcome Wagon. So here I am! Seconds, anyone? I'll treat.''

"No, thanks," Carol said.

"Me, either," Joan declined. "But do sit down, Bethie Girl, unless you brought a brass band with you, and they're tuning up outside!"

Beth laughed brittlely and flopped into a chair. "It would have been a novel idea, at that. They could've played the American and British anthems, mingled or mangled in one version. Don't you think, Carol?"

"I hadn't until now," Carol murmured.

"Seriously, dear. You and Jeff should have gone to England together. It could've been a second honeymoon, if you believe in such things. Frankly, I don't. I don't believe you can recapture the glow after twenty years, no matter how or where you try. Frank and I couldn't after only ten years—and we tried in the supposedly romantic, enchanted Naples.'' As she chattered, Beth primped in an enormous jeweled compact, her eyes reconnoitering the room in the mirror.

"Maybe you didn't try hard enough," Joan suggested.

Beth closed the compact with a sharp snap and dropped it into her huge straw tote bag. Then she scrounged for her jade holder, fitted a cigarette into it, and flicked a jade lighter. "We tried," she said somewhat wistfully. "I did, anyway. You know what they say—'See Naples and die'? We did and died as far as love is concerned. Age might improve wine and cheese, but it stales marriage."

"Speak for yourself," Joan admonished, but Carol only stared at the residue in her coffee cup.

"Well, you and Ken may be on a perpetual honeymoon,

and more power to you. But I think going to Europe was our biggest mistake. Frank was in Italy during the war, and I couldn't help wondering if he'd known some gorgeous, chesty babe there, like Sophia Loren or Gina Lollobrigida, and balled her whenever possible, maybe even given her a bambino along with chocolate bars. There's a lot of truth in those jokes about the oversexed American soldier starting the world population explosion. GI Joe scattered his virile seed all over the earth, and many came to fruition. Orphans, orphans everywhere! But that's the nature of the beast, isn't it? Why be a Pollyanna about it?''

"No one could ever accuse you of being a Pollyanna," Joan said, trying not to glare at her.

Beth drew on her smoldering cigarette, smiling through the smoke screen. "I bet, deep down, Carol agrees with me. And I envy her, having a young Englishman to break the monotonous routine of twenty years. Seventeen, is he? What a wonderful age! If I were seventeen again, I think I'd kill myself and die happy."

"I doubt that," Joan told her. "Teenagers have problems, too. I should know, I have one."

For a few moments Beth's expression and voice mellowed in retrospect or regret. "You're lucky in many ways," she said. "I know that's an odd statement from someone who's been the abortion route, but I happen to believe it's more important for children to be born in love than in wedlock. A single woman shouldn't be denied the right to motherhood, any more than a wife should be forced into it against her wishes."

"We've heard your theories on that subject before, Beth. Why don't you go out and start a movement?"

Beth grinned. "I'm just a realist, Joan, which is more than I can say for some of us. But God forbid that I should shatter any fairy tale illusions!"

"Yes, God forbid," Joan muttered, fuming.

Carol began to tremble again, and from the depths of her seemingly fathomless bag Beth hauled up a familiar initialed gold box and extended it across the table. "Nervous, darling? I have just the thing for you!"

"I have my own, thanks."

"Oh? I didn't know you used them? That is, I didn't think you had need of pills. The ideal couple, and all that! Remember that satire Skeets composed about The Perfect Courtlands?"

"No marriage is perfect," Carol said.

"But, sweetie, that's exactly my point! Only a naive and stupid fool would argue it. And isn't it nice that Jeff kept in touch with that British kid's family all these years? Few men were so faithful to wartime acquaintances."

"Our flight is due," Joan interrupted, rising. "We don't want to miss it."

"No, indeed." Beth popped a colorful capsule into her wide orange mouth. "Coming, Carol?"

Jeff was waiting at the flight gate. He took Carol's hand and pressed it reassuringly, but there was no response.

"She's tranquilized," Joan whispered.

"What?"

There wasn't time to explain. The plane was down and taxiing along the runway. Glimpsing her father in a window, Kay began waving to him. "There's Daddy, Mom! He sees us! Wave to him!"

10

Christopher was tall for his age and slim, an angular, athletic slimness peculiar to adolescence, but which, nevertheless, assailed Jeff with the thought that perhaps he had never had enough to eat. His eyes, neither the pale blue of his mother's nor the deep brown of his father's but a cobalt blend of the two colors, were alert and intelligent, and the blond fuzz that had covered his head in infancy had thickened and darkened to a burnished bronze. His facial features—fine straight nose, full mouth, square jaw—were patterned as accurately after Jeff's as if they had been cast in the same mold. Except for the Eton crop of his hair and his British accent, Christopher seemed as American as Penrod or Holden Caulfield. He was a child to be proud of, and Jeff greeted him with immediate pride, affection, and realization of what he had missed.

"Hello, son! Welcome to America!"

Son, Carol thought, wishfully comparing them. No doubt

about it. His son, Anne Bentley's son, *their* son. Why couldn't he have been mine, *ours*? Dear God, *why*!

Composing a smile, she clasped his hand warmly, trying to divest her mind of all extraneous intrusions about his conception. "We're so happy to have you, Christopher, and hope you'll enjoy being with us."

"Thank you for inviting me," he replied stiffly.

He was reserved, polite, formal to a fault, as if his manners had been imposed by preadmonition. But he seemed more at ease with the Cranshaws, delighted to meet Ken's family.

And Kay was visibly impressed, her pretty face turned up to his like a dewy flower to the sun, her diminutive figure at its female best in a short pink skirt and fuzzy white sweater. Few youths in her acquaintance had such straight, braceless teeth and smooth, unblemished skin, and none was taller or better looking. "I'm so pleased to know you, Chris, and hope you'll stay ever so long!"

"I'm just here on holiday," he said, and even his accent thrilled her.

Soon Beth was jogging his hand like a pump handle and giggling like a silly schoolgirl. "I don't blame Kay. If I were twenty years younger . . . So jolly meeting you, Chris Boy! You'll like America, and America will love you, I'm sure. Now I must dash, darlings. Cheerio!"

Her orange skirt swirled past a Turkish diplomat escorting a dark elegant woman in a flowing white sari. The last Carol saw of Beth she was trying to disentangle herself from a brace of Afghan hounds led by a French ballerina come to entertain at the White House. Carol relaxed somewhat, talking to Joan, while Christopher, ignoring the adults, concentrated on Kay Cranshaw, and Ken went to collect the luggage.

*   *   *

Christopher sat in the back seat of the big, shiny sedan, watching the traffic on Mount Vernon Memorial Highway.

"How was the trip?" Carol asked him.

"Fair."

"Was it your first by plane?"

"Yes."

"What do you think of America so far?"

"Haven't seen much yet. New York looked all right from the air, but I think London is bigger."

"It was almost leveled when last I saw it," Jeff said.

"It's being rebuilt."

"Did you go to London often?"

"I lived there for a while. It was interesting."

"Well, we'll try to make it interesting for you here, too," Jeff said. "We want you to like it so much that you'll want to stay a long time, even consider making it your home."

Bloody little chance of that, Christopher thought grimly, and fell silent.

Soon they were in a town which he was told was Alexandria, Virginia, and that they lived in the Old Section. Here the streets were named King, Queen, Prince, Princess, Duke, Royal. Some were cobbled and sentineled by great majestic trees. On Prince Street, which sloped toward the Potomac River, the houses stood close together, touching in fact. They were made of brick and frame and stucco, some painted yellow or red or pink, with dormer windows and bright shutters and beautiful old doors fronting on the sidewalks. Chimneys towered above the steep roofs, and there were secluded gardens in the rears.

Christopher, who had seen such homes in England, was not surprised to learn that some of these had been built by Englishmen. But he was surprised that the Courtlands

lived in one of them. He had expected something modern
and flamboyant and American, like the houses in Hollywood films: a split-level, rambling design in suburbia of
native stone and glass, with an Olympic-sized swimming
pool. This fine old Georgian mansion on a corner somewhat aloof from its neighbors would have set well in
London's Mayfair or Belgrade Square, or on the estate of a
country squire.

The car turned into a brick-paved driveway and stopped
before an ivy-latticed garage, presumably once the carriage
house with servants' quarters above, and Carol said, "This
is our home, Christopher."

"Did George Washington sleep here?"

Jeff smiled. "Ask Mrs. Courtland's mother," he said as
Margaret came out to meet them. "Mrs. Wilton knows all
about those things."

Margaret was beaming. "So this is Christopher? My,
what a handsome lad! I baked a cake for you, son. I hope
you like chocolate?"

"I'm not hungry," he said, evading her embrace.

"You will be, dear. Later. Now I think you should see
the charming room the Courtlands have for you."

It was the finest residence Christopher had ever been in,
and all so splendid he expected to see Don't Touch signs
and restraining ropes around the heirloom furniture and
other fine museum pieces. He estimated that the cost of the
Venetian chandelier in the elegant drawing room would
have bought clothes and shoes for him for many years.
The silver tea set on the Sheraton sideboard in the dining
room would have provided a good supply of fuel for the
Cotswold cottage, with money left for repairs. The excellent paintings could have sent him through a choice college. The magnificent furniture could have paid for the
best specialists in the world for his mother. The bric-a-brac

alone could have taken care of Agatha Linton's taxes and amply stocked her larder for many seasons.

All this, he thought bitterly, while his poor mother, ill herself, had nursed sick people, worn darned uniforms, purchased bargain items, and was buried in a cheap wood box in a markerless grave! While Sister Bentley had administered enemas and emptied slops, Mrs. Courtland had likely attended auctions and searched antique shops for more rare treasures to enrich her extensive collection.

How gracefully she mounted the curved stairway, this fine American lady in her expensive clothes, and how gracious she was trying to be, gentle smile, soft voice, when she probably despised him! He could not believe that she could know the truth and not despise him.

She led him to a large bright room on the second floor. His feet, accustomed to bare stone floors and rag rugs, sank into the deep luxurious carpet. The paint and fabrics smelled fresh, and even the books and globe on the maple desk were new. His shabby bags, carried in by Courtland, were as incongruous as himself in this house—and he hated them for that, too.

"Shall I help you unpack?" Carol offered.

"I can manage alone," he declined.

"Well, I'll just show you where to put your things."

"Must I put them in special places?"

"Not unless you want to, Christopher. But it's easier that way, don't you think? 'A place for everything, and everything in its place.' "

"I suppose so," he agreed, examining the portable television set. "Thanks for the telly."

"I hope you enjoy it, Chris. There's a radio too, by the bed, which will wake you with music and put you to sleep with it, if you wish. And your own personal telephone."

Joan Cranshaw had told her that teenagers preferred a private line to any other gift.

Christopher realized that they had gone to considerable trouble and expense for his benefit, and perhaps he should express more enthusiastic appreciation. On the other hand, wasn't he entitled, by blood and birthright, to much more than these small presents and concessions?

"Thank you," he murmured grudgingly.

"Can I do anything?" asked Margaret eagerly.

"You can make some tea," Carol told her. "And take him with you." She meant Jeff, who was standing rather helplessly in the doorway.

The first thing Christopher removed from his luggage was a carefully wrapped package, which had been cushioned between some woolen garments to prevent breakage. It contained two photographs in tarnished gilt frames: one, an ordinary looking young woman wearing her light hair in the long simply waved style of the 1940's; the other, a rugged young man in a British army uniform, branch of Combined Operations, popularly known as the Commandos, his tunic adorned with decorations. He placed the photographs on the dresser, side by side, and moved the bowl of fresh flowers near his mother's.

Watching, Carol felt a sudden chill and silly superstition that Anne Bentley's spirit had entered the room, and chided herself for the occult notion. Nothing like a ghost to haunt an old house! A friendly ghost, she hoped, gazing at the woman's picture. *You do seem friendly, Miss Bentley. Were you kind to my husband? Will you be kind to me now? Help me forgive and forget? Oh, please, do help me!*

"I say, Mam, are you all right?"

"What? Oh, yes, of course, Christopher. Just day-dreaming. Women sometimes do, you know."

He nodded, remembering his mother's fantasies. "Do you suppose tea is ready, Mam?"

"I'll see," Carol said, leaving.

11

There are some barriers more formidable than walls, and Christopher began to construct them around himself at an early age. When his vulnerability was threatened, he re-enforced his barricades and retreated deeper into his fort.

The Courtlands were after him, and if he did not protect himself, they would breach his defenses and capture him. Then he would belong to them, like a pet, and they would put him on a leash or in a cage, and he could never escape. This house, this life, these people, would imprison him. *Own him!* And he did not intend to let that happen.

Seclusion was a part of his vigilance, and his first week in America was spent largely in voluntary confinement, watching television, listening to the radio, reading, and writing letters to Agatha Linton. When he had read every book in his room, he ventured down to the library, waiting until late afternoon, when he thought Mrs. Courtland was dressing for dinner and Mr. Courtland had not yet returned from Washington.

The walls seemed to be made of books, the shelves reaching from floor to ceiling and filled with a magnificent collection: classics in matched bindings, current fiction in inviting jackets, history and biography, poetry, some rare old volumes bound in hand-tooled leather, and even some unpublished manuscripts. To a deprived scholar they were adventures waiting to be experienced, dreams offering a few magic hours of reality, treasure chests containing all the wisdom and wonders of the world. A veritable store-house of knowledge and entertainment, and Christopher stood in the center of it, like a beggar in the midst of plenty, awed and angry, remembering the tattered books his mother had slaved and saved to buy for him, often denying herself some necessity. His eyes fell on the full crystal inkwell and silver letter opener on the desk, and he had a sudden wild impulse and vision of dark stains, ripped paper, irreparable damage, and chaos. A movement in a dim corner startled him out of his mischievous meditation, and Courtland materialized in the shadows, drink in hand.

"Hello, Chris."

Instantly he recoiled, feeling spied upon, and resentful. "Excuse me, sir. I didn't know anyone was here. May I borrow some books?"

"Help yourself, son. I don't think there's anything here you shouldn't read."

He smirked. "High moral standards, eh?"

"What?"

Christopher shrugged and stepped swiftly to the nearest shelf, removed several volumes without regard for title, author, or content, though he had originally intended to browse and perhaps try one of the lounge chairs, with its ottoman and proper lamp. But Courtland had spoiled even that simple pleasure and anticipation, and he could not conceal his hostile resentment. He would have left immediately except for the restraining hand on his arm.

"What's your hurry, Chris? Sit down. Talk."

The hand was brushed off as if it were a fly or something dirtier, while his eyes gazed eloquently at the drink in the other hand. "You're busy, sir."

"You mean this? Just a predinner cocktail. An aid to digestion." He felt foolish in his rationalization, exasperated with the boy's silent contempt and condemnation. "All right, it's straight bourbon. Jack Daniel's, the tired businessman's friend. But I rarely touched it before—"

"I came?" Christopher finished. "Well, cheer up, sir. I shan't be here long. I may as well tell you now that I want to go home. Back to England."

"So soon?"

"I've been here long enough."

"I don't agree, Christopher. We've tried to make you comfortable and happy. You owe it to us and yourself to stay a while longer."

"You're wrong, sir. I don't owe anybody anything."

"Not even your mother, or Aunt Agatha? They wanted you to come to America, didn't they?"

There was no denying that. His mother's wishes had been painfully evident and, toward the last, so also Aunt Agatha's. He shuffled restively, anxious to be gone, and mumbled, "They thought I'd like it here."

"And you would, Chris, if you'd give yourself a chance. You could have a bright future, too. Education, a good position. I know you finished high school. Do you think you could pass a college entrance examination?"

"I almost won a scholarship," he said proudly. "I may have been the village bastard, but I wasn't the village idiot!'' His tongue had spoken independent of his will, and now he was embarrassed and confused, afraid he had dropped his guard too far, left himself open to disaster. ''May I be excused?'' he asked and ran out of the library.

''Wait, son.'' Jeff followed him into the hall and shouted after him, his voice echoing in the stairwell. ''Chris, come back here! *Christopher!*''

He did not answer, leaping the stairs in pairs, reaching the safety of his room and turning the key in the lock, wondering what he would do if Courtland pursued and demanded entry. Fortunately, he did not have to make that decision. He placed the books on the desk and spun the globe thoughtfully, defeated in the knowledge that the narrow strip of luminous blue plastic between the United States and Great Britain represented three thousand miles of ocean, and he lacked the price of fare by sea or air. Aunt Agatha would have to send it to him, and he would write and beg her again tonight.

''What was all that commotion?'' Carol asked, as Jeff was pouring himself another drink.

''I think Christopher knows.''

''I have that feeling, too.''

''Should I level with him, Carol?''

''I don't know, Jeff. He's a strange boy.''

''Just strange to us, and we to him.''

''He's proud and independent.''

''Like his mother,'' Jeff reflected aloud, unintentionally hurting her.

Carol sighed. ''He's devoted to her memory, Jeff. He makes a shrine of her photograph, with fresh flowers every day. But why would he have brought the Commando's picture if he knew the truth?''

''To rile me, probably. Who knows the workings of the adolescent male mind?''

"You should, you were one once."

"Not in his position. My father may not have been much of a man, but at least he was around and I knew who he was. Maybe that makes him more of a man than I, and a hell of a lot more of a father." He paused, drank. "I wonder how Dad would have handled this situation. To my knowledge, the greatest dilemma ever to confront him was a torn ligament in his favorite stallion's right foreleg, when it jumped a fence to get a neighbor's ready mare on the eve of the season's biggest hunt. But at least Dad had the sense not to jump any moral fences, or get tangled up if he did. That's more than I had. God, the way that kid looks at me! As if I were a monster! He hates me, Carol."

"He doesn't even know you, Jeff. Not as a man, and certainly not as a father. You can't expect a filial relationship to blossom overnight."

Jeff stared into his glass, absently swirling the amber liquid into a miniature maelstrom. "He called himself the village bastard, so he knows he's illegitimate. I wanted to find out what else he knows, but he ran off and locked himself in his room. Have we a key to his door?"

"Not the right one, I'm afraid."

Behind his barricade Christopher brooded, refusing to appear for dinner and rejecting the tray sent to him. They simply would not let him alone! They had not brought him here to give him solitude and privacy, had not lured him to this bloody land of the brave and the free to let him be either brave or free. They had a devious scheme, he thought; a predetermined strategy in their Campaign to Capture Christopher, and apparently everyone, including the domestics, was committed to it.

The housekeeper hovered over him at the table, her syrupy voice promising to "put mo' flesh on yo' po' bones.'' He had read mucky novels about the Old American South and thought that this bountiful Negress was giving a good imitation of a matriarchal mammy. But he had been raised on simple fare and practical etiquette, and the fancy food of this house and formality in which it was served amazed and sometimes nauseated him. Every day was like the feast in honor of the Prodigal Son. The Prodigal Father was soaking up liquor like a sponge, and the Fine Lady was in some kind of trance or quandary half the time. It was a ménage worthy of a Noel Coward drama.

The yardman was less officious in his attentions, but even he seemed to keep a dark eye on Christopher when he wandered about the place, examining the cars in the garage—her conservative blue Buick sedan, his lusty red Thunderbird—and the sporting gear in the shop.

''Good fishin' in the Potomac,'' Toby said.

He was a raw-boned old fellow, shiny black with grizzly kinks, his clothes drenched in pungent sweat. But neither the sun nor hard work seemed to dampen his spirit. Toby whistled at his job, as Ella sang at hers, and Christopher wondered what made them so happy. From the news in the papers and on the telly, their black brethren, especially the younger generation, were not so content. There were protests, bloody race riots, freedom marches—apparently as many apartheid problems here as in South Africa. But, of course, it wasn't exactly easy for underprivileged whites like himself, either.

''That so?'' he asked.

''Sure it's so.'' Toby grinned, resting on his spading fork. ''I wouldn't lie to you, boy. I caught me a big old blue cat there just yesterday.''

''Cat?''

''Catfish, boy. Ain't no better eatin', when fried all nice

and brown in cornmeal and hog fat. Plenty of fresh grubs in the garden, if you wants to try yo' luck.''

"I might, sometime.''

"Don't go swimmin', though," Toby cautioned. "Mighty powerful river, the Potomac. Strong currents. Drown you sure—and sweep you out to sea.''

"Back to England, maybe?''

"Don't talk crazy, boy," Toby admonished, turning peat into the rich loam, where Mrs. Courtland wanted another annual bed. "And get along with you now. I got work to do!''

Mrs. Wilton was a somewhat different case, often puzzling. She baked him scads of scones and crumpets and English rock cookies, and hauled him around town, pointing out the landmarks and Alexandria's British heritage, as if to convince him that he belonged there as much as any native son. She'd have got real mushy about it had he let her. She asked him how he addressed Mrs. Courtland, and when he said he just called her Mam, she beamingly suggested that he call her Grand Mam. A hoary cheek, Christopher thought, since he'd never gone that far even with Agatha Linton. He missed the old lady now, missed the cottage and the hills and the dog. He inquired about Bounder in his letters, but so far Aunt Agatha had written him only two, both dated within a week after his departure.

One day, in desperation, he took the money she had given him, exchanged it at a local bank, and was gone all afternoon. His disappearance caused some anxiety in the household. Mrs. Courtland thought he had got lost, or run away, and was in a mild panic when finally he returned. His explanation sounded lame even to him.

"I went to the cinema. They had an English film. It was good. I saw it twice. Just forgot about the time.''

"That's all right, Christopher. But try to remember to tell me next time, will you? I was worried."

"Yes, Mam."

"Guess who called while you were out?"

"Queen Elizabeth?"

"Now, Chris, be serious. It was Kay Cranshaw. She wants you to go with her to the Independence Day parade in Washington next week and watch the fireworks display in the evening. We have great Fourth of July celebrations."

"Why should an Englishman be interested in celebrating American independence?" he asked reasonably.

Her jaw dropped slightly, but she quickly lifted it again, and smiled. "No reason, I guess. But you would like to see our nation's capital, wouldn't you?"

Although he affected a negligent shrug, his usual response to anything American, Carol detected a flicker of interest and curiosity difficult for a student of history to suppress. "I might."

"Fine. I'll tell Kay. She's a lovely girl, don't you think?"

"I don't know her."

"Of course you do! You met her at the airport when you arrived. Mr. Cranshaw's daughter. Don't you remember?"

"I met her," he said. "I don't *know* her. You don't know someone just by meeting them. It's hard enough to know people when you live with them."

Out of the mouths of babes, Carol thought.

"That's very true, Christopher. And it means we must all try harder to understand one another, doesn't it, if we expect to get along. Families, friends, neighbors, nations. Now it's almost time for dinner. Are you hungry?"

"Not if it's that bloody meat we had last night."

They had prime ribs of beef yesterday. "Was the roast too rare for you, Chris?"

"It was raw."

"Not quite, dear. But tell me, what kind of meat do you like?"

"Boiled mutton and leg o' lamb and roast beef if it's done. Kidney pie and wet hash, too."

"Wet hash?"

"That's lamb stew, with potatoes, tomatoes, and bits of ham. Aunt Agatha makes the best wet hash in the Cotswolds. The best black currant pudding, too."

"I'll bet she does. Next time you write, ask her to send her recipes, and Ella will make them for you."

"I'm not going to be here that long, am I?"

"Why, I don't know, Christopher. That will depend on Mr. Courtland, I suppose."

His blood rushed in swift anger and disappointment, flushing his face, and he snapped, "Mr. Cranshaw said it would depend on *me!*"

"Did he? Well, I'm sorry, Chris, but I'm not familiar with any promises Mr. Cranshaw may have made to you."

"You're a liar!" he accused furiously. "You're all liars, and you got me here with lies!" He was thoroughly disgusted, for he had considered Cranshaw a nice chap for an American, and had liked and respected him. But he had lied and tricked him, too, and was a part of this whole rotten conspiracy!

"Now, Christopher—"

"Let me alone!" He headed for the stairway.

"Will you come down for dinner?"

"No, I'd rather starve!" he shouted over his shoulder.

But he knew they wouldn't let him starve, even if he wanted to. Mammy Ella would tote him a loaded tray and wheedle at the door until he accepted it. And he would cat the rich, gooey stuff if it killed him. And he almost wished it would.

12

Jeff had brought some work home and was trying to concentrate on it when Carol walked into the room, wearing a hostess gown of iridescent silk that shimmered across her breasts and emphasized her hips. He had never thought of her as voluptuous before, but lately everything about her seemed sexy and seductive. Her eyes, mouth, figure, walk, voice, scent—the very sight and sound and smell of her stimulated him. The physical separation had intensified his senses, honed them to a keen and quivering edge not unlike that of adolescence, and he was suddenly inflamed and tormented with sexual desire.

"Are you busy?" she asked.

"Nothing that can't wait," he answered quickly, searching her face, mistaking the anxiety there for response to his own urgency.

Then she sat in the chair opposite the desk, like a client come for consultation, and he knew he had been a fool crazy with heat. It wasn't sex disturbing her, but his son. After a slight hesitation, she said, "I'm worried about Christopher, Jeff. He's not adjusting."

"Give him time, Carol. It's only been three weeks."

"Four," she corrected.

"All right. Four weeks. Could you tear up your roots, replant them in another land, and flourish in that length of time? He's not acclimated yet, that's all."

"We're talking about a person, Jeff, not a plant. The human system is considerably more complicated, I'm afraid. And don't pretend you're not worried, too."

He frowned. "Yes, I'm worried, Carol. But I don't know what to do, how to approach him. He's not only shut up in his room most of the time, he's shut up in himself. I've been waiting, hoping for a signal, a chink in his armor . . ." He sighed, reaching for his drink. "Where is he now?"

"He went to a movie. That same English film. He's seen it five times already."

"Anything to get away from us, I guess."

"I was afraid we might fail, Jeffrey."

"It's too early to concede failure, Carol."

"Oh, Jeffrey, be realistic! The boy is miserable. If we can't make him happy, what good are we as parents? What good are material things to him if he doesn't feel loved and wanted and that he belongs? A month in this house and he's still as much of a stranger as the day he arrived. Worse even, he feels shanghaied and wants to go home."

"This is his home, Carol."

"He doesn't think so."

"He'd better," Jeff said doggedly, "because he has no other now. Agatha Linton is dead."

Carol caught her breath. "Oh, no!"

"Yes. Ken had a cable from her attorney this morning. Tary said a letter would follow."

"Oh, that poor boy! How will you tell him?"

"I won't. Not right away. He'd want to return for the funeral, and that would be bad for him and pointless. There's nothing he can do now and nothing for him in England anymore. Besides, if he leaves us, he might never return."

"But he writes to her almost every day and waits for an answer! She must have been too ill these past few weeks to write. It's wrong to keep this from him, Jeff, and you're losing an opportunity to get closer to him. He'll need sympathy and comfort."

"Let me handle this, Carol."

"Very well, he's your son. But I think you're making a mistake, and it's not going to improve our relations with him any. He already considers us liars and hypocrites— conspirators who got him here under false pretenses and intend to hold him against his will. This deception might be the last straw."

"It's for his own good," Jeff insisted. "And another thing for his own good would be friends. Boys and girls his age."

"I'm ahead of you there, and though we don't know any teenage boys, I thought Kay Cranshaw might help. He seemed interested enough in her at first. But he hasn't bothered to return her calls, or accept her invitation to show him Washington. Maybe he feels he's not going to be here long enough to need friends."

"Well, he is, and see that he bothers with Kay. Get them together somehow, Carol. Ask Joan to help. Once Christopher comes out of his shell and shares himself with someone, anyone, we'll be getting somewhere with him, accomplishing something. Half the battle will be won."

"I'll try, Jeff. I'll talk to Joan tomorrow and get Kay to call him again."

"Thanks," he said. "Maybe by the time I get back . . ."

"Get back?"

"I have to go to New York tomorrow."

"Oh? You didn't tell me, Jeff. Were you saving it for a surprise?"

"Well, our communications haven't been the best lately, have they? Beckenheimer beckons. He wants to expand his investments, both domestic and foreign. I'm studying his portfolio now. It'll mean a big commission."

"Do we need the money?"

"Every little bit helps," he joked wryly. "That's how Waldo Beckenheimer became one of the world's richest men."

"I wonder if he's also one of the world's happiest."

"If not, he has compensations. And he can buy some reasonable facsimiles."

"What is that supposed to mean?"

He looked at her. "You figure it out."

"I'll pack for you," Carol said, rising.

It was an obvious escape, but Jeff did not try to detain her. He watched her leave, thoroughly frustrated.

Carol was putting shirts into a bag when he came up later. He had remained for another drink, wondering how to approach her, feeling foolish—a husband pondering the seduction of his wife and fearing rejection. It shouldn't matter so much to a man his age, and after all these years, but it *did* matter. Goddamn it, she had no right to cut him off cold! She had never used sex as a reward or punishment before, why was she being capricious now? And what the devil did she expect him to do? Become celibate?

"Will six shirts be enough?" she asked.

"Plenty."

"Select your own ties, Jeff."

He grabbed a handful from the rack in the closet, tossed them on the bed. She arranged them neatly in the luggage. "You'll wear your gray silk suit, I suppose, and take your blue sharkskin. What about evening clothes?"

"This is a business trip, Carol."

"Business is often mixed with pleasure, isn't it? Better be prepared with a dinner jacket, anyway. If you need anything more formal, rent it."

Jeff went to the dresser, opened the liquor decanter.

"Didn't you have enough downstairs, dear?"

"It's just something to do, *dear*."

"It's a crutch, Jeff, and you're leaning on it too heavily of late."

"Genetic weakness," he muttered. "And what are you leaning on, Mrs. Courtland? Pills? Yes, I know about your prescriptions, Carol. Do you expect to limp through the rest of your life on drugs?"

"I'm hoping it won't be necessary," she replied.

"It'll be necessary, Carol, as long as you build walls between us instead of bridges. They're getting higher and wider, and one day I'll be too damn old and feeble to even try to climb them."

"Are you too old to walk across the hall, too feeble to open the door? Use your crutch, if you need assistance."

"There shouldn't be any halls to cross or doors to open," he said, pouring himself a stiff shot.

"You're wallowing in booze and self-pity."

"What's your excuse?"

"If there are walls between us, Jeffrey, I didn't build them alone. You helped, and you could tear them down, if you're man enough."

"I don't like challenges, Carol."

"What are you proposing, then? Accommodation?"

"No, goddamn it! I can get that from a whore."

"Washington has some gorgeous ones, I understand."

"I wouldn't know. Are you suggesting I find out?"

She shrugged. "That's up to you."

"No, my dear, it's up to *you*."

"I don't like challenges either, Jeff."

"Then don't goad me into issuing them."

"I think the difficulty is primarily with you," she accused. "You feel guilty about Christopher and me, and you're trying to conquer your guilt with liquor."

"I'd rather conquer it with love," he rebutted, drinking.

"So would I," she murmured, taking the glass from him.

"Don't do me any favors, Carol."

"I won't, but maybe you can do me one."

But something was wrong, seriously, demoralizingly, dreadfully wrong. This was not love, this was sexual aggression, with an element of violence that astonished and disgusted Carol. Her partner was a brutal, determined stranger, neither drunk nor sober, and she felt violated. Lust could be exciting and satisfying when mutual, but this was a mere fusion of bodies with orgasm the ultimate object. When it was over she lay in tense silence, reluctant to speak, relieved when he withdrew from her.

"Did that help any?" she finally asked.

"Not much," he answered sheepishly. "I guess I was a bit of a precipitous brute. I'm sorry, Carol. Blame the bourbon."

The separation was more than physical now, it was mental and emotional as well. "Were you ever a brute with her?"

"So that was your trouble? I knew it was something. You just can't forget, can you? It was like having a ghost in bed with us."

It was true, and she could not help herself. Anne Bentley had become a haunting obsession. She found herself wondering if he had kissed and caressed her the same way, whispered the same passionate endearments, practiced and improved his art not only with the Englishwoman but with others as well. How many? Who was the last one, and when and where, and under what lustful circumstances?

"You didn't answer my question," she said. "Did you screw her the same way you do me?"

"Don't talk that way."

"I want to know! A man has a sexual technique, and it's the same with any woman, isn't it?"

"More or less, because the end result is the same. But women are different. She was nothing like you, Carol. There was no comparison."

"Yet she took my place in your life for months. Was she just a convenience, a substitute—or was there a deeper attachment you won't admit even to yourself?"

"Oh, God, I don't know, Carol! I don't remember. It was all so long ago. And what does it matter now? Love or lust, what difference does it make now?"

"Did you ever just take her, or was she always willing and eager?"

"I didn't often revel in rape, if that's what you mean."

"Reserved it for special occasions? What kind of relation did you have the time you made her pregnant?"

"Stop it, Carol! Stop this inquisition."

"Do I sound sick? A shrink would make me talk about it."

"Do you think you need a shrink?"

"No more than you," she said, rising abruptly and getting dressed in the dark.

The bedside lamp flashed on. "What're you doing?"

"Dressing! Christopher will be home soon."

"So what? He's seventeen, Carol. Don't you think he knows what goes on in marriage?"

"And outside of it," she murmured.

"Thanks," he said grimly. "I needed that reminder, I was in danger of forgetting. But he's old enough to know *that*, too."

"Then why don't you tell him?"

"I will, if ever he gives me a chance."

"Cover up, Jeffrey."

"Embarrassed? You never used to be. Look at me, Carol. I may not be an athlete anymore, but I'm not exactly a slob, either. And you look as good to me as ever. Take those things off and come back to bed."

"For a repeat performance?"

"No. But you're going to stay here awhile, naked in the light. I'll be goddamned if we're going to be embarrassed by each other's nudity after twenty years!"

Carol hesitated a few more moments, then obeyed, humoring him. "If Christopher should open the door—"

"He wouldn't, without knocking. Besides, it has a lock. Stop worrying and relax, Carol." He did not touch her, except with his eyes and his smile. "Still shy?"

"No, but this is rather silly, isn't it? Like a couple of exhibitionists."

"I think it's pleasant, and so did you, once. Now you act as if one or the other of us is deformed. We're not, you know. Not physically, anyway."

"What time does your plane leave tomorrow?"

"Early."

"Wake me in time, and I'll drive you to the airport."

"Thanks. Shall we talk some more?"

"I'm a little tired," she hedged. "And you must be, too?"

"After all that strenuous activity?" he asked with rueful

chagrin. "Yeah, I reckon we both need some rest. Good night, my dear."

"Good night."

But she had to resort to her usual sedative for sleep, and Jeff did not disturb her in the morning. He called a cab. Carol found his note when she woke. *"Darling, you seemed to be having a pleasant dream, and I didn't want to interrupt it. Will call you from New York. Love, J."*

Carol tried to remember what, if anything, she had dreamed, but all was darkness and oblivion.

13

"They hurry like ants," Christopher remarked. "Everyone in a bounding rush, as if afraid of missing something."

"Maybe they are," Kay said. "Most of them have only two weeks to see the country—the whole world, in fact. And we'll miss something too if we don't get in the race."

They were caught in the stampede of tourists, which, while worse in summer, was apt to occur at any time in Washington: the blossoming of the cherry trees, the Easter Egg Roll on the White House lawn, the Independence Day celebrations, the lighting of the nation's Christmas tree, or the inauguration of a president.

The glare of concrete and hot pavement was blinding, the jockeying for position frantic and often comical. There were noisy children in blue jeans, bowlegged men in Bermuda shorts, bulging women in Capri pants. The heat was appalling, melting the ice cream bars, Popsicles, and snowcones of the vendors as rapidly as they sold them.

Cameras clicked while guides chanted information, most of which was only superficially absorbed. Instant Americana, like other instant products, was a commodity in the national economy.

Kay's protégé was interested enough, but not particularly impressed. He had seen the capital of England, which he regarded as the center of the universe with the rest of the world on its periphery. "Why don't we just park somewhere?" Christopher suggested. "I'd like to sit in the gallery of your Senate or House of Representatives and witness democracy in action. See how it differs from our Parliament."

Kay could not imagine anything less exciting. "Oh, you can watch Congress some other time, Chris. It's not very interesting, really, unless you want to be a politician. I was bored the time my class went on a civics assignment. All they do is argue and yield, filibuster and caucus and call quorums."

"That sounds like the observation of a good healthy ignoramus," he teased. "I bet you flunked that course."

"Almost. Got a C minus. But you needn't be so nasty about it. Some girls don't care about such things. I suppose you'd like to be a congressional page?"

"That's for *American* boys," he said.

"Are you an exchange student, Chris, or what?"

"I'm a what," he said wryly.

"I don't understand?"

An evasive shrug dismissed her curiosity, and they crossed the long green sweep of the Mall, once a handball and bowling court, moving with the horde toward the marble obelisk of the Washington Monument. They stood in line to enter, to ride the elevator, to view the capital and its environs from the observation cap. Kay passed Christopher the binoculars and pointed out the Pentagon across the

Potomac, Arlington National Cemetery with its thousands of markers like white dots on the green turf, General Robert E. Lee's mansion, and the guarded Tomb of the Unknown Soldier.

"Our Unknown Soldier is buried in Westminster Abbey," he said. "With the kings and queens."

"That's nice. I'd love to visit England, and we're going abroad when I graduate from high school. Mother says I'll appreciate travel more then, and it'll help me in college. Are you going to college, Chris?"

"I don't think so," he said. "We'd better queue up for the down lift."

Kay smiled. "We call that an elevator."

"Whatever, it's better than all those blasted stairs. Eight hundred and ninety-eight, the guidebook says."

They were borne down swiftly and ejected like exploding atoms from the tight, perspiring nucleus of humanity into another procession marching on the Lincoln Memorial. The only serenity seemed to lie in the long quiet reflecting pool, and Kay longed to sit on the concrete edge and dangle her bare feet in the cool clear water.

"It looks like a Greek temple," Christopher criticized the magnificent marble structure. "Fit for a god. I should think the humble Mr. Lincoln would have preferred a simpler monument. A log cabin, perhaps."

"No doubt he would have," Kay agreed. "But his grateful country thought he deserved a noble shrine. He saved the Union, you know."

Ascending the high wide steps and terraces and passing between the fluted Ionic pillars into the central chamber, they met the colossal statue of the man, bearded and solemn, with sorrow and tragedy etched into the marble features, and strength and determination in the great hands gripping the arms of the massive, flag-draped chair. Christopher read the inscriptions on the walls seriously, concentrating on the Gettysburg Address, with which he was somewhat familiar.

"Mr. Lincoln freed the slaves during the American Civil War, didn't he?"

"That's right, when he issued the Emancipation Proclamation."

"When are the people going to recognize it? I mean, why are they still fighting and oppressing the Negroes in some places? I read it in the papers and see it on the telly and hear it on the wireless."

Kay quoted her elders. "It takes time."

"Like a hundred years or so? You celebrated your Civil War centennial last year, didn't you?"

"How do you know so much about America?"

"I read a lot."

"I haven't studied much about Britain yet," Kay said. "I hope you're around to tutor me when we get to English history in school. It sure would help."

His mind still on the previous subject, he asked, "Do you go to school with black kids?"

"I go to a private school."

A cynical smile quirked his mouth. "That's what I thought, Miss Cranshaw. What's next on the agenda?"

"The Jefferson Memorial is a must," Kay said. "But it's across the Tidal Basin, and I don't think I could walk that far now. I'm beat. We should have taken a tour bus, like Mother and Aunt Carol suggested."

Accustomed to long hikes in the country, Christopher was not in the least tired. "That's the trouble with Americans. They ride everywhere they go, have two or more motor cars, and think bicycles are only for kids. Walk a block, and they're exhausted. A soft breed, I think."

"Not according to our history," Kay snapped. "Besides, I don't think you've appreciated anything you've seen. You're a cold fish, like most Englishmen.''

He grinned. "Is that so?"

"Well, maybe not, but—"

"You expect me to wave the Stars and Stripes, sing your national anthem, and swear allegiance?"

"No, I wouldn't expect to convert you in one day! But do you have to be such a drag? Couldn't you act just a little more enthused?"

"Sorry," he apologized. "I'm not bored, Kay. Not with you, anyway. And I'm enjoying this, really I am. And learning a lot, Teacher."

"Well . . . want to recess for lunch?"

"If you do."

"We'll go Dutch at a drugstore."

"They sell most anything in American apothecaries, don't they? Is the chemist also a cook?"

"You mean the pharmacist? Sometimes," Kay laughed.

Her hair, tied in a ponytail when first Christopher saw her, was loose now, dark and damply curling about her pretty wistful face, and her soft fair shoulders were already pink above the white sunback dress. No English girl had ever looked lovelier to him, nor stirred more impulses, not even sultry Sally Sawyer. Was Kay another trick the "hunters" were employing—a decoy to lure him if all else failed?

"Better walk in the shade," he said. "You're getting sunburnt. Don't you use an umbrella?"

"Only when it rains."

"Most Britons carry them."

"It rains there often, doesn't it?"

"Rather."

They found a pharmacy with a vacant booth and ordered the standard American teenage fare, hamburgers and cokes,

although Christopher would have preferred fish and chips.
The sullen, gum-popping waitress brought the food so
promptly, Kay knew it had been previously prepared in
anticipation of the noon-hour rush. Their request for straws,
paper napkins, and separate checks plainly irritated her.
She grumbled, "You kids sure expect a lot of service,
considerin' you *never* tip!"

"It says no tipping on the menu," Kay pointed out.
"Right there at the bottom, see? 'No tips, please; it's our
pleasure to serve you.' "

"Hah," she snorted, scribbling out two tabs and slap-
ping them down on the Formica-topped table. "Hurry it up
now, we need the booth."

The buns were soggy from the steam table, the meat
dry, the drinks weak and mostly ice. Kay frowned. "Pretty
awful, isn't it? But we can take the paper cups with us. I
like to chew ice, though it's supposed to be as harmful as
sugar to teeth. They say the English have lots of dental
problems because they eat so much candy, but your teeth
are very good."

"Not many sweets in childhood."

"I had flouride treatments and was just glad I didn't
need braces. You were lucky, too."

"Yeah."

"It'll take weeks to see all of Washington, Chris. Will
you come in every day and let me show you?"

Having nothing better in prospect, he agreed. "Where
shall we meet tomorrow?"

"How about General Grant's statue in Union Square.
It's that huge bronze man and horse. Ten o'clock, and
you'd better get an early bus out of Alexandria. The
morning traffic is snailish."

"I'll be there."

And he was, considerably before the appointed hour. But Kay, missing her bus, was late. She ran to meet him.

"Thanks for waiting."

"Didn't you expect me to?"

"I wasn't sure, Chris. You're strange sometimes."

"Queer?"

Kay blushed, and he realized that she had another interpretation of the word. "Just different," she murmured and started walking toward Constitution Avenue. "We're going to the National Archives today."

In Exhibition Hall they stood on a marble platform, viewing the Declaration of Independence, the Constitution, and the Bill of Rights. While waiting for Kay in Union Square Christopher had read in the guidebook that the glass cases were filled with helium gas and the light filtered to protect the fragile parchments from the damaging effects of air and dust, and that they were guarded during the day and stored in vaults at night. The public attitude was more respectful here, almost reverent, the visitors moving and speaking quietly.

"These are the American people's most priceless documents," Kay whispered. "They are to the American what— well, what the Magna Carta is to the Englishman."

"But they were rebels, those colonists," Christopher rejoined in a firm voice. "They took up arms against their king and motherland."

"Not without cause," Kay retorted, embarrassed by the curious glances of the other spectators.

His mercurial temperament had changed overnight, back into that of a bitter cynic again. And because there were so few subtleties and variations in her own personality, Kay was at a loss to understand and cope with his sudden transformations. "What did you do last night, Mr. Hyde? Take an evil potion!"

"They started a revolution," he insisted.

"They were oppressed," Kay argued and ushered him swiftly out of the Archives under the somewhat amused surveillance of the guards. "The White House is next, although I know it's not going to compare to your Buckingham Palace!"

"Now who's being nasty?"

"Your attitude is contagious."

"You think America is the greatest country in the world, and I think England is," he temporized. "Neither of us is going to convert the other, so why don't we stop fighting and call a truce?"

"You mean it, Chris? I want so much to be friends."

"Me, too," he said huskily, taking her hand. "Is that a common across from the White House?"

"Lafayette Park? Yes, it's public."

"The guidebook calls it the Park of Presidents, and says some congressmen fought duels there in the past."

"They still do," Kay said. "Verbally."

A long line of tourists stood waiting to enter the President's home and staring at the upper windows in the hope of glimpsing the First Lady or one of the children. Another crowd hung around the fence of the grounds where Caroline Kennedy sometimes rode her pony Macaroni, with her glamorous mother walking along beside her. With a few variations of dress and demeanor, it was the same group they had encountered everywhere else, and Kay was relieved when Christopher suggested waiting in Lafayette Park until the queue shortened and the next tour started.

He bought a bag of popcorn from a vendor to feed the pigeons. Kay sat on a bench and watched him, wondering why she had not realized before that he resembled Jeffrey Courtland. When she told him this, he smiled ironically.

"Really?"

"Yes, and don't act insulted. I think Uncle Jeff is very handsome for an older man."

"Why do you call the Courtlands uncle and aunt? They're not your kin, are they?"

"No, but they're my godparents. I've known them all my life and love them very much. Do you like them?"

He shrugged, tossing a handful of popcorn to the cooing, strutting, begging birds. "Not especially."

"Then why are you staying with them?"

"Questions, questions! I hate questions, Kay."

"Is that why you never answer them?"

"I don't like talking about myself."

"You want to be a mystery or something?"

"Look here, Kay, if we're going to get along—" He glanced at the diminishing line across the avenue. "Let's go over there now and have done with it."

"Why bother, if that's how you feel?"

"Damn it all, Kay! I thought we had a truce?"

"You broke it."

"No, you did, with your infernal female curiosity. You've got to learn to stop probing me."

"I'm sorry," she murmured, standing. "But you don't know much about girls, do you? They're not curious about things—or people—that don't interest them."

"Kay—"

"Oh, come on! Let's get on with it."

She stepped off the curb into the street—and directly into the path of a car. Christopher shouted and grabbed her back. She lost her balance and would have fallen without his support. They stood together thus, hearts pounding with the sudden fright, trying to smile at her folly. Then, suddenly, his smile faded and his eyes darkened passionately. "You little fool," he scolded hoarsely. "You might have been killed."

"Would you care?"

Kay thought he was going to kiss her right there on Pennsylvania Avenue, but he did not, and she felt cheated. Releasing her as abruptly as he had caught her, he joked, "Sure! I'd hate to lose my guide."

"You saved my life, Chris, so now I belong to you. That's an old Indian custom."

His face sobered. "We're not Indians, Kay. Furthermore, that axiom is Chinese."

"You're always so literal," she accused. "Where's your imagination? Didn't you ever pretend even in childhood?"

"I pretended, Kay. Plenty. I still do, occasionally. But pretense is a game we play mostly to beguile ourselves—and it's not really clever, fooling yourself. Sort of stupid, actually. Because you tend to believe it, and it's a rude awakening—the jolt back to reality."

"Are you having fun?" Carol asked when Christopher returned to Alexandria that evening. "Enjoying Washington?"

"It's all right, I guess. We're going to the Smithsonian Institute tomorrow. Kay says it's just a stuffy old museum, but I want to see it."

"By all means, Chris. The Smithsonian is called the Nation's Attic, and you'll understand why when you rummage through it. The curator never throws anything away. You must visit our art galleries, too. And our wax museum."

"I've seen the London galleries, and Madame Tussaud's is the best wax museum in the world."

"Naturally. It's British." She smiled, teasing him, and Christopher responded in spite of himself.

"I suppose I sound a bit waxy myself, sometimes. We

had a gosh-awful lunch in an apothecary, lucky we didn't get ptomaine. What's for dinner?''

"Something you'll like, I hope.''

There was the usual feast, and Ella serving him like the master at the head of the table. It was bearable only because the master was away on what the mistress evidently believed was business, but Christopher wondered. How many other women had Courtland betrayed? How many other bastards did he have scattered over the earth? And how much longer could this one delay the reckoning?

14

The phone rang shortly before noon. It was Joan with a problem. "Carol, I'm in a bind! Ken invited a new client to dinner this evening, and we're shy a partner. I know this is awfully short notice, but I didn't have much more myself. I met the man only yesterday, at the office."

"What man?" Carol asked.

"Major Mark Lawrence. I've no idea why he consulted Ken, but he's new in town, a bachelor, and before I knew it Ken was inviting him to dinner. I didn't think he'd accept, but he did, and—will you be an angel, Carol? The only single gals I know are away on vacation—one in Europe, the other in Canada. I'm desperate, and I'm sure Jeff wouldn't mind."

"Why do you say that?"

"Well, he told Ken before he left that he thought you were staying in too much these days. He probably didn't know you've been declining invitations from some of us.

You can't become a recluse, now can you? Bring Chris along if you feel you need a chaperon, though I assure you the major is quite harmless. Big as a Saint Bernard, and just as gentle and friendly. Will you come, Carol?''

"I'd be delighted, Joan. What time?''

"Eightish. And try not to be late, darling, because I suspect the major is going to be early. Now I'd better organize the maid and menu. See you!''

Carol replaced the receiver slowly. So Jeff wanted her to socialize in his absence? That was undoubtedly the motive behind the Cranshaws' impromptu invitation, and Jeff had known she could not refuse. There was an unwritten law about a social SOS. Friends could not ignore them, never knowing when they might be in the same predicament. It would serve Jeff right if she enjoyed herself, although such trumped-up affairs were usually boring, and Carol was tempted to invent a headache or other last-minute excuse. Finding a replacement for her in a city where females outnumbered males six to one shouldn't be too difficult; indeed, there must be dozens among Ken's clients.

She went to find Christopher and met him just coming in from the garden, a single red rose in his hand. She knew the perfect bloom was intended for the bud vase before his mother's photograph. He had not missed a day of this tribute since his arrival, and it saddened Carol to realize that she would never have a child to love and cherish her memory. Even in death, Anne Bentley was more blessed than Carol Courtland in life, she thought.

"There you are!" she said, smiling. "Don't go anywhere this evening, Chris. We're dining with the Cranshaws. Take a shower and shave and wear a jacket.''

"You didn't have to tell me to do any of those things, Mam. I'm not a clod.''

"Certainly not, Chris, and I didn't mean to imply that at all. I just want you to look your best."

"And be on my best behavior? What do you want, Little Lord Fauntleroy?"

"Heaven forbid! He was a bit of a prig, wasn't he?"

Sometimes he liked this woman and felt genuinely sorry for her. She tried hard to be nice and kind, and he wished he could respond. Then a thorn in the rose stem pricked his finger, the pain pierced his heart—there was no room there for anyone except his poor dead mother.

"He was that, all right," he agreed and passed on.

As Joan had predicted, Major Lawrence was painfully punctual. Military habit, perhaps, and a part of his training, like his stance and bearing. He stood tall and erect in his dress uniform, so raptly at attention that Joan wanted to put him at ease. Men of his rank were usually more sophisticated, but somehow his lack of urbanity was refreshing. She was so tired of aging Lotharios like Frank Benedict and pathetic buffoons like Skeets Martin—plastic people with synthetic emotions. Major Lawrence appeared real, solid, unaffected.

"I hope I'm not late, Mrs. Cranshaw. I had some difficulty finding this place. All the streets seem to end in circles, squares, or monuments."

Joan smiled, her own dressing still incomplete, fastening on emerald earrings to complement her formal gown. "Blame it on the Frenchmen who designed this metropolitan puzzle," she said. "And you're not late at all, Major. Make yourself comfortable, won't you? Ken will be out in a few minutes." She indicated the ebony bar with chrome fittings and white leather stools, excused herself, and returned to the bedroom to hurry her husband.

"Christ," Ken muttered, pulling on his trousers. "Doesn't

the poor guy know that nobody's ever on time for anything in Washington except the President's press conference?''

"He's as uneasy as if he'd been invited to an embassy reception and was unsure of the protocol," Joan said. "But he's nice, Ken, and appealing in a bucolic sort of way. Like a big cuddly bear."

"This morning he was a big lonely Saint Bernard, now he's a big bucolic bear." Ken closed his zipper sharply. "Maybe he's really a big bad wolf who just hasn't learned the trails through this government preserve yet. Are you sure this will be all right with Jeff?"

Joan straightened his tie and held his coat for him. "He asked us to entertain her, didn't he?"

"Not with another guy."

"They'll be dinner partners and bridge partners later. What could happen?"

"I doubt that Mark Lawrence is much on bridge, baby. Poker and craps, maybe. But bridge . . ." He paused, shaking his head.

"What'll we do, then?"

Ken grinned. "Play parlor games? Post office, or spin-the-bottle?"

"He's already spinning the bottle," Joan said. "Better get out there before he falls on his face."

"Don't worry about that. Unless the Army has changed a hell of a lot since I was in it, he'll be proficient at that pastime, able to lap up a fifth of one hundred proof anything, and still recite the Manual of Arms verbatim."

Carol was a few minutes late, and there was some additional delay when the kids decided that they would rather go out to an old movie than remain for dinner—and rushed off to catch a bus. Only blithe youth could have preferred *Dracula* and theater snacks to vichyssoise, caesar salad, Maine lobster and Maryland crab, white Bordeaux—

all prepared by an excellent cook and served by a Swedish maid.

The conversation, as it invariably did in Washington, turned to politics, Ken's bailiwick beyond law. He pursued it through dessert, over coffee and cordials, and Joan indulged him for the sake of amenity.

"The only reason we maintain that white elephant residence in Baltimore is because it's Ken's hometown, and he has an ambition to represent his district in Congress."

"Congress could do worse," Major Lawrence said.

"He'll have my vote," Carol promised, smiling.

"Not mine," Joan said seriously. "I don't want him in that bloody game. It's killing in more ways than one, and he knows my objections. I've warned him that I'll get a soapbox and campaign against him."

Ken regarded her musingly. "And so, Ladies and Gentlemen, if I'm defeated, I can only blame my wife," he said in a sonorous voice, and all but Joan laughed.

"He thinks I'm kidding," she said. "But honestly now, Carol, would you want your husband in politics?"

"I've never thought much about it," Carol said. "And I don't think he has, either."

She realized that she was not contributing much to the evening. She had said nothing wise or witty, had almost ignored the major, and Joan was probably disappointed in her. But she had never been clever at pretense of any kind and simply could not enthuse and sparkle when she felt dull and flat. And amplifying her sense of social inadequacy was the realization that Mark Lawrence was experiencing one of his own—and not concealing it as well.

He sat uncomfortably in a customized chair in the living room, as if afraid he would inadvertently soil or damage something—spill a drink, drop cigarette ashes on the white carpet—plainly unaccustomed to penthouses and the people who occupied them, and out of his element.

What had brought him here? she wondered. Loneliness, boredom, the need for human companionship? Or, as in her own case, politeness: the inability to offend by declining an invitation. An attractive man physically, with a pleasant personality, she might have found him interesting and even exciting under other circumstances. But now he was just someone to remind her of something she would rather forget: the uniform, the decorations, the war.

Ken rose to fix more drinks, Joan to refill the cigarette boxes, and Carol found herself under the major's observation, his keen gray eyes measuring as though he were trying to calculate the range of a distant target. When he spoke, his voice was low and carefully calibrated.

"It was good of you to come this evening, Mrs. Courtland. I'm afraid I put the Cranshaws in a corner by accepting their invitation, and I hope I'm not a bore?"

"Not at all," Carol protested, embarrassed by her transparency. "It's been very pleasant, Major."

His gallant smile told her he knew better but appreciated her efforts and the possibility that she may have been cornered, too. Then he glanced toward the broad expanse of plate glass, which caught the myriad reflections of the city lights through the open drapes.

Seeing his captive look, Joan sought to free him. "Carol dear, why don't you show Mark the view from the terrace?"

Carol obliged, seeking release herself, and led him out to a miniature garden of potted plants and shirred shrubs, brightly cushioned chairs and lounges, and sun-bathing mats. Standing at the molded balustrade, she gestured grandly. "The District of Columbia, Major!"

"Nice," Mark commented inadequately, for the view

from The Towers, an exclusive apartment hotel near Woodley Park, was spectacular.

"You don't get the impression of height here that you do in New York or Chicago," Carol said. "The capital goes out instead of up, and I think it's fitting that the Washington Monument dominates the skyline."

"Yes," he agreed. "I'm not a skyscraper enthusiast myself. I'm a flatlander, born and raised on the Kansas plains, where a silo or grain elevator looks tall."

"Oh? I thought I detected a Midwestern accent. How long have you been in the Army?"

"Twenty years, but only about twenty days at the Pentagon. My first official assignment there, although I've been in and out of it a number of times. Is Washington your home?"

"No, I'm a native Virginian. My husband, too. We live in Alexandria, and have been married as long as you've been in the military." Now why had she told him that? He couldn't possibly care about her marital status. They were virtual strangers and probably would remain so. But apparently he was interested enough to pursue the topic.

"Children?"

"Unfortunately, no."

"Who's the young man?"

"Christopher? He's visiting us. My husband knew his family in England, during the war."

"Where is Mr. Courtland now?"

"New York, on business. He's a broker, with offices in Washington."

"He's lucky."

"Lucky?"

"To be so well established."

Carol was silent, her profile tilted to the moon. Such a lovely face deserved an appropriate compliment, Mark thought, but he had never been facile with flattery. Margie had told him that often enough, calling him rube and rustic, and she was right, for he had come off a farm. He was still a farmer at heart, looking for a place to retire. He thought he had found it in California, Florida, Texas. Now he thought he might find it in Virginia.

"Washington architecture has an aspect of strength and permanence," he said, gazing at the illuminated dome of the Capitol and the shadowy bulks of the other federal buildings. "But that's no guarantee of security these days."

"A madman somewhere pushes the wrong button?"

"Well, there's considerably more to it than that," he said. "At least the Pentagon brass think so."

"That's comforting. But is anything on earth really permanent and indestructible, Major? Isn't it all temporary, subject to ruin and decay?" She paused, mocking herself with her dire philosophy. "Forgive me, Mark. I'm not usually so dramatic in my pessimism."

"Sounds more like disillusion, Carol, and that's just another hazard of living. It comes to us all, sooner or later. For most it's sooner, I'm afraid."

"I guess that makes me a late-blooming flower."

"Beg pardon?"

"Nothing." She pinched off a leaf of rose geranium, crushed it between her fingers to release the fragrance, then let it drift away. "Shall we go in, Mark?"

"Will you have dinner with me tomorrow, Carol?"

"Alone?"

"I'll invite the Cranshaws if you wish."

"It doesn't matter. But what will it mean, Mark?"

"Only that you don't find me repulsive."

"Of course I don't!"

"Then you will?"

"Why not?" she murmured.

*   *   *

The ice melted in the martinis, weakening them. Ken poured the contents of the pitcher down the bar drain and mixed a fresh batch. "That view must be damned fascinating. I'll have to look at it again myself."

Joan held out her glass. Ken filled it and tossed in an olive on a plastic pick. "Worried about Carol?"

"Maybe."

"She's not a child likely to fall off the terrace, Ken, and I don't think she's desperate enough to jump."

"Mark likes her, Joan."

"Yes, but she doesn't know he's alive. Might be a good thing if she did."

"That's a wild thing to say."

"Why? There's never been anyone in her life but Jeffrey. Maybe she should find out if there ever could be. She still hasn't recovered from her shock, you know. She's in a kind of emotional catalepsy, alive but not really living, feeling, reacting to life. She needs a stimulant rather than those sedatives she takes."

"Sleeping Beauty and perhaps the Handsome Hero's kiss can awaken her to reality? Are you tight, or just giddy? That's fairy tale stuff, and even Kay has outgrown it. Carol's life is complicated enough without an affair."

"Could she have an affair if she's still in love with her husband?"

"I don't know. Could you?"

"Not the way I feel about you now," Joan said, nibbling her olive. "But if ever I doubted my love, or yours—"

"Is that a threat?"

She laughed. "Now don't turn prosecutor and start cross-examining me. My case is purely hypothetical at this point. But Carol is in a bit of a dilemma now, unsure of her man and her marriage. She has some puzzling doubts and problems to resolve.''

''Well, she'll never do it moon-gazing with another guy,'' Ken said. ''Apparently she's not as unaware of Mark Lawrence as you seem to think, and I feel like a traitor to Jeff.''

''Hush,'' Joan cautioned. ''Here they come! How was the view, Major?''

''Beautiful,'' he answered, his eyes on Carol.

15

It was midnight before they got back to Alexandria, and Christopher went to bed immediately. Carol sat up for a while reading, and then impulsively decided to call New York. She could hear the phone ringing in the hotel room and finally his voice answered, hoarse with sleep.

"Jeff? It's me, Carol. When are you coming home?"

"Carol! Do you know what time it is?"

"Two A.M.," she replied and repeated her question.

"Why? Is anything wrong?" He was awake now, alert and tense. "Something must be wrong for you to call at this hour. Problems with Christopher?"

"No, nothing. I'm just lonesome, that's all."

It was irritating, in view of the fact that he had called her yesterday to tell he would be away longer than he had expected, but he explained again. The reasons were logical: meetings, conferences, expansions, taxes, heirs, wills, trusts. There were considerations and ramifications in an account the size of Waldo Beckenheimer's and personal attention necessary to a client of his stature, and Jeff had sent for his secretary to assist him.

Carol was aware of all this and annoyed with herself for disturbing him. His secretary often accompanied him on his business trips, or joined him later with portfolio and portable typewriter. Someone had to handle the paperwork, and it was better to have someone familiar with it than to hire a public stenographer. She had regarded Miss Ledlow as a part of the office equipment, efficient and necessary, and had not asked questions about her any more than she inquired about the desks and office machines. But suddenly Carol found herself wondering about their relationship and accommodations, if their rooms adjoined, if perhaps they were in bed together then . . .

Oh, God, wasn't this exactly what Joan had warned her she must guard against; regarding any and every woman her husband came in contact with now as suspect! But Doris Ledlow wasn't just any woman. She was someone important to Jeff, someone he confided in, depended on, trusted. She had been with him so long, over ten years, and Jeff was very fond of her. He remembered her with bonuses and gifts on special occasions. Carol herself had chosen some of them—impersonal items such as books, stationery, a silver carafe for Doris's apartment. And undoubtedly Doris had helped to select some of her boss's presents to his wife when he was too busy, possibly even reminded him of important dates he may have forgotten. But to imagine Miss Phi Beta Kappa in the role of femme fatale was absurd, and Carol forced the suspicion out of her mind with an idiotic but typically wifely question.

"Do you need more shirts?"

"No, the Waldorf has excellent laundry service."

"That's good."

"How is Chris?" he asked. "I was afraid he was sick or hurt, or had run away or something?"

"No, he's fine. Having a ball with Kay. He has come out of his cocoon, and they're flitting about Washington like butterflies."

"Well, don't let them get too cozy, Carol. They're just kids, you know. Eager and intense."

"And Christopher is your son," she murmured.

"What?"

"Static on the line."

"Are you sure everything is okay, Carol?"

"A-okay, darling. All systems working. And I shouldn't be lonesome anymore, thanks to you."

"We must have a bad connection," he said, stifling a yawn. "Listen, baby. I've got to get some sleep. I'm meeting Beckenheimer's brain trust at his Long Island estate early tomorrow, and I'd like to be at least partially awake."

"Did you just get to bed?"

"As a matter of fact, yes. I had a busy day and a late dinner, and then I had to give Doris some dictation—"

"Of course, dear. I understand, and I'm terribly sorry I interrupted your rest. Give Doris my regards."

"Good night, darling."

"Good night," she said and rang off.

Driving along Mount Vernon Highway toward the Rochambeau Bridge and the bright lights of the capital, Carol thought the Potomac River was more than a physical boundary; it was the threshold of another world. And why, exactly, was she entering that world again this evening? Why had she spent most of the morning in the beauty salon and most of the afternoon trying to decide what to wear? And why did she feel this curious mixture of tension and guilt and excitement now, as if she were going to an assignation? It was important to keep this thing in focus, perspective, lest she mistake its scope and significance. What it amounted to, she assured herself, was the prospect of a pleasant evening with a pleasant companion, which, ironically enough, had evolved from her husband's meddling and connivance. Just as the companionship of Christopher and Kay, which he had originally wanted to promote and now wanted to curtail . . .

She said to the boy, "You don't think perhaps you and Kay are getting a bit too chummy?"

His sigh was sheer disgust. "I wish you'd make up your mind! Two weeks ago, you were pushing us together."

"But you mustn't monopolize all of Kay's time, Chris. She has other friends too, you know. And Mr. Courtland thinks—"

He interrupted, "What does Mr. Courtland think?"

"Well, that you and Kay may be seeing a trifle too much of each other. Kids can become seriously involved before they know it, and you're both too young for that. We wouldn't want either of you to get hurt."

Christopher pondered this a moment, then asked abruptly, "Since when is my welfare of such concern to you and Courtland? Since you discovered that you couldn't have kids of your own!"

Carol kept her eyes riveted on the road. "Who told you that, Christopher?"

"Nobody. I'm not stupid. You've been married a long time and have no children. That's Courtland's interest in me now, isn't it, and it's a bloody bit late!"

Her hands gripped the steering wheel. Apparently he knew, and had probably known for years! What should she say, do? It was unwise for her to react in any way; she might only make matters worse. Let Jeff handle it.

"Why don't you ask him, Christopher?"

"I will," he muttered, "if I'm around long enough."

He sat against the door of the sedan, brooding. Always in a mood of some kind, Carol thought. An enigma, ever deepening, defying her comprehension, threatening her serenity and perhaps even her sanity.

"What do you and Kay plan to do tonight?" she asked.

"Play records, I guess, while her folks play bridge. What do you and the major plan to do?"

Carol ignored the impertinence, relieved to reach The Towers. "Well, here we are! Have fun, Chris."

His grin, insolent and insinuating, accompanied Carol to the Ambassador Hotel, where she was meeting Major Lawrence. Why did Christopher hate her so, want to mock and hurt her, as if she were personally responsible for his plight? Friend one minute, foe the next. She felt as if she had fought and lost a battle, and the emotional scars were as visible to Mark as a bruised eye or swollen jaw.

"Problems?" he asked after they had ordered dinner.

Carol nodded. "But I won't bore you with them, Mark."

"You couldn't ever bore me, Carol."

She was wearing a black lace Dior, daringly décolleté and sirenish, she thought. But to Mark she looked like a madonna in mourning, sad and sacred. Take the lace stole from her shoulders, drape it over her head, put a babe in her arms—and she could have posed for Raphael or Michelangelo. Surely she could not be deliberately childless? Only a perverse nature could have denied such a woman motherhood!

She picked up the corsage of white camellias by her plate and smiled at him. "Thank you, Mark. They're exquisite. But why not orchids?"

"Do you prefer orchids?"

"No, but how did you know?"

"Just by looking at you. It'll be violets the next time, or forget-me-nots, but never orchids."

"You'll have me weeping in my wine," she murmured.

"Is that where women weep now?"

"Only the sophisticates, the orchid types. The violets and forget-me-nots still prefer men's shoulders. Yours are very strong and sturdy, aren't they? You're good for me, Mark."

"I'm not sure that's a compliment, Carol. It makes me feel like a therapist."

"Perhaps that is what I need. Therapy."

"I was afraid you wouldn't come tonight," he said.

"Maybe I shouldn't have."

"Conscience?"

"I have one, Mark."

"Everyone has, Carol. The inner voice. Some people listen, some argue, some compromise. Which did you do?"

"Well, obviously I didn't listen. I argued awhile, and then I guess I compromised."

"And now you expect me to propose a compromise? You can't conceive of a man wanting to be with a woman for any other reason, can you?"

"It doesn't enter your mind, Major? You're so different from other men?"

The waiter brought the châteaubriand for two, and Mark began to divide it. "That sounds bitter and cynical, Carol. What did he do to you?"

"Who?"

"The guy who soured you on men and sex."

"You're presuming."

"I'm prying."

"And you have no right."

"My dear, you've been hurt. Badly, deeply. A blind

person could see it, and I have twenty-twenty vision. I don't flatter myself that you're with me now because I'm so damned handsome and irresistible. I think you're here because of that conversation we had on the Cranshaws' terrace last night, the one about disillusionment. Yours has been rather recent, hasn't it?''

Carol had scarcely touched her salad and was dawdling with the delicious steak. ''Your talents are wasted in the Artillery, Major. You should be in Army Intelligence.''

''It doesn't take any special talent or perception to recognize disenchantment, Carol. The victim usually betrays himself, one way or another. I may be wrong, but I have an idea yours is associated with your visitor from England.''

Carol gazed into her champagne glass, contemplating the bubbles rising in the hollow stem, breaking, vanishing. ''Am I under interrogation, Mark, or analysis?''

His hand, big and warm and gentle, covered hers. ''Forgive me, Carol. But I had to know and didn't want to play charades to find out. The music's back,'' he said, as the orchestra returned from intermission. ''Want to dance?''

She went into his arms eagerly, with a sense of belonging, and needing something solid and stable to cling to in a precarious world. And when later he whispered, ''Tomorrow?'' she responded, ''Why not?''

To avoid the Cranshaws, Carol called from the lobby, and Christopher came down alone. They spoke little on the way home, each preoccupied with personal matters, and when she told him he could see Kay again the next evening if he wished, Christopher only smiled—that same cynical, too-old smile incongruous on such a young face.

The restaurant, small and dimly lit, did not live up to its gourmet reputation or romantic mystique. The food and wine were second-rate, the service poor, the tablecloth stained—and what was more clandestine than dirty linen? They were both disappointed and embarrassed.

"I'm sorry, Carol. Someone recommended this place to me, I can't imagine why. A bird colonel, yet!"

"The decor, probably. Some people like faded murals and candles stuck in wine bottles."

"And snails? Hell, I'd rather have a hamburger or pizza. Let's get out of here! Take my car and go somewhere."

He had brought her flowers again, an old-fashioned nosegay of pink sweetheart roses reminiscent of her sixteenth birthday. She had not thought florists made such bouquets anymore, or that a soldier could be so sentimental and nostalgic. His admiration was sincere, his attentions flattering—the buffer, the reassurance she had needed for months now, perhaps for years. She felt young and lovely and desirable, and that in itself was important to a woman her age. Eager to escape the shoddy little rendezvous before the feeling passed, she quickly agreed.

The city was beautiful at night, with shafts and domes of light, illuminated fountains and statues, but Carol had seen it all before, and Mark was preoccupied with other thoughts, too. On Massachusetts Avenue they passed the building that housed Courtland Investments, and Carol shivered despite the warmth of the summer night. Mark drove aimlessly, wandering across Rock Creek into Georgetown's narrow, bowered, hilly streets and old homes, around Dumbarton Oaks and the Naval Observatory, finally swearing in confusion.

"Damned if I know where we are! I'm lost, Carol. Lead me out of this labyrinth."

She directed him to the parkway which followed the creek to the river, past the Titanic Memorial and the

Watergate. Soon they were on Ohio Drive, where it edged East Potomac Park, and Carol was watching the willows along the sea wall, their branches dipping into the water, the fallen leaves floating, shimmering like gold flecks on the dark surface.

"A dollar for your thoughts," Mark said.

"Dollar?"

"Inflation."

"Oh. Well, I'm afraid they're not worth that much. I was thinking that we shouldn't see each other anymore."

"Why not, if we enjoy being together?"

"It's not that simple, Mark. I'm married."

"I'm aware of that, Carol."

"Then you must realize it's an impossible situation, and indefensible. Isn't a soldier supposed to retreat when a position is untenable?"

"You're not a military objective, Carol, and I'm not going to launch a sudden attack. That's not my mission."

"What is your mission?"

"To be with you as often as possible."

"A platonic relationship?"

"If that's how you want it."

At Hains Point, the southern tip of the peninsula park, he found a vacant niche among the parked automobiles and expertly eased into it.

"You've been here before, Major," Carol accused.

"Once, with a girl from the Pentagon. But she was only twenty, a child, and I felt more protective than romantic. She told me I reminded her of her father back home in Missouri. I never saw her again."

The beacons of Bolling Field and Washington National Airport blazed across the water, left and right, and farther down the Potomac old Alexandria glowed hazily. In days past Carol had watched the President's Cup Regatta from

Hains Point, and met Jeff at the Tea Room for lunch after golf on the park course. They had sat on the terrace, enjoying the view and planning the future, and memory and nostalgia hammered at her now like an anvil chorus.

"On a clear day you can see the Virginia hills from here," she said. "They look blue."

"Virginia's a beautiful state," Mark said. "I'd like to retire there if I can find the right place. A farm in the Shenandoah Valley. Raise apples, maybe."

"What did you raise in Kansas?"

"Hell and dust, mostly. But my folks tried to raise wheat, when they weren't battling weather and insects. The Great Plains are rugged, brutally cold in winter, abominably hot in summer, and I'm getting too old and lazy to wrestle the elements and worry about crop failures."

Carol clucked her tongue in mock sympathy. "Oh, I'm sure you must be about ready for the Old Soldiers Home, Major Lawrence."

"I'm forty-one," he told her. "That's no kid."

"It's not ancient, either. But if farming's your ambition, why have you made a career of the military?"

"I started with Pearl Harbor, then there was Korea and other brinks of war, as Dulles called them, and there just didn't seem to be any good time to get out of uniform. And after I lost my wife—"

"Oh, I'm so sorry, Mark!"

"It was divorce, not death," he clarified. "I got a Dear Mark in Korea." He paused in wry reflection. "I was on Heartbreak Ridge at the time."

"It must have seemed terribly cruel, Mark, but maybe it was actually a kindness. At least she was honest with you."

"Wasn't he honest with you?"

Unexpectedly, her damned emotions broke and threat-

ened to inundate her. And suddenly she was in Mark's
arms, weeping and volunteering bits of information, while
he extracted more, until he was able to piece the puzzle
together and confirm his suspicions. He held her close,
quieting her sobs, drying her tears with his handkerchief.

"We have a lot in common, Carol. Do you still think
we shouldn't see each other anymore?"

"Why not?" she murmured.

"Will you sleep with me tonight?"

Startled, Carol twisted out of his embrace. *"What?"*

"I just wanted to see if you were listening," he said,
smiling. "You've answered 'why not?' to almost everything I've asked you since we met, and I was curious to
hear your response to that question."

"Why not?"

"Don't tease me, Carol. Not about that."

"I'm sorry, Mark. I'm not good at jokes or clever
repartee. We'd better go back now, it's getting late, and I
still have to pick up Christopher. He must have worn out
Kay's records and his welcome by now."

"Are you going to adopt him?"

"That's our hope and plan, if he's agreeable. So far,
however, Christopher hasn't given much indication of wanting us for parents."

"You must love him a great deal?"

"I would, if he'd let me."

"I don't mean the boy, Carol. What you're doing for
him is because of his father. You realize that, don't you?
Lucky bastard, Courtland! Both of them, in fact."

"That's ugly talk, Mark. I don't like it."

"Sorry." He started the motor, racing it in anger or
frustration. "When will he be back?"

"Who?"

"You know *who*!"

"Say his name, then."

"Okay. When will your husband, Jeffrey Courtland, broker and lucky bastard, return?"

"I don't know."

"Doesn't he keep you informed?"

"I thought so, once. Now—" She shrugged.

"Marital faith is a fragile thing, isn't it? Constructed like a matchstick house: remove one support, and the whole structure topples. Catch a spouse in one lie, and his or her veracity forever after is doubtful. Uncover one intrigue, one infidelity, and all future acts and motives come under suspicion."

"That's essentially what Joan Cranshaw told me."

"Well, it doesn't matter, Carol. We're going to see each other again, regardless."

"No, Mark, please. I'd only hurt you, and I don't want to do that."

"I've been hurt before, Carol. Disillusioned and disenchanted, too, like you. We're comrades-in-arms. We need each other, my dear, for comfort if nothing else."

They continued around the park, which bordered Washington Channel, and drove to the parking lot where Carol had left her car. There Mark drew her gently against him and kissed her mouth, silently, tenderly persisting until she responded in a brief burst of passion.

"Oh, Mark, we met too late! Years too late."

"It's never too late, Carol."

"It is for us," she insisted. "Later than you think, Mark. I've got to go now."

He escorted her to the sedan, put her behind the wheel, leaned inside, and kissed her again, longingly. "That's good night," he whispered, "not good-bye."

16

Carol volunteered to drive Christopher and Kay to Arlington National Cemetery the following afternoon, and after the solemn and impressive changing of the guard at the Tomb of the Unknown Soldier, they visited the massive Iwo Jima Memorial on the west bank of the Potomac.

Carol saw the Army officer standing there, his profile in partial shadow, cap in hand, gazing pensively at the simulated Mount Suribachi and the six valiant figures raising the flag in the celebrated victory, as if he had been one of them.

"Major Lawrence?"

He turned swiftly—and at first she was not sure it was Mark. He looked older in the sunlight, with obvious gray in his dark crew cut, and sharp lines etched in his bronzed face. But his smile and voice were the same. "Carol!"

"Hello, Mark. Do you sometimes feel that it *really* is a small world?"

"I did, until I traveled over most of it."

"The South Pacific, too? Iwo Jima?"

"No. My younger brother. David was a Marine. To me, this monument is a sort of personal shrine to him. He was twenty, just a boy, forced into manhood too quickly and killed before he actually reached it. Which is some kind of indictment against humanity, I guess, and a mockery of civilization. But war has never been either humane or civilized."

Carol nodded, thinking of Christopher. The spoils, the horrors, the tragedies of war. "Never," she agreed.

Mark said, "It's peaceful here in the evening, and rather beautiful at sunset. You can watch the lights go on in Washington, and remember how they used to go off in other cities. I come here often on my way from the Pentagon."

He seemed to be telling her where she could find him if she inclined, suggesting a positive meeting place, and the plea in his eyes was unmistakable. Carol remembered the embrace of the night before, the impulsive, sensual kiss in the parking lot, and knew he was remembering, too. Then the children appeared, laughing congenially as they came around the great granite base of the memorial.

"Why, it's Major Lawrence!" cried Kay, obviously both surprised and pleased to see him. "How are you, sir?"

"Fine, thanks, Kay." And to the boy, "How're you, son?"

"All right," Christopher mumbled, shaking the hand he offered briefly. It embarrassed him to be called "son" by any man, particularly one in American military uniform.

"What do you think of this?" Mark asked him, indicating the monument.

"Iwo Jima? 'Twas a bloody good battle, no doubt. But

the British put up some fierce ones in that war, too. I've read about it."

"You bet they did, Chris! It couldn't have been won without them. You can be proud of your country."

With a teasing glance at Christopher, Kay said, "Chris and I have a regular seesaw going on England and America. But it's fun showing him around, and we're learning from each other."

"Have you taken him to the FBI shooting exhibit yet?" Mark suggested. "He might like to compare their marksmanship with Scotland Yard's."

At Chris's nod, Kay said, "We'll go there tomorrow. But we'd better go home now, Aunt Carol. I promised Mother I wouldn't be late for dinner this evening."

"You won't be, dear," Carol assured her. "Good-bye, Major. So nice seeing you again." She hoped her manner was as casual and noncommittal as she tried to make it.

Mark donned his cap, touching the bill in salute, and Carol marveled that he should still be alive, considering the campaign ribbons on his chest. Had his life been spared for a reason? How romantic and superstitious! He was alive because he *was*, and they had met because they *had*, that's all! Fate, destiny, the gods, had nothing to do with it.

Yet she could not explain the magnetism that drew her inexorably, compelling her to return to the scene. For she was there at five o'clock the next day, in a white linen sheath and high-heeled white pumps, as lovely and feminine as her jasmine fragrance.

Mark arrived directly from the Pentagon, apparently less surprised than pleased to find her waiting.

"There's a Marine Band concert at the Watergate this evening," she began nervously. "I thought you might like to take me there, Major, after dinner."

"Bless you," he said simply.

A man's home is his castle, Mark thought, and Courtland just about had one in Alexandria. His wife was a fitting chatelaine for it, too.

Could a man ask a woman accustomed to such luxury and ease to share a farmhouse with him? Incredibly enough, that idea had occurred to him last night, while dining at the Mayflower Hotel, while listening to the Marine concert under the stars in the Watergate Amphitheater, and again in his quarters in Arlington after he and Carol had parted. It was, in fact, the reason he had asked her to drive out with him this morning to look at some property in the Shenandoah Valley, and her acceptance had been encouraging. But these things had a different aspect in daylight, and he wondered now if Carol had merely taken the opportunity to show him that difference in the invitation to her home.

The black servant admitted him, scrutinizing him as critically as an inspector general before leading him to the elegant white and gold chamber too formal to be called a living room. "Miz Courtland will be down directly, sir. She say for you to have a drink if you like."

But it was too early in the day for liquor. And he had better not smoke, either, soiling a clean ashtray and leaving a telltale butt. He glanced about furtively, feeling like a trespasser on forbidden property. Was Carol's delay deliberate, to allow him to cool his ardor and come to his senses in this magnificent room, to impress upon him as perhaps nothing else could the incongruity of their relationship? When finally she appeared, casually chic in beige silk slacks and a floral blouse, her flaxen hair smoothed back with a grosgrain band, he felt even more rueful. The Country Boy and the Country Club Girl!

"Am I late, Mark?"

"No, I'm early," he apologized. "I'm afraid I operate by bugles, stopwatches, and countdowns—and sometimes I jump the gun." Anxious to escape what seemed like a gilded cage, trapping her, barring him, he urged, "Ready?"

"Quite."

Mark did not speak again until they were in the car and out of the neighborhood, heading for the highway. "The realtor gave me some directions, and I picked up an area map at the service station. You can be my navigator."

"What's our destination?"

"The Fenton Higby farm, Rockingham County."

"That's a far piece, Major. Cigarette?"

"Light one for me, please. There's a carton in the glove compartment. Several packs of your brand, too."

"I'm not hooked on any special kind, Mark. As a matter of fact, I hardly smoked at all until recently."

"I've tried to quit a few times, cold turkey, and went through withdrawal symptoms. Kicking the habit will have to be a gradual process with me."

"Remember when 'Lucky Strike green went to war'? Few kids today would know what that meant. And it's still hard to believe there was enough olive drab dye in their original package to make it necessary."

"Probably just a concession to patriotism," Mark surmised. "Civilians made a lot of patriotic gestures those days."

Carol lit two cigarettes and handed him one with traces of strawberry-flavored lipstick on the cork-tip, which he seemed to savor. "You should be smoking a pipe, you know. Whoever heard of a country squire smoking anything else?"

Mark laughed. "Country squire suits me about as well

as a goatee and fancy cane would!'' He didn't like affectation, nor cared much for officers who did.

"Add another twenty years, and the image will fit. You may even become a horse-and-hound enthusiast, Major. Have you ever gone fox hunting?''

"Not in the tallyho style. I suppose you're an expert?''

"I've ridden in many hunts,'' she admitted. "Jeffrey's paternal grandmother owned some fine horses and hounds. Until her death and the sale of the old family place, we never missed a season.''

Carol had enjoyed the long weekends in the country, the walks in the woods, the gaiety of the hunt season, and thought that Jeff had shared her pleasure. Sometimes she missed Belle Manor terribly, but if Jeff did it was not enough to accept the invitations from the new owner, a rather ribald Texan who was attempting to ingratiate himself into the horse set in all the wrong ways: with invitations to people he did not know, gifts of valuable quarter horses from his ranch on the Rio Grande, and silver-tooled Western saddles which no respectable Eastern horse would abide. Jeff refused to sponsor the man's social ambitions, or cater to his gargantuan ego. Lacking a base of operations, the Courtlands gave up regular stays in the country, although Carol still rode and visited occasionally with old friends.

Jeff did his hunting on foot now, however, with rifle or shotgun, and he went with other men and their dogs, or alone. The few times Carol had accompanied him, she had proved to be more of a burden and nuisance than helpful companion, losing her way in the brush, collecting scratches and bruises, ending up with a cold or dysentery, or both. She found no coziness in tents and crude cabins, no convenience in improvised privies, and thought that romance in a sleeping bag was highly overrated. Invariably a thorn or pebble under her buttocks spoiled the ecstasy, and she was always terrified that a wild animal would wander into camp while Jeff was too busy to notice. After a few such experiences he had agreed that she should do her hunting on a horse, wearing black coat, canary-yellow breeches, and velvet cap. He urged her to go without him, which Carol did only because he left her to pursue his favorite sports. And she used to think how wonderful it would be if he had a son to join him . . .

"We're in the heart of the hunt country," she said, as they neared Warrenton and the former Courtland estate.

Sleek thoroughbreds grazed in blue grass pastures and exercised in white-fenced paddocks. Old mansions sat back from the road, half-hidden by trees and shrubbery. Here and there an open entrance gate afforded a glimpse of tall white columns and lovely gardens. Wooded hills rolled westward to the Blue Ridge Mountains. Green, peaceful country, with markers to commemorate past violence.

"In the heart of history, too," Mark said. "It's everywhere in this state, including the first settlement at Jamestown. No doubt your ancestors were involved?"

"Some of them."

"Courtland's, too?"

"Yes, but we don't practice ancestor-worship, Mark."

"That's comforting," he said, although it was not what he had heard about the First Families of Virginia. "Because my coat-of-arms reads more like a coat-of-alms. Pioneer stock, some folks might say, since anyone who ventured west of the Missouri River in those days was a pioneer. My great-grandparents were Pennsylvania Quakers, who went to Kansas on a prairie schooner. They were poor and pious and plain as dirt, and remained that way throughout life. If their crops survived the weather, the locusts destroyed them. But they kept trying and praying, because farming was the only thing they knew how to do and faith was inherent. They had ten children, most of whom died in infancy, and they left the hardy survivors a legacy of poverty, piety, perseverance, and failure. If there's a spiritual reward for such humble virtues, the Lawrence souls should be on golden thrones in heaven.''

"Maybe they are," Carol said solemnly. "But if things were so bad, how did you manage college?"

"I managed only two years of it, by slinging hash. I can make better buckwheat cakes than Aunt Jemima, and I invented a beef stew that made Dinty's Diner near the Kansas A & M campus famous. I don't regret my experience in the kitchen, however. It's come in handy all these years of cooking for myself."

"You know you're a bachelor by choice, Mark. And just because one woman failed you—"

"Maybe I failed her," he said.

"Did you?"

"I couldn't be what she wanted."

"What did she want—a general?"

"That would have been a nice start, but I was a long way from it when she requested her freedom." He paused, his features grim in reflection. "Naturally, my ego couldn't stand in her path. I consented to a divorce by return mail. Oh, I was suave as the devil, wishing her happiness and good luck. Unfortunately, she didn't have much of either. The guy married her all right, gave her a set of twins, and then went AWOL. Her mother wrote me about it, said Margie wasn't well and had two little girls to support, and I could see tears on the paper."

"So now you're helping her?"

"A little," he admitted reluctantly. "But Margie doesn't know it. That's why I consulted Cranshaw. A fellow officer, who had some domestic problems which your friend solved, recommended him to me. Ken worked out something that Margie thinks is a trust fund established by her late father and administered by her mother.''

"You're a remarkable man, Mark."

"Yeah, sure. Santa Claus in olive drab. Maybe that's why I'm always left holding the bag."

"But you don't have to help her, Mark."

"Her kids are hungry."

"They're not yours."

"No, but I've seen hungry children all over the world, and it's a sad sight."

"Are you sure it's just the youngsters you're concerned about, Mark? Isn't it possible that you're still in love with their mother?"

"No." He shook his head. "I thought so until—well, for a long time. Now I know it's over and could never be revived. It's hard to realize how much she once meant to me, and how torn up I was about losing her. For a while I didn't give a damn what happened to me in Korea and half-hoped some gook would finish me off. But I knew I wasn't alone, other guys had gotten the same raw deal, and some went home to find another man's child. At least I was spared . . . Oh, Jesus, Carol, I'm sorry!"

"It's all right," she murmured.

The foothills gave way to the mountains, the blue ridges blending with the sky, cresting in the white clouds. In the lookout area, where Mark parked, an artist was committing the scene to canvas, brushing on oils of emerald and indigo, sapphire and turquoise, ochre and terra cotta.

"I should have brought my camera," Mark said.

"It'll be here next week, Mark. And next year."

"But I may not, Carol. They've been shifting me around like a hotrod transmission lately. The Army's a great life if you have some gypsy in you, but my youthful wanderlust was dissipated long ago. I want to settle down now, dig in some roots, accumulate something besides mileage records.''

"Can you retire at will?"

"I could get a medical disability anytime, Carol. I have some shrapnel wounds, mementos of the Battle of the Bulge, which discomfit me at times. I just haven't mentioned it to the medicos.''

"Wouldn't farming be a little strenuous for you?"

"Not if it's mechanized, and I wouldn't consider doing it any other way.''

"Well, I hope it works out for you, Mark. I hope you get what you want.''

"So do I," he said and was momentarily silent, surveying the scenery. "It's like being in church, isn't it? A great cathedral with a vaulted nave and magnificent stained glass windows. Sort of makes you want to pray.''

Carol nodded wistfully. "I always expect to hear a mighty organ playing 'Rock of Ages,' and an invisible choir singing. And I feel so small and mortal and insignificant. You know what I mean?''

Mark was gazing somberly into infinity, eternity. "I think so, Carol. Ashes to ashes, dust to dust.''

"Oh, Mark! I don't want to pass from this earth without leaving some imprint. So many people leave only a memory, which soon fades, and a piece of stone that just gathers moss. I want to leave something vital to live on after me.''

"There's only one way to do that, Carol.''

"I know. And I know why Jeff needed his child, why he could never be happy or whole without him.'' Her voice cracked, and tears threatened. "I don't want to think or talk about it anymore, Mark. Please drive on.''

They crossed the ridge and descended into the valley.

Embarrassed by her sudden emotional outburst, Carol reached for another cigarette.

"Careful with that match," Mark warned humorously, as they passed a government forestry sign. "Smokey the Bear might be watching."

"Don't worry, we won't start any fires, Mark."

"None we can't handle, anyway," he said.

Realizing what he meant, Carol only hoped he was more certain of his control than she was of hers.

17

Deep summer in the Shenandoah—an easy, languid time with most of the crops harvested and only the apples still green in the orchards.

"In spring," Carol told Mark, "when the fruit trees are in bloom, the valley smells like a perfume factory. It's the loveliest sight and sweetest scent on earth."

"I'd rather smell ripe fruit, especially apples," Mark said. "They always remind me of Thanksgiving and Christmas, because that's about the only time I had them as a kid."

"Were you really so poor, Mark?"

"We were destitute during the Depression. Remember the long droughts of the thirties? And the dust storms called Black Blizzards?"

"I remember the Depression," Carol said. "My father was in real estate, and business was bad. People were trying to sell property; no one wanted to buy it."

"Ours was mortgaged to the hilt, and we'd have lost it except for the presidential moratorium. Kansas was in the center of the Dust Bowl, and for several years the fields were barren and desolate as dunes, the topsoil blowing away with the wind, the livestock dying of thirst or choking to death on sand.

"Our farm was one of those that President Roosevelt visited on his tour of the region. He was wearing a white Panama hat with the brim turned up all around, smoking a cigarette in a long tortoise-shell holder, and sweating in the back seat of an open touring car. He talked seriously with Dad for a while, but about the only consolation he could offer was a new farm program, that famous smile of his, and a warm handshake when he was leaving. But that was enough for Mom. She could never forget that she had met the President of the United States. Roosevelt was a savior to her, a second Messiah preaching the gospel of 'Nothing to fear but fear itself.' She lived on the memory, the hope, and promise, and probably died happy and unafraid because of it. But I was sixteen, an eager youth with my future enveloped in dust—and that was what impressed me most: the seeming hopelessness and futility. Strange, how childhood memories linger."

"Not strange, Mark. Tragic, because they're more than memories now. They're complexes and traumas."

"Really, Doctor?"

"Of course. This need of yours to own some land, to possess something solid and permanent, stems from the poverty and insecurity of your youth. Surely you realize that? You've probably remained in the service primarily for the security it offers."

He smiled ironically. "I wonder why I didn't feel secure in Europe and Korea."

"I don't mean the fighting part, Mark. The benefits.

The regular paycheck and commissary privileges, the medical care, and pension on retirement. You want your future insured because there was a time when you knew only dust and grasshoppers and cold and hunger.''

"Maybe," he agreed.

"No maybe about it, Mark. Childhood affects adulthood, psychologically and other ways. I have living proof of that in Christopher, and I'm not sure he could ever really adjust without professional therapy. Possibly not even then. His surliness toward you at the Iwo Jima Memorial was due to your uniform, I think."

"He sees his father in every American military man?"

"More or less."

"Poor boy! Don't ever take him to a veterans' parade. He's liable to run amuck."

"I worry about his hostility," Carol admitted, "and wonder if he's capable of violence. He's so full of bitterness and resentment. It's hard to know what an illegitimate child actually feels toward his father, and what sort of revenge or retribution he might contemplate. Jeff speaks of taking him hunting this fall, but I'm actually afraid it would be a mistake to put a loaded gun in Christopher's hands."

"He would have to be severely disturbed to do anything that drastic, Carol. I've seen plenty of Section Eights— psycho cases—in the Army, but usually they were born that way, and military life, discipline, and war merely triggered their abnormalities. Christopher appears normal and rational enough to me. Very bright, really."

"Oh, I'm certain of his intelligence, Mark! He has the makings of a scholar and could have a wonderful future here. Jeff would give him a fine education, but it can't be forced on him. He'll have to recognize the opportunities and advantages himself, and so far he hasn't. Perhaps he just needs more time. But this isn't your problem, Mark, and I'd better watch the map. That farm road we need should be at the next junction. Yes, I see it up ahead. Take the left fork, and then exactly a mile down the lane to Higby's farm . . .''

It was there, where the realtor had said it would be, the RFD mailbox on a post, at the entrance to a red dirt lane edged with weeds and wild flowers. To Mark, it was Paradise and Shangri-la rolled into one, but he did not think it affected Carol that way. She stayed in the car, held at bay by several lean, spotted, barking hounds, until the old farmer emerged from the house and called them off.

Higby was in overalls, and in need of a haircut and shave. "What can I do for you folks?"

Mark introduced himself and showed him the advertisement in the *Washington Post*.

"Yep, it's for sale, all right, Major. The place and everything on it. Make you a good retirement living, too. Best pippins in the whole valley! Winesaps, too. I ought to know, lived here all my life. Borned in the Shenandoah.''

"Why do you want to sell now?" Mark asked.

"Lost my wife last year. Also gettin' old, as you can plainly see. Farm's a lonesome place for a man without a woman. Why don't you and the missus look around a bit for yourselves, if you've a mind to? Dogs won't bother you none," he said, leading them into the house with him.

"You should have corrected him about the missus," Carol admonished, getting out of the car.

"Why? I like it.''

"That's not the point.''

But Mark was already surveying the property.

In the orchard he scooped up a handful of soil, trying to analyze its composition by appearance and texture, forming it into a soft, moist clod, dissolving the lump and letting it sift slowly through his fingers. "Limestone base," he said. "Friable, holds moisture well. With proper fertilization and tilling, this earth would grow anything. It's a gold mine with a replenishable lode. There's a lifetime of security here, Carol. Freedom from want and worry. Peace and contentment. The Constitution doesn't guarantee much more."

"It doesn't guarantee that much, Major."

His eyes measured the big gambrel-roofed barn, visualizing it full of hay and grain, as he saw the smokehouse hung with hams, bacon, sausages. He envisaged these things as other men did stocks and bonds in bank vaults. He took mental inventory of the equipment, marking the usable tools and machinery as assets. He estimated the flock of chickens scratching in the yard at fifty and thought he could handle a hundred or more. And a bull servicing only two cows was wasted energy, he told Carol; there should be at least six or eight.

"Why not a dozen?" she quipped. "A bovine harem should make him happy."

"His happiness is incidental. A paying farm produces, and impregnating two cows a year is not enough production for a healthy bull. The male calves could be sold, and the heifers could produce more calves."

"What happens to the sterile ones?"

"To market, or the meat grinder," Mark replied. "Everything on a commerical farm produces."

"No exceptions?"

"None. And no slackers, either. Hen doesn't lay, into the pot. Rooster gets too old, off with his head. Lazy pigs, pork chops. And that bull should earn his keep, too."

"Oh, I don't imagine he'd object too much, if he's anything like his human counterpart."

"My dear, you're generalizing again," he said. "What do you think of the house?"

Carol considered the weathered frame structure, sadly in need of paint and repairs, a random design built by rudimentary carpenters. The lilacs near the front porch were overgrown with honeysuckle, the boxwood untrimmed. Marigolds and zinnias bloomed bravely in the neglected garden, which had obviously been Higby's wife's domain and showed her absence as pathetically as the house. The only homey aspect now was the old tabby cat in an upstairs window and the aroma of bacon and eggs from the kitchen, where Higby was preparing his lonely meal.

"It's shelter," she said. "Utilitarian. The land's the important thing, isn't it?"

"Not to a woman. Tell me the truth, Carol. Does that shanty have any feminine appeal whatever?"

"Not much in its present state, I'm afraid. But it's not hopeless, Mark. With a little imagination and a lot of expense, it could be made quite livable. Even attractive."

"It could never compare to Courtland Castle on the Potomac though, could it?"

"Why would you want it to compare, Mark? Such a house wouldn't be practical on a farm."

They had reached one of the property boundaries, a split-rail fence erected when the region was still a wilderness, and Mark leaned against it, facing the farmhouse. "I'm just trying to picture you in another setting, my lady. Somehow I can't."

"Mark—"

"I love you, Carol. I didn't intend to say it so unromantically—but there it is, blunt and bucolic. I'm in love with you."

"You've only known me a week!"

"The world was created in less time," he said. "Surely

it's long enough for a man to fall in love with a woman and want to marry her.''

"Oh, Mark, we can't speak of marriage!"

"Can we speak of love?" Without waiting for an answer, he drew her into his arms, immediately aroused. "You know how I feel about you—"

"This isn't doing you any good, Mark."

"Yes, it is. More than you know. Didn't I make the proposal clear enough? I want to marry you."

"You're besieging me, Major. Firing all your big guns at once, and my only defense is a wedding ring. You know marriage is not possible for us, Mark. Even if it were, it wouldn't be practical. I know nothing about farming, and I'm not young anymore."

He smiled. "You're young enough."

"Be serious, Mark. Remember what you said? Everything on a paying farm produces? Well, I'd be the exception. The slacker. The unproductive liability. I couldn't bear children—and what's a farm without kids?"

"How many would you like?"

"Stop it, Mark! You know I told you—"

He interrupted, "You told me you couldn't have children with Courtland. That doesn't necessarily mean you couldn't with another man, Carol. Didn't any of those specialists you consulted tell you that?"

"I'm thirty-eight, Mark."

"You could still be a mother, Carol."

"No, Mark. Get yourself a healthy young woman."

"So her offspring could seem like my grandchildren? I don't want that, Carol. Nor do I want to marry just anyone, either. I want you."

"Are you asking me to divorce my husband?"

"No, you'd have to make that decision alone. I'm only telling you how I feel, and what I'm willing to do about it.

The next move has to be yours." He took her hand eagerly. "Come on, now! Let's go find that farmer and see if he's in a bargaining mood . . ."

Carol sat with her shoes off, legs curled up on the car seat, listening to the radio, as they drove along the highway. They had eaten dinner at a mountain inn and watched the bonfire blaze of the sun setting on the valley. Now the stillness of the summer evening was upon the countryside. The woods were deep and shadowy, scented with pine, their dark solitude somehow more romantic and stimulating than a brilliant moon.

She was keenly aware of the intimacy, all her senses responding to it, her body amenable to his groping hand. She wanted him to unbutton her blouse and fondle her breasts, kiss the nipples, and explore beneath her slacks. And it came as a surprise, almost a revelation, that another man's touch could evoke intense and pleasurable sensations.

"Can you drive and do that?"

"Not very well," he replied, his voice hoarse with total sexual arousal. "Should I stop?"

"Driving?"

"Playing with you."

"No, I like it."

"Reciprocate."

"I'm afraid."

"Of what?"

"Wanting you."

"And that frightens you?"

"A little. I've never wanted any other man that way. Never even thought I could."

"That's the best news I've heard all day," he said, as a mournful commentator came on the air. "Oh, Christ!

Gloomy Gabriel Heatter blowing his doomsday horn again. Turn him off, darling. Get some music.''

Carol spun the dial to a singing voice and a tune popular during the war. ''They reached back for that one.''

''Way back! 'Sentimental Journey' was 'our song' for a lot of wartime couples. Remember 'You'd Be So Nice To Come Home To' or 'I Don't Want to Walk Without You, Baby.' ''

''Ours was 'White Cliffs of Dover,' '' Carol reflected, and suddenly the mood was shattered, the spell broken. ''I guess because he was in England.''

''I was partial to the 'Warsaw Concerto,' '' Mark reminisced. ''I saw Poland and Czechoslovakia after the war. Warsaw, Danzig, Lublin. And the ruins of poor brave little Lidice, which was razed and every adult male killed in reprisal for the assassination of its beastly Nazi ruler, Reinhard Heydrich. In Warsaw there was an old man sitting on the edge of a bomb crater, where once his home had stood, playing a concertina, and I recognized the tune. Haunting music; I brood whenever I hear it.''

''Don't brood now, Mark.''

''No, darling. Not until I leave you.''

''You don't have to leave me.''

''You're sweet, Carol, but your motives are as transparent as cellophane. Those memory lane songs just now made you remember something you want to forget, and you think going to bed with me might help. But it wouldn't, Carol. It'd only make it worse because you still love the guy. It hurts like hell for me to say it, but at least I realize what I'm up against. I just wonder if you do.''

''You're refusing me?''

He swung the car off the road, cut the motor, and yanked the emergency brake. ''Listen to me, Carol! I love you, and if I thought it was mutual, I'd take you here and now. I'd force the issue any way I could. But I know it's not mutual, at least not yet, and that's why I can't force any issues prematurely, nor let one indiscretion on your part force any, either. That's no way to end a marriage."

"No? That's how most marriages end, Mark. Irrevocable involvement."

"Not on the spur of the moment, Carol. Spontaneous passion is great if sex is the only object. Otherwise it requires some thought and consideration."

"That night in Potomac Park you said you weren't afraid of being hurt, Mark. But you are, aren't you? And you're using my marriage as a shield now."

"I'm afraid of having and then losing you," he said, "and that would be infinitely worse than not having you at all. Maybe I'm just greedy and selfish—and you can trace that to my hungry childhood, too. But half a loaf wouldn't satisfy me, Carol, or be enough. I want the whole thing."

"All or nothing?"

"You're not the kind of woman who sleeps around for kicks, Carol, or could cheat without qualms. And you don't want just an affair any more than I do. Do you?"

She shook her head and moved away from him, tidying her clothes. Mark started the car and took her straight home. At the door, she said, "Congratulations, Major. You still have your Good Conduct Medal."

He smiled sheepishly. "Sort of silly, isn't it?"

"No, sort of wonderful, actually. Chivalry isn't dead, after all."

"It's staggering, though. Don't ever tempt me that way again, lady. I'm no tin soldier."

"On the contrary, sir, I think you're the real thing. Will you call me tomorrow?"

"Negative." He handed her a card with an address and telephone number. "You can reach me here, if you want me. That is, if you want me for something more than a buffer for your loneliness and frustration.''

"I thought you weren't going to force any issues?"

"I'm not," he insisted. "As I told you on the farm, my love, the next move is yours."

"Mark, I can't make any decisions now. They might be wrong. I'm so mixed up."

"I know, Carol. Think about it. And don't call me unless you're sure. I'll wait."

"How long?"

"Well, not more than ten years or so."

"Oh, Mark!" She smiled, touched his face, kissed him quickly on the mouth, and went inside.

18

A noise somewhere outside woke Carol early. She lay drowsily in bed, a little surprised but relieved to find herself alone. For a while last night, in Mark's car and in his arms, she'd had a dream, a vision of happiness. But it had been only illusory, a chimera chased in the madness of night, vanished in the sanity of day.

It was too late for her. She was approaching middle age, the climacteric which some women entered at forty, or soon thereafter. This was a physical, biological fact, inevitable and inescapable. Even if it were possible that her bodily chemistry had just been incompatible with Jeff's all these years, possible that she might experience motherhood with another man, there were serious factors to consider. She had read enough medical books on the subject to know the risks and dangers involved in childbirth after the age of thirty-five. Did she really want to take that chance and hope for two miracles, pregnancy and a normal child? Would Mark, if he considered it objectively? No, he deserved better. She would destroy his card, destroy the temptation ever to use it, destroy the memory itself.

With this resolution firmly in mind, she got Christopher up, down to breakfast, and off to Washington for a scheduled picnic with Kay Cranshaw. Then she helped Ella plan a week of menus, completed some neglected correspondence, checked her household accounts, and finally went out to cut some flowers for the house.

While selecting and snipping, she discussed the garden with Toby and admired the new bulb bed he had just designed, which would be bright with tulips next spring. She noticed with some dismay, however, that the trellises needed painting again, and the terrace flagstones needed resetting. The garage doors were sagging slightly, making them harder to open, indicating a necessary foundation check. Also, another termite inspection was due. Always something, she thought. And repairmen were getting harder to find and more expensive every day.

The scare talk about Russia and Cuba had stimulated interest in bomb shelters and country real estate. Even President and Mrs. Kennedy were building a retreat on Rattlesnake Mountain in the Blue Ridge. That secluded little Higby farm in the Shenandoah Valley had its attractions, all right, and if Mark didn't buy it, someone else surely would. Realtors and survivalists were predicting a mass exodus from the crowded East Coast cities.

When her basket was full, Carol went inside and removed her sun hat and canvas gloves. She was arranging yellow roses in a Chantilly vase for the living room when she heard the front door open, luggage being set down in the foyer, and her name called. Composing a smile, she went to meet her husband.

"Welcome home, Mr. Courtland!"

"I left as soon as I could," he said, kissing her cheek perfunctorily. "Any problems here?"

"Just the ordinary. No emergencies."

"Where's Christopher?"

"Picnicking with Kay."

"Doesn't he ever stay home?"

"Not if he can help it," Carol said. "Did you get squared away with Beckenheimer?"

"For the present, but he's liable to summon me back tomorrow. The man simply has too much money, still wants more, and hates to part with any through taxes or other ways. It can get complicated."

"Everyone should have such complications," said Carol, stepping back into the living room.

Jeff followed. "I tried to call you several times. In the evenings, mostly. I tried last night until midnight to tell you I'd be home today."

"I'm sorry, Jeff. I was out."

"Another dinner party?"

Carol glanced at him, wishing he did not appear so tired and edgy. "No," she murmured.

"Want to tell me about it?"

She resumed her floral arrangement. "There's nothing to tell, Jeff. I met this man, Major Mark Lawrence, at the Cranshaws, and I've seen him a few times since. He wants to buy some land in Virginia—a place to retire—and asked me to go with him to look at a farm. It's in the Shenandoah Valley, so naturally we were late getting back."

A wry smile twisted his mouth, increasing the fatigue in his eyes, and he went to the cellaret. "Naturally."

"Don't be cynical, Jeff, and don't reach for the bottle. This isn't something to drink about."

"I happen to be thirsty," he drawled, filling a hobnail glass with bourbon and bolting most of it before turning back to her. "I guess I'm to blame, Carol. I didn't expect you to sit at home with my pipe and slippers and a candle burning in the window. But I didn't intend the Cranshaws' invitation to be a liberty pass, either."

"It wasn't," she replied, maintaining her composure and patience. "But I resent your method of getting it issued. Don't try to play Perle Mesta for my benefit again, Jeff."

"Don't worry, I won't."

"Shall we forget it, then?"

"Just like that? Forget it? I rush home, slighting my client and my business, thinking I might be needed here. And instead, I find my son roaming more than ever, and my wife occupied with the Army!" He sloshed more whiskey into the glass, overflowing it on the marble-topped cabinet. "Would you mind telling me what that was the night before I left, Mrs. Courtland? I thought it was reconciliation, now I suspect it was just placation."

"Stop this, Jeffrey, before it gets out of hand."

"And creates a scene? You hate scenes, don't you, and would do anything to avoid one, even let yourself be raped!"

"I didn't regard it that way."

"Like hell you didn't! I trust your officer friend is more considerate?"

The remark would have infuriated Carol, except that she knew it was fermented in alcohol. "Don't judge all men by yourself," she rebuked him quietly.

"Is the major a wooden soldier?"

"Just a gentleman."

"Yeah, sure." He drank, his hand trembling on the tumbler. "Aren't we all, my dear? Ladies and gentlemen of the Old School."

"Be careful, please. You're spilling liquor on the carpet, and it stains."

"So what? A few stains won't hurt and might even help. This place has always been too neat, too clean, too goddamned perfect!"

"And sterile?"

"Perfect, I said. Maybe that's why Christopher doesn't care to stay in it much. If I were his age, I wouldn't want to hang around here either, afraid of spoiling something."

A blow from his fist could not have stunned or wounded Carol more; indeed it might have been kinder than this sudden, brutal revelation. All her years of devotion to this house, the time and energy and money expended to make it as nearly perfect as possible, because she had imagined he liked and appreciated perfection—and he had *let* her believe it. But apparently he did not want that at all. Apparently he was bored with the place, tired of the responsibilities and expenses, tired of commuting to Washington, tired and bored with everything, perhaps, including his wife and marriage. And instead of pitying their lease-hopping friends in their District apartments, maybe he was envying their personal freedoms and follies.

Tears stung her eyes, but she forced them back and spoke calmly. "I never knew you felt that way, Jeffrey. I never suspected, never even dreamed it. All these years I thought . . . you let me think . . . why did you, Jeff? Why did you lie and deceive me about the house, too? Why didn't you tell me the truth?"

"Because I don't honestly know what the truth is, even now," he said, sighing gravely. "I don't know if this place is a pleasure to me or a pain. I don't know if I love it, Carol, or hate it."

"Or if you love or hate me?"

"My God!" he gasped, crossing the room to her. "Is *that* what you think?"

She shrugged, lowering her eyes lest he see the hurt and bewilderment in their depths. "I don't know what to think anymore."

"Did your little escapade confuse you so much?"

"It wasn't an escapade."

"Whatever it was, it affected you, Carol. More than you seem to realize. Perhaps you should continue to see this guy, if you feel you must prove something to me or yourself? But don't think you can do it without any emotional involvement, my dear. And don't imagine you can forget twenty years in a week or month or year. But if you want to try, and I'm in the way, I can always go on another trip."

"And take your secretary?"

"Doris?"

"Do you have another one?"

"No, just Doris."

"You couldn't do without her, could you? Is she as competent in the bedroom as in the office?"

He laughed, drinking from the bottle now. "I can't believe this conversation, Carol. Tell me, who else do you suspect? Shirley Martin? Maybe even Beth Benedict? Frank would get a charge out of that!"

"You're drunk, Jeffrey."

"Celebrating, darling. My happy homecoming."

As always, his self-pity evoked her compassion. "I'm sorry, Jeff. I didn't intend it to be like this, believe me. And I don't want to quarrel now. I know you're tired and upset. Go upstairs and rest. You'll feel better later."

"Come with me," he pleaded, anguish and apology in his voice, and Carol agreed, wondering why he no longer seemed able to approach her sober.

And so it has degenerated into this? she thought sadly. Liquor and quarrels, accusations and recriminations and apologies—and wallowing in bed until a sexual climax was achieved. His, not hers, for she was still too beset by the critical comments and uncertain circumstances to respond adequately to his lovemaking.

Other doubts assailed her, too. Was her domestic fanaticism basic insecurity and fear of failing as a wife and homemaker because she could not bear children? If so, she was a functional neurotic in need of therapy, and she must have made him fairly miserable all these years with her idiosyncrasies and fastidiousness. Running behind him with coasters for his liquor glasses and emptying ashtrays before he was finished with them! Fretting if he got hair oil on a chair or sofa pillow, sat on a bedspread, or threw a wet towel down in the bathroom. Setting the table and serving every meal as if Amy Vanderbilt were a houseguest.

God only knew how he lived, what he ate and did on his escapes into the wilderness, but he always appeared healthy and happy upon returning from his hunting and fishing expeditions. Sometimes bearded and unbathed, always relaxed and visibly rested. And usually amorous, until she cooled his ardor by suggesting that he shower and shave first.

Once he had complained, "Some people enjoy primitive, spontaneous sex occasionally! Why must we always be so civilized and organized about it? You practically bathe in Arpege. Did it ever occur to you that a woman's natural scent isn't necessarily offensive to a man? And that there's more than one way to make love? With us, anything more than face-to-face missionary acts are a rare novelty—and then I don't think you really enjoy it, or want to reciprocate. Just once, I wish it'd be *your* idea! Jesus, Carol, you're a twentieth-century Puritan!"

The next day she had gone out and bought Dr. Kinsey and some other explicit, clinical sex manuals. Not so much to educate herself for her own benefit and pleasure as to please and placate him. *Love me, need me, want me.*

Timidly now, and with slow reluctance, she touched his naked shoulder. "Are you awake?"

"Uh-huh," he murmured.

"I want to talk, Jeff."

"Can't it wait? I'm wasted, baby."

"It's important, Jeffrey."

"Okay, I'm listening."

But his eyes were closed, his breathing heavy, and Carol knew she would be talking to herself.

19

They rented bicycles and pedaled along Beach Drive, laughing as they splashed through the shallow fords of Rock Creek. They toured the park and zoo and went up on Ridge Road near the Maryland state line, a steep climb that left Kay breathless. Tiring of riding, they walked pushing their bikes through the woods to a miniature waterfall on the creek, where they ate the lunch Kay had packed.

Her brief denim shorts slung low on her slender hips revealed a cute little navel like a big dimple and beautifully shaped legs—a much more mature body than Christopher had suspected in her dresses and jeans. Braless, her breasts were full and more provocative than in blouses or sweaters, the tiny nipples prominent at times under the scanty halter. He tried not to stare at them. He wanted to touch her there and wondered what she would do if he did. Sally Sawyer had liked to be touched, there and everywhere. Just thinking about it gave him an embarrassing erection, but Kay was either too innocent or timid to notice. No doubt she was still a virgin, possibly even an unkissed virgin. Did she ever get itchy that way, so stimulated she had to relieve herself? Every normal teenager he knew had a keen and curious interest in sex and at least some knowledge, if not practical experience, of its adolescent agonies. But Kay didn't seem to know much about such things—or anything else for that matter.

"Don't you like the sandwiches, Chris?"

"Sure, they're good."

"You're not eating much."

"Peanut butter goes down slowly."

"Not if it's mixed with jelly, and I used plenty. But maybe you don't like blueberry?"

"Well, I like strawberry better."

"I'll remember next time," she promised, apparently still unaware of the bulge in his jeans. "Here, have some potato chips. And cookies."

"Thanks." He took a handful of each and began to juggle them, his appetite gone. God, he was beginning to ache in the groin, as if he had a stone-bruise.

"Want an apple?"

Was that how Eve said it, so naive and direct, completely ignorant of what Adam really wanted? Or did Kay realize more than he imagined and was actually tempting him? In his state, it was hard to distinguish between innocence and coyness, and girls were a natural enigma, anyway. Their minds were practically inscrutable, and they rarely revealed their true thoughts or emotions. A chap could go flaky trying to understand them, especially the "nice" ones.

"Later," he said. "You think we might stretch out here

for a while? It's bloody hot, and I saw other picnickers catching forty winks.''

Some were doing more than napping, or hadn't she noticed? How could she *not* notice? That energetic couple under a tablecloth, for instance. And the pair thrashing behind a bush along the trail. The used condoms shriveling in the sun. Maybe she had never seen a rubber and thought they were just strange balloons. Then again, she might be just pretending. The ''good'' ones were usually clever pretenders, too. It was part of their feminine instinct.

''Are you tired, Chris? So am I, from all that cycling. My legs hurt clear up to my hips, and I know I'm getting sunburnt. Look how pink my skin is! Should have brought a shirt along. Reckon I could borrow yours?''

Oh, Christ! He was sweating, and not just from the heat.

''I guess so, if you need it. But it's shady here. Wish we had some newspapers to lie on.''

''We can use paper napkins and dispose of them in the litter barrel afterwards, not like the mess-cats before us. Somebody must have had a bad cold. All those filthy Kleenex!''

Christopher gazed at her. It was naiveté, not pretense. She honestly didn't realize what was on those tissues and the man's handkerchief a few feet away. What kind of biology, if any, did they teach at Abbey Hall?

''Yeah,'' he said, pillowing his head on his folded arms and concentrating on the sky visible through the tree branches, as he used to do in the Cotswolds. Often he and Bounder would rest beside a brook when the trout weren't biting, or when he just wanted to read, think, or be alone in the hills.

Odd, how the sky looked the same everywhere in the world. This one was Wedgwood blue with fluffs of white clouds like marshmallow meringue. But there was also a slight haze, which meant summer was ending, and a faint yellowish tinge to the foliage overhead. Kay would be off to school soon, and he should be on his way to England. But Aunt Agatha had not answered his last six letters. She must be terribly ill to neglect him so, or else the Courtlands were intercepting his mail. Perhaps he should write to Mr. Tary or Vicar Tisdale and ask if anything was wrong.

Thinking of the Cotswolds, of the cottage and Aunt Agatha and his dog, nostalgia filled him and overflowed in a favorite verse by a little known poet.

> I want to go home
> To the dull old town,
> With the shaded street
> And the open square;
> And the hill
> And the flats
> And the houses I love,
> And the paths I know
> I want to go home.

"That's beautiful," Kay said. "Yours?"

"No, I don't write poetry. It's called *Home*, by Paul Kester, and may be the only poem he ever wrote."

"Well, it's lovely, but sad. And you sounded sad reciting it. You really want to go home so much, Chris?"

"Yes, but I don't have the fare."

"Uncle Jeff would give it to you."

"I suppose, if I insisted. But I hate to ask."

"Gee, I thought you planned to stay and go to school here? I mean, if you're an exchange student—"

Christopher sat up abruptly, took an apple and bit into

it. The juice trickled down his chin, and he wiped it off on his sleeve.

Kay sat up too, resting her back against the tree trunk. "Don't you want to nap?"

"Can't," he said, almost harshly. "This is an Albermarle pippin, isn't it? Queen Victoria used to order them for Windsor Castle, along with hams from Smithfield, Virginia. Pippins are still the favorite apple of the House of Windsor."

Cabbages and kings, apples and queens. He knew so much, Kay thought, and she so little. Sometimes it seemed that she had learned nothing at Abbey Hall, except morals, manners, and horsemanship. But she wondered if he was making small talk now to keep his mind off other things. She had seen him looking at her breasts and legs, her navel and her mouth. He had never kissed her, or even tried. Why not? Did she have bad breath, or something? She brushed her teeth regularly and chewed chlorophyl gum and mints. She bathed every day, sometimes twice, shaved her underarms, and used a deodorant. She tried to be especially fastidious during her period, so he wouldn't notice that she was having the curse.

"That's nice," she said.

"What's nice?"

"That the House of Windsor likes our apples and hams."

"Have you ever been hungry, Kay?"

"Not really. You?"

"Yes. I've even stolen food."

"That's awful, Chris."

"Not if you're hungry enough."

"What other bad things have you done?"

"Depends on what you call bad."

Kay picked up a stick and scratched in the earth, wanting to draw a big heart with a piercing arrow and initials like the one some lovers had carved on the oak against which she rested. "You know," she murmured, blushing.

"Yes, and it wasn't bad. It was good."

"Did you love the girl?"

"I thought so, at first. But she had other guys. Half the Teddies in Bethnal Green, I think."

"What's Bethnal Green?"

"A slum in London, and a Teddy Boy is a hoodlum."

"What were you doing in a slum?"

"I lived there for a while. Worked there."

This admission was even more surprising than the other. Kay had never associated with anyone from a slum before and wondered if her parents knew his background. Nevertheless, she was glad he had not loved the slum girl.

"What was so great about England if you lived in a slum and had to steal food sometimes?" she asked.

He finished the apple, tossed the core almost violently into the creek. "You don't understand, Kay. You don't know who I am, or why I'm here. You don't know anything at all about me, actually, and would likely hate me if you did."

"No, I wouldn't, Chris. I could never hate you, no matter what. Tell me, please?"

She leaned toward him, her eyes pleading, and he was erect again. The spontaneous arousals were frequent and obsessive when he was with her, confusing his logic.

"It doesn't matter, Kay. When I go back you'll forget me soon enough. You'll be a debutante one day and marry some rich, fancy fellow. You're pretty, you know. And your folks have money."

"Money isn't everything, Chris."

"Only if you don't have any, like me. Hell, I can't even afford a ticket to England."

"Maybe you don't want to go back as much as you

think," Kay suggested. "If so, you'd ask the Courtlands for the fare. Pride and prejudice wouldn't stop you."

He grinned wryly. "Very cute, Miss Cranshaw."

"Oh, I've read Jane Austen, Mr. Bentley! She's a 'must' at Abbey Hall, along with just about every other English lit classic and author, except Joyce and D.H. Lawrence."

"The ones the goody-gals want most to read, eh?"

"I didn't say that."

"We still have lots of cycling to do," he said, standing. "Better mount our wheels!"

By the time they returned the bikes to the rental agency and rode the bus to The Towers, it was evening. Her parents had already gone out, the servants had left, and they were alone in the penthouse.

Christopher was fascinated anew each time he went there. If London had such places, he had never seen one. All he had known were rented rooms in shabby tenements or boardinghouses. He was lucky to have a window or two, even with cracked and grimy panes. Bare floors, lumpy and squeaky beds, walls so thin he could hear his neighbors fighting or frigging. It was a long way from that ratty cubicle in London's Bethnal Green to this crystal tower in Washington's Woodley Park, from Sally Sawyer to Kay Cranshaw, and Christopher was keenly aware of the distance.

"It's like heaven up here," he said, gazing through the expanse of polished glass.

"But scary in a storm, especially at night," Kay told him. "The lightning seems nearer, the thunder louder. Sometimes I get frightened and run to my parents, or hide under the covers."

"That's childish."

"I know, and I'm outgrowing it."

"Where are your mum and dad now?"

"Partying, which never seems to end in this city. Cocktail parties, dinners, embassy receptions. Daddy says alcohol lubricates the axis on which Washington revolves, including society, government, and diplomacy."

"No doubt," he agreed, as Kay read him her mother's note attached by a magnet to the refrigerator door.

"Darling, we hoped you'd return before we had to leave. Names and numbers where we can be reached on pad by your phone. Plenty of food in fridge, help yourselves. Snacks, too. Tell Chris to call home. Uncle Jeff is back from New York and anxious to see him. Be a good girl, and we'll see you later. Love, Mom and Dad."

"Are you going to call Uncle Jeff?" Kay prodded.

"No."

"That's mean, Chris."

He merely shrugged.

"Cold chicken?" she offered, opening the refrigerator. "Ham, cheese, caviar? Milk, cake, ice cream?"

"I'm still stuffed from the picnic," he said. "Just a coke for now, please."

"Okay." She removed two bottles, handed him one, and indicated the opener. "TV or records?"

"Records."

Kay selected her favorites, including the latest Elvis Presley, from the cabinet in the den and put them on the stereo. Then they sat cross-legged on the huge floor cushions, sipping the sodas.

"This beats the park," Christopher said.

But Kay was uneasy, flipping the pages of a new movie magazine, unable to get comfortable or maintain the yoga lotus position on the slippery vinyl, finally sliding off onto the carpet. She had never been so completely alone with a boy before. School affairs were always chaperoned, and though some of the older girls dated and discussed sex at slumber parties, none ever admitted to doing anything really wrong. Immorality was simply not condoned at Abbey Hall. The faculty made this eminently clear at every orientation session, and any breach of the Rules of Propriety could result in expulsion. A girl could go so far with a boy and no farther, and Kay had hardly gone any distance at all. A few inept kisses, wet and sticky, not particularly enjoyable. She kept her mouth tightly closed, because some of her friends said you could get pregnant just by French kissing and swore they knew of such cases.

"Maybe we should to go a movie?" she suggested. "*Dracula* is showing somewhere, I think. Do you want to see it again?"

"I've seen it several times. I don't like horror films that much. Besides, vampires give me ideas." He bared his teeth in a Bela Lugosi grin. "I might bite your neck, and you'd probably scream bloody murder."

"Well, I don't like hickeys."

"Oh, I wouldn't mark you, baby. Just nibble a bit. Did you know horses show affection by biting each other's necks? I watched a stallion and mare in a pasture once. I bet you've never seen any animals mate, not even dogs? Country kids learn a lot more about nature than town kids. You don't know much about anything, do you?"

"Not much," Kay admitted.

"Are you afraid of boys?"

"No."

"Then why are you fidgeting now?"

"I'm not fidgeting."

"You are, Kay."

"Well, so are you! And looking at me like you did in the park. You didn't think I noticed?"

"You don't have much on," he explained, "and nothing under that halter. You didn't *expect* me to notice?"

"I don't want to talk about it," she said piously.

"Talk about what—sex?"

"Is that what's on your mind now?"

"Isn't it on yours?"

"No!" she hotly denied.

He smiled. "It is, and you're scared to death."

"Well, I'm not Sally Sawyer."

"I know that, Kay. When do you leave for school?"

"First week in September."

"That's not far away. Are you glad?"

"Is anybody ever *glad* to go back to school?"

Christopher stroked his coke bottle, his fingers tracing the curves almost sensuously. "I wasn't going to tell you this, Kay, because I thought you were bright enough to guess. I'm not an exchange student, not just a visitor to this country. I'm half-American. Your Uncle Jeff, as you call him, had an affair with my mother during World War II. Courtland is my father."

Kay was surprised and yet she wasn't. She was aware of the resemblance between them, which she had dismissed as coincidence. Many people not even remotely kin resembled one another, and Hollywood stars had such stand-ins. But the revelation unnerved her, for she had never known anyone to admit to illegitimacy before, and she didn't know what to say. He looked so tragic, so bitter and cynical, as if he were a disfigured outcast. Suddenly the rock-and-roll music sounded harsh and tinny. She reached over to turn it off and spilled her coke, staining her shorts and frowning, abashed.

"Don't crack up, Kay. It's my problem, not yours."

"That's why you hate Uncle Jeff, isn't it? And Aunt Carol, too. But it's not her fault, Chris."

"Nobody seems to think it was anybody's fault," he said, brooding. "They just say such things happen in war. And nobody really gives a damn about the poor kids."

"That's not true, Chris!" She had to believe it wasn't true. "The Courtlands care about you."

"Kay, I'm seventeen! Where was their care all those other years? I wish Courtland had died in the war. Then I'd never have known who was my father, or be faced with this damnable dilemma now."

"Oh, Chris." She wanted to comfort him somehow, take him in her arms and assure him that it didn't matter to her. "I care, Chris. Believe me, I do."

"You feel sorry for me, Kay. Poor bastard, is that what you think? You know something? A few times I've thought about making some nice American girl pregnant, and then running off and leaving her to do the best she could."

Tears glistened in her eyes, spilling on her cheeks. "Did you consider doing that to me?"

"Maybe, when I first met you. Before I got to know and like you. Then I knew I—I couldn't be that kind of dog, just because my father was."

"Is that why you've never even kissed me?"

"You're such an infant, Kay. I'd better go now."

"Will I see you tomorrow?"

He hesitated, shaking his head. "I don't think so. It's not such a good idea, you and me. Anyway, I won't be here much longer. I've decided to ask Courtland for the money."

Kay raised a hand, as if to stay him. "I—I don't want you to go back to England, Chris."

He touched her hair, his hand lingering gently. "You're sweet, Kay. A sweet girl."

"I love you," she cried unexpectedly. "Oh, Chris, I do! And I think you love me, too."

Chris turned to her, taking her in his arms. They lay on the carpet together, and Kay let him hold and kiss and fondle her; he was not clumsy and embarrassed like the other boys she knew. He untied her halter, baring her breasts and running his tongue over the taut nipples, tasting her. "God," he shuddered. "Oh, God."

"What's the matter?" she quavered.

"This," he answered, pressing his genitals against her. "I'm half-wild, Kay."

"Me, too. Kiss me some more."

His voice was husky, his breathing labored. "You don't know how to kiss."

"Teach me."

"Open your mouth. Suck tongues."

At first Kay thought she would strangle, or that their teeth would interfere, but then she realized how easy it was, and how pleasant and exciting. His right leg lay across her thigh, and even through his clothing she could feel his throbbing erection, hot and hard and seemingly huge against her bare flesh. His hand stroked her crotch, and she moaned and clung to him, on the verge of orgasm.

"Are we doing it?" she asked breathlessly.

"No, you goose." Suddenly the spell was broken. He stopped and scrambled to his feet, checking his fly to make sure it was still closed. "Don't you know anything? Better read some books."

"But the way we kissed—?" She was remembering the girlish secrets and confidences, the fantasies and rumors and half-truths.

"That's all it was, kissing. And playing. But nothing happened, Kay. You'd know if it had."

Her eyes gazed up at him, languid with love and admiration. "You're something, Chris. Really something."

"Yeah, I'm something, all right. The question is, what? Get yourself together, Kay, before your folks come home."

"Where're you going?"

"To the lavatory—and then to catch a bus to Alexandria!"

"Don't leave, please?" she begged, extending her hand.

"You want to get raped?"

"You wouldn't do that," she said, fixing her halter. "But I wouldn't care if you did. I love you."

"Stop saying that."

"Chris—"

"Kay, for God's sake, let me go!"

20

The Courtlands were in the study watching a television newscast when Christopher arrived home. Something about Khrushchev and Cuba. Americans were always suspicious of Russia, and currently Castro was the bogeyman of the Caribbean. On the bus to Alexandria he had heard people talking seriously and excitedly about building air raid shelters and storing up food and water. Suddenly the spotlight had been shifted from the Black Freedom Crusaders, and folks were more afraid of Communists taking over the country than the Negroes. Another reason why he wanted to get away from this crazy, panicky place!

"Good evening," he greeted them with his customary reserve, adding before they could reply, "may I speak with you, sir, when that's over? I'll be in my room."

He was writing a letter when Jeff knocked and entered. Several filled pages and an addressed envelope lay on the desk, in the circle of light from the green-shaded lamp.

"You wanted to see me, Chris?"

"Yes, sir. I'd like to borrow some money, please. To go home. I'll repay it somehow, I promise." He was very businesslike. "I'd be willing to sign a paper."

"You're writing to Aunt Agatha?"

"Yes, telling her to expect me. I'll send it airpost."

Jeff hesitated slightly, then plunged ahead swiftly, realizing no valid purpose would be served by further delay of the vital information. Nor was there any kind way to relay it, best to be direct. "It won't do any good, Christopher. I should have told you before: Agatha Linton is dead."

Christopher's face blanched. He dropped the pen, spattering ink on the stationery, and furiously accused, "You're lying again!" But this time Jeff knew he believed and was trying to suppress his tears. "When?" he asked slowly, swallowing the painful lump in his throat.

"Two weeks ago."

"And you kept it from me all this time? You let me write letters and wonder why they weren't answered. You and Mrs. Courtland and the Cranshaws—liars, all of you! Bloody liars! Monsters!"

Jeff winced at the piercing barbs. "There was nothing you could do, Chris."

"I could have gone to the funeral, done that much at least for the kind old lady who helped to raise me." He visualized the small procession headed by Vicar Tisdale, the plain wood coffin, the villagers carrying flowers from their gardens. Two raw graves in the churchyard cemetery now without tombstones! The cottage empty, still guarded by the faithful collie. What would happen to Bounder now?

"That wouldn't have helped either of you," Jeff said, trying to console him with judicious counsel. "And if you go back now, you'll be going against both your mother's and your aunt's wishes. Don't you understand, Christopher? There's nothing for you in England anymore, not even the cottage in Tilbury. Miss Linton's will directs that it be sold and the proceeds put in trust for you, although a quick sale or good sum is unlikely. This has to be your home now, son.''

But prudence, expedience, rationalization, momentarily escaped the confused, bewildered boy. He felt dizzy and a little sick, as if he had drunk too much cheap wine. His head was like a string-held balloon floating in space, and it would have been a relief to cut the cord and let it drift away. But it was attached to leaden feet. He discovered this when he tried to stand and move. Somehow he made it to the bed and sat on the edge of the mattress, staring at the deep blue carpet as if it were a fathomless sea. Minutes of hopelessness, futility, frustration, passed before he finally spoke, dragging the words out reluctantly.

''I—I guess that's what they would want, all right. Mother and Aunt Agatha . . . for me to stay in America . . .''

Touching his shoulder tentatively, Jeff felt Christopher's flesh recoil and removed his hand. ''Christopher, look at me. You know I'm your father, don't you?''

He nodded grimly without raising his eyes. The thing he had feared most had happened: he was trapped with no immediate or even ultimate prospect of escape. But he didn't have to become a docile monkey responding obediently to his captor's every command or whim; nor was he obliged to lick the hand that fed him.

''How long have you known?''

''A long time,'' he replied, still downcast. ''The boys in the village used to sing a dirty ditty left over from the war. 'Oh, woe is me! Oh, woe is me! He left me with empty arms and a full belly!' I was eight before I learnt they were singing about my mother. They didn't mean to be cruel.

They were just mouthing their elders, but it hurt worse than if they'd hit, kicked, and spat on me. Until then, you see, I thought the Commando was my dad and that he'd died in the war at Dieppe, a great hero. Then one day I overheard Mum and Aunt Agatha talking—and later on Mum told me the truth herself. She didn't intend to, I know, it was just one of her bad times when she was muddled in the head. She forgot what she said, but I didn't.'' After a long pause, he finally looked at his father. ''She killed herself, Courtland. Did you know that?''

Jeff was visibly shaken by the news, and Christopher was glad. He wanted him to suffer in the knowledge, to suffer and repent living with it. Jeff's face was ashen, his voice grave as he answered, ''No, I didn't know that, Christopher. I thought it was an accident.''

''Well, it wasn't! She didn't break her neck in a fall. She hung herself in the garret. Suicide, sir, and you *drove* her to it!'' There was no mistaking the hatred, the bitterness in his accusation.

''You despise me, don't you?''

''What do you think?''

''I think it's probably natural and normal under the circumstances,'' Jeff allowed. ''But I also think it's a little unfair to me, not knowing my side of the story. I'm very sorry that your mother took her own life, Christopher, but no one can be sure why, unless she left a note of explanation. Nor should we attempt to analyze her motives now.'' He glanced at Anne's photograph. No condemnation in the forlorn eyes, only a kind of poignant resignation that cut across his memory like a whiplash. She had looked that way standing on the crowded dock in Southampton, holding the baby in her arms and waving good-bye to him. ''It wasn't the sort of relationship you seem to think, son. And you must understand one thing clearly: she knew I was married.''

"You knew it too, didn't you?" he snapped.

How to answer that clever charge, how could he defend himself?

"Of course! But I didn't just abandon her and you, Chris. Nor was I ruthless and callous, as you *also* seem to think. I tried to help. Your mother refused.''

"A few crummy gifts," he reflected bitterly. "That's how much you helped, how hard you tried! Remember the electric train? We didn't even have electricity in the cottage! The red wagon? I hauled wood from the forest in it to help keep us warm in winter. The erector set? I built a gibbet with it—and hung you in effigy!''

Jeff tensed, flinching. "My son, my nemesis! But your mother didn't hate me, Chris. She loved me. Didn't she tell you that, along with the rest?''

"She told me," he admitted grudgingly. "And love was the reason for what she did. What's *your* excuse, sir?'' He waited, his cobalt eyes boring into his father's like pneumatic drills. "She was just a strumpet to you, wasn't she?''

"No, Christopher, never that! I swear to you, on my honor. She was a fine person, and I respected and admired her. You must believe me.''

"On your honor?" he scoffed. "Did you love her?''

Jeff, hesitating under the skeptical, demanding glare, knew the truth would estrange them permanently. And what was the truth? If he didn't know then, how could he know now, or ever. "Yes, I loved her," he said evenly.

"And would have married her, I suppose, if you could?''

"Yes." Lie or not, what did it matter now. Justification lay in the hope of solving their problems and bringing them closer together.

Christopher's expression altered somewhat as belief struggled with doubt, and lost. "I don't believe you, sir! But even if I did, it wouldn't make any difference now. I don't want any part of you or your life—and nothing you say or do can change that!"

"But you *are* a part of me and my life, Christopher, whether you like it or not," Jeff reasoned. "You are my flesh and blood—and nothing *you* say or do can change that, either. Listen to me, son . . ."

Bolting from the bed, Christopher stood before him with clenched fists. "No, you listen to me, Courtland! I know why you want me now. Your wife is barren, so you're willing to settle for Anne Bentley's bastard! Yeah, Pops, that's what they called me in Tilbury, though not often to my face. It was something to titillate the ladies at tea, and the men in the pub. Every English hamlet has at least one American bastard, so it wasn't as bad as it might have been in another age, when my mother might have been publicly whipped, stoned, branded, or put in the stocks! And she was always telling me I'd grow up to be somebody someday, big and important. Show the village. And the world, I guess. Poor Mum, and her 'great expectations'! She doesn't even have a grave marker."

"She will, Christopher. Aunt Agatha, too, just as soon as I can arrange it."

"You'd better! A white marble angel. I promised her."

"Whatever you want," Jeff assented, measuring him, searching for some hopeful sign of acquiescence, however slight. "I realize I have a great deal to make up to you, son, and I'll do my best."

"You owe me, all right," he agreed, unrelenting.

"I want to adopt you, Christopher."

"And make me your heir?"

Jeff gazed at him, taken aback, trying to read the inscrutable face. "Why, yes, along with Mrs. Courtland, if that's important to you."

"It's important," Christopher declared. "I guess I've got enough American blood in me to feel that money's important."

"I trust you're also intelligent enough to realize where your future lies," Jeff told him.

"I realize the alternative, sir. And like you said, there's nothing in England for me now."

"You won't be sorry, Chris. I promise you."

"Promise my mother," he muttered, wincing as Jeff tried again to finally embrace him.

The rejection embarrassed Jeff. Apparently the boy wanted no show of paternal affection. What manner of father-son relationship would this be? "I'll talk to Mr. Cranshaw in the morning, Christopher, and get the legal ball rolling. Then we'll discuss your education. I think perhaps, since you're only seventeen, a year at my old prep school might be advisable before college."

His old prep school. His bloody alma mater for his bloody bastard. No, thanks! Eton and Oxford had been his mother's ambition for him.

"I'd rather go to school in England, sir."

"That's not necessary, Chris. We have excellent schools in America. And we've been separated so long—well, I want you here, in Virginia. You can come home on holidays, and I can visit you during semesters. We'll do some fishing before the season closes, and some hunting in fall. Do you like those sports, son?"

Son, son! How about pal, buddy, chum? If he doesn't stop, I'll puke!

"Yes, sir."

"Ah, that's great! I'll buy you some fine tackle and guns. We'll have fun together, Chris. You'll see." A warm clap on the back. "I'm very happy about this, more pleased than I can tell you. And I'm sure Mrs. Courtland will be, too. I'm anxious to give her the good news. Try to get some sleep now. Good night, son."

"Good night, sir." Cool, formal, as if he were bidding the amenity to a stranger.

On his way out of the room Jeff turned the Commando's photograph face-down on the dresser. "I think we can dispense with this now, don't you?"

Christopher only smiled, later resurrecting the fallen hero and saluting him. *You get under the old boy's skin, Commando! So if you don't mind, I'll keep you around a bit longer. Should be a jolly good show, what?*

He thought he knew his father well enough, that he had met him many times in fiction and films. One of those wealthy cads who spent their years like money, with little concern for the consequences, until one day they realized they were no longer young and the bank of life was nearly exhausted. Then, suddenly, their earthly possessions, accomplishments, and feminine conquests didn't mean much anymore, and all they wanted was a legitimate son and heir to perpetuate their bloody name and dynasty. The climax came when Only Son rejected Pater and walked out—perhaps to vindictively steal away his beautiful young mistress—and Pater either drowned himself in alcohol, or dropped dead of a coronary.

Now the character, the image, had materialized for him in Jeffrey Courtland.

Over breakfast the next morning Mrs. Courtland told him how happy she was about everything, and what a nice family they would be; and though her voice sounded sincere enough to Christopher's ears, she didn't appear to be smiling much. And Courtland, whose meal consisted of several cups of black coffee, rushed off to consult with his attorney. Soon the mistress of the manor was telephoning her mother, and Christopher seized the opportunity to get away by himself.

Mrs. Wilton called the waterfront a commercial canker on the fine old face of Alexandria, and Christopher agreed with her. The shipping industry had long ago moved to Hampton Roads, leaving a few polluting chemical and fertilizer plants behind. Fishing vessels, stinking garbage scows, and private pleasure craft shared the berths now. Debris littered the narrow alleys behind the mossy old restaurants, taverns, hotels, rooming houses, and the area was as dirty and odorous as a refuse dump.

He wandered downriver several miles, past some Negro youngsters fishing with cane poles, and settled himself in the shade of a weeping willow. A ferryboat whistled on its way to Norfolk, and his eyes trailed it wistfully. He knew from study of the globe and maps that the Potomac flowed into the Chesapeake Bay, then the Atlantic Ocean, and that ships sailed from Virginia to all ports of the world. Once he had considered trying to stowaway on one bound for Britain, now he knew he wouldn't be sailing anywhere for a while.

Christopher Courtland, Son and Heir! He supposed he should feel some satisfaction, but all he felt was wonder at his consent. For in all honesty the status of heir appealed to him far more than that of son, and he had not realized there was that much greed in him. Just how rich was Courtland? And how long would he have to wait for his legacy? The way he was hitting the booze, probably— hopefully—not long. Somehow he would stomach the interim . . .

A sleek cabin cruiser was motoring down the river with a small party aboard. He watched it longingly. A boat like that would be nice. A sports car, too. British, of course. A gold Jaguar, or a silver Aston Martin. Girls would cater to him then, and he wouldn't have to go around horny all the time, and afraid to take advantage as he was with Kay last night. Christ, what a little ninny! Where had she got such stupid ideas about sex? From other dumb virgins, no doubt, who had never even seen a hard male organ, much less felt one inside them. Probably her Abbey Hall sorority sisters, who didn't know the difference between their mouths and vaginas if they thought tongue kissing was "doing it" —and a penis was just for urination. What kind of guys did they date, anyway? Prep school creeps who only grinned and held their hands while dancing! Kay went wild when he touched her breasts and body, and he had damned near exploded himself. Two shakes was all it had taken in the bathroom, and she probably thought he just had to pee. Damn, he was rising again just thinking about it!

A plunge in the Potomac might cool him off, but Toby had warned him about the currents. No use taking any needless risks now, Son and Heir, he chided himself.

The black boys upstream were having some luck: a couple of fish and a turtle. Maybe he could borrow a pole and some bait from them. No, they didn't have any spares and undoubtedly needed the catch for food. The rainbow trout he'd caught in the Cotswold brooks had always ended up on the table—and sometimes made the difference between a full belly and an empty one.

Once, when he was fourteen and they couldn't afford a goose for Christmas dinner, Christopher had simply stolen one, telling his mother that a neighbor had given it to him for watching his gaggle in the meadow. Later, he had confessed his guilt and was sentenced by Aunt Agatha to minding that farmer's geese for three months. Fortunately, he was not caught lifting food in London. Ah, but the lean years were over! He was in the midst of plenty now, a cornucopia of U.S. dollars. American green. Son and Heir.

An excursion liner loaded with tourists bound for Mount Vernon passed. Perhaps tomorrow he'd visit the plantation home of George Washington. They had something in common, he and Georgie. He, Christopher, also lived in a mansion on the Potomac, a part of his bounty and future inheritance. According to Mrs. Wilton, the grounds had been landscaped by slaves and had once stretched in terraces to the river and private pier of the Englishman who had built the place. Unlike her mother, however, Mrs. Courtland refused to open her historic home to the public, even during the annual garden pilgrimages, saying that she valued their privacy too much. A logical reason, Christopher thought, remembering some of his own unpleasant experiences with curious and careless tourists. Yet he would not attribute such logic to his future stepmother, perversely preferring to consider her selfish and possessive—afraid that someone might soil or damage one of her precious antiques, steal a souvenir, trample a flower. Things would change when *he* owned it.

Carol was in the garden when he returned at noon, and Christopher regarded her resentfully, as if she were a stranger trespassing on private property. "Your father's already back from Washington," she said. "Due process of law has begun. He wants to drive out to the school tomorrow. You'll like it, I'm sure."

"I'm not so sure," he argued. "It's a bloody military academy, and I don't want to be a bloody American soldier!"

"Few Hitchfield graduates enter military careers, Christopher. But the training and discipline are invaluable. We have a draft in this country, you know."

"Yeah, and I'll be caught in it!"

"Not necessarily. The draft may be abolished before you get out of college. If we don't have war with Russia before then. Last year it seemed we'd have to fight over Berlin, and now something is happening in Cuba. My mother is making a bomb shelter in her basement, and perhaps we should do likewise. At any rate, you'd be safer at Hitchfield Academy than here. It's in Charlottesville, in the foothills of the Blue Ridge Mountains. It's also considered an excellent preparatory school for young men privileged enough to attend it."

"I thought Groton was the Eton of America?"

"Hitchfield is just as prestigious, in the Southern tradition of military schools for boys."

"It must be expensive?"

"Comparatively."

"And you have no objections?"

His challenging tone offended her. Was he deliberately taunting, baiting her? "Of course not, Christopher. Why should I object?"

"I'm taking money from you, aren't I?"

"Oh, don't worry about *that*, Chris! There's enough to go around."

He gazed at her suspiciously, sullen and cynical. "You want me to go away to school, don't you? Out of sight, out of mind, you think? You hate me because I'm not your child, and because your husband was in love with my mother."

Carol saw his sardonic lips moving but couldn't quite assimilate the words. "What did you say?"

"You heard me! My father was in love with my mother and would have married her if it weren't for you."

Her face drained of color, and her heart seemed to falter

before rushing into spasmodic thudding. "Did Mr. Courtland tell you that, Christopher?"

"Yes," he said, feeling triumphant until he saw her terrible defeat. She was deathly pale, and her mouth had a bluish tint under the coral paint. She looked quite ill, as if she might faint or something, and he regretted his wrath and cruelty. Kay was right. This lady had not harmed him or his mother, why should he hurt her? Kay would be angry with him, disappointed, and disgusted.

"I say, Mam, are you all right?"

Her head nodded as if worked by a string. She was obviously stunned speechless.

"I'm sorry, Mam," he apologized. "I guess he lied to you about *that* too, didn't he?"

Carol stood motionless, her eyes remote, her hands unconsciously destroying a rose, its crimson petals falling at her feet, seeming to bleed in the dust.

"I'm sorry," Christopher repeated sincerely, wishing he had never spoken of the matter. "Truly I am, Mam. Can I do anything for you?"

She began to shake now, as if the earth were quaking beneath her, and Christopher was genuinely alarmed. He wanted to support her with a steadying arm around her waist, but feared an adverse reaction to his touch, and merely offered his help again.

"No, thank you," she murmured tremulously at long last, her bowed head preventing a clear view of her moist eyes. "You've done quite enough already, young man. Leave me alone, please. Go find your father . . ."

21

Joan Cranshaw had spent the day preparing for her daughter's return to Abbey Hall. She had received no assistance whatever from the sullen girl, who moped and fretted about the house, insisting that she was not going back to that "moldy convent." Joan ignored Kay's tantrums, diligently packing her clothes, pretending more confidence than she felt. What, after all, could they do if Kay flatly refused to go when the time came? Take her under restraint? Threaten her and risk her deliberate failure and expulsion or, worse, her running away?

Kay seemed to have undergone a sudden transformation this summer, from an obedient, amenable, almost model, child to an obstinate, restless, rebellious teenager. There was a curious youth rebellion rising in the country, the world, along with a dangerous drug cult, and it appeared to be gaining momentum on the college campuses. The old morals and ethical codes were being ridiculed and flaunted, colonies of twentieth-century rebels were congregating in communes in New York and California, parents were losing control, and society was in a quandary to cope. Hopefully, it was just another of the temporary manias, like the Gay Nineties or the Roaring Twenties, which afflicted civilization periodically. Every generation seemed to go through a transitional phase and craze, and parents could only hope and pray that their children would either be immune or escape unafflicted.

Still Joan could not suppress her worry and anxiety and expressed it to her husband that evening while preparing for bed. "Kay doesn't want to go back to school—not to Abbey Hall, anyway. She told me in no uncertain terms."

Ken was putting on his pajamas. "That's ridiculous. She still has a year to graduation. What did you tell her?"

"Nothing. Just pretended it was a mood that would pass. The trouble is Christopher, of course. I'm sure she thinks she's in love with him."

"At sixteen?"

"It's possible, Ken."

"Nonsense! Infatuation, maybe, but not love. She'll get over it."

Joan frowned skeptically. "I don't know, Ken. Perhaps we shouldn't ignore this thing, whatever it is, between her and Christopher. According to child psychologists, nothing humiliates and annihilates an adolescent more than being treated like one: dismissing their emotional and sexual problems as immature, imaginary, puppy love, et cetera. Kay used to confide in me, but she's hardly communicative now. She avoids me, in fact. She's reticent and distant, even secretive, brooding in her room, or wandering about listlessly. Maybe she thinks I failed her when she needed me most. This is some sort of crisis in her life, Ken. She's desperately unhappy. And vulnerable. That boy could hurt her deeply, badly. He's like a young bull in a rage, determined to gore someone.''

Ken began some routine exercises. "Oh, he's just flexing his muscles, which is natural enough. And his anger is aimed at his father, mostly. Anyway, he won't be able to do any real damage here. Jeff is sending him to Hitchfield Academy, and that's about as strict discipline as a boy can get.'' He lowered himself to the floor for some pushups, which grew harder to do every year. "Kay is going to Abbey Hall, and that's final. They'll forget each other in a few weeks. Placate her somehow, buy her something she wants.''

"She already has everything," Joan said, "except perhaps what she wants most.''

Ken rose, winded and flushed. "Well, she's not going to have Christopher or any other boy at her age! Talk to her, Joan. You're her mother. Make her realize, understand, and accept what's best for her.''

"And if she won't listen?''

"She'll listen. My God, she's not all that incorrigible, is she? I think you're making too much of this, honey. There's nothing unusual or terrible about Kay's attraction to Christopher. She hasn't known many, if any, boys like him. He's special to her, the kind of guy naive young girls dream about. But that doesn't necessarily mean she's in love with him, or that her fantasies will last forever. Forget it for now, darling, and come to bed.''

She stood at a window, gazing at the night sky. "There's lightning in the west, and heavy clouds. A storm is moving in. Kay will be afraid. Shouldn't I go to her?''

"No, let her grow up, Joan.''

"Maybe she has, Ken, and we just refuse to recognize it. Parents often do, you know. And Christopher is older and wiser than his years. I bet he's had sex already.''

"Most boys his age have," Ken said. "As long as he doesn't have it with Kay . . ."

"How can we be sure?"

"By the way you raised her, Mommy. Your little girl is still a virgin, and she'll get over her childish crush on Chris. Didn't you have several before me?"

"Yes, but kids weren't so intense, then."

"The hell they weren't! I was on fire half the time, and you had hot pants, too. Like a good Boy Scout I was always prepared with at least three condoms, but you had a hang-up about your virginity and wanted to save it for marriage. You didn't think I'd 'admire' or 'respect' you if you surrendered prematurely. You did a lot of moralizing— but there wasn't much difference, really. We were all over each other, everywhere but inside you. The upholstery of that old Chevy convertible was saturated with my spilled seed, and some of your juice, too."

"Oh, Ken, do you think Kay and Chris are behaving that way?"

"Oh, honey, I don't know! Probably. Kay has quite a provocative figure already. Chris would be less than human if he didn't try to play with her a little, but I think he knows better than to do more. Jeff and I would both clobber him."

"How would we know, unless she becomes pregnant? I can't take her to the doctor for a pelvic examination, can I? She'd know I suspect something and despise me. Nor can I have her fitted for a diaphragm, or put her on that new birth control pill that Shirley Martin raves about. What if they are doing it, and he's not using any protection?"

"He'd damn well better!"

"Then you think they *are* doing it?"

"Doing it, doing it," he mimicked. "Why can't you just say the word? No, I don't believe he's actually screwing her, and I can't castrate him on mere suspicion. Let's hit the sack, Joan. I'm getting horny myself.''

Lightning flashed across the glass wall, thunder crashed and rumbled over the building. ''God's angry at the world,'' Joan said. ''That's what my mother thought about storms.''

''My father had a different idea. He imagined the devil was making love, and if he was home he tried to usher Mom into their bedroom and lock the door. But she always had a ready excuse. She had to cook, wash the dishes, iron, sew—or the kids were around.''

''And I'm using Kay's fear of storms, is that it? Don't you remember her bursting in on us a few times, screaming and crying in terror?''

''Well, she's a big girl now and would knock first. Besides, I already locked the door.'' He waited. ''Joan, what's the matter? Wrong time of the month?''

''No, I was just wondering . . .''

''About what?''

''If I'm too old to have another baby.''

''At thirty-six? My mother had a perfectly healthy child at forty-four. Those days women didn't know about all the great 'hazards and risks' of late pregnancies. They bore children naturally until menopause, and there didn't seem to be any more defective births than there are now. Why, do you want to get pregnant?''

''I've thought about it lately.''

''Why lately?''

''Oh, Ken! I'm afraid of losing Kay!''

''And you want a replacement? You can't replace one child with another, Joan. Jeff would have wanted Christopher even if he'd had a dozen kids with Carol. And you couldn't replace Kay with quintuplets.''

''No,'' she agreed, ''of course not. And if we're not

going to make a baby tonight, I'd better put in the damned diaphragm. Wouldn't want to be a pregnant grandmother."

Ken smiled. "Don't worry about that, darling. Kay's going to finish college and have a debut before she marries. And there'll be many boyfriends before she meets Mr. Right."

"Suppose, in her mind, she already has met him?"

"Then they'll wait for each other."

"I hope so," she said, moving toward the bathroom.

A month later, when Kay was safely enrolled at Abbey Hall and Christopher at Hitchfield Academy, Joan confided another, almost equally disturbing, concern to her husband. In town for the day, she dropped by his office, poured herself a glass of sherry, and sat on the edge of his desk. "Busy?"

He glanced up from the brief he was studying. "Not very, and I know you didn't come here just for the Harvey's Bristol Cream. I thought you and Carol were shopping today?"

"We did this morning."

"And?"

"Her mind was elsewhere."

"Well, there's always tomorrow."

Joan set the wine down, touched the onyx paperweight. "I think there's a new affair in our group."

"Oh? Who is it this time?"

"You'd be surprised."

"I doubt it, and don't be so mysterious."

Joan took a deep breath. "Carol and Major Lawrence. Surprised?"

"Somewhat, if it's true. Did she tell you?"

"No, Carol doesn't talk much these days. I may as well

have shopped and lunched alone. She's quiet, preoccupied. Just not herself anymore."

"She hasn't been since that letter from Britain."

Joan sighed. "But there's something tragic about her now, Ken. Something sad and hopeless. Pathetic, really. I'm afraid she's seriously involved with Mark."

Ken shook his head. "I can't believe it."

"Well, it may not be a fait accompli yet. It's just my feminine intuition at this point, which isn't always as accurate as radar, and I hope is one hundred percent wrong this time."

"The Perfect Courtlands," Ken mused wryly. "Remember when everyone called them that?"

"Nobody's perfect," Joan said. "What can we do, Ken?"

"Nothing, Joan. It's none of our business."

"How can you say that? They're our best friends! And this whole mess, if such it is, started with us."

Ken tapped a pencil on his desk. "You didn't think it could do any harm, remember? You thought it would be good for Carol to test her love for Jeffrey with another man. Now you're afraid the experiment might have backfired and blown up their marriage!"

"Aren't *you* worried?"

He pondered a moment before replying. "Well, I don't exactly relish the prospect of a Courtland *ménage à trois*, my dear. But Carol and Mark are not kids, like Kay and Chris. We can't just send them in opposite directions and hope for the best."

"There must be something—"

"There isn't!" he interrupted. "Just stay the hell out of it, that's all."

"And let them break up?"

"Now you're speculating."

"It's just that I love Carol so much, like a sister, and want her to be happy, Ken."

"Then don't meddle, Mrs. Fixit." He peered at her. "Did you hear me?"

She nodded pensively. "But I still think—"

Ken stood up, leering at her across the desk. "You want to get laid, lady? That seems to be the only way to shut you up lately!"

"In the middle of a conversation? You have the most impetuous penis! Just thinking of other people's sex—"

He laughed. "Just thinking of sex, period. How about a quickie, like the old days in Baltimore?"

Joan smiled, remembering his one-room walk-up office over a pharmacy, when he was a struggling young lawyer and she was his wife and secretary. There were few clients then, and lots of leisure, and they would hang out the OUT TO LUNCH or IN COURT sign on the locked door almost every day. It was exciting then—and now. Flattering, too, his spontaneous lust for her after all these years. She felt her juices flowing. God, how she loved him! She would die, simply wither and die, if ever he stopped loving her. Had there ever been anyone else since their marriage? Would he admit it if she asked? What would she do in Carol's position?

"We'll have to be careful," she said softly. "I didn't come prepared."

"I can get a rubber in the men's room down the hall."

"That convenient, huh?"

"For sudden emergencies," he grinned. "In case somebody's spouse or lover visits the office unexpectedly."

"Ken—"

"Yes?"

She hesitated, struggling with an imp of curious jealousy. "That's a new sofa, isn't it?"

"Fairly, and still a virgin. Time to initiate it. You'll find it more comfortable, I think, than that old Baltimore couch with the broken spring."

"I loved that couch," she said wistfully. "It was beautiful, cracked leather, lumps, stains, and all. Some of the loveliest moments of my life were spent there, and I sort of wish we had kept it."

"For the Smithsonian? Don't go away, I'll be right back."

"Better tell your secretary to hold your calls. Can't just take the receiver off the hook, the way we did."

"Anything else?"

"No, darling, just hurry back."

During his absence Joan surveyed his office. There was more than just another expensive sofa. Different end tables, too, and a marvelous pair of bronze lamps. Why hadn't she noticed the new furniture before? Oh, she was being silly! Just because he hadn't consulted her prior to doing a little redecorating didn't mean anything; it was just a previous habit with him, as with her and their residence. He still had the same faithful secretary, who was no younger or better looking than Jeff's loyal Doris Ledlow. If ever Ken replaced Lois Aiken with a young, pretty girl—*that* would be the time to wonder and worry. Skeets Martin and Frank Benedict averaged at least one new secretary every year!

22

"Can you spend the night?" he asked.

"If you like."

"That means he's away?"

"Visiting Christopher at school," she said. "He's trying hard to be a father to the boy."

"Is the boy trying hard to be a son?"

"I'm not sure. It's difficult to tell about Christopher, and I haven't seen him lately. But Jeff is a different man. His life, his whole personality has changed, taken on new facets and dimensions. All these years I thought I knew him so well, but now . . . it's like living with a stranger."

Mark hesitated, dreading to ask the question that had plagued him since her first visit to his apartment. "Does he still make love to you?"

"He hasn't recently."

"How recently?"

"A month or so."

"Then he must know, or at least suspect?"

"No, he'd do something if he did."

"Is he violent?"

"He could be, I think."

"Well, he has sufficient provocation, and I don't like cuckolding him, Carol." He paused, looking at her. "When are you going to tell him about us?"

"Don't rush me, Mark."

That remark sounded like a delaying tactic, which he feared and had to bridge. "Carol, I'm on temporary duty at the Pentagon. I could receive orders any day. I think we're getting involved in that mess that France pulled out of in Vietnam. Kennedy is sending military advisors to South Nam, and I could be one of them."

"But it's just a police action, isn't it?"

"So they say, but these things have a way of escalating," he told her. "We can't procrastinate too long on our personal issue, Carol. It has to be resolved, settled."

After a long, solemn moment, she said, "All right, Mark. I'll tell him Sunday, when he returns from Charlottesville. Or should I call his hotel now?"

"Sunday will do," he said, touching her breast. "Remember the first time you came here?"

She nodded, shame welling up inside her. "I was hysterical."

"I felt terrible afterwards, as if I'd taken advantage of a sick and helpless woman. You've never told me the reason for that, Carol."

"Reason for what?"

"Coming to me that way and abandoning yourself."

"Weren't you pleased? You seemed so."

"Tell me why, Carol."

"I'd rather not, Mark."

"Are you always going to keep secrets from me?"

"Secrets? We're naked in bed, Mark. You can see and feel everything . . ."

"It's what I can't see and feel that worries me," he said. "Inside your heart and mind. What's there, Carol? What's there for me—for us?"

"Happiness, I hope."

"And love? What about love?"

"It'll come, Mark. I'm certain of that. In fact, when we're together like this, I think it has come."

"And when we're apart—what do you feel, then?"

She smiled, touching his face, pressing her palms tenderly against his cheeks. "It's flattering, actually—your eagerness to marry me. According to the moralists, you're not supposed to be anxious at this stage. What's that old rustic joke—'why buy the cow when you can get the milk free'? And don't frown! It fits your situation perfectly— the farm, you know? Of course, if you want breeding stock, it's customary to establish ownership, isn't it?"

"That's not funny, Carol."

"No," she agreed ruefully. "And my mother, who's a stickler for the conventions, would be astonished at my behavior now. You must meet her, Mark. I'll go to her when I leave Jeff, and I won't take anything but my clothes with me. No alimony, no settlement. I shall come to you rather poor, darling."

He frowned. "I'm not after a dowry, Carol."

"I know, Mark. Kiss me now—quickly."

Before I change my mind, she thought. Before I begin to think and wonder what I'm doing here, in your arms, in your bed, in adultery, and become as hysterical as I was on that first occasion, when I couldn't decide whether to take all of my Seconals at once, jump in the river, or drive to Arlington. Was it only a month ago?

"Don't think," Mark pleaded. "You leave me when you think. Come back and cooperate . . ."

Carol had known for twenty years that a woman must employ self-hypnosis in coitus, must induce or simulate a state of enchantment to achieve ecstasy. This vital emotional factor and total physical involvement were probably instinctive, inherent—an innate precaution against promiscuity of which the female of the species was far more aware than the male. Nature had given the she-animal heat periods during which she would accept her mate, and society had instilled other barriers in her human counterpart. Drummed into well-bred girls from puberty, and even before, "decent" young ladies were expected to protect their virginity with an invisible chastity belt to be removed only by the husband on the wedding night. *No sex without marriage.* The ancient edict was delivered—and often arbitrarily imposed—by generations of distaff ancestors, with no reassuring explanations as to how the resultant fears and inhibitions would be miraculously removed when it was permissible; how the naive virgin would suddenly evolve into a satisfactory mate capable of giving, receiving, sharing complete sexual fulfillment when finally the act was legal.

How different the truth, the facts! In reality and practice, it was a damned lucky lady who reached climax every time—so rare, indeed, that numerous articles and books were now being written and published on the subject of "the human female orgasm." Too long deprived of the vital information and social sanctions, many women simply became clever actresses in bed, inspired by fear of bruising the precious phallic ego and being considered frigid. Carol had had some great moments with Jeff and even a few with Mark. She tried hard to concentrate now, to divest her mind of everything but the physical contact and rhythm of their bodies, ultimately succeeding. His face loomed over hers, his eyes dilated and glowing.

"Now?" he asked, thrusting vigorously. "Now, darling?"

"Now," she murmured, flinging her arms around him, holding the deep kiss until his convulsive release seconds after hers. And God how pleased he was, the almighty male, the triumphant stud gloating over his satisfied mount, as if totally unaware how easily she could have faked her response and orgasm.

"We're terrific together, baby. You know that, don't you? We make it. Jesus, I love you!"

"Because I came, or because you made me?"

"Both, I guess," he smiled, savoring his triumph. "But more than that, Carol. So much more."

"You're sweet, Mark, and I'm glad you love me. I'm glad we're sexually compatible, too. It would be awful if our chemistries clashed in that respect, wouldn't it? Unhappy lovers rarely make happy spouses."

"Then you're happy with me?"

"Yes," she whispered, closing her eyes before he took her lips again, lest a treacherous tear betray her.

She left before daylight and hated sneaking along the corridors of the apartment building, down the rear stairs, and out to her parked car in his space in the lot. But she had this silly hang-up from the days when supposedly "nice" girls did not stay out with boys all night, as if the time element made any difference to the sexual glands. Mark teased her about it when he kissed her good-bye, trying to persuade her to stay for breakfast, offering to cook it himself and serve her in bed.

"There's no curfew on love, darling. A few more hours won't matter. You don't turn into a pumpkin at dawn, do you?"

She laughed nervously, organizing herself. "No, a witch. Honestly, Mark, I'm a fright in the morning. I can't sleep in a net, so my hair's a mess. I can never remove all of my makeup and usually have a black-ringed eye and a red-smeared mouth. Wait. You'll see."

"I'm looking forward to it," he said, holding her close and stroking her back gently.

Carol pressed her face against his bare chest, where his robe had parted. Except for the scars from old shrapnel wounds partially concealed under the mat of thick dark hair, it reminded her of another chest. She had wept at first sight of the scars, because they reminded her of the war, as his uniform and medals recalled the war—and that had been part of her hysteria that first time in Mark's quarters.

It was misting as she drove through the deserted streets of Arlington toward Alexandria. The arc lights were fuzzy yellow haloes. She drove faster than was safe on the slippery pavement, as if fleeing the scene of a crime, glad that the autumn nights were longer and darkness lingered. She slowed down only as she approached her own neighborhood, suddenly reluctant to proceed. Returning home after being with Mark was becoming increasingly difficult for her—one more reason, in addition to those he had given, for ending these liaisons via her divorce and their marriage.

Cobwebs of fog were spun about the old mansion, the chimneys lost in it, the trees sodden and scraggly in seasonal defoliation, giving the place a vacant, haunted appearance. Once the mere sight of this historic house had filled her with joy and warmth and welcome; now it seemed to repel her. More of her Victorian conscience, no doubt, but she couldn't shrug off the eerie, tenacious mood.

It accompanied her into the dark and chilly interior. She

was jittery and exhausted. They had slept little, talking, planning, loving through most of the night, and she felt dull and depressed now, as if she had taken too many tranquilizers. She climbed the stairs, trailing her sable stole on the carpet, removing her black suede pumps before reaching the bedroom. Without cleaning her face or brushing her teeth, she undressed and crawled into bed, too tired to dream.

When she awoke at eleven o'clock, it was raining. Torrents drummed on the slate roof, splashed at the windows. She had slept five hours but did not feel refreshed. Her head throbbed, her eyes burned. She slipped on a negligee, stuck her feet into scuffs, and padded downstairs to brew some coffee.

The house was warm, and she thought her mother had come in and turned up the thermostat, for Ella was off on Sundays. Margaret had probably come in hopes of taking her to church. Dear God, how long had it been? Months since she and Jeff had attended services together, weeks since either of them had gone alone. Pastor and parishioners were probably wondering, perhaps even getting suspicious.

"Mother?" she called. No answer.

She wandered through the rooms, the large beautiful old chambers with their high ceilings, paneled and papered walls, corniced windows, marble fireplaces. She remembered the months of planning with the decorators, the consultations with the Historical and Conservation Society, the searching in antique shops and attending auctions for authentic pieces to supplement the priceless originals and expensive reproductions, and Margaret's insistence that they share it all with others at least once a year during Garden Week. But the owners wanted no curious and insensitive tourist traffic, and so Courtland House was listed in the brochures as: *Private residence. Positively no admittance.*

Except to the ghost of the master's former British mistress, Carol thought mournfully, for Anne Bentley's presence seemed almost tangible this morning, and stubbornly pervasive, following her about. She called again impatiently, almost shouting, "Mother, I'm up! Where are you? *Mother!*"

Her search ended in the study, where a fire burned on the hearth and a figure reclined on the long leather sofa. "Why didn't you answer me?" Carol demanded, snapping on the light. "Oh, my God!" she gasped, staring.

He rose slowly, like a reluctant materialization. "Don't be frightened, Mrs. Courtland. It's not an apparition, only your humble husband."

After minutes of speechless immobility, she murmured tremulously, "How long . . . I mean . . . when did you get back?"

"Last night." His eyes peered at her, and through her. "Chris is in the infirmary with a cold. I got home about ten o'clock. I heard you come in this morning."

"It wasn't quite morning," she said stupidly.

"Almost. I looked at the clock."

"Why didn't you say something?"

"Thought you might need some rest," he replied ironically, and Carol was aware of the sight she must be: tousled hair, smeared lipstick, mascara-smudged eyes.

He was a sight himself. Rumpled trousers, shirt-collar open, tie hanging like a loose noose about his neck. But at least he was sober. Thank heaven, for she could not have faced him otherwise. A head taller than she, he towered over her now, his back to the fire, a giant silhouetted in flame.

"We . . . we have to talk, Jeffrey."

"Yes, I'd say it's about time, Carol."

She hesitated, not wanting to hurt him or betray herself. "If I could think of a kind way to say this I would. But I can't, so I'll just have to be blunt and specific. I want a divorce, Jeff."

"I see," he said calmly, as if he had been expecting the request a long while and hearing it was anticlimactic. "On what grounds?"

Oh, Lord, he was going to be difficult—and she had no choice now! "We both have grounds, Jeff, if we want to use them. But let's not make this any harder or dirtier than necessary. If you agree, I'll use incompatibility."

"And if I don't agree?"

"Then it'll be messy."

"When did you decide this, Carol?"

"Last night."

"With the major's assistance? I figured you were together at his place and tried to find you. Lucky for him, he's not in the book."

"Try to be adult about this, Jeffrey."

Irony etched his face, sharpening his features, deepening the lines of fatigue and despair. "Like you were adult when you learned about Anne Bentley?"

"I think I can understand now how that happened," she said. "If it's any comfort to you."

"You're admitting infidelity and asking me to be comforted? And you think the circumstances are equal? The son-of-a-bitch! I ought to kill him. Would you understand *that*, my dear?"

"Pistols at twenty paces, in the old Courtland tradition? Don't be medieval, Jeff! Your pride and ego are affronted, not your honor. Or your heart. Let me go—quietly, peacefully. You don't need me anymore, if ever you did."

"How do you know what I need, Carol?"

"You needed your son, Jeffrey, and you have him now. And except for me, you'd probably have his mother, too. The woman you really loved and wanted!"

He stared at her as if she were speaking incoherently, a nerve flicking in his tense jaw. "What are you babbling about?"

Carol shook her head, averting her face. She would be civilized, sophisticated, mature about this if it killed her. No scenes, no dramatics, no hysteria. "It's no use, Jeff. I know. Christopher told me."

"Told you what?"

"Oh, stop pretending! You're only making it worse. You were in love with Anne Bentley, weren't you, and would have married her if you could? You told the boy that, didn't you?"

"Good Lord," Jeff sighed.

"Well, didn't you?"

"Yes!" he shouted. "Yes, I told him that! He asked me pointblank. What else could I tell him and not have him hate me for the rest of his life?"

A tremor seized Carol, then a series of them. She clutched the back of a chair for support. "It was better to have him hate *me*, regard *me* as the obstacle in his path to legitimacy?"

"He doesn't hate you, Carol. He doesn't hate anybody, really, although he thinks he hates the whole world. This part of it, anyway. We all disappointed and failed him in some way, including Kay. He's just mixed up, Carol. And so are you. All of us are confused, I'm afraid."

Her control was slipping; she caught at it frantically. Her irrevocable actions, promulgated primarily on the strength of his son's accusations, horrified her. "*Why* didn't you tell me what you had told Christopher?"

"I had a lot on my mind. I just forgot."

"Forgot?" Her fists hammered the chair, lest they hammer him. "How could you *forget* a thing like that?"

"I didn't expect him to tell you," he rationalized. "But you should have known better, Carol. My God, how could you believe it after all these years! And what did you do? Run immediately to Mark Lawrence?"

"Not immediately," she answered miserably, remembering the desperate alternatives she had considered: the long sleep, the plunge into the Potomac. "But it doesn't matter now, Jeff. I shall consult Ken tomorrow."

"I haven't agreed to a divorce, Carol." He started toward her, but she lifted a hand to stay him.

"No, please. It's over, Jeffrey."

It had to be over now. She had gone too far to turn back, and she did not want him feeling sorry for her, pretending to forgive and forget—a pair of emotional cripples comforting each other in their splendid sorrow. Nor could she renege on her promises to Mark.

From somewhere deep inside himself, he summoned the dreaded question: "Are you in love with him?"

"I'm going to marry him."

"That's not what I asked."

"He's in love with me," she hedged. "And, in a way, I think I love him, too."

"In what way?"

"How many ways are there?"

"A good many, my dear, but they don't all add up to love."

"You should know," she said, her fingers working in the upholstery of the Queen Anne chair.

"Yes, I should know. And so should you, or you'll be far more miserable than you imagine you are now. Just thinking you love this man isn't enough, Carol. Not nearly enough. You should be sure. Positive."

"Is anyone ever absolutely sure about love, Jeff? I was absolutely 'positive' that you loved me, and I was wrong."

"You weren't wrong, Carol."

"Then how could this have happened to either of us?" she asked tearfully, shaking her head.

"A while ago you said you knew how," he reminded her.

"Maybe I was mistaken about that, too. Maybe nothing ever really happens by chance or circumstance. Maybe things, with the exception of sickness and death, happen because we, unconsciously or not, want them to happen and make them happen. Maybe we're masters of our own destiny, after all. But that's neither here nor there, is it? The fact is, it *has* happened and how or why isn't important now, only that it can't be undone."

"Don't you even want to try?"

She touched the prized heirloom, stroking the soft velvet fabric like a cherished pet. "Remember that beautiful old vase I broke and tried to glue back together? The cracks were always visible, weren't they? I kept patching it up, but finally it fell apart completely and had to be discarded. Trying to save it was a waste of time, but I had lots of time then. I don't have much now, at least not enough that I can afford to waste any."

He smiled ruefully. "You may find that you have more time than you need, Carol. More than you can use in any one day, much less for the remainder of your life. But you'll have to discover that for yourself, the hard way." He paused, waited, shrugged. "Well, I guess I might as well start packing?"

"No, I will, Jeff. This is Christopher's home now, and it should be his heritage. I'll always have Mother's place, you know, and I'll go there now. Of course, I'll ask Ella to stay on with you."

His despair exploded in sudden, desperate anger. "Don't be so goddamned amenable, Carol! You know you love this house, and it has always meant more to you than to me. I'd as soon have an apartment in Washington, near my office."

Her mournful gaze made Jeff wish he had not spoken, for he was not at all sure he meant what he had said; he only knew that she loved her home dearly, and that it was traditional for the husband to vacate the domicile. But her tragic expression showed what she was thinking: all the wrong things, the sad and wistful and enigmatic things which she believed lay at the core of their marital failure, like debris at the bottom of an outwardly placid pool.

"Keep it for your son, Jeffrey. He's never had a proper home of his own, *he* might appreciate it," she said, turning away and hurrying from the room.

23

Home again in her old room, Carol unpacked her bags and put her clothes away, while her mother stood by, shocked, helpless, incredulous. "Am I to understand you have left Jeffrey? That you intend to divorce him, marry somebody named Mark Lawrence, and move to a farm in the Shenandoah Valley?" Margaret Wilton asked, watching in dismay.

"Major Lawrence will have to retire from the Army first, or resign his commission," Carol answered. "But that's the general idea, Mother."

"How did all this happen so suddenly, Carol? Where did you meet this man, and how did you become so deeply involved with him?"

Carol, now arranging toilet articles on the dressing table, which was still skirted in girlishly ruffled white organdy, resented the personal questions. "Please, Mother, not now. I'm too tired to give you a detailed account."

"Never mind," Margaret said with a catch in her voice. "I think I can guess the details, and they're not very pretty, are they? If you ask me, you were motivated by desperation. In my day we called it rebound. But whatever you choose to call it now, I cannot believe it's love, Carol, or that legalizing it will bring you happiness or whatever else you seek."

Carol sighed. "I suppose you must say these things, Mother. You must be properly outraged and scandalized. It's your maternal duty to chastise and lecture me and it's my daughterly duty to listen. But I'm not a child anymore, Mother, and don't have to agree or obey. Now if you'll excuse me . . ."

She went into the bathroom, poured bubble bath into the tub, and turned on the taps. All she needed was a hot bath and some rest, she told herself. It would all vanish while she slept: the tension and malaise, the anxieties and apprehensions and perplexities. Tomorrow she would be recuperated, refreshed, ready for a full new life.

She undressed and stood before the mirror, examining herself critically, and the reflection was reassuring. Her figure was still physically attractive, almost virginal in appearance, for there had been no pregnancies to stretch the abdominal muscles and tissues, to enlarge the hips and sag the breasts. Mark had not said much at the first sight of her nude—he was never lavish with compliments—but she had known he was pleased and stimulated. And after her initial hysteria had subsided, she had felt young and desirable, loved and wanted and needed. He would be overjoyed when she gave him the news, and they could begin planning immediately. She might even become pregnant when they stopped the precautions, though she felt her mother would scoff at this dream too, even if it made one of her own come true.

Carrying the thought into the tub with her elevated her spirits somewhat. She lay with her head on a rubber cushion, relaxing in the warm fragrant billows. The bubbles enveloped her in iridescence, arching like a miniature, frothy rainbow. Whimsically, she reached out for a handful, but they broke and vanished at her touch—not even one could she capture and hold in her hand.

Ella's call came early Monday morning. "I's sorry, Miss Carol, but I's got to push the panic button already."

"Yes, Ella, what is it?"

"It's Mister Jeff," Ella said. "I come to work this morning like usual and got his breakfast ready and went to fetch him, but he won't budge. He locked in his room."

"He's just drunk, Ella."

"I knows that, honey. What I don't knows is what to do 'bout it. If he was my man I'd bust in, strip him to the buff, and put him under a cold shower, but I can't do that with your man. An' just talkin' and pleadin' with him ain' gettin' me nowhere.

"I says to him, 'Mister Jeff, sir, you got to sober up, 'cause this here's Monday and you got to go to work.' An' he say, 'Why, Ella? What for I got to work now?' I say, ' 'Cause you got to live like civilized folks.' An' he say, 'They ain't no civilized folks, Ella. They all savages. They all wild animals that belongs in cages. I's in my cage now, and you let me be.'

"Well, by now I's gettin' upset, Miss Carol. I rattles the doorknob, and he holler at me, 'Get away from that door, black woman!' I tell him I's gonna call you, and he say if I does, I's fired on the spot, and that why I's talkin' so low now, Miss Carol, so's he won't hear me, though I reckon he done passed out cold by now. I can't handle that white man! You's got to come home, honey!"

"I can't, Ella."

"Why can't you?" Ella demanded reasonably. "He still your husband, ain' he? You ain' got rid of him already, is you?"

"Don't you see, Ella? He knew you'd call me, and if I come back now, he'll use this trick over and over. I'm not going to nurse him through such spells. When he realizes that, he'll behave himself."

"Honey, he past realizin' anythin'. An' I don't think he pullin' no trick, neither. I think he just don't care no more what happen to him, if he live or die."

"He won't die, Ella. He'll sleep it off today and go to the office tomorrow. This isn't his first bout with the bottle, you know. Don't worry about it. Just let him alone, as he wishes, and go about your business."

"You ain' comin' home?"

"No, Ella. I'm sorry."

"I's sorry too, Miss Carol. Everybody powerful sorry, seems like, but ain' nobody doin' nothin' 'bout it."

"You'll manage, Ella. Bye, now."

Margaret, who had been listening to her daughter's end of the conversation, shook her head as Carol replaced the receiver. "How can you be so cold, Carol? If ever you loved Jeffrey, how can you not go to him now?"

"Mother, don't you understand either? It's because I did love him that I can't go to him now! I couldn't bear to see him in that condition, locked in a room with his bottles, like a caged animal with its bones, snarling and snapping like a sick animal when someone tries to help him." Half-sobbing, she cried vehemently, "I don't want to remember him that way!"

"No, of course not," Margaret consoled, wondering what else she could say or do, except agree. "Well, what are your plans for today?"

"I have an appointment with Kenneth Cranshaw this afternoon," Carol replied. "And then . . ." She paused, chewing her lower lip.

"You'll live happily ever after with Mark Lawrence? What a charming idyll! Darby and Joan in the Shenandoah."

"That's not funny, Mother."

"Indeed not! It's quite sad, actually. What training, what preparation have you had for farm life? You weren't in the Four-H Club and couldn't even raise a good Victory Garden during the war. You've never done anything more agricultural than cutting flowers nor more rural than fox hunting. And you think your behavior now is rational? It's insanity, Carol, and I only hope it's temporary."

"Crazy or not, my mind is made up, Mother."

"You're not well, Carol. You need psychoanalysis."

"And a hysterectomy?"

"Perhaps," Margaret nodded. "I think you're afflicted with middle-age mania. Men don't have a monopoly on it, you know. A fortyish female can be the most foolish fool of all! Haven't you proof enough of that in Beth Benedict and Shirley Martin? Pathetic creatures, both of them, and it breaks my heart to think you might become equally pathetic."

"I'm not forty yet, Mother! I'm only thirty-eight, and I'll try not to disgrace you."

"Just try not to disgrace yourself," Margaret advised.

"You wouldn't say that if you knew Mark."

"When will I have that pleasure?"

"This evening—and please be nice to him, Mother. He's not a boor, really. Just because he was born and raised on a farm in Kansas—"

"Darling, you're the one apologizing for him."

"I'm not apologizing for him!" Carol protested. "Oh, why don't you go knit something? I'll get breakfast."

"My, aren't we domestic this morning? Don't burn the toast or overcook the eggs."

"This is the age of electronics, Mother. There are gadgets to prevent such accidents."

Margaret picked up her knitting basket. "Ah, yes! Automation, and people have become automatons, pressing buttons, flicking switches, setting timers. Robots on jets and rockets bound for God knows where and what! President Kennedy even expects to land an astronaut on the moon before the decade's over. A wonderful, exciting age for youth, I suppose, but rather frightening for old fogies like me. The potential is simply awesome. Man is in danger of becoming dehumanized."

"That's progress, Mother."

"Perhaps," Margaret conceded. "But I'm glad I can remember a time when life was less mechanized and scientific. Less convenient, possibly, but also less hectic. And much happier. Maybe that's why I prefer the past and fear the future; why I love candlelight and open hearths and Strauss waltzes. Why I like to grind my own coffee and spices and time my eggs by an hourglass. And you'd better learn a few practical household hints too, my dear. Your farmhouse may not be equipped with all the latest electronic marvels."

"Watch those needles, Mother. You wouldn't want to drop a stitch. What's that you're making, anyway?"

"A sweater for Christopher."

"Sweater? It looks more like a cover for a cricket bat. He's not *that* thin, Mother."

Margaret smiled. "This is a sleeve, dear."

"All right, Mother, you've made your point," Carol murmured, retreating rosy-faced to the kitchen.

*　　*　　*

It was two o'clock in the afternoon, and Carol was seated in Ken's office. He had lit a cigarette for her and one for himself, and both were contemplative, the big semicircular desk between them, neither as yet fully able to believe the reason for the meeting.

Ken still hoped it was all a mistake that could be rectified by rationale and reconciliation. Finally, he said, "After your call this morning I phoned Jeff and asked him to come here, too. These things should be discussed in person. Both parties have rights, and neither is expected to forfeit them. But I couldn't persuade him, which is probably just as well, considering his condition and attitude. He's drinking."

"That's not news, Ken. According to Ella, he had a lost weekend."

"Every man has a weakness and a breaking point, Carol. It usually takes a personal crisis to reach them, and Jeff has had his share lately."

"I can't be held responsible if Jeff turns into an alcoholic over this, Ken. He made his own crises, and part of his weakness in that respect is inherited from his father. Clarence Courtland wasn't exactly a strong character."

"I'm not blaming you, Carol."

"In a way, maybe it is my fault," Carol relented, sighing. "I've babied Jeff so long. Frustrated mother instinct. I had so much of it, I had to use it somehow. And Jeff humored and indulged me—as much out of pity, I suspect, as anything else. But it wasn't a healthy situation, Ken. Nor a truly happy one, either. Something was wrong, missing. I realize that now, as never before, and perhaps this is the best thing for both of us."

"Divorce is rarely the best thing for any couple, Carol. It's radical surgery and generally requires anesthesia. Jeff is anesthetizing himself with bourbon. What are you using—barbiturates?''

Carol shifted her position uneasily, inhaled deeply on her cigarette. ''I engaged you as legal counsel, Ken, not medical or marital advisor.''

''You need both, my dear, and there's no charge for the extra service.''

A ponderous silence ensued during which Carol glanced curiously about the office, as if she had never seen it before. It was one of a commodious suite of six rooms in a new professional building, richly paneled in walnut, handsomely furnished. Law volumes filled the wall shelves. The file cabinets were neatly recessed, the bar discreetly closed. The Capitol dome was visible from the windows, as it was visible from the windows of Courtland Investments, several blocks away.

''Courtland versus Courtland,'' Ken mused. ''I never expected to see that on my legal calendar. Six months ago yours was one of the few marriages in our crowd that I'd have bet on lasting forever. And here you and Jeff are at the parting gate, while the others are still together.''

''Together how, Ken? Like the Martins and the Benedicts? They're not together, they're merely sharing the same stable; not even the same stall, only the same stable. That's not marriage, it's coexistence, and I want no part of it.''

''Where does Major Lawrence fit into this stable, as you call it? Has he been playing stud with you?''

Carol gasped, outraged. ''Look here, Ken!''

''Oh, come on now, Carol. A woman shouldn't have secrets from her physician or attorney. That's what I am now, your attorney. And I expect—in fact, demand—truth and honesty from my clients. Have you been in the hay with that old war horse?''

"He's not old," Carol murmured.

"He's old enough to know better, and so are you."

"You want a corespondent?"

"No, but Jeff might. Could he charge Mark?"

Her expression of rueful remorse betrayed her, and it was Ken who was the more embarrassed. And disappointed, as if he had discovered something unpleasant about his sister.

"I'm sorry," he apologized. "I wish it hadn't been necessary to ask. It's so damn ironic."

"Life is full of ironies, Ken. And travesties. It's one long bitter satire."

Ken gazed at her sadly. "Now you sound like the others, Carol. The cynics and skeptics."

"Why not? I'm a member of the club now. I've been initiated. God, how I've been initiated! Nothing in my Sweet Briar sorority prepared me for a hazing like this."

"Try to preserve a few dreams and illusions, Carol. A few principles and ideals. Cynicism can satiate quickly, and a steady diet of it can sicken. Sicken unto death. Save a few beautiful memories to cherish. Even divorce doesn't have to be mean and ugly."

" 'Parting is such sweet sorrow'?" Her wistful smile was forced, for tears threatened her eyes. "I've already discovered that, Ken. Sorrow can be splendid, did you know that? Even erotic. It can reach such an exquisite crescendo that the pain becomes ecstasy. Oh, poor Ken! You look so unhappy. You had some illusions about me, didn't you? And I've spoiled them."

"More tragic, you've spoiled them for yourself, my dear. And for Jeff. Try not to repeat the tragedy with Mark. I presume you're going to marry him?"

After a weighty pause, she nodded. "Yes."

"You're sure that's what you want, Carol?"

"As sure as I'll ever be about anything in my life again, Ken." She stared at the ember of her cigarette a long moment, then ground it out resolutely; she didn't actually enjoy smoking, it was just something to do with her idle, nervous hands. "Shall we get down to the specifics that will make it possible? The clinical approach, please. We're counselor and client now, remember?"

Ken sighed. "I wish it were that simple."

"Would you rather I took my business elsewhere? Do you want to recommend someone?"

"No, it's not that," he said, frowning. "It's just that I feel guilty, having introduced you to Major Lawrence."

"Don't be silly, Ken! You know very well that Jeff instigated that little soiree. It just boomeranged, that's all. Backfired."

"Yes, and Joan and I were caught in the crossfire."

"There's someone else caught in it, too," Carol said gravely, "and that's the biggest and worst tragedy of all, Ken. That poor boy . . ."

Part Three

Alas! how easily things go wrong!
A sigh too much or a kiss too long,
And there follows a mist and a weeping rain,
And life is never the same again.

George MacDonald,
(1824–1905)
Phantastes

24

Carol went out with Mark that evening. They drove to an exclusive restaurant in Chevy Chase, Maryland, for dinner at prices she knew Mark couldn't afford, and she wondered why he didn't use more discretion in his entertainment. Then she realized he was doing it for her because he thought she was accustomed to the best and wanted to give it to her at least during the courtship. He was primarily a steak-and-potatoes man, and he preferred his wine and brandy in glasses rather than in the rich sauces and desserts that were specialties at this famous French house. And rather than tell him the events of the day had left her stomach in knots rebellious to food, she let him order a full-course meal and wine and pretended to enjoy it. God, the pretenses lovers practiced when honesty would have been the best policy! But Mark was not much fooled, withal.

"Was it very rough on you today?" he asked.

"About what I expected," she said. "Ken missed his calling. He should have been a minister. And, of course, Jeff didn't help matters by refusing to appear for the preliminaries."

"Is there a chance he'll contest?"

"I don't think so, Mark. It would mean a fight, and we've fought enough already." Anxiety creased her brow. "I just wish it were over."

"Ditto," he said.

"What do you think of my mother?"

"I like her, but I'm not sure it's mutual."

"It's nothing personal, Mark. Mother's just of the old school. Not exactly a Puritan, but far from a feminist. She doesn't believe in free love or divorce, and she thinks I'm making a mistake. But she thought the same thing when I married Jeffrey. Don't worry, darling. She'll learn to love you, too. Like a son."

The faint purple shadows under her eyes, which not even the whimsical chic black veil could conceal, disturbed Mark. Her skin was pearl-pale, almost translucent against the somber black costume, and she appeared frail and withdrawn, rather wraithlike. Too delicate to long endure the rigors of farm life, he thought, even with hired help in the house. He might have to give up the idea of retirement and farming, stay in the service; they would travel around like gypsies. Could she take that? There was nothing nomadic about her, either; no wandering vine, she needed firm roots and pillars to sustain her. She was like a woman left over from another era, the kind he thought about when he heard a Stephen Foster ballad. She belonged in that old mansion on the Potomac, with her rosewood and mahogany and petit point, her magnolias and mimosas, and faithful servants. But still he could not relinquish his dream, his hope.

"I spoke with the real estate agent again," he said, "and he thinks Higby might accept an offer of twenty-seven thousand. That would be a saving of three thousand over his original price. We could buy some new equipment and livestock with it. And fix the house."

"Three thousand dollars wouldn't begin to remodel that shack and buy decent furniture, Mark, much less new equipment and livestock."

"Well, I know it's not Courtland House, but—"

"It's a shack," Carol interrupted.

"You're right," he agreed, chagrined. "And we'll fix it first. Do you know any architects and contractors?"

"Several, but they're expensive."

"I have some savings, Carol."

"So have I, from my father's estate."

"Let Jeff invest your money for you."

"Most of it is in stocks and bonds already, but we can cash them in," she offered, tasting her Chablis.

"No, Carol." He shook his head emphatically, set his jaw firmly. "Your securities are your own. I want you to keep them that way."

"Oh, Mark, don't be a medieval mule!"

But he was adamant. "You can spend your money on clothes or any other personal things, and I'll accept some tools or an implement for a wedding gift. But don't try to remodel the house and buy furniture at your expense, Carol. We've already nixed the dowry bit! You said you'd come to me poor, remember?"

Carol sighed, flaking the French pastry to crumbs with her fork. "We're quarreling, Mark. In public."

He was instantly apologetic, and affectionate, reaching across the table for her hand. "I'm sorry, darling. I'm a clod. But we had to clear up that issue immediately and definitely. I'll be able to support you, Carol. Not in the style to which you're accustomed, but without too much hardship, I hope. I won't expect you to wear rags, work in the fields, and account for your cookie jar savings. You can manage the house any way you please.''

''As long as I don't dip into my private funds?''

''Darling, will you trust my judgment in this?''

She nodded, giving him a smile poignant with deference, and the desire to make love to her suddenly overwhelmed Mark. ''No point torturing that poor napoleon further,'' he said, signaling the waiter. ''I think we're finished here.''

In the car he kissed her hungrily and pressed his face into her hair, breathing the familiar Arpege fragrance. ''Shall we go to my billet?''

''Do you think it's safe?'' she worried. ''It might be under surveillance.''

''My God, you think he'd resort to that?''

Carol shrugged. ''I don't know, Mark. But he could name you corespondent. Ken says we have to be careful.''

''I hope Cranshaw's as competent as he seems,'' Mark said, frowning. ''A long delay will be hell on everyone . . .''

The sun, shifting its position with the season, no longer struck the windows in Carol's room in the morning. Often there was fog floating up from the river, or rain and gusty wind, and wet leaves littered the sidewalks. As her mother's yardman raked and put them in plastic bags for the garbage collectors, Carol thought of her own garden going dormant. No, not *hers* anymore! She would have to devise a substitute on the farm, for she simply could not live without the beauty and pleasure of fresh flowers.

Farmers naturally preferred to grow vegetables, and Mark had a philosophy about everything on a paying farm producing, but he would surely let her have her mind about the house and garden. Humoring and indulging her, perhaps, as Jeffrey had done. Maybe she should just live with Mark for a while and see how things developed? No, her mother would have a stroke—and Jeff might actually kill Mark. Why did everyone, including Ken and Joan, think she must be protected? Did she unwittingly give the impression of frailty, helplessness, dependency? An antiquated clinging vine image that was possibly more accurate than she imagined, or desired? Or was it just some kind of sentimental conspiracy to make her feel that way?

Margaret knocked and entered with a breakfast tray and cheery greeting. "Good morning, dear!"

"You shouldn't have, Mother," Carol scolded. "I wanted to come down to breakfast. Stop treating me like an invalid. I'm not ill."

Margaret smiled indulgently. "Louise fixed popovers for you. Strawberries and Persian melon, too. You used to love them, especially when they were out of season."

"Looks like a last meal," Carol mused. "I'm going to be divorced, Mother, not executed. Or is this your quaint way of showing me what I'll miss in the country?"

"Well, I doubt you'll have many breakfasts in bed, dear. A farmer's wife must be up and stirring before dawn. Pamper yourself while you can."

Shunning the tray, Carol rose and slipped on a robe. "Think you're clever, don't you? Well, it won't work. I *know* it's not going to be easy."

Margaret unfolded the morning paper. "There are some pressure cookers advertised on page six. Better buy a couple and a book on canning. Learn to do it properly, or you might as well label your pantry jars with a skull and crossbones. Botulism, you know."

Her daughter tried to suppress her irritation by brushing her hair vigorously. "Are you enjoying this, Mother?"

"Enjoying it? My heart is bleeding, Carol. For you. And Jeffrey. And Christopher. You could have been a family together—and maybe that's what God intended when He denied you children of your own."

"If so, He botched it, wouldn't you say?"

"The Lord moves in strange ways."

"Ah, sweet mystery of life!"

Ignoring the sarcasm, Margaret continued cogently, "Nature is often strange too, and just as mysterious. Did you know that chickens are subject to over a hundred different diseases?"

"I read *The Egg and I*, Mother."

"That hardly makes you an authority."

"Nor you, dear."

"Well, I've been doing some research on animal husbandry," Margaret said. "Very interesting. Rather indelicate, though. Cows can get contagious abortion, and they can also die calving. Boars sometimes get hung in sows and have to be extricated. Foaling is often difficult and dangerous for young mares and more so for *older* ones. Better find a good vet in that wilderness, darling. And a good doctor for yourself. Remember when you got pneumonia sitting in a cold duck blind? And Jeffrey told me he couldn't take you hunting because you wept every time he shot anything. How are you going to slay a chicken, or watch your pet pigs and calves slaughtered?"

"Mark will do the butchering, Mother. When a man has killed other men in war and seen women and children bombed to death, preparing animals for food shouldn't be too terribly traumatic."

"You'll just stuff the sausages and smoke the hams and bacon? Gather the eggs, clean the coops. Milk the cows, separate the cream, churn the butter. Practically nothing for a big sturdy woman like you. But who's going to do it if you can't? If you become ill, or pregnant?''

"We'll hire it done.''

Maternal pity surfaced in Margaret's comprehending gaze. "So you still cherish the hope of pregnancy? Oh, Carol! Are you going to put yourself through that kind of pain and heartbreak again? Go on hoping and praying for a miracle until menopause, and even during it? Frustrate yourself and drive that poor man to despair trying to impregnate you? *Why* can't you accept things as they are?''

Carol flung the hairbrush down with a clatter, scattering perfume and cosmetic bottles and jars. "Why should I, as long as there's a chance?" she cried, tears brimming.

"Christopher was your chance for motherhood, Carol,'' Margaret reasoned gently, suppressing the ache in her own heart. She shared her child's tragedy and pain, felt her frustration, and longed to comfort and compensate her.

"I tried to be a mother to him! He didn't want me.''

"I think he did, Carol, but didn't know how to show it. He's only a boy. A hurt, bewildered, embittered adolescent who feels betrayed and rejected. But you were too busy feeling sorry for yourself to realize and understand his feelings.''

"That's not quite true,'' Carol protested, wondering at her quick denial. "Am I supposed to feel guilty now, accept the blame for Jeffrey's transgressions years ago? Anyway, I see no point in discussing this matter any further!''

"Very well.'' Margaret turned to leave. "Oh, I almost forgot. Kenneth Cranshaw called. If it's convenient, he'd like to see you at his office this afternoon.''

*   *   *

But it was only another conference, and Carol complained that they did not seem to progress beyond that stage. "I'm no nearer to the judge now than when first I came here, Ken."

"It takes time, Carol. Due process of law."

"Due rigamarole."

"Releasing the bonds of matrimony is somewhat more difficult and involved than tying them, my dear."

"You're deliberately stalling," Carol accused.

Ken smiled blandly. "Yours isn't the only case on my docket, honey. I have other clients too, and most are just as impatient as you. What's the big rush?"

"I just don't like waiting, Ken."

"Waiting? I understood that you and Mark . . ."

She blushed. "That's not what I mean. But we're waiting that way now, too. On your advice, Counselor."

"If it's a great imposition, maybe you should go to Reno for six weeks. Or Mexico. Or to Phenix City, Alabama, where it only takes twenty-four hours. That's the latest divorce mill for impatient lovers."

"Oh, my God! More preaching and moralizing?"

"Listen, Carol. Jeff isn't as anxious and cooperative as you, and I can't bludgeon him into submission. He refused to come here, so I went to him. He was in his office, but he wasn't accomplishing much. He looks bad, Carol. Thin and haggard. I think he's living on whiskey, coffee, and tobacco, and if it weren't for his trips to Hitchfield Academy, he'd probably never sober up or go anywhere. If he continues this way, he'll be a candidate for AA."

Carol winced, unable to suppress her emotions at this news. "Ella only called me once," she said. "Jeff must have threatened her into silence. But I'm not exactly robust myself, Ken, as should be obvious. Mother thinks I'm about ready for Menninger's Clinic."

"And you still insist that divorce is the best thing for the Courtlands?"

"Maybe not the best, but the only thing now."

"Oh, hell, Carol! Because you've been in the sack with Mark doesn't mean you have to marry him. Jeff isn't that old-fashioned, or narrow-minded. He still loves you and wants you back, but he's wrestling with his pride. After all, *you* left *him*. That's tough on the male ego."

"Has he signed the papers yet?"

"They're not ready for signature yet. I have a CPA checking his books. Jeff's a very solvent man and a very generous one. He insists on giving you alimony *pendente lite*—pending trial—and extra compensation if you waive it afterwards. In other words, a settlement, whether you want it or not. Don't be proud, stubborn, and foolish, Carol. It will only complicate and delay matters. You're entitled to something after twenty years, and you and Mark can make good use of it on that farm."

"So you've been talking to my mother? And naturally she agrees with you?"

"Naturally. *You* on a farm? Holy Jesus, Carol!"

She crossed her nyloned legs, uncrossed them; reached for a cigarette, put it back. "Why does the idea of me on a farm strike everyone as absurd and even pathetic? What's wrong with farming, for heaven's sake? It's an ancient and honorable occupation, and the world couldn't survive without it!"

"Sure, honey, and you can go right over to the Capitol and start lobbying with the Farm Block," Ken grinned. "But buy yourself a new hat first. That's last season's you're wearing, and so is the rest of your outfit. Are you trying to economize already, or just getting used to looking like a farmer's frau?"

"Does last year's mink make me Ma Kettle? Remember the Eisenhowers? They're living on a farm now."

"Why don't you write and ask Mamie the secret of her rural success?" Ken suggested. "Get a few pointers on country living from Jackie, too. They're building a place on Rattlesnake Mountain, in the Blue Ridge, you know. But buy that new chapeau first—something bright and frivolous and frightfully expensive. A new dress wouldn't hurt, either. That suit's not your type, too tailored, a crime against femininity. And black, *always black*—you in mourning or something? You'll be a divorcée, not a widow. And even widows don't wear weeds much anymore. Go shopping, Carol. Your charge accounts are still open, but if you don't want to use them, bill me. Maybe Joan will see the bills and get jealous, and we'll have a delightful fight. We're so monogamously happy, people are beginning to call us The Perfect Cranshaws, and it scares hell out of me . . ."

25

The elevator seemed to descend too swiftly. Carol had a vision of broken cables and a free fall to the basement of the building, crashing, crumbling in the concrete. She clawed at the switch, lost her balance, and fell backwards against the wall, clutching the rail for support. Her heart leaping, her head spinning, she had a sense of compression in the compact enclosure, and of suffocation. It was her first experience with claustrophobia, and when she was safe on the ground floor she could not imagine what had brought it on. Psychosomatic or not, it was utterly terrifying.

The day was bleak and gray with the promise of winter, and though she had intended to go straight to Alexandria from Ken's office, she hailed a taxi and went to his home instead. The driver launched immediately into a conversation on politics as if an authority on the subject, and his idiotic chatter set Carol's teeth on edge. She tried to ignore him. He stole a glance at her in the rearview mirror.

"You okay, lady?"

"Fine."

"You a Democrat or Republican?"

"Independent," Carol replied. Oh, so independent!

"Well, if you ask me, what this country needs is—"

"A silent cabdriver," she interrupted.

"What?"

"Nothing. Just watch the traffic, please."

"Don't worry," he grinned. "Never had an accident yet, and I had some important people in this old hack. Just about every senator and congressman on the Hill. Even the Veep once. That Johnson fella, he's something. Was wearing a Stetson hat and cowboy boots with his silk suit. Invited me to come down to his Texas ranch and ride a horse. I think he meant it, too. Wish Kennedy'd invite me up to Hyannisport."

He sped along Massachusetts Avenue toward Woodley Park, weaving recklessly through the murderous traffic, recalling the glories and advantages of his position as a capital cabbie, confusing and mispronouncing names and personalities with no care or comprehension of his errors. "The Towers, eh? That's a classy joint. I drove Perle Mister and Cara Boot Lace to ritzy parties there a couple times. You want I should wait, lady?" he asked, screeching the brakes before the building, nearly jolting Carol's head against the front seat.

"No, thanks," she said, so relieved to arrive in one piece that she overtipped him.

He whistled appreciatively. "Gee, thanks, lady! Some folks is so tight-fisted nowadays, you'd think they was trying to balance the national budget . . ."

Another distressing ride in an automatic elevator, more vertigo, the fear of being trapped, and the inclination to pound the walls and scream for help. Whatever was wrong

with her lately? Elevators had never affected her this way
before, garrulous cabmen had never irritated her before,
nor had she dreaded the coming of winter before this
season. Trivialities upset and depressed her now, and mi-
nor incidents were easily magnified into major calamities.
She could cry or throw a tantrum on the slightest provocation, or slip into a long deep dark mood of somber intro-
spection. Were these the insidious, ominous symptoms of
mental disturbance bordering on a nervous breakdown?
That would be the awful crux, the terrible finale!

At last the cage released her at the pinnacle, and she
hurried down the corridor to the Cranshaws' penthouse,
pressing the bell anxiously. Anxiety was another thing she
felt too often and keenly these days. All her emotions were
intensified, in fact, seeming to work on a self-winding key
which she was unable to control, growing tighter and
tighter, so that she kept expecting to hear an internal alarm
or explosion.

Joan answered, wearing black velvet Capri pants, a
white flamenco blouse, red satin cummerbund, and gold
harem slippers. With her lovely dark hair swept sleekly
back and loops of gold at her ears, she looked as if she had
been posing for a high fashion magazine. No wonder Ken
was amused by last year's clothes on herself, Carol thought.

Even when surrounded by superficiality, Joan's charm
was incandescent and sincere. "Carol darling! Now I believe in mental telepathy. Shirley and Beth dropped in a
few minutes ago, and we were just wishing for a fourth for
bridge. Come in, stranger. That's what you've been lately,
you know."

"I've been busy, Joan."

"So we hear," Beth crowed, sitting on a huge white
hassock before the fireplace and sipping gin from a teacup.

Shirley lounged on the sofa in a molded black wool

sheath with a rope of jet beads dangling from her throat. "Welcome to the club, Mrs. Courtland."

Beth patted a cushion beside her. "Yeah, park it and join the powwow. Enjoy the fire. I love an open hearth. That stupid place of ours just has fakes and gas logs. I told Frank we were moving this winter if it's the last thing we do. Trouble is, we can't find another pad we like as well at the same price. The District is just getting too goddamned crowded for comfort. We may have to take to a split-level trap in the suburbs."

"Try a farm," Carol suggested.

Shirley laughed, stretching her long shapely legs toward the fire. "We heard such rumors, but you can't be serious, sweetie. Unless it's a horse farm in the hunt country?"

"No, it's a dirt farm in the valley."

"What valley?"

"When a native Virginian speaks of 'the valley,' he means the Shenandoah," Joan explained.

"For some women it could be the Valley of Tears," Shirley murmured, as if quoting Carol's mother. "But I hope it'll be Eden for Mrs. Mark Lawrence."

"You don't have to explain anything to these maudlin cats," Joan told Carol. "Just tell them to shut up and go to hell, they'll understand."

"Sure," Shirley nodded, unaffronted. "We're used to such finesse from our friends. It's her own business, anyway. Her own affair."

Carol winced and wondered why she should at the truth. It was an affair, and it was her own business, but in the company of women who made a farce of marriage and a mockery of fidelity, she felt cheap and promiscuous. She should avoid such associations, excuse herself and leave. But she remained, mesmerized by Beth's chatter, her tongue clacking like a castanet in her excitement over an embassy ball to which she and Frank had wrangled an invitation.

"It's just one of the banana republics," she said, "but I'm thrilled about it. Blew eight hundred and fifty bucks on my gown. An original by Oleg Cassini, and I'd better not see a duplicate on You Know Who or I'll sue the old boy." She giggled, gulping avidly from the teacup. "Let me tell you about it, girls! It's silver lamé and strapless and—"

"Strapless?" Shirley interrupted. "Isn't that a bit risky with your proportions?"

"My proportions are highly fashionable this season, thank you! Who's more chic or flatter than Jackie?"

"With her face and other assets she could be the titless wonder of the world," Shirley drawled, "and still have half the men on earth lusting for her. And before you repeat the gossip about her husband lusting after that Hollywood sex goddess who swallowed too many barbs in August, there's no real proof of that! Just because he flew out there occasionally to visit his brother-in-law doesn't mean he was sleeping with her. Besides, we were discussing *your* bosom, not Marilyn's. You're still wearing a training bra, aren't you?"

Beth poked her tongue out. "Only when I'm in training, smartie. Furthermore, they make some mighty realistic boob facsimiles, you know, and I bought a pair for the strapless creation."

"That's cheating," Shirley scoffed. "It's also false advertising."

"Only if you're trying to attract men. I'm not, never have. That's your line, Shirl. Who's your latest sheik? I know there's someone because Skeets has been doing his pocket dance regularly."

"Skeets is a clown."

"And you keep him around for laughs?"

"No, because I love him."

"Oh, brother!" Beth reached for the bottle of Beefeater's. "I'll have another shot on that."

"It's true," Shirley insisted.

"You just sleep around for kicks?"

"That's Skeets's fault, too. And since you can't possibly know or understand my motives, Bethie Girl, I'll thank you not to poke around in my libido."

Beth snorted. "Your motives are self-explanatory, and there's not much mystery to your libido, either. Only a nympho or whore makes herself available to any man who wants her. Which are you, Shirl Girl?"

Joan said sternly, "Knock it off, Beth."

"Oh, let her rave, Joanie. Let her practice amateur psychology. What other fun does she have in life? But Skeets is the one she should analyze. Ask him why he sics his friends on me, why he's always making nasty cracks and insinuations, like at his weekly poker game the other evening. The boys were telling dirty stories, and out of the blue Skeets pops up with, 'I bet I'm the only guy here who saw his wife raw before he even met her.' He has a complex about my career on the stage."

"Career?" Beth slapped her thigh, laughing hilariously. "Is *that* what you call it?"

"I was an exotic dancer," Shirley defended her act. "I can move my pectoral muscles clockwise and counterclockwise simultaneously and ripple my tummy with a jewel in my navel. That took years of practice and control to master, and there's art to it whether you realize it or not, Beth."

"To quote H. Allen Smith, 'I never met a stripper who didn't believe she was guilty of art.' "

Joan intervened again, "Don't be so bitchy, Beth."

"Oh, she's just quoting Skeets, too. To him, I was just a bare body, a bust and belly twirler, and fair quarry for the sex hunters. He gave me the name among his friends, and after a while I didn't give a damn and played the game. He thinks he discourages interest with his crude remarks, but he only promotes it. The lechers can hardly wait till they think he's safely away to come sniffing at the door."

"My lech included?" asked Beth.

And mine? Carol wondered.

"You don't have to answer that," Beth said. "I know my Frank. He'd cuckold his own brother if he could. But he blames me for his chasing. Philandering husbands usually blame their wives. The little lady is either fat, frumpy, fickle, frigid, or forty, and the last is apparently the worst of the wifely offenses. The cardinal sin, growing old. Unforgivable."

"Not necessarily," Joan reasoned.

Beth raised her hand like a stop signal. "Hold the big pep talks about middle-age and The Prime of Life. My mother warned me, and she was right. It's a drag and a disaster. Maybe the ancient Chinese had the right answer: put the wife aside at forty and take a young mistress. Unfortunately, most men don't wait that long. Some start leering on the honeymoon, or soon thereafter."

"You have the wrong attitude," Joan told her.

Beth frowned. "Wait till you can speak from experience, Saint Joan."

"Well, glory be!" cried Shirley gleefully. "Listen to the woman! Admitting menopause. I never thought I'd see the day."

"Oh, you will," Beth assured her. "It's inevitable, if you keep living, and those big mammaries will shrink with your ovaries, and you'll be popping hormone pills like jellybeans. But Skeets will probably welcome your change. Not so Frank. He thinks it's a curse and women should be taboo at this time, like they are during menstruation in some jungle tribes.''

"He'll be taboo himself at sixty or so," Joan said. "Or doesn't he know that?"

"He knows it, that's why he's so frantic now. I suspect he'll seek aphrodisiacs when his wane comes. I hope it leaves him impotent. That's a terrible fate for a wife to wish her husband, but I think we could be happy then. Compatible. Strangely enough, I still love the beast. But it's like loving something that doesn't exist—a dream, shadow, phantom. Impotence might give him substance, reality. I mean, if he doesn't need or want anyone else, he just might need and want me. To grow old with, if nothing else. A companion to accompany him down the twilight path to the sunset years in a golden age community in Florida.'' She paused, glancing at Carol. "You've been sitting there like a sphinx. What's your opinion of all this?"

Carol shrugged. "I don't know."

"Oh, come on, darling! Give. Relate. Communicate. You should be able to speak with some authority now."

Joan, who rarely used profanity, suddenly exploded. "Goddamn it, Beth! Must you sharpen your fangs on other people's sensibilities? Claw away even at your friends? Sometimes I wonder why I put up with you."

"Shall I tell you? Because you enjoy the smug sense of superiority you feel around me, the Lucky-Me and Poor-Beth syndromes. Carol had it too, before her husband got a CARE package from Britain. Then suddenly she knew what it meant to have the props knocked out from under her, and have the things she loved and cherished and built her future on collapse in ruins and dust. Believe me, it can shake you up, set you reeling—even into the arms of another man, if one is handy. One wasn't handy when I got my first blow from Frank's infidelity, so I had to comfort myself in other ways, and I guess it made me bitter and bitchy.''

The others said nothing, as Beth continued, "Even so, I'm not actually as venomous as I seem, nor as vindictive. I'm glad Carol had a handsome hero to catch her on her first fall. And regardless of my perpetual vendetta with Shirley, I don't really resent her male conquests, nor envy her much, either. Her erotic fascination won't last forever, I'm sure she realizes that, and she'll be just another aging beauty, another sad sex symbol.

"But you, Joan, are still in the clouds, an unsullied madonna on a marble pedestal, wearing your happiness and virtue like a triumphant white banner across your pure and noble breast—and sometimes I just can't resist the temptation to try to rip it off, expose a few raw nerves, a little torn and bleeding flesh, just to prove you're as human and vulnerable as the rest of us mere mortals.'' She grabbed the gin again. "Oh, shit and hellfire! I need another bolstering potion. Frank says I suffer from dysentery of the mouth, and I'm afraid he's right. Well, here's to Adam and Eve and *Paradise Lost*! Drink up, Eves. It's only juniper juice.'' She drained her cup, refilled it, grimaced. "How I wish it were hemlock . . .''

"Don't be an idiot,'' Joan said gently.

"Oh, don't worry. I'm not going to exterminate myself, at least not in some horribly messy way; I'll do it subtly, via the pickling in alcohol process. I lack both the courage and instinct for violence. Otherwise, I'd take the plunge off your terrace now. But even drunk, I'm a coward. So I'll just whimper and simper through life, wounding my friends because my wise enemies won't let me get close enough. Thanks for suffering me, darlings. Especially you, Saint Joan."

"Forget it," Joan murmured, embarrassed.

"Yeah, sure. All I need is a tranquilizer and a hormone shot, and my cup runneth over. With gall and tears. Crying towels, anyone?"

"Take it easy," Joan soothed, and Beth finished off the gin, curled up on the hassock like an emaciated cat, and passed out, snoring quietly.

Shirley shook her head sympathetically, beginning to feel the straight vodka she had been consuming. "Poor bitch. I feel sorry for her. I feel sorry for all us poor bitches at the mercy of bastards. Pardon me, while I repair to the powder room before I pee in my pants . . ."

Carol watched her wobble away. "I feel worse than either of them, Joan. Do you know, I'm beginning to believe that stuff about middle-aged women?"

"Nonsense, Carol. I expect to go through menopause without growing a mustache or neurosis."

"Or losing your husband?"

"You needn't lose yours," Joan said.

"I already have, dear. Divorce is just a formality."

"There is such a thing as reconciliation, Carol."

"No, it wouldn't be fair to Mark."

"Is it fair to marry a man you don't love?"

Carol sipped her Dubonnet. "Who says I don't love him?"

"You do, with everything but words. Put it into words, Carol, speak them aloud, and you won't marry Mark Lawrence. You couldn't be that unfair to him or yourself. 'To thine own self be true,' et cetera . . ."

"You're sweet to worry about me, Joan."

"I want you to be happy, Carol."

"I want me to be happy, too. I want everybody to be happy." She gazed wistfully at the mother-daughter portrait over the mantel. "How is Kay?"

Joan frowned slightly. "Well, she doesn't write as often as she should. Studies are harder this semester, I suppose. She didn't want to return to Abbey Hall, you know."

"Christopher wasn't keen about Hitchfield Academy, either," Carol said. "He acted as if he were being sent to Coventry, as the British say."

"Do you think they've forgotten each other?"

After a pause, Carol shrugged. "First love is not easily forgotten, Joan."

"Is that what you think it was?"

"Don't you?"

"Yes. But Ken—well, Kay is still his baby, his little girl, too young and innocent to even think about love, much less experience it. It's amazing how brilliant he can be about other people's problems, and how benighted about his own daughter's. But that's a paternal failing, I guess. To tell the truth, I'm worried about Kay. I hope she won't do anything rash or foolish, like running away from school . . ."

Shirley returned, yanking on her two-way stretch girdle, giggling self-consciously. "Who's running away?"

"I am," said Carol, rising and putting on last year's hat, suddenly feeling old and frumpish in it. Ken was right. She should buy a new one, something chic and extravagant. And she *was* wearing too much black lately. Too much tailoring, too. A woman could defeminize herself that way, neuter her emotions. She needed a whole new wardrobe, and there was a fine shop in the arcade of The Towers . . .

But there was the automatic elevator again, the horrifying claustrophobia, and she barely made it to the drugstore for a Coke to wash down a tranquilizer. Her second—or was it her third or fourth that day? Either the nepenthe was losing its efficacy, or she was developing an immunity to it, for the expected euphoria never came, and the would-be shopping spree ended in the purchase of a fashion magazine.

26

"*Vogue?*" said Margaret with mock surprise. "Farm journals and seed catalogs would be more helpful, dear. What's the latest in sunbonnets and milking-aprons?"

Carol decided to banter with her. "Think how nice it will be to have fruit and vegetables raised with your daughter's own fair hands."

"Your hands won't be fair long," Margaret predicted. "Nor your face. The elements will brutalize your complexion, dry your skin, fade your hair. You'll age rapidly."

"Not if I take care, Mother, wear hats and gloves. I don't intend to just abandon myself! And you should be proud of my ambition—weren't your and Daddy's ancestors farmers?"

"Planters," Margaret corrected. "There's a difference. First slaves and then hired hands and sharecroppers worked their fields in the Tidewater. You and the major will be dirt diggers, *The Good Earth* variety, and you're not prepared for it."

"I've told you before, Mother, we're not planning to live like peasants, plowing with mules and sticks. Farming is a science now, and we intend to do it scientifically, with books and machinery."

The older woman chuckled. "That should be an interesting sight for your neighbors. You in dungarees and sombrero, driving a tractor with one hand and holding a manual in the other. Maybe you can sell tickets, earn some extra money, since you're too proud to accept any from Jeffrey."

"Have you been talking with Jeff again?"

"Only to ask about Christopher," Margaret lied. "I finished his sweater, and Jeffrey will take it to him when they go hunting next week."

"Hunting? But Jeff can't go to the mountains now! We'll need him to sign papers. And in court, if Ken ever gets us that far. Oh, you're all in league against Mark and me, and if you think you can keep us apart that way forever . . ."

"Carol!" her mother interrupted harshly, comprehending her meaning with shock.

"I don't care, it's true! Jeff has even hired a private detective to spy on us."

"That's preposterous!"

"Is it? Then who are the strange men taking shifts watching Mark's apartment building?"

"Security guards employed by the management?" Margaret suggested.

"*They* wear uniforms! These are plainclothes sleuths, reading newspapers in the lobby or tinkering with cars in the parking facilities, as if they suspect foreign agents or Mafia connections among the residents."

"Probably just figments of your imagination and guilty conscience, Carol. I can't believe that Jeffrey would—"

"I can," Carol cried, throwing aside the magazine. "And I should have known he wouldn't fight fair."

"He's not fighting at all, Carol. You are."

"I'm going to win, too."

"It will be a Cadmean victory," Margaret said, adding at Carol's blank look: "In case you've forgotten your mythology, that's a victory in which both sides lose."

"How erudite," Carol muttered.

"Is the major calling this evening?"

"Yes, and I wish you'd call him Mark, Mother, and make him feel more welcome and comfortable. Major this and Major that! Can't you see how uneasy it makes him? I'm surprised he doesn't stand at attention and salute you. Limber up, General! Give Mark a chance to know you, and yourself to know him. You'll both profit. He's really a very fine man, Mother. A wonderful person."

"I'm sure he is," Margaret agreed seriously, after a slight hesitation. "I should hate to think my daughter could be attracted to any other kind."

Carol met Mark in a mood reckless and defiant. When he asked where she would like to go, she answered swiftly and positively, "Your place."

"It's still under surveillance," he said.

Unconsciously quoting her mother, she suggested, "Maybe we just imagine it."

"Maybe, but why take the chance?"

"Mark, you have to take some chances in life! And especially in a situation like this. Every adulterous liaison can't be a sure thing. If we hadn't taken some risks in the beginning, we wouldn't be in this mess now."

"Mess?"

"Face it, Mark. It's a predicament, and it's not improving. I feel like a mouse in a maze."

"Darling, I know the waiting is tedious, but it can't be much longer."

"No? Jeff is taking to the hills next week! He's just liable to spend the winter."

"He can be subpoenaed."

"His cabin is as secluded as a moonshiner's still," Carol informed. "It would take an army of revenue agents to find it."

"What do you suggest?"

"I was hoping you'd have a suggestion," she sighed.

"Get another attorney. Go to Reno, or Mexico."

"Or Alabama, like the author of *Peyton Place* did, so she could marry her disc jockey? We're behaving like a couple of characters out of that book right now! Anyway, Ken already suggested a quickie divorce—but Jeff would still have to cooperate. I want it to be legal, Mark. Valid."

"Then we'll just have to be patient, Carol."

"Aren't you tired of patience?"

"Well, I'm not exactly an ardent young swain."

"That's precisely what they're counting on, Mark."

"Who?"

"Mother and Jeff. They're allies in this. Conspirators. And they're expecting us to behave exactly as we are, like a pair of scared rabbits."

"But Ken advised—"

"Damn Ken! He's on their side, too. After all, he's Jeff's best friend!"

"But he's also *your* friend and lawyer, Carol. And a highly ethical guy. I trust him. Don't you?"

She relented, ashamed of her outburst. "I suppose so. I have to, now. Don't mind me, Mark, I'm just in a snit this evening. Mother and I had words today. She thinks she's being so damned rational and practical about this, and I guess I'm being a little paranoid."

"Come over here," Mark urged softly. "I can still drive with one hand." As Carol obliged, his free arm circled her waist. "There's always a drive-in theater."

"And park in the back row? That's kid stuff."

With wry humor Mark began to sing, "Hello, middle-aged lovers wherever you are, are you having a tough time, too?"

Carol was not amused. "When you proposed a few months ago, you said we were still young, with a lot of future before us. Is it behind us now, Mark? How did we suddenly get old?"

"Looking for a place to prove we're still young," he joked without much humor. "And we can't drive all night, can we?"

"No."

But it seemed as if they would before he found a suitable country lane and followed it into a woods, up a hill, and down to a small pond, apparently a swimming and fishing hole in summer, but deserted now in late autumn. A sickle moon hung above, its light pale and wintry. They sat gazing at it in silence, the car intimate with the warmth of the heater and fragrance of her perfume, and then they embraced desperately. Neither spoke, though each was intensely aware of the other's preparations: the metallic rasp of his zipper and papery crackle of the condom wrapper; the twisting necessary to remove her panties.

It was a fiasco, comic in its contortions, pathetic in its frustrations. They rushed together and rushed apart, as if a detective were behind every bush and tree, as if the night itself had eyes and ears—a camera and tape recorder. Carol felt naive and stupid. It was her first sexual intercourse in an automobile, and she was ignorant of the arts and intricacies involved. Jeff had neglected her education in that respect, marrying his little virgin soon after they met. She should have warned Mark. He should have warned her, too: abstinence breeds prematurity. A cloud eclipsed the crescent moon, obscuring his face, but she sensed his chagrin, remorse, humiliation.

"You were right about the rabbits," he said contritely. "Me, anyway. I'm sorry, darling, but I guess this isn't the answer, either."

"No," she murmured, grateful for the darkness that concealed her own mortification.

"I used to be pretty good at auto acrobatics," Mark continued to apologize, "even when there were floor-shifts to wrestle with. Guess I'm not agile enough anymore."

Carol did not know how to explain her disappointment, but it was more than the failure of a clandestine coitus, more than the involuntary revulsion she felt when he tried to comfort her. It was claustrophobia in reverse, and she wanted to hide in a hole and never come out.

"Don't, please," she begged at his touch. "I feel like a tramp."

"You're not a tramp, Carol."

"I know, but I can't help how I feel."

"Well, I feel like a dog," he said. "A damned precipitous cur. Forgive me, Carol."

"It wasn't your fault, Mark. I was just clumsy and wriggling too much. Believe it or not, it was a first for me. That's something, isn't it, at my age? Never in a car, back or front seat!"

"Something," he agreed. "You were a chaste bride?"

"There were some those days."

Why didn't he leave her alone now, let her organize herself? Was he just going to sit there, talking, with his pants still open and hers still off? Hick! she thought and feared she had spoken aloud, for he was opening the door, getting out, walking to the pond. She saw the flame of his cigarette lighter, smelled tobacco smoke. He stood on the bank, remote and brooding, a specter himself, unreal even in reality.

Carol caught her spike heel in the lacy undergarment. Jesus God, she hadn't even removed her shoes, much less her hose and garter belt, and her footprints were probably embedded in the dashboard. Her brassiere was hanging by one hook, and his blasted zipper had gotten tangled in her hair, scraping and pulling it excruciatingly. Why hadn't he put the car seat on the ground? Teenagers probably knew that much. And for Christ's sake, was he going to stand out there forever now!

She called to him. He tossed his cigarette into the water, returned to the Plymouth coupe, got in and under the wheel. They sat apart, staring at the faint phosphorescence cast upon the pond by the reappearing silver sliver of moon. Finally, Mark made the first move, and this time she did not reject his embrace.

"I love you," he said, burying his face in her hair.

"I know, Mark."

"That was lousy for you, wasn't it?"

"Not much fun for you, either."

"More than for you, though. I could help now."

Not knowing whether to laugh or cry, Carol made an idiotic excuse. "I already put my pants on."

"Take them off. We'll try it again. It'll take me longer this time. Oh, shit—that was my last rubber!"

"It's all right," she said, actually relieved.

"Will you trust me not to fumble withdrawal?"

"Forget it!" Her voice was on edge.

"But you're still tense, darling." His hand touched her knee, then slipped under her skirt. "Manual is better than nothing, and I have a fairly talented forefinger."

"Mark, I'm not a nympho, and I won't go ape if I don't have an orgasm! Furthermore, I don't want to rely on that kind of sexual relief. Make a habit of it, like some women. I have a friend neglected by her husband who resorts to vibrators and other quaint dildoes. That's little better than masturbation to me."

"Do you miss Jeff in bed? Is he a great stud?"

"Aren't most men?"

"Not most, no. And some are much better than others, as some women are better partners than others."

"On a rating scale of one to ten, where would you put me in that category?"

"At the top."

"How chivalrous!"

"No, I'm serious. You're terrific when you concentrate on it. It's instinctive, you know, but you also had a good technical instructor. You're somewhat shy about one particular aspect of coitus, however, and I hope to change that after marriage. Maybe I can teach you a few new tricks and variations, too."

"Maybe," she agreed, surmising that he meant the same kind of innovations Jeff encouraged.

"I love you," he said again, prompting response.

"Yes."

"It'll work out for us, Carol."

She nodded, but could not restrain the tears.

Mark held her close. "Don't, baby."

"I'm sorry," she wept. "I'm an idiot."

He smiled, stroking her hair. "Just a little retarded in some respects."

"You're teasing, but it's true. Good thing I never had kids, they'd probably have been imbeciles."

"Hush," he commanded angrily. "That's utter nonsense, and you know it. Please stop crying, honey, it guts me."

She yanked a tissue from the box on the dash. It was silly, a mature woman bawling on a bleak country lane like a deflowered maiden afraid of pregnancy and unwed motherhood. "It's getting cold out here, Mark. Let's go home."

"To Alexandria?"

"Arlington. Damn the detectives! Full speed ahead!"

"Nice try," he said, releasing her and starting the motor. "But I think not, darling. Not tonight, anyway. How about tomorrow evening? We'll make an occasion of it, start with dinner. I'll cook for you. Okay?"

"Okay."

"You like Japanese food? I'm handy with a habachi, and teriyaki is my specialty. We'll drink hot sake, too."

"Fine. I'll don a kimono and play geisha. May I have a cigarette, please?"

"Of course." He offered his pack.

"Why, for your lungs' sake, don't you buy filter-tips? I suppose you'll roll your own from a sack of Bull Durham on the farm?"

"Yep, might even grow my own, ma'am. This here's tobacco country, ain't it?"

Carol laughed, truly amused for the first time that evening. "Oh, Mark! Rhett Butler, you're not."

"Rhett Butler? Fine mimic, I am! It was supposed to be Gary Cooper in *Bright Leaf*. But, Miss Scarlett, if you want to rebuild the old family plantation and take Mammy Ella with you . . ."

He was better as Clark Gable, who had a natural Midwestern twang, but Carol was tired of the comedy and ready to weep again. Premenstrual nerves and tension, she decided, increased by the other emotional events. Her period was due in a few days, and she was already having familiar and distressing symptoms. That damned precaution had been an unnecessary nuisance! Condoms were something else she hadn't experienced before Mark. Her husband had certainly never needed them with her, for contraception was the least of their marital problems. Had he practiced it with his British mistress, or left that messy detail to her medical knowledge? She smoked quietly, wondering what Jeff was doing about his sexuality now. Surely he had someone to appease his lusty appetite? Sex was vital to him, and he was—oh, God, yes!—he *was* a terrific lover. Again she wondered, had his knowing nurse been the perfect paramour?

27

Architecturally, Abbey Hall consisted of twelve beautifully symmetrical buildings of red brick with clean white limestone trim, occupying two hundred landscaped acres near Baltimore. There was a classically-spired chapel with stained glass windows, hard pews, and heavy hymnals. The campus, called the Quadrangle, was big and shady, with walks, benches, Grecian fountains and statuary, tall fluted urns of flowers, and shirred boxwood. At the edge of the property, partially screened by woods, were the stables, horses, and grooms' quarters, for riding was an important part of the curriculum.

Academically, Abbey Hall ranked with the finest finishing schools in the country, and its graduates received preference at such prestigious women's colleges as Sweet Briar, Radcliffe, Vassar, Bryn Mawr. Socially, it was the peer of Virginia's Foxcroft School, and like the students and endowments of that famous institution, those of Abbey

Hall came mostly from old Southern families: the daughters, granddaughters, and great-granddaughters of the alumnae.

The girls said that "abbey" was an appropriate name for the school, and the headmistress, Miss Constance Ferth, an appropriate abbess. Rules and regulations were as rigid as those governing the novice nun, and infractions punished accordingly. A completely incorrigible young lady was tolerated only one semester before expulsion.

Kay Cranshaw had experienced neither scholastic nor disciplinary difficulties before enrolling for her senior year in September. Although not a scholar, she had managed to maintain the required average and had excelled in at least one subject: horsemanship. She rode as if born to the saddle, and the Master of Horses assigned her the finest jumper in the stables. Kay took Pegasus over the hurdles as if he did indeed possess winged feet. Always the star attraction in the annual horse show, Kay had already won several trophies for Abbey Hall. Sometimes she suspected that her scholastic abilities were judged in part by her equestrian accomplishments, for Miss Ferth enjoyed winning the competitions in the meets with comparable schools. The silver cups were displayed as prominently and proudly in the lobby and her office as the merit and academic awards.

Looking back on summer vacation in Washington, Kay felt as if she had been on parole those three months and returned to a correctional institution because of a violation. For she had done something forbidden for a sixteen-year-old girl who still had a year of finishing school, four years of college, and a debut facing her: she had fallen in love.

But her parents, those wise adults who knew all about everything, thought this was impossible, could not happen, was just infatuation, kid stuff, and she would get over it.

Well, they were wrong. She did not forget Christopher.
Kay thought more of him now than she had in Washington. He monopolized her mind so completely sometimes that she could not concentrate on her studies at all and feared she would fail some of the imminent examinations.

She sat glumly in the dormitory now, in one of the prim white-walled rooms which the girls called "cloister cells." The simple furniture consisted of a dresser and mirror; a chest of drawers, which, along with the clothes closet, had to stand frequent inspections; a desk and chair; and a narrow candlewick-covered bed with a reproduction of Sir Thomas Lawrence's *Pinkie* over it. A reproduction of *Blue Boy* hung in the community room downstairs, where they were permitted to receive male visitors on weekends and special occasions, and which Kay had been forlornly avoiding because the picture reminded her of Christopher.

There were no roommates at Abbey Hall—a precaution, some students surmised, against the sort of gossip and scandal that sometimes touched non-coed schools, and they conversed about it privately, referring to Lillian Hellman's play *The Children's Hour*. But they were allowed to visit in one another's rooms from four to six in the afternoon, at which time the bell rang for the evening meal, and they filed down to the Refectory.

Kay's best friend, Linda Fulbright, was just across the hall. Linda was seventeen, blessed with a high intelligence quotient and retentive memory, which made cramming for exams unnecessary. Kay envied her these gifts almost as much as she envied her sophistication and invitation to the annual military ball at Hitchfield Academy, one of the male counterparts of Abbey Hall. The Cadet Hop, a social tradition at Hitchfield, was held in December preceding the Christmas holidays, and Kay was hoping and praying that Chris would invite her. Of course, there was still plenty of time. So far no formal requests had arrived in the mail. But the boys usually extended oral bids far in advance, to get the girl of their choice. The engraved gray cards from Hitchfield Academy were merely a formality.

Abbey Hall had no uniform other than the riding habit, although there were restrictions as to the manner of appearance in class. Casual clothes, low heels, no strong perfumes or obvious makeup. After class, the girls could lounge informally as long as they were "decently covered," and Linda considered a corduroy brunch coat decent enough coverage in which to call on Miss Cranshaw.

"Still fighting French?" she asked, tapping the open text on Kay's desk. Linda had memorized tomorrow's vocabulary at a glance and never had to struggle with translation and conjugation as did Kay.

"It's fighting me," Kay replied morosely. "English history, too. I don't think I'm going to crash out of here next spring, Lin. That'll just about kill my parents."

"Cheer up, baby. There's always cribbing."

Surely she was joking? Linda had the kind of sense of humor that laughed at complications and even frustrations, possibly because she had experienced so few of either. The daughter of a prominent Georgia banker, she lived in a lovely old antebellum mansion in Savannah. Visiting Linda was like visiting Scarlett O'Hara at Tara. Her mother, like that famous heroine's, was even of French descent; her name was Monette. Mrs. Fulbright was a graduate of Abbey Hall, a charming lady of impeccable manners, graceful movement, and soft voice. She looked young enough to be Linda's older sister, with the same luxuriant blue-black hair and exquisitely delicate features. Mr. Fulbright had iron-gray hair, a trim gray mustache, and well-manicured hands. Kay, judging from their home, servants, clothes, and cars, presumed they were millionaires.

"Fat chance," she said.

"Oh, it's been done, honey! There's no teacher with eyes in the back of her head, not even Miss Ferth, though I reckon her intuition is better than radar."

"Well, I'd rather flunk than try it."

Linda offered a pink satin-covered box she had brought along. "Candy? Mom sent me another batch yesterday. Real French bonbons. I'm sick of 'em. Besides, if I eat any more, my face will break out."

"No, thanks. I haven't finished my last box from home yet. Hey, I hear you got a bid to the Hitchfield Cadet Hop?"

"Umm," Linda nodded.

"Accepting?"

Her friend shrugged. "Only if the Maryland U and Navy game doesn't interfere. They're on the same day, I think, and I have a tentative date with this terrific college tackle, and he's more fun than the Hitch cadet. More mature, too, though they're the same age. Nineteen."

"I know what you mean," Kay said. "Chris seems older than his years, too."

She had confided her summer romance to Linda, including her parents' negative reaction and ultimate uptightness about it. Linda understood and sympathized, aware that her family would also object to her serious interest in any boy now.

"Did you write to Chris like I told you?"

"No, I was afraid he wouldn't answer."

"So you waste a stamp."

"More than that, Lin."

"Your precious pride would be hurt? Well, what's a little jolted vanity on the bumpy road of love?"

"He knows where I am," Kay said obstinately. "He could write to *me* if he cared."

"Maybe he thinks the same about you," Linda reasoned. "Or maybe he got the parental message same as you. The you're-too-young-for-that spiel. My mother sends me 'Dear Abby' clippings about teenage girls in trouble. And she once told me that breasts and menstruation don't necessarily mature a girl, any more than shaving and wearing an athletic support automatically transform a boy into a man."

Kay gazed down at the Quadrangle below the windows. The fountains were bathing the marble statues. But the deciduous trees were bare, the birdbaths empty. A couple of girls strolled there arm-in-arm, and apparently everyone but the faculty knew they were in love with each other. Kay had only suspected it, however, until Linda enlightened her.

"There go the Sapphos! I bet their folks are real happy they're not serious about boys yet."

"You think they're really lesbians, Lin?"

"Sure. They make out from four to six, in their rooms, while they're supposed to be studying."

"But there're no locks on the doors!"

"They shove furniture against them. I tried to visit Debbie once and found the barrier. Later I hinted at the truth, and she neither admitted nor denied it. Sort of silent assent. Who cares? To each his own."

"They could be expelled."

"If the brass knew—but who's going to tattle? Not me. They're brilliant students, you know. Lisa's all A's."

Kay frowned. "I don't understand it. What do they do, just kiss and pet?"

"A lot more than that," Linda grinned. "You mean you've never been approached by a dyke? A dreamy doll like you? Well, I have. One made a pass at me in the showers last year. She kept admiring my body, and then suddenly reached over and began groping me. I was so startled I slapped her face, like she was a fresh guy.''

"What did she do?"

"Smiled and shrugged, like a fresh guy who got slapped."

"Who was she?"

"A senior. Graduated last June. I hear she found an accommodating roomie at Smith."

"I feel sorry for them."

"Don't. It's their way—and perfectly natural and normal for them. They're not freaks, just different in their sexual preferences. Most of the girls are friendly with them, and so am I. Lisa's kind and gentle, and Debbie's very generous about sharing her hefty allowance. The spendthrifts are always borrowing from her, and some never repay. Debbie never asks for the money, nor refuses additional loans. You can't beat that kind of generosity and friendship."

Kay's mind wandered off that subject and onto one closer to her heart. "Linda . . . have you ever been . . . intimate with a boy?"

"How intimate?"

"You know, do it."

"Almost, but not quite."

"He didn't go inside you?"

"Only his finger," Linda reflected. "I wonder if Gidget lost her virtue to a male digit, or Tammy surrendered her plum to a thumb. It didn't hurt much, but the blood scared me and surprised him, because our hot petting made him doubt my virginity. I cried, he comforted me and said I was confused about my morals, I agreed, and it all seemed pretty damned silly. But still I wouldn't actually go all the way with him later, and so technically I'm still a virgin. You must have guessed by now he's the football hero?"

"Uh-huh. Maryland U or Naval Academy?"

"The first, and a psychology major. He says I have some Freudian hang-ups. 'What do women want?' he quotes Freud, and answers, 'Finger-fiddling, Herr Freud. That's all mine fräulein wants, anyway.' And maybe that's all most of us do want, Kay. Maybe that's how we think we can hang on to ourselves, by not giving guys what they really want. I don't know. It's just that Mother drummed chastity until marriage into my head, and no matter what my body craves, my mind forbids, 'No, no, Linda! Wait for the golden ring.' Which all too often is brass. Reckon there's any chance of Kinsey taking a survey at Abbey Hall?''

Kay expressed serious doubts of that, and asked, "What's doing in Rec Hall this evening?"

"Nothing exciting, you may be sure."

Entertainment was limited to games, educational films, lectures, selected music, and television programs—all subject to the nine-thirty curfew.

"Well, I have to study, anyway, in case we have a pop test tomorrow. Miss Fontaine loves to surprise us."

"Probably how she gets her kicks."

The chapel bell tolled, a lonely mournful sound echoing across the twilight campus, and Linda jumped up from the bed. "Oh, Christ! The Angelus already, and I'm not properly dressed. Another infraction of the 'holy rule,' and 'Mother Superior Ferth' will put me in a hair shirt and permanent penance. See you at sustenance, honeychile!"

The food was nourishing, prepared under the supervision of a competent but unimaginative dietician, and less than appetizing during emotional disturbances. Kay had not eaten heartily in months and was becoming thin and leggy as a new filly. Her mother had noticed this on one of her visits and bought her a huge bottle of vitamins and minerals, but they had not helped much. Now she was sending boxes of cookies and candy and other delicacies.

Miss Ferth sat at the head of the staff table, like Christ at the Last Supper, and no one dared leave the refectory without her permission. After the thanksgiving grace, she announced that two short films were being shown this evening, one on the French ballet, the other about the famous white Lipizzaner stallions of Vienna. Kay had seen both features before, enjoying the horses more than the dancers. She went to her room and tried to study, gave up, and lay in bed thinking of Christopher, finally dreaming of him—a passionately romantic dream that seemed amazingly realistic. She awoke trembling and clutching her pillow.

Somehow she fumbled through French the next morning, and in riding class she conceived an idea. Why not let Pegasus run away with her and head for Virginia? In her jodhpurs and jacket and little black derby, she could pass for someone going to a fox hunt, or left over from one. She discussed it with Linda that afternoon, but The Brain was skeptical.

"Miss Ferth would send out an immediate alarm, and the law would be hot on your trail. Hunting hounds could track you, along with helicopters and the National Guard. But even if you eluded a sheriff's posse, how could you convince the Gorgon that an expert rider like you couldn't control your mount?"

Kay sighed, deflated. "I didn't think of that."

Linda pondered the problem as if it were one in algebra and as easy for her to solve. "I've got it!" she cried triumphantly. "Next week is Thanksgiving, right? And we get a temporary parole, correct? Well, why don't you leave a few days early and catch a bus to Hitchfield

Academy?'' At Kay's puzzlement, Linda cautioned, "Don't tax the gray matter, honey. I have the perfect plan! I'm leaving Sunday and going through Washington. I'll send Miss Ferth a wire requesting an early dismissal for you and sign your mother's name. Ingenious?''

"Oh, yes," Kay breathed. "But *dangerous*! If it should backfire, we'd both be kicked out.''

"Think, girl, think! Who'd blow the whistle on us? Your Mom? Mine? Hardly!''

"Not likely, anyway.''

"Well, it's foolproof then, isn't it?''

"I guess so," Kay agreed. "Okay, it's a deal. I'll be waiting for the wire. And thanks a bunch, Lin. You're a true friend. A smart one, too.''

Linda grinned, winked. "Those are the best kind.''

"Oh, Linda, what would I do without you?''

"Stay out of trouble, probably. You won't goof this up, will you, Kay? Get scared, chicken out—and land us both in the frying pan?''

"No, I promise. Even if there's an unfortunate foul-up, heaven forbid, I'll keep your name out of it. I'd never rat on you, Lin. You know that. *Never*.''

"Just be careful," Linda cautioned, hugging her. "And have fun, baby. That's all I ask . . .''

The telegram was delivered signed as promised. Kay received the necessary permission from the headmistress, and immediately boarded a bus for Washington, since she could not travel any other route without arousing suspicion.

But she felt guilty and sneaky when the Greyhound pulled into the capital station and was tempted to go home. She had fine parents, why was she doing this to them, and to herself? Was Christopher worth it? Was anything in the whole world worth the way she felt sitting incognito in the bus depot, her eyes wary behind dark glasses, and the beaver collar of her coat turned up to shield her frightened face. She worried that something might go wrong, that some emergency might arise at home and make it necessary for her family to contact the school—and she would be exposed, disgraced, expelled. And for what? Chris may not even want to see her, may already have forgotten her, or wish he had never known her at all.

She bought a movie magazine and thumbed through it, her shaded eyes shifting on the incoming and departing passengers, fearful that an acquaintance might recognize her despite the disguise. She got a soda from the vending machine, but her hands were trembling so badly she could hardly hold or drink it and she put it aside.

Finally, the bus for Charlottesville, Virginia, was announced on the public speaker. Kay rose, clutching her ticket and small weekend case, and walked out of the waiting room to board with the other passengers.

Her throat tightened and her stomach churned nervously as the Greyhound crossed the Potomac and rolled westward into Virginia. Although no heavy snows had fallen yet this season, hard frosts had frozen the countryside. Dead leaves drifted across the highway, grassy meadows were strawy-brown, haystacks and corn shocks were weathering in the fields. The Blue Ridge Mountains, ablaze with the glory of Indian summer a month ago, were a dim misty bulk in the distance now, and only the pine forests were still green.

Charlottesville, in the foothills of that formidable barrier, loomed before the runaway girl like a gigantic truant officer. There was still time to reconsider, return home on the next bus, and no one but Linda and herself would be the wiser. Instead, she claimed her piece of luggage from the overhead rack and debarked with the others. Quickly, before more doubts plagued her, she engaged a taxi and gave the driver the name of a hotel she had seen advertised along the route.

28

It was a nice room in a good hotel, more expensive than Kay had expected, and she was glad she had accepted a loan from the always solvent and generous banker's daughter. "You might need some mad money, and I won't charge interest," Linda said, stuffing some bills into Kay's purse, "which is more than Daddy does for his friends."

But now that Kay was here, the thought of a rendezvous was somewhat terrifying. For one thing, she had no idea how to arrange it. She had only the knowledge gleaned from sexy novels, which were forbidden at Abbey Hall and had to be smuggled in like contraband, sanitary napkin boxes being a favorite and fairly safe cache, and passed furtively from room to room. In these exciting and romantic adventures, the hero was usually the aggressor, a mature sophisticated lover who took command of the situation without a hitch. When callow novices tried it, the result was often chaos, complications, and ultimate calamity.

But Linda said this was merely a moralistic warning to precocious adolescents and was not to be taken too seriously; she knew of several clever and ingenious Abbey Hall girls—and even one from a Catholic convent boarding school—who had managed clandestine meetings and matings without any undue obstacles or dire consequences.

Assuming that Christopher would be in class until three o'clock and would go immediately to his dorm afterwards, Kay allowed fifteen minutes before placing her call. The Hitchfield Academy operator transferred it to the appropriate building, where a boy answered and told her to hold on, and Kay almost panicked and hung up. At the sound of his voice she lost hers, and he repeated rather impatiently, in his crisp British accent, "Courtland here!"

Kay recovered and choked out, "Chris? It's me, Kay."

"Kay who?"

"Cranshaw," she murmured, crestfallen. If he couldn't recognize her voice or even remember her name . . .

"Oh. Hullo, Kay. How are you?"

"Fine. You?"

"Well enough."

"I'm glad."

"Where are you?"

"Here. Charlottesville. In a hotel."

"Alone?"

"Yes." With a sudden rush of courage, she added, "I came to see you, Chris. Will you meet me somewhere?"

He hesitated before replying, "I suppose so. Where?"

That was the question. And for several hours she had been trying to think of some place that wouldn't attract undue attention to a couple of kids. Suddenly she had an inspiration, so simple she wondered why it hadn't occurred to her before. "Monticello? We could pretend to be . . .

just tourists. I'll take a tour bus and meet you there, on the north terrace. Okay?"

Silence hummed on the line, and for a few suspenseful moments Kay feared he would refuse and almost wished he would. Then she could go home and forget the whole wild fantasy. But finally he agreed. "Okay. Better dress warmly. It's deucedly cold up there now, you know."

"I know, Chris. See you."

An hour later she was pacing the wooden promenade over President Thomas Jefferson's ice house, stables, and carriage house, trying to keep warm. Without a camera she did not look like a tourist but a lost, bewildered child afraid of not being found. If he stood her up, made a fool of her, she would simply die! Throw herself off the mountain, she thought dramatically, if she didn't freeze to death first.

Her previous visits to Monticello had been in the spring and summer, when the town in the valley below was a green and shady place, and once in October when the surrounding hills glowed with autumn brightness. Mr. Jefferson's beloved home had been the subject of an English composition titled, How I Spent My Summer Vacation, and subtitled, My Visit to Monticello. Similar themes were called, My Visit to Mount Vernon; My Visit to Yorktown; Appomattox; Jamestown; Williamsburg; Fredericksburg, et cetera. Later, she had used essentially the same material in American history, but luckily her teachers had never compared notes.

It was easy to understand why President Jefferson had loved Monticello, his "Little Mountain," and preferred the Italian pronunciation. Even in the bleakness of winter, the view was magnificent, encompassing scenery so absorbing that Kay almost forgot her chattering teeth and gloveless hands. He may have stood on this very spot, watching through a spyglass the construction of the University of Virginia, the white-columned, white-domed red brick rotunda of which bore his architectural trademark. But it was farther west that Kay gazed now, to a cluster of gray stone buildings in the red clay hills—Hitchfield Academy. Maybe there was some silly rule that prevented a cadet's leaving the premises? All sorts of strict rules governed Abbey Hall, and Linda said the locked gates were as much to keep the students in as trespassers out.

The numbness in her limbs was cold, but the ache in her breast was love, and no pain could equal it at sixteen. At times its severity incapacitated her physically and mentally and threatened to become fatal. If he would only be kind to her, she would be and do whatever he wanted. How else could she prove that she loved him?

Christopher saw her first, with her dark ponytail whipping in the wind, her mouth made petulant by too much lipstick, which she kept applying to prevent chapping.

"Hi," he said behind her.

She turned swiftly and, rigid with cold a moment ago, went suddenly limp. His smile, as cynical as ever and uniquely his own, touched her with a magic warmth, and she responded instantly, melting like wax under flame. "Hi, yourself."

"Let's walk."

The lawns and gardens were mostly dormant, only a few chrysanthemums still blooming in the borders, but the enchanted girl might have been strolling on the Schloss with the Student Prince, viewing the University of Heidelberg in the Odenwald Mountains, so handsome did the boy appear in his uniform of Confederate-gray twill with black braid and brass buttons polished like gold, and a black-visored cap worn at a rakish angle.

"Do your parents know you're here, Miss Cranshaw?"

"No, Cadet Courtland."

"You shouldn't have come, Kay."

Her heart missed a beat, her feet a step. "Aren't you glad to see me?"

"I think you're balmy, taking such a chance," he scolded. "You could get into trouble, at school and home."

"I don't care." She shrugged recklessly, thinking that this experience would be worth almost any kind of punishment, even expulsion. "Besides, I'm already in trouble at Abbey Hall. Bad grades. How're you doing at Hitchfield?"

"Hacking it," he replied in American slang.

"Don't be so modest. I bet you're somewhere near the top of your class?"

"Well, your schools are easier than ours."

"To a genius, maybe. I'm a moron. I'll never get out of Abbey Hall, much less college."

"You just don't keep your mind on your work."

"That's true," she admitted. "Shall we buy tickets and go through the house? It's warm inside."

"Too many people, don't you think? We can't talk while the guides are explaining things. Besides, I've already been through the house. I wanted to see what made Mr. Jefferson tick. You can learn a lot about a person from his home."

"What did you learn?"

"That he was a fine architect and fair inventor. He liked novelties—dumbwaiters, disappearing beds, folding chairs, and that odd clock in the entrance hall on which he goofed a bit. He also liked comfort and luxury. He kept slaves and horses and enjoyed good food and entertainment. But I think he honestly believed what he wrote in the Declaration of Independence and wanted it to succeed, so I suppose he was a truly great statesman and educator, and America was fortunate to have him on her side."

This was the most voluble offering of peace and detente that Kay had ever received from him, and she grasped at the olive branch, encouraged enough to slip her arm through his, only to be abruptly rebuffed for the gesture.

"Don't," he said, removing her hand. "This is not a lovers' lane. We do have one at Hitchfield, though. The cadets call it Flirtation Walk Junior, after the famous one at West Point, you know. There's a kissing rock, too."

"Do you spend much time there, Cadet Courtland?" Kay asked, both curious and jealous.

"I don't have much leisure time, Miss Cranshaw. Studies keep me busy, and Mr. Courtland comes on weekends." He still could not call the man Father. "He's coming tomorrow, in fact, to take me hunting over the holiday."

"Aren't you going home for Thanksgiving?"

He laughed. "That's an American custom, it means nothing to me. But Courtland said we'd shoot our own turkey, a wild one, and cook it at the hunting lodge."

"Is Aunt Carol going along?"

Christopher paused, peering at her. "Don't you know?"

"Know what?"

"The Courtlands are getting a divorce. Your father is handling it."

The news could not have shocked or saddened Kay more if she had heard it about her own parents. Why hadn't *she* been told? Did they think she was too young to understand such things? Still treating her like a child. Well, she'd show them. She'd show them good!

"Do you know the reason, Chris?"

"I think so," he nodded but did not volunteer more, and past experience had taught Kay that prying was useless.

They had circled the west lawn of Monticello and come to the Honeymoon Cottage. A door plaque stated that young Thomas Jefferson had brought his bride here by horseback in a blizzard in 1772. Kay thought this highly romantic, but Christopher said he was just eager and impatient, like any other bridegroom.

"Would you be anxious?" she inquired, abashed at her own audacity.

"You ought to know, after that wrestling at your pad."

"But nothing happened."

"Damned near, Kay. Damned near!"

"Is that why you stopped seeing me afterwards?"

After a long gaze at the faraway hills, he answered slowly, "Not exactly. That night I learnt that Aunt Agatha had died, and I couldn't go back to England. Courtland and I came to an understanding of sorts, and immediately the bloody Organization Man began planning my future in America. I didn't really want to go to school here, especially not to a military academy. But now I'm adopted and subject to the draft . . ." He paused, shaking his head ruefully.

"Gee, I never thought of that, Chris. As a citizen, you will have to serve, won't you? But you can get a college deferment for four years. And then if you go into the Peace Corps or National Guard, or get married . . ."

"I won't," he interrupted. "I'll probably just get the hell out of this country. Go to Canada, and then home."

"But America is your home now, Chris!"

"Not to me, Kay."

"Does Uncle Jeff know how you feel?"

"He should—he's not a fool."

"And Aunt Carol?"

"She *is* a fool! Leaving the way she did, virtually empty-handed, giving it all to me. I didn't expect that. I'll likely inherit a great fortune someday."

It hurt Kay when he talked this way; worried and frightened her, too. "Is money so important to you?"

A sardonic grin increased her fears. "Why not? Christopher Bentley, Poor Boy Bastard, is now Christopher Courtland, Rich Son and Heir. Legitimate at long last!"

"You just can't forget, can you?"

His cobalt eyes focused grimly on something in the distant Blue Ridge Mountains, remote and intangible to Kay. "No, I can't forget. Nor forgive."

"That's paranoid, Chris."

He smirked. "You don't even know what that word means."

"I do, too! I may not be a prodigy like you, but—"

"You're stupid," he cut in brutally. "What you've done today proves it. Who helped you in this, Kay? I doubt that your feeble mentality could conceive such a cunningly clever brain child without assistance."

Intimidated by the harsh criticism, and made wretched because of it, Kay confessed the conspiracy.

Christopher listened, shaking his head sadly. "You're growing up, baby. You're learning to lie and scheme and cheat, like the elder generation. You're an adult now, Miss Cranshaw. A stupid one, I'm afraid, but an adult."

Crushed, bewildered, Kay broke away and ran past the servants' quarters, the dairy, smokehouse, summer kitchen of Monticello, past the ingenious privy, which the guides sheepishly skimmed over, across the terraced walks, and out into the trees bordering the property. She stumbled and stubbed her toe and did not care if she tumbled off the mountain and rolled, broken and bleeding, into the valley below.

"Go away!" she cried when Christopher caught up with her, and turned away, trembling with cold and humiliation.

"I'm sorry," he apologized, somewhat breathless from

the chase. "But you know I'm right, Kay. Coming here wasn't the brightest thing in the world."

"Leave me alone!"

"Maybe you're not grown up, after all," he said. "You're certainly acting childish now. Don't you realize the bus is going to leave soon, and there won't be another today? You'll have to walk back to town."

"I'm sure that would bother you greatly."

"Yes, it would, Kay."

His hand lifted her sulking chin. Her lipstick was smeared, and he used his clean handkerchief to wipe her mouth. "Don't wear so much of that junk," he told her gently. "It looks cheap, and you're not."

As he stood gazing at her, smiling slightly, Kay swayed irresistibly toward him. He didn't speak, but she knew he felt as she did. Her head tipped back, her eyes closed, and he was the Student Prince again, kissing her on a high and windy hill. But it didn't last long enough, his kisses never did, and she clung to him desperately.

"Oh, Chris, what're we going to do?"

"Nothing," he muttered, releasing her. "Not here, anyway. People are watching." They were, too, and smiling.

"I know, darling." The endearment, secretly practiced, slipped out. She waited for him to take the initiative, make the decision, but apparently he was deferring to her. "Will I see you later? We could have dinner together. I noticed a nice restaurant near the hotel—"

"It'd have to be early," he said, consulting his watch. "Taps is at nine."

"Is there a bed check?" There was at Abbey Hall.

"Not actually. They just ask at the door. We use the honor system."

"Then you could get someone to cover for you?"

He looked at her, and she dropped her eyes in shame.

"Sorry. Mature thinking again."

"Why don't we go to that place and eat now?"

"Good idea," she agreed.

"Come on, then. The bus is boarding. Hurry!"

He took her hand and they ran out of the trees, laughing, but it was no longer carefree young laughter, nor indeed very happy.

They ordered the house specialty, baked ham with cherry sauce, and glazed sweet potatoes. Kay ate little and chattered much, her eyes appealing to him for help, a plan. He let her flounder, suffer alone.

"I don't know what to do," she said finally. "Where to go from here. I suppose we could sit in the Courthouse Square, but it's awfully cold. I think it's going to rain or snow and—oh, if only you weren't wearing that uniform! Everybody in town must know it's Hitchfield." She paused, swallowed painfully, and compromised herself. "Maybe if I went to the hotel alone, you could come later and just take the elevator or stairs to my room? The stairs might be better, because . . . do you think it would work?"

"I'm not sure, Kay."

"Well, do you want to try?"

"I guess so. If you do."

She nodded, unable to meet his gaze. "I'm not hungry anymore, Chris. I'll leave now. Have you enough to pay for the meal?"

"Plenty. Courtland is very generous with my allowance. Blood money," he added grimly.

"Room 420," she whispered, eyes downcast. "Knock softly, three times."

Still not facing him, she tried to walk sedately out of the restaurant, but her knees were trembling, her insides quivering. She hoped she would not collapse, or worse, throw up. The block to the hotel seemed a mile. Using the side entrance, she went straight to her room. She dropped the key in the corridor, found it, fumbled it in the lock, and almost panicked before the door opened. Inside she felt safer, but not safe. She hung her coat in the closet, then lowered the window shades and pulled the draperies together.

As usual when nervous she had to urinate frequently and had almost wet herself during the kiss at Monticello. Idiotically, she wondered if the occupants of the adjacent rooms could hear her flushing the toilet and washing her hands. Was that *her* face in the mirror above the lavatory? She looked like a terrified juvenile delinquent. Maybe that's what she was, and the house detective would burst into the room in the middle of her delinquency and haul them both off to the local police station, where they would have to wait in horrified shame until their parents arrived.

She removed the rubber band from her hair and let it fall free on her shoulders. Her casual clothes appalled her. No girl could be seductive in a Scotch-plaid skirt, fuzzy yellow sweater, and saddle-oxfords. Nor could the pink nylon pajamas and matching robe in her luggage be considered fascinating. There was nothing to drink, nothing to smoke, and it would be ridiculous to order Cokes or ginger ale from room service.

For some anxious minutes she wondered if she would get pregnant and wished she knew more about life and her own body. Her mother had discussed certain necessary aspects with her, and the school nurse had lectured the students on feminine hygiene, but the information seemed pitifully inadequate now. Linda said smart boys knew what to do, and Christopher was smart. But he was only seventeen and may not be able to purchase the things over a drugstore counter. If Christopher had to produce an identification card, he was sunk, for it was unlikely that he would have acquired a forged ID, as did some underage youths in order to purchase cigarettes and alcohol. Would it help to pray? Hardly. One could not expect God to answer such a prayer, be a willing accomplice to mortal sin.

Last year an Abbey Hall senior had been expelled for pregnancy in her final semester, and the scandal had fascinated the virgins for months. Laurie Bennington might have concealed her condition until graduation had she been clever or deceitful enough to report herself periodically indisposed. The physical ed instructress became suspicious and consulted the resident RN, who consulted the headmistress. At first Laurie denied the accusation. Then she took off on a horse, galloping and jumping the hurdles wildly, while shouting over her shoulder at Miss Ferth: "I am, so what, screw you! Screw Abbey Hall! Screw the whole goddamn system!" Naturally, such language would have caused her expulsion, even if she had been perfectly innocent of any other infractions. If nothing else, the dramatic incident had served as a grave warning to others so inclined.

Kay remembered it now, but it was not enough to deter her. She loved Christopher and was prepared to risk anything—pain, pregnancy, her reputation and entire future, to please him and prove her love. Her apprehensions were mostly curiosity now. Would it hurt terribly, would she bleed much? Neither her mother nor the family physician had delved into such details with her. Indeed, chastity was so strongly exhorted, advised, inculcated, she was afraid to experiment privately with her natural sexual instincts, or to use sanitary tampons for fear of rupturing her maidenhead. Was the male penis a "foreign object"? Christopher would have to teach her everything from scratch.

Time dragged, raced, dragged again. An hour passed, almost two. *Why didn't he come?*

Finally, the telephone rang. She leaped to answer it.

"Kay?" His voice sounded hoarse and distant, as if he was whispering in a tunnel.

"Yes! It's getting late, Chris. Where are you?"

"In a public phone booth and can't talk loudly or long. Don't wait for me, Kay. I'm not coming."

"Why not? Did something happen?"

"No, nothing. I'm all right. I just remembered, I have a Latin test tomorrow and have to study for it."

"Latin means more to you than—" She couldn't finish.

He cleared his throat twice. "Go home, Kay, as soon as possible. Don't mention this folly to anyone, and I won't, either. You hear?"

"I don't understand, Chris!" She was almost frantic. "I thought—are you saying you don't care? Is that what you're trying to tell me?"

"I'm trying to tell you to go home," he said roughly. "Is that so difficult to comprehend? Must I spell it out? I'll give you a couple of words not prominent in my Latin text: *virgo intactus*. That's what you are—that's your present, premarital condition. Understand?"

"No," she sniffed, fighting nausea.

She heard his heavy sigh. "I was afraid not. Kay—now, don't cry! Please?"

"I'm not crying," she quavered, half-retching. "Good-bye, Chris."

"Wait a minute, Kay! Listen to me—"

"Good-bye," she repeated and hung up.

Hurrying to the bathroom Kay sobbed through a seemingly endless urination, flushing the commode frequently so her immediate neighbors would suspect no more than kidney trouble. Where was it written that natural human bodily functions must be discreetly disguised and concealed even from transient strangers? Uninhibited Laurie

Bennington would probably have shouted "Piss on you!" through the walls. But she wasn't bold Laurie, she was timid Kay Cranshaw, with some Latin affliction called *virgo intactus* (a horrible contagious disease?), and Christopher didn't love or want her.

She washed her hands and face, dried her eyes, blew her nose. Then she called the desk clerk and asked to be awakened at six o'clock in the morning because she had to catch an early bus to Washington. "I want to rest now," she added. "No more calls, please." But she could not rest. She lay on the bed and continued to cry, no longer sure if the tears were from rejection or relief.

Part Four

It ever has been since time began,
And ever will be, till time lose breath,
That love is a mood—no more—to man,
And love to a woman is life or death.

Ella Wheeler Wilcox
(1855–1919)
Blind

29

Although she had dressed carefully, Carol knew she did not look her best for her engagement with Mark that evening. The cosmetic camouflage did not effectively conceal her darkly circled eyes, and while hollow cheeks might accentuate the glamour and sensuality of some women, they did nothing for her. Nor had her mother helped matters by saying that her hair needed a brightening rinse and her plain gray wool coat resembled a horse blanket.

But what hurt Carol most was that Mark had not told her recently that she was beautiful, nor tried to convince her that she was still young. In fact, a few times she had caught him observing her anxiously and treating her with exaggerated tenderness and compassion, as if she were a sick person. And he spoke less of retirement, more of the perilous international situation and the possibility of foreign duty. The Cuban Crisis, which had alarmed the nation for the past month, had apparently been resolved with the dismantling of the Soviet missile bases in Cuba, but Mark feared that another threat might develop elsewhere: Germany, Laos, Vietnam, or any of a dozen other potential trouble areas. He would not be surprised, he told Carol, to receive orders soon, and something in his tone made her wonder if he had not actually sought a transfer.

"What about the farm?" she asked.

"It may have to wait. Would you mind terribly?"

"I want you to do what you feel you should, Mark. If you don't think this is the time to retire, then don't. Of course I hope they won't send you to a hot spot—but, if so, I can wait. I've waited for a soldier before."

"Under different circumstances," he said. "He was your husband."

"You will be too, Mark. If we can't marry before you leave, we'll do it by proxy."

"You mean bigamy."

"Mark, I'm sure Jeff will sign the divorce papers when he returns from his hunting trip. Ken expects the case to go before a judge soon after Christmas. I told you that when I called you earlier at the Pentagon. We're supposed to be celebrating now."

But the charcoaled steak was burned, the sparkling Burgundy did not sparkle, and the combo band played so loudly they virtually had to shout across the table. The once sedate nightclub had become a popular discotheque, with weird wall murals and garish revolving lights, utterly devoid of romance, sentiment, relaxation—part of the new psychedelic craze and culture sweeping the country, the world. The dancers seemed to be in a perpetual frenzy, intense, resentful, and even violent about something of which they were only vaguely aware.

"Whatever happened to candlelight and string quartets?"

Mark mused. "That's the craziest goddamn music ever created, and surely that's not dancing?"

"It's the rage with youth," Carol said.

"Rage is right. They act furious, wild, possessed. If I twisted my torso like that, I'd need a chiropractic adjustment to straighten up again."

"It does look painful, doesn't it? Definitely not for the Geritol and Ben-Gay set." She sipped the flat wine. "I wonder if they're really enjoying themselves, or just pretending. Releasing hidden fears, angers, frustrations. Maybe it's only pretense, masquerade, and we're out of costume and character."

"Maybe," Mark agreed. "The drummer is high on dope and imitating Gene Krupa, and the singer thinks he's Elvis Presley. Let's get out of this mixed-up madhouse!"

Carol picked up her purse and gloves, thinking how drab and dull her sedate clothes must appear compared to the vividly colored and extreme fashions of the other women. She was eager to escape the clamor, the smoke, the wild, partially drunk cult, like alien creatures from another planet. Her poor head had begun to ache and her nerves to quiver.

Although there was no longer any need to avoid Mark's apartment, he did not suggest it, and Carol could not do so herself. Perhaps he thought she was having her period. Men, including husbands, could never remember a woman's menstrual calendar. Jeff had always been confused, even when she was counting days to ovulation and marking dates and temperatures on her chart, and invariably imagined she was ill when he saw the thermometer in her mouth. Moreover, he preferred spontaneous to planned sex and thought routine adversely affected performance and enjoyment. Possibly Mark felt the same way and did not want to make the obvious proposal now.

Miles ticked away on the speedometer, and they were on the road to Richmond when he said, "You need a vacation, Carol. A few weeks away from Alexandria. Some sun to tan that lily complexion. I think Florida is safe enough now that Khrushchev has removed the Russian missiles and bombers from Cuba, and Kennedy has lifted the naval quarantine. Why don't you jet down to Miami?"

"Alone?"

"Well, I don't think a premature honeymoon would be in your best interest, darling. Rest and sunshine would benefit you far more."

"Do I look so hideous, Mark?"

"Of course not. Just tired. And too pale."

"It hasn't been easy," she sighed, "for either of us."

"No, but it's almost over now, thank God. So don't try to analyze it, Carol, and fix guilt or innocence. Regard it as something that just happened, and try to believe it happened for the best and will turn out all right."

She smiled ruefully. "Have you ever known anything like this to turn out all right?"

"Divorce? Certainly. There are thousands of them every year, and most of the people involved go on to better, happier lives. Why shouldn't we?"

"No reason, I guess. Don't mind me, Mark. I'm like the Burgundy tonight, I'm afraid. Flat."

"Not *flat*," he teased, reaching for her. "But you have lost weight, honey, and that's why I think a nice quiet vacation would be good for you."

His concern exasperated her. "Mark, what is all this about my health? I've never been robust, but I'm not exactly sickly, either. And I resent being treated like an invalid."

"My God, I'm just concerned about you, that's all, Is that so strange? I love you, you know."

"Then what are we doing on the highway now? Why aren't we in bed together? Or do you think I'm not well enough for such strenuous activity?"

"I think you're hysterical," he said gently.

"Neurotic, you mean? Between you and Mother, I'm beginning to feel like a schizoid Camille."

"We can go to a motel if you think that's the answer, Carol. But it isn't. We're not celebrating anything tonight. This is a wake, for your dead marriage—and I don't want to cry in bed with you."

He was right, of course. She was grieving, mourning. She could not dismiss twenty years without a tear or thought, forget so much time with one man in a few minutes of sex with another. Mark was sensible enough to realize that.

She tightened his arm about her waist. "Sorry, dear. I guess I'm just not the 'gay divorcée' type. Severing the bond is painful, traumatic. It hurts."

"Because you still love him, Carol. No matter what he did, you still love him. Nothing between us has changed that. And you don't *really* want to marry me, do you?"

"Yes, I do, Mark! As soon as possible. Why don't we drive out to the farm again tomorrow?"

"To hell with that," he muttered. "I'll stay in the Army, be a thirty-year man, retire to the Old Soldiers Home in Washington. You can be a Red Cross Gray Lady and visit me sometimes. Bring me cookies, magazines, puzzles. Play honeymoon bridge with me . . ."

"Don't, Mark. Please."

"Sorry. I'm the maudlin one now. I just don't see how I could come so close to winning and still lose. But that seems to be the story of my life."

"You haven't lost, Mark."

"Haven't I?" Exiting onto a rural road, he finally parked in some farmer's lane. "It won't work for us, Carol. I was a fool to think it would."

"Is there someone else?"

"Oh, Christ! Why do women always think there has to be someone else?"

"Because there usually is," she said cogently.

"Not this time. At least not for me. The someone else is your husband, and it kills me to say it. Go back to him, Carol, before it's too late."

"It's already too late, Mark. The divorce is going through, whether you and I break up or not."

"That's foolish pride," he said, removing his arm. "You can patch it up."

"Patching is for clothes and plaster, Mark. This isn't just a torn dress or cracked wall. I walked out on Jeff and ran to you. I can't beg him to take me back, nor will I hold you to any marital promises."

"You think I'm trying to renege? You're wrong, Carol. But you're not a very good actress, and I think you were hoping all along that Jeff wouldn't let you divorce him. Ken's news this morning was a shock, wasn't it? Do you have any idea why Jeff suddenly decided to be so agreeable?"

"No," she murmured. "He just told Ken to get the legal documents ready for his signature and the case on the court docket in a hurry. Maybe he has a girl."

"There you go again."

"Well, he's still potent, Mark. Highly potent. I don't imagine he's been celibate while I've been with you. I'm not that naive. And it wouldn't be his first affair."

He touched her breast tentatively, then her thigh. "Still in the mood for a motel?"

"If you are."

"That wasn't the question."

"I don't know, Mark."

"Okay. Forget it."

"Now you're angry."

"No, at ease."

"How can you be at ease?"

He laughed shortly. "That's Army lingo for the male sexual syndrome. Advance, retreat. Attention, at ease. Up one minute, down the next, and it's one military member that doesn't rise on command."

"Oh, Mark—I've spoiled the evening, haven't I? I'm great at ruining special occasions. I seem to have a genuine talent for what used to be called SNAFU."

"Let it rest, Carol. Contrary to what women may think, sex isn't the only thing on the male mind. It's an important part of life, sure, but not everything." He lit a cigarette and sat smoking pensively, hands resting on the steering wheel, eyes gazing at the dark mountains lining the western horizon. "I bet winter's a bitch in the Shenandoah."

"But a beauty in spring," Carol said, "wearing a bright green dress and apple blossoms in her hair. Fertile and voluptuous and yearning to produce. Enchanting, Mark, and you'll love her once you get to know her."

"I'm afraid not, Carol. It's been my unhappy experience that Mother Nature is the most fickle of females, and a man is a fool to entrust his heart and future to her." He shook his head resolutely, as one who recognizes a vision, illusion, fantasy as no more than that. "What do I know about raising apples in Virginia? No more than I knew about raising wheat in Kansas. What do I know about anything but weapons and war? I'm a soldier, not a farmer. It was a dream, Carol, but I'm awake now. I know where I belong. And I hope, my dearest, that you know your place, too.''

Mark smoked silently and incessantly on the drive back to Alexandria. Carol, absorbed in her own deep, private thoughts, did not disturb his. At the door he embraced and held her, as if reluctant to let go, but his mouth kissed her hair and cheek instead of the lips she offered. No words of farewell were spoken, only good nights, yet the finality of the scene was unmistakable to Carol. There would be no tomorrows for them.

She lay awake most of the night thinking about it, unable to believe the end had come so easily. But perhaps it had been inherent in the beginning, the relationship having begun for all the wrong reasons. Mark had just realized it sooner than she and dealt with it more honestly and realistically. She would probably have gone through with the ceremony, vacillating all the way to the Shenandoah Valley, and fouling up his life even worse than Margie had. And her own even more than it was now.

But she did not need to tell her mother any of this. Margaret's uncanny perception sensed it at breakfast. ''So you finally came to your senses?''

''No, he did.''

''Intelligent man,'' Margaret remarked seriously. ''You should be grateful to him.''

''I am, Mother. But no postmortems, please.''

''Sometimes it helps to talk about it,'' the older woman encouraged, pouring coffee.

''Not this time, Mother.''

''Very well. What will you do now?''

Suddenly Carol wondered how she could have come this far without asking herself that same question. And what was the answer? Until last night she thought she knew. Now she shrugged, shaking her head.

"Well, I won't try to advise you, dear."

"Promise?"

"You wouldn't listen, anyway. But you know—"

"*Mother!*"

"Oh, all right! I'm due at the club at ten, and then I'll shop for Thanksgiving dinner. Should we have oyster or chestnut dressing? Pumpkin or apple pie?"

"It doesn't matter."

"Your food is getting cold."

"Go ahead, Mother. You'll be late."

Margaret hesitated, reluctant to leave her daughter in such obvious and gloomy bewilderment. "Why don't you dress and come along?"

"No, thanks. I wouldn't be good company. Besides, I have some thinking to do. Bye, Mom!"

The florist arrived as Margaret was leaving. Two dozen white roses. No card. But they could only be from Mark. He had a thing about white flowers. Fair ladies, marble pedestals, and white flowers. Was the gallant gesture a token of his esteem? Was he leaving the door open between them, or closing it forever? Puzzled, Carol put the roses in water, inhaling their lovely fragrance, and then wept.

30

The passenger beside Kay tried to initiate a conversation, but she was too absorbed in her private misery to respond. Her pride and propriety were in tatters, she felt cheap and common and was sure that Christopher now regarded her as he did that slut in the London slums. Was he feeling noble and superior now for not having taken advantage of the situation? She could never face him again and was certain that she never wanted to. But she had to face herself, and her family . . .

There was no place to go but home when she arrived in Washington, and Kay was not prepared to go there yet. She was not due for a couple of days, and her mother would think her premature arrival and red tear-swollen eyes indicated a cold or allergy and rush her off to the doctor for a shot or something. She sat in the bus terminal, the same confused and apprehensive girl in dark glasses and upturned coat-collar who had sat there twenty-four

298

hours ago, watching the clock on the wall until it seemed the phenomenon had at last occurred, and Time was indeed standing still.

What could she do, where could she go to idle away some hours? The theaters were not open yet, the parks were dangerous for a girl alone, and she had seen the capital sights too often to take another guided tour. A boat trip to Mount Vernon would occupy much of the day, but she lacked both the fare and inclination. Besides, she had to get her mind and emotions together, or she would go to pieces under maternal questioning, betray herself, and that would be her doom. Her parents might send her farther away to school, to New York or Boston. Maybe even to Switzerland or France—and with her French, that would be the worst kind of punishment and exile.

Oh, God, she had to go to the toilet again!

In the ladies lounge a girl about her own age was lying on the couch. She was shabbily dressed, with long stringy hair, and obviously pregnant. Had she spent the night there because she had no family or was afraid to face them in that condition? After a swift appraisal of Kay's appearance, she smiled slightly, lifted a languid hand, and murmured in a Brooklyn accent, "Hi."

"Hi."

"Got a cigarette?"

"No, I don't smoke."

"Lend me a dime for a Coke?"

"Sure." Kay gave her the coin.

"Thanks. It'll help settle my tummy. Have you ever been bombed?"

"Bombed?"

"Knocked up."

Kay blushed. "No."

"It's no fun, believe me. Especially when you're alone. My guy left me."

"Your husband?"

"No, just my boyfriend. We was sort of traveling around together. It's his kid inside me now. But the bastard just abandoned me last night, right here in this station, and caught a bus to Florida. Fort Lauderdale. I ain't got the dough to follow and can't walk or hitchhike."

"Call the police," Kay suggested. "They'll help you get back home."

"I can't go home," she said. "Not like this! I'll go to one of them places for unwed mothers."

"I'm sorry." Kay didn't know what else to say.

"Hey, don't use the free john! I puked in it. But you don't have to use free pots, do you? Not with that coat."

Sympathy for her overwhelmed Kay and inspired a sudden magnanimous gesture. "You want it?"

"You kidding?"

Kay removed the expensive garment, handed it to her. She had an extra sweater in her luggage, and she would tell her mother that she had lost the beaver-trimmed cashmere coat, left it somewhere.

The recipient's eyes filled, glistened. "You're the greatest, baby. God bless you."

Someone else came in then, and she was able to bum a smoke. Kay went about her business, thinking of something Johnny Carson had said about happiness being an empty bladder. The inspiration to go to Alexandria came while she was washing her hands. She counted her money. It was not enough to hire a taxi, but Kay was confident she could borrow the rest from the person she intended to visit.

*   *   *

Carol was resting on the chaise longue in her room, alone in the house except for the servant. She would have to find something to occupy herself. Money would not be an immediate problem, but leisure and boredom would. What did women like her do with themselves under the circumstances? Travel? Take up hobbies? Become perpetual club members chairing perennial committees and projects, like her mother? Try to launch a career?

Thousands of women worked for the government in various offices and agencies, but Carol could think of no position for which she qualified, either by experience or education. She had not finished college, or even taken a business course. She could not type, take shorthand, keep books, file. Furthermore, competitive examinations were required to even get one's name on the civil service lists. What could she put on the application blank? Twenty years of housewifery. Meticulous, neurotic homemaker, she thought ruefully. She could probably run the White House efficiently, but that post was already competently filled . . .

Her godchild's entry into her emotional wasteland was like rain on a desert, refreshing until she realized that a personal storm had brought her.

"Why, Kay, what are you doing here? Oh, darling, you didn't leave school without permission?"

"Not exactly," Kay stammered after the maid left. "I mean—Aunt Carol, can I talk to you?"

"Of course, dear."

Carol opened her arms maternally, and Kay ran to her and sat on the lounge sobbing out her story.

"I know it was wrong . . . a bad thing to do . . . but I couldn't help myself, Aunt Carol. I—I had to see Chris again. I couldn't sleep or study or hardly eat for thinking of him. Then a friend of mine got this idea how we could get together, like I told you. Oh, I don't know what to do now! Mother wouldn't understand . . ."

"I'm sure she would, Kay, if you explained it to her as you have to me."

"But what would she think? And Daddy?"

"That you've grown up," Carol said. "But more important, perhaps, that Christopher has grown up. And he must care for you deeply, Kay."

"He sent me away," she wept. "Would he have done that if he cared so much?"

"Yes, dear, I think that's exactly what he would have done." If only Mark had sent her away when she had flown to him on wings of hysteria! "In time you'll realize that, Kay. You'll understand what Chris did, and why, and appreciate how difficult it must have been for him."

Kay wiped her eyes with a tissue from the box Carol offered. "You've been crying too, haven't you?"

"Woman's lot," Carol nodded, "to cry over man."

"Chris told me about . . . about the divorce," Kay ventured. "Is it true, Aunt Carol?"

"It's true, Kay."

"Why didn't Mother tell me?"

"Maybe she thought it would upset you, or that you wouldn't understand."

"Adults always use that excuse when they don't want to explain to kids," Kay said, "or when they're afraid they might understand too well."

"Possibly she didn't want to disillusion you, then," Carol amended, "about love and marriage."

Kay toyed with her skirt, arranging the pleats precisely. "I guess I shouldn't ask what happened, but I think I should tell you that I know Uncle Jeff is Christopher's father. Chris has known a long time, and he feels simply terrible about it. Calls himself a—a bastard, which sounds dreadful because people use it like a dirty word. But it isn't really, is it? It's just a poor kid without a legal father, and there're lots of them in the world. But Chris acts like he's marked or something. Some kind of freak or outcast. He's so bitter and cynical about life and everything.''

''I think that's an act, Kay. That he takes refuge in cynicism, uses it as a shield to guard his true feelings. Boys his age hate to show emotion. It has to do with manhood, the masculine mystique. Girls can cry and be temperamental, but boys are taught in childhood that such behavior is sissified. They're supposed to be strong and brave and all that, you know.''

''But that's silly! They're as human as girls. Why must they pretend and act differently when life hurts or disappoints them? I don't believe God expects it.''

''No, just society. But that's how it is, Kay. Since Genesis men and women have been wearing certain labels and playing certain roles, and the male of the species seems to prefer it that way. There are periodic female rebellions, but the status quo doesn't change much.''

''And girls aren't supposed to chase boys,'' Kay said, sighing. ''Mother was certainly right about that. I should never have gone to Charlottesville.''

''Well, no harm done, Kay. Tell me—how is Christopher? Has he gained any weight?'' Her voice was as anxious and interested as a mother's inquiring about an estranged child.

''No, he's still very slim. But he looks fine, and ever so tall and handsome in his uniform.'' Her eyes gleamed with the mere memory.

Carol smiled. ''Most men do.''

''Major Lawrence looks good in his uniform, too,'' Kay said. ''And he's very nice. But I like Uncle Jeff better.''

''You know him better, dear.''

Kay hesitated slightly, reluctant to pry but curious to know. "Why did you leave him, Aunt Carol?"

Her godmother glanced at the gray November sky beyond the windows. "It seemed like the thing to do at the time, Kay. Like getting caught in a revolving door, you keep spinning until you reach an exit. Whether it's the right one doesn't seem to matter at the moment, just so you get out. When marriage goes into a spin, divorce is the usual exit. Not necessarily the right one in my case, as your father tried to tell me."

Her last words heartened Kay. "Daddy tried to keep you and Uncle Jeff together?"

"Oh, yes. But my pride and vanity were hurt, and I wouldn't listen. Now it's too late."

"Are you going to marry Major Lawrence?"

"I don't think so, dear."

"Then why is it too late?"

"To use an old cliché, I've reached the point of no return," Carol explained. "Now why don't you call your mother, Kay?"

"Will you speak to her first?" Then, quickly, "Never mind. If I was old enough to take the risks, I'm old enough to take the consequences."

"I don't think there'll be any consequences, Kay. Not serious ones, anyway." She paused, looking at the girl significantly. "Although you realize, of course, that there could have been?"

Kay nodded, pink to the roots of her ponytail. She would not soon forget the poor wretched abandoned creature in the bus station. Could *that* be why Christopher had sent her away? If anyone had reason to know about such consequences . . .

"Oh, Aunt Carol, I'm so glad Chris did what he did!

And Mom and Dad couldn't possibly be mad at him, could they?''

"Not possibly," Carol assured her.

Kay picked up the telephone, her face suddenly wreathed in smiles, brilliant in mature comprehension. I'll tell Mother the truth, she thought. About everything, including my coat . . .

31

On the long drive from the academy to the cabin, Christopher was quiet and pensive, thinking of Kay. Had she cried much when he had not come to her in the hotel? Did she finally understand his reasons? Not likely. Girls were notoriously dense about such things, and Kay was more naive than most her age. She probably considered herself a "scorned woman" now, and hated him as passionately as she might have loved him. And maybe he was a fool for not taking all he could get from any American. The trouble was, he cared for Kay Cranshaw more than he had wanted or expected to, and his life was difficult and complicated enough coping with Courtland without adding an emotional female.

The bloody bloke was trying hard to redeem himself, and the game of life would have been considerably easier to play if they were on the same team. But they were opponents, and this trek to the mountains would not change that. How many more defeats must the old sport experience before he realized it?

Although the rented Jeep was curtained against the cold, it still was not comfortably warm, and Christopher wished he had followed Courtland's advice to wear more practical clothing before leaving Charlottesville. But Nimrod was prepared with an assortment of coats, caps, boots, U.S. Army blankets, groceries, battery-powered radio, binoculars, and the weapons: two shotguns, two rifles with telescopic sights, and a veritable arsenal of ammunition.

And once again the awesome urge struck Christopher. He'd had it before, often enough to recognize it immediately: at target practice on the range and skeet shooting at Courtland's gun club; while practicing archery and fencing, traditional sports at Hitchfield Academy and in which Courtland had, and still, excelled and Christopher was fairly adept. A frightening sensation, this urge to kill, leaving him slightly giddy when it passed and apprehensive that one day it might not pass.

After crossing the Blue Ridge and leaving the main highway, the road became a twisting trail through a remote wilderness. Courtland explained that it had begun as an Indian path and eventually served pioneer scouts and explorers in the exhausting quest for a practical route across the Appalachian Mountains, which ranged over the eastern North American continent, from Quebec, Canada, to Alabama, and had forged a great natural barrier to potential settlers of both countries. Christopher replied that he had read about the Lewis and Clark expedition, the Cumberland Gap, the Missouri and Mississippi rivers, and was currently studying American history in school.

"I think you already know more about it than most of our natives," Jeff told him, "who get a somewhat distorted picture from Hollywood."

"You mean the cowboy and Indian cinemas?"

"Yes. Most are far from authentic. The American West wasn't really won that way. Not every pioneer man was a gunslinger. Naturally they knew how to shoot and fight, but homesteading was the principal goal and ambition of most of the families in the wagon trains that crossed the High Plains and the Great Divide of the Rocky Mountains. Whenever possible, they left the duels to the outlaws and the Indian battles to the Frontier Cavalry. The real progress came with the railroads."

"Your saccharine romances of the Old South are sort of synthetic and farfetched, too, aren't they? Slavery wasn't all that romantic."

"Hardly. Things usually seem more romantic in retrospect and sugar-coated nostalgia. The truth is, only a small percentage of antebellum aristocracy held slaves."

"And both your and Mrs. Courtland's ancestors were in that privileged minority, according to Mrs. Wilton. Planters with thousands of acres of land and hundreds of slaves. Wealthy, genteel First Family Virginians."

"Did she also tell you they were English?"

"She told me," he admitted grudgingly.

"The Courtland history is recorded at length in one of John Randolph's volumes in my library, Christopher. Read it sometime. You might be pleasantly surprised."

His lips curled cynically, for he was secretly familiar with the recommended passages. "Should I be proud that you're my father?"

"Not necessarily, Christopher. But you need not be too ashamed, either."

"What I'm ashamed of, sir, is how you became my sire."

"I've explained that to you, son, and it can't be undone now. Why not try to make the best of it? Look ahead to the future. Perhaps you noticed, when Kay Cranshaw was showing you Washington, what's written over the portals of the National Archives? *The Past Is Prologue.*"

"Americans like slogans, don't they? Every commercial product has one, and the promotions on the telly are really quite ludicrous. But I'm not so sure the slogans can be applied to people, or that they're words of wisdom to live by."

"I guess you hear a different drummer, Chris. Shall we drop it?" Another impasse, Jeff thought wearily, as the boy withdrew into one of his moody silences.

Scattered stands of pine, spruce, hemlock, showed green in the forests, but the bare gray skeletons of hardwoods predominated. There were jagged peaks and sheer gorges, rushing streams and foaming rapids, thickets abounding with game and other wildlife. A hunter's paradise and a hermit's refuge, and it did not fit Christopher's preferred image of Jeffrey Courtland as a bloody businessman interested only in success and the pleasures money could buy: country club membership and other class privileges, including a prestigious mansion and servants, fine clothes and cars, booze and broads.

There was no visible softness or slack about the man beside him now, in leather jacket and paratrooper boots, skillfully maneuvering the Jeep around hairpin bends and along precipitous rock ledges, alert to the potential dangers of a sudden landslide or unexpected animal. He looked lean and flint-hard, and for the first time Christopher was curious about what he had done in the war. His question brought a gratified glance from his father and a brief résumé of his participation in the European theater.

"Were you wounded?"

"Fortunately not."

"Afraid?"

"At times, yes. Every sane man is afraid at times, Chris. Especially in war."

"Decorated?"

"A few medals and citations. Yours, if you want them."

The offer offended Christopher, and he regretted asking. Discussing that war with Courtland was like walking over his mother's grave, which suddenly loomed large and naked in his mind. Had it sunk level yet and the grass effaced the raw earth? Was some kind volunteer pulling the weeds, or was maintenance of the Linton family plot in St. Andrew's Cemetery a community project like potter's field? Was the painted name on the wood cross still legible, or had the weather faded it into obscurity and anonymity? What had Courtland done about the monuments he had promised Anne and Aunt Agatha?

Anger and frustration fermented in him. The road here was chiseled into the shoulder of the mountain, and the vehicle hugged the curve under Courtland's competent control. But one swift pull of the wheels to the right would plunge them into the ravine—and almost certain death. The peace of deep dark eternal oblivion!

The demon of violence possessed him again, and he tried to exorcise it through conversation. "This is very rugged country. Reminds me of a film I once saw about the Scottish Highlands."

"I've never been to Scotland," Jeff said. "Would you like to go there, Chris? Next summer, perhaps. Take a long trip. We'll be alone then, you know."

"We're alone now," he murmured, gazing into the awesome, strangely beckoning chasm.

"I mean permanently alone, Chris. Mrs. Courtland is not coming back home. I'm sure you realize that?"

"Yes, sir."

This was another subject he did not like to discuss with

Courtland. He was taking the divorce as hard as death, and Christopher felt some guilt and responsibility. He had not thought Mrs. Courtland would react so drastically to the truth, and if she was happy believing her husband's lies, he should not have disillusioned her. She had not hurt him, why had he wanted to hurt her? And Kay. And, Mrs. Wilton. And why did he feel this fierce and terrible desire to destroy Courtland? Kay had called it paranoia, insisting that she knew the meaning, and maybe she was right. Maybe he was mentally and emotionally disturbed, and the worst mistake Courtland could make was to put a loaded gun in his hands . . .

"We could visit Ireland and England, too," Jeff continued. "You might like to see the Cotswolds again."

"The village?"

"Yes. I'd like your approval of the tombstones."

"You ordered them?"

"Of course. Through Mr. Tary. A white marble angel for Anne. That's what you wanted, isn't it?"

His throat tightened dryly; he swallowed to moisten it. One taut word issued: "Right."

"Well, it's done, Chris."

Not quite, the boy thought. *Not quite!*

"Has Mr. Tary sold the cottage yet?" he asked.

"I don't think so."

"I hope he never sells it."

"You miss Tilbury?"

"Sometimes. My dog, too." Had someone adopted Bounder, or was he still guarding the property and scavenging or begging the neighbors for food? Perhaps he had taken to the hills hunting for his master, or was keeping a vigil by the graves. He had heard of dogs doing that, and he knew from experience that they could be more faithful than people. Few animals of any species deserted their young, he thought bitterly, contemplating his father again.

"Would you like another dog, Christopher?"

Another bribe, Pops? I'm not a temperamental kid to be distracted by a new plaything!

"No, thanks. No pets allowed at Hitchfield, you know. I hear a cadet was expelled for stealing a white mouse from the laboratory, and another for smuggling in a hamster."

"I was thinking of a hunting hound, Chris. We could train him ourselves. Maybe a couple of them. A Labrador retriever for ducks and other waterfowl, a beagle for land birds. Think about it, anyway."

Jeff shifted into low gear to brake the motor down a steep grade, and finally the Jeep entered a long narrow valley virtually hidden in mountainous shadows. The cabin nestled there was the first sign of civilization that Christopher had seen in many miles, and it was something less than he had anticipated. Some old settler or hermit must have built it a century or more ago, and later died or moved on. Had Courtland inherited it? Surely it was not the kind of place a man of his position and taste would buy intentionally.

"Is this it?" he asked, hoping his reaction did not betray his disappointment.

A brief nod, a slight smile. "You expected something quite different, didn't you? Rather like a king's lodge on a royal preserve?"

"Rather," came the reluctant admittance. "You own it?"

"No, I have a long-term lease. An old moonshiner used to live here."

"Moonshiner?"

"Illegal whiskey-maker. His still is back in the hills.

The Treasury agents never did find him. He eventually moved to Roanoke, Virginia, where he now operates a legitimate liquor distributorship.''

"The place is well-hidden, all right. A real hideaway! How do you get out when it snows?''

"You don't. Not for a while, anyway. But that's the beauty of it. Bad weather on the mountains drives the game below for food and shelter. It's just a matter of being prepared with necessities of your own. I've been isolated here a few times—and enjoyed the peace and solitude. But it doesn't happen often and the ice thaws rapidly—the elevations are not high enough for perpetual snow. Give me a hand with the gear, and then we'll build a fire. You forage for your fuel and water here. No electricity, no gas, no telephone. This is truly God's country, and even the animals can get lost in it.''

Christopher did not doubt that. He had consciously tried to establish mental landmarks, roads and junctions and guideposts, but a scout with a map and compass would have difficulty navigating this territory. The whole experience was becoming a challenge, and he sensed that Courtland was aware of it. Wordlessly, with his arms full, Christopher followed him into the cabin.

There was one fairly large room, plus a lean-to kitchen. Sleeping quarters consisted of a pair of cots before the native stone fireplace. The ceiling was open-beamed, the log walls chinked with clay mortar. Because his wife had objected to dead, stuffed animals in their home, a few of his trophies were displayed here: a bearskin rug, several deer heads with magnificent racks, and a large black bass on a varnished plaque over the mantel. Books, magazines, pipes, were handy. Kerosene lamps, lanterns, candles, provided light, and the plumbing was an archaic outhouse.

"Better than a slit trench," Jeff said, gesturing toward

the leaning board structure with a crescent moon cut in the door, "which is the kind of sanitation the army uses in the field. Just watch for spiders and scorpions. You'll go through the roof if one hits your cock."

"Even an ant sting is no fun there," Christopher reflected. "One crawled up my pants when I was twelve, and I thought I'd die. The damn thing swelled up twice its size, and I couldn't touch it for a month, except to pee and even that hurt and burnt like hellfire. I almost began to believe Aunt Agatha's gospel about what she called 'that nasty habit' of youth and wondered if I was being punished for my sins."

Jeff laughed knowingly, remembering his own adolescence, and his grandmother's serious admonitions in that respect. Suffering none of the supposedly dire consequences and afflictions, however, he couldn't understand why something so enjoyable should be called self-abuse. Upon entering the academy at thirteen, he learned that most boys were given similar unheeded advice and warnings in puberty.

"How do you like Hitchfield, Chris?"

"I'm not exactly gung ho on it."

"Made any close friends yet?"

"Not real close."

"Not even your roomie?"

"He's a toad, with hang-ups about his acne and ears."

"What's wrong with his ears?"

"They'd make good jug handles."

"He can't help his looks, Chris."

"I know, but he smears all kinds of salves and lotions on his face at night and picks at his pimples almost constantly. It's disgusting! I advised him just to wash his skin twice daily and keep his grimy paws off it, but he won't listen. Most irksome, the frog considers himself a prince and super stud because he's got an expensive foreign carriage at home, souped up for drag racing, and he brags about his female conquests last summer. I hate that in a guy, and so do most of the other cadets. Rodney Landers will never win any popularity contests at Hitchfield."

"It's reprehensible," Jeff agreed, happy that Chris was opening up, "and probably more fiction than fact—an ego trip because he knows the truth is something less. There are always some fellows like that, at all ages. Just be glad he doesn't have adenoids and keep you awake half the night snoring like a bullfrog. That's what I had to contend with my first semester. All my efforts to get him transferred to another billet failed, until I complained that lack of sleep was affecting my studies. Use that excuse if this jerk's personal habits get on your nerves too much. But, believe me, you could get somebody worse. Know what I mean?"

"Yeah. I've been to London . . . and saw more than the Queen. Soho and Chelsea were enlightening experiences. I've also read some forbidden books."

"I don't suppose there's much I can teach you about sex, then?"

"No, we don't need one of those corny man-to-man talks," Christopher replied, and changed the subject. "Is there a larder in the lodge?"

"Pantry? Just the cupboard."

"I don't see any pump. How do we get water?"

"Carry it from the spring. It's not far away, you'll see the path. Go after a couple of pails. I'll get in some wood. May have to swing the ax."

"Any poisonous snakes around here?"

"Several, but they're in hibernation now. Watch your step, anyway. And put your boots and leather leggings on before you go. Better safe than sorry, and a wise man takes precautions."

Not always, Christopher thought wryly. You sure as hell didn't with my mother! Did the rubber shortage then affect the Yank condom ration, or didn't you care enough to even try to protect her?

He smirked. "An ounce of precaution is worth a pound of cure, eh? More of your American axioms!"

"Most of which originated in the United Kingdom," Jeff informed, handing him the galvanized buckets.

Hatred and resentment accompanied Christopher on the trail to the spring, which bubbled crystal-clear out of the base of a mountain. He recalled the time he, his mother, and Bounder had hiked to the source of the Thames in the Cotswolds and picnicked under the old tree with TH carved in the trunk. Sometimes it seemed as if he were two people in two different places at the same time. One of them longed for England while the other tried to adjust to America. Individuals and strangers to each other, often antagonistic and threatening to clash, and he wondered which person would ultimately triumph.

Returning with the water, he found his father building a fire in the relic cook-range left behind by the moonshiner.

"That's a fine spring," he commented. "Does it ever freeze solid?"

"Occasionally. Then you chip and melt the ice and drink real mountain dew. Hungry?"

"A trifle."

"How's the chow at school?"

"Fair. Southern style, mostly."

"Well, the chef was never cordon bleu when I went there, but the food was always palatable—though naturally we thought it was loaded with saltpeter. We'll have simple fare this evening, but if we kill our bird tomorrow, I'll show you I'm not such a bad cook. The first Thanksgiving was actually celebrated in Virginia, you know, although

New Englanders like to think they invented it, as they like to believe they made the first settlement. Of course, they know better on both scores, but it helps to preserve the traditional rivalry between the North and South.''

"I prefer roast goose to turkey," Christopher said. "I stole a goose once, a big fat gander, because we couldn't afford to buy one for Christmas."

Jeff flinched, laying bacon rashers in the frying pan. "I'm sorry, son. If I'd known, I'd have sent you a carload of geese. Were you punished?"

"Yes, and I didn't even enjoy eating the goose."

"I stole a watermelon from a neighbor's field once," Jeff recalled. "I wasn't hungry, and we had our own patch on the plantation, so I don't know why I snatched that melon. But I didn't enjoy it much, either. Matter of fact, I've never cared much for watermelon since."

"Were you punished?"

"Not corporally. My grandmother was too fond of me, and my father was too busy punishing himself. Someday I'll tell you about your paternal grandfather."

"Lord of the manor and all that?"

"Well, he lived like one," Jeff said, as the bacon sizzled in the skillet. "Damned near broke the family."

"Wastrel, eh? How did he punish himself?"

"Booze, mostly. Trying to forget something. He finally succeeded—in death. Ruptured liver."

"That's the hard way," Christopher murmured, thinking of his mother's even harder way out, and retreating into himself again.

The rapport was suddenly gone, and Jeff knew it. He concentrated on fixing supper while Christopher set the table with plastic dishes and paper napkins, a far cry from the china and linen they used at home. Crisp bacon and scrambled eggs, baked beans from a can, fresh fruit and nuts for dessert, also vastly different from the fancy food served in the mansion.

Later, after the kitchen was cleaned, they sat on the cots before the fire, Jeff smoking a pipe, Christopher cracking English walnuts.

"Where's the best place to hunt turkey, sir?"

"Around their feeding grounds. They like nuts and berries and seeds. But they're wary, wily birds, given to roaming the ridges, difficult to stalk and even more difficult to kill."

"Can't you call them?"

"Only if you know their language and 'talking turkey' is exactly that. If you don't speak it, better keep quiet. Is your shotgun ready? Did you clean and oil it after that last skeet shoot?"

"Thoroughly, the way we have to do our weapons at school. May I take my rifle along too, in case I see a deer?"

"If you wish, Chris—though I've found it best to concentrate on one quarry at a time."

There was a significant tone in his voice, almost an insinuation, which his son deciphered merely as paternal advice. He rested a foot on the head of the bearskin rug before the hearth. "Where'd you bag this brute?"

"A few feet from the back door. He got hungry and reckless and came calling. Not many bears around here anymore, however. More in the Smoky Mountains of Tennessee and the Dismal Swamp down near North Carolina. Plenty of deer in the Blue Ridge, though. Great specimens, like those mounts on the walls."

"Do we hunt together or alone?"

"Either way. I brought plenty of shells, to allow for misses." Another significant pause. "Even the sharpest shooter occasionally flubs, you know."

"Uh-huh."

Jeff smoked in silence for a while, one hand cupping the bowl of the well-seasoned, imported British briar pipe. The moon had not yet risen, and the windows were still dark, shadeless rectangles. A hard wind was blowing off the mountains, shrill as a screaming woman.

"The wind sounds like that in the Cotswolds sometimes," Christopher reflected. "Eerie, haunting. Aunt Agatha called it a banshee wail."

"Was she Irish?"

"Part. And very superstitious. She claimed when a wind made such noise, or a dog howled mournfully, it meant someone was going to die."

"Someone is always dying somewhere sometime," Jeff told him. "But I don't believe screeching winds or howling dogs have anything supernatural to do with death." He paused thoughtfully, to organize his next words. "I may not have time to tell you this tomorrow, Christopher—or may forget it—so I'll do it now. If anything should happen to me, don't panic and lose your head. If you need help, follow the Jeep tracks to the main road. Blue Rock Junction is exactly five miles from here, and there's a telephone at the general store."

Christopher tensed, fearing his mind was transparent. "What could happen, sir?"

"An accident, perhaps. Hunters have accidents, you know. Every season other hunters are mistaken for prey. A red cap in a tree appears to be a gobbler, a gray or brown jacket resembles a deer, or God knows what in the woods. People are shot, wounded, even killed, accidentally." Another long, weighty pause and narrowed eyes peering through the cloud of tobacco smoke. "Of course, it's not always an accident. Sometimes it's murder, but difficult to prove. The moral is, never go hunting with your enemies. And even good friends can't always be trusted not to err, or get trigger-happy.''

"I suppose not," Christopher concurred, his voice taut as a bowstring. "You think there might be other hunters up here?"

"Possibly." Jeff puffed his pipe, gazing pensively into the orange-red flames. "Natives, poachers. Just remember what I said about finding your way out. And call Mr. Cranshaw. He'd know what to do."

"About what, sir?"

"About everything, Chris. Everything."

As if by sorcery the weird, evil obsession returned, projecting macabre images on the screen of memory: a child building a gibbet with an American-made erector set, ceremoniously hanging a tiny wax effigy and then melting it by blaze into an unrecognizable blob; a lad shooting arrows and throwing rocks at a nameless target; a desperate youth once beating a bramble bush to pulp in a helpless rage; and more recently, an angry young chap exploding clay pigeons bearing the now recognizable countenance. A shiver chased along his spine, radiating to his right arm and finally down to his trigger finger. That itch again, that insidious itch! Unconsciously, he scratched it.

"You have a premonition, sir?"

Jeff rose to stir the coals and add another log. "Let's just say I'm aware of the potential dangers."

Moments passed during which the ticking of the alarm clock sounded loud, harsh, prophetic to the boy unable to control his own racing heart. Was time running out for both of them? Tossing the nutshells into the fiery crucible of the hearth, he stretched out on the cot and pulled the surplus U.S. Army blanket up to his chin. "Think I'll turn in now, sir. Good night."

"Good night, son. Sleep well."

Christopher did not close his eyes immediately but lay watching the elfin shadows on the crude ceiling beams, so like the naked rafters in the garret of the Cotswold cottage, where his poor mother had hanged herself.

32

The fire kept the cabin cozy through the night and was blazing brightly when Courtland woke him before dawn. Breakfast was already on the table, and nothing had ever smelled or tasted better to Christopher than the ham and eggs, biscuits, and hot coffee.

Anticipation of the hunt excited him, honed his senses to a keen and quivering edge. But the man across the table appeared quite calm and somewhat preoccupied. In the yellow lamplight his unshaven face showed a shadow of heavy beard, some silver bristles mingled with the dark. There was more gray at his temples than Christopher had realized too, and deeper facial lines. Had he lost sleep, quaffed a few drinks during the night from his supply in the Jeep? No, his eyes were not bloodshot, nor his hands unsteady. Still, he bore no resemblance to the suave, white-dinner-jacketed host or distinguished, briefcase-carrying broker. He might have been a native mountaineer or woodsman, hard-bitten and tough as his leather boots. Aware of his weaponry skill and hunting prowess, Christopher knew he would have much ado to match wits, guts, or shots with him.

Frost glazed the landscape, glistening on the evergreens, etching the bare gray hardwoods like steel engravings against the pale morning sky. Christopher had never known a sharper, more penetrating cold and was glad he had worn the long thermal underwear and hunting togs Courtland had brought along for him.

They walked together without speaking, pausing every fifty feet or so to scan the area with binoculars. Now and then a gravel-throated tom turkey gobbled like a barking dog and was answered by the lighter warble of a hen. They came upon the tracks of a small flock. Jeff pointed to them, Christopher nodded, and they eased their steps on the frozen leaves and twigs, their steaming breaths mingling.

"How much farther?" the boy whispered during another pause for reconnaissance.

"Not much," Jeff murmured. "But I think we're too late for the first spot I had in mind."

Reaching it, they saw that the turkeys had already been there, feasting on the beechnuts and dogwood berries, roosting temporarily in the trees, their moist droppings and lost feathers betraying them. Not much food remained, but enough possibly to entice the greedy and the stragglers to return.

"What now, sir?"

"Well, I'll wait here for a while. Why don't you take up another post? That stand of maples to the left is a likely spot."

"I'd rather try for a deer," Christopher decided.

"Leave your shotgun here, then. And remember, males only. Make sure he has horns before you shoot. Game wardens are scarce in this territory, but it's the principle of the thing.''

"The honor system, eh? Like Hitchfield.''

"Sportsmanship, too,'' Jeff said. "Good luck, son.''

"You too, sir,'' Christopher mumbled and left.

His eyes searched for deer tracks, but the accumulated mulch of centuries did not easily retain hoof imprints. The grove of maples Courtland had suggested was a thin one affording insufficient camouflage, and forest scavengers had already combed the fallen red leaves for the edible berries. He chose a copse of bronzed oaks instead and hoped a lone stag would come foraging for acorns. Stationing himself sentrylike with ready rifle, he raised the binoculars.

The land he surveyed was a vast pristine wilderness apparently little changed since creation. The American Appalachians made the Cotswold Hills seem like knolls, and yet he knew there were far greater ranges, some permanently snow-clad, in the western part of the country. The Canadian Rockies, the Grand Tetons, the Sierra Nevada, the Cascades—he had read about these in his American geography. They harbored larger, wilier, and more dangerous game, too: moose, elk, big horn sheep, cougars, fierce grizzly bears. Last night Courtland had said that they might go hunting "out West" when he finished college, and Christopher had mentioned the draft.

"If you take ROTC—Reserve Officers Training Corps—at Washington and Lee University, you'll graduate with a commission. Second lieutenant.''

"What if I don't want to serve this country?''

"As a citizen you'll be obligated, Chris, in one of the services. It's the law. That's why I wanted you to go to a military academy.''

"You have some stupid laws here, and you're always getting into wars somewhere."

"If I recall my world history accurately, Britain has been involved in some international conflicts herself. And a couple of times she was probably damned glad of our 'stupid laws' and penchant for meddling in other people's wars—and somehow ending up fighting and dying in them to save other nations' hides. Paying for them, too. And, incidentally, winning most of them."

"Oh, sure. There wouldn't be an England anymore if it weren't for the rich, powerful, almighty Yanks," Christopher jeered cynically. "They did a lot for the Empire, including increasing the population!"

The argument had ended there, abruptly, with Christopher striking the coup d'etat.

Now he focused the glasses on Courtland, his father and foe, and his heart began to thud fiercely. He could feel his pulse beating drumlike in his ears, vibrating in his skull. He stared, fascinated, almost hypnotized, and time seemed to recede. He was a kid again, seven or eight, wishing he had a daddy to show him how to do things, how to make a kite from sticks and newspaper and string, a sailboat out of a sardine can, a motor car from a block of wood. Then he was ten and learning to do things alone, assuring himself that he had no need of a father, that he was the kind of confident, self-sufficient chap who could get along just fine without an old man. Next he was twelve and stalking a faceless enemy, destroying him in dreams and fantasies. And then he was sixteen and at a Piccadilly shooting gallery, firing at steel ducks whose billed heads became visored American Army caps . . .

Courtland stood in a clearing, motionless as a statue, a perfect target in his bright red jacket. "If anything should happen to me . . . hunters have accidents . . . of course, it's not always an accident . . . sometimes it's murder, but difficult to prove . . . let's just say I'm aware of the potential dangers . . . don't panic and lose your head . . . follow the Jeep tracks to the main road . . . and call Mr. Cranshaw . . . he'd know what to do . . . about everything . . . everything . . .'' Courtland had spoken those words himself, preparing him for any eventuality. Preparing himself, perhaps, as well?

The cold was bone-chilling. Christopher blew on his hands to warm them and forgetfully stamped his half-frozen feet. Several grouse exploded with a frightening flutter from a nearby bush, and he thought Courtland might fire at them but he did not. A disturbed rabbit scurried for its burrow, and a mother possum waddled by with her young on her back. The distractions unnerved Christopher. His hands trembled so much he could hardly hold the rifle. He rested the barrel in a tree-fork and trained the scope on Courtland, lining him up in the cross hairs, steady now as a transit. The Winchester was loaded, cocked, he had only to squeeze the trigger . . .

Why was the fool standing out in the open? He knew better! A half-blind turkey could spot him. What was wrong with him, anyway? He did some peculiar things lately. Like the time they were practicing archery with steel-tipped arrows, and Courtland stood before the target and called, ''Could you hit the bull's eye from here?'' And though Christopher was no Robin Hood or William Tell, he could scarcely have missed from that distance. And the other time, when they were fencing with genuine swords, not foils, and Courtland deliberately dropped his guard, and Christopher could easily have thrust his own blade into the red-felt heart on the white twill uniform. And now the bloke was exposing himself even more recklessly and perplexingly, poised there with his whole chest a red bull's eye, a bleeding heart . . .

His muscles twitched and tightened. Painful cramps surged through his belly and bowels. If it wasn't visceral fear, he was getting dysentery. Soon he was dizzy, belching bile, and had to urinate. Jesus, he was going to be sick!

He placed the rifle on the ground and leaned his spinning head against the oak, hoping the wretched sensations would pass. But they only increased, and he knew he would have to vomit. Dropping to his knees, he retched as if to expel his guts, and prayed that Courtland would not hear him. As the nausea abated, his bloated bladder leaked down his legs, stinging hot urine at first, then clammy cold, and he held his buttocks together manually to prevent an even worse seepage.

Afterwards, while he was cleaning his face, the report of a shotgun startled him. Courtland must have found his prey. Another blast, closer, rumbled like thunder through the valley, echoing across the hills. Then he heard approaching footsteps, light and stealthy earlier this morning, heavy and obvious now. Rising rapidly to his feet, Christopher kicked debris over the vomitus, picked up his cap and set it on his head. Courtland must not see him in this sorry state, must not suspect the insane treachery he had contemplated, nor the horrified terror that had tortured him in his moment of truth.

His father walked up smiling, smoking a cigarette. "How're you doing, son?"

"No luck," he murmured with averted eyes. "You?"

"Missed," Jeff drawled, nonchalantly flicking ash on the ground and grinding it with his boot. "Those birds will run for a mile or more now. Probably won't have another crack at them today. We might as well go back to the cabin and brew some java."

"You go ahead, sir. I'll be along later. I—I might still see a deer."

"Not after those shots, Chris. Every wild creature within hearing took cover." A long intent pause. "I'm sorry if I spoiled your hunting, son."

Christopher thought he would be ill again, certain now that Courtland knew. Possibly he had watched through his own binoculars his convulsion of cowardice, and the shots had not been misses at any kind of game but signals to organize himself, save face and honor. What kind of man was this, his father?

"I'd like to wait a bit longer, anyway, sir."

"Sure, son. But don't stand too still, move about some. You'll freeze otherwise."

"I wet my pants," he admitted unexpectedly, afraid the evidence was visible.

"Next time don't wait so long, although I know it's hard to pull out when you think it might turn into an icicle. Well, come on when you're ready, Chris."

"Yes, sir."

An hour later, he was ready. He rose from the ground where he had sat yogilike, nearly stiff with cold, wishing his clothes would dry. But they were still damp when he walked shivering into the cabin, racked his rifle, and went quickly to the fire.

Jeff handed him a mug of steaming coffee. "The hunter's home from the hill."

"Empty-handed."

"There's always tomorrow."

"Guess we won't have turkey, though."

"Oh, maybe we'll both have better luck next time."

Christopher gazed at him intently. "You know, don't you." It was a statement, not a question.

Jeff nodded, reluctantly.

"And yet you stood there, tempting me!" Christopher accused angrily. *"Why?"*

Jeff answered slowly, choosing his words carefully: they must make an impression but not a scar. "Because I knew it wasn't the first time that thought had crossed your mind, Christopher. It was one of the reasons I brought you out here, in fact, and mentioned what I did about accidents. To give you the opportunity. You see, I had to know if you hated me enough to kill me. And if you did—well, the way things are now," he shrugged, "I'd as soon be dead. You'd have done me a favor, actually. I mean, if there wasn't even you to live for . . . But you couldn't do it, could you? You just couldn't pull the trigger when you had me in your telescopic sight and couldn't possibly have missed. You're not a killer, Chris, and you couldn't murder anyone. That's the important thing, son, and all that matters—really matters—to me now. I guess you don't hate me so much, after all."

"Maybe I'm just a coward," Christopher surmised. "And I thought *you* were. But I was wrong about you."

"You're wrong about yourself, too. You couldn't stand here telling me this if you were a coward, Chris. But we don't have to analyze it now. We don't have to discuss it at all ever again."

It seemed incredible to the boy that there should be no parental recriminations, no reprisals. Treachery such as he had harbored—indeed, patricide!—should be punished. A beating was the least he deserved. He knew Courtland could thrash him severely and thought he would feel better if he did. No man had ever laid a hand on him in anger or discipline, and there had been times during childhood when he had rather envied naughty and incorrigible lads whose fathers cared enough to chastise them.

"Don't patronize me," he bristled. "And don't be kind

to me, either. That's the same as saying you're strong and I'm weak. I think we should fight this out, sir. Go outside and have at it!''

"You've been seeing too many of our TV westerns," Jeff temporized. "Violence is not the answer, Christopher. But if you think so, if you imagine it's the only way to clear the air and settle this thing between us, we can go out and beat up on each other. But I warn you, boy, I won't let you win. I'll bloody your nose, blacken your eyes, and break every bone in your body if that's what it takes to break your hostility—and make you realize, you obstinate, arrogant young fool, that I love you!''

"Like a son?"

"*As* a son! Because that, too, is an unalterable fact. I'm your father, I'll always be your father, and you'll always be my son. I just wish you were as proud and happy about it as I am, Christopher.''

Christopher stood irresolutely, measuring his father skeptically. Then in a swift, almost violent motion he turned away, toward the wall, beating his fists on it, hammering his humiliation, frustration, despair like pegs into the wood, until there was nothing left but adolescent emotions against which he had no defense and no release except the natural one. And at seventeen, tears were the greatest pain and mortification of all he had suffered that miserable day, including the abominable accident with his bladder.

Putting his arms around the heaving young shoulders, Jeff waited apprehensively for the remembered revulsion, resentment, rejection. They did not come, not perceptibly, possibly not at all. "They say men are like bricks, Chris, worthless until they've been through fire: the human crucible. We've been through it, son, in different forms and degrees, but we've been through fire, you and I, and should be tempered, stronger, better men for it.''

Christopher knew he must say the words, the meaning-less words which meant nothing and everything, not be-cause they were expected or demanded, but because they might serve to establish some genuine empathy and effec-tive communication. "I—I'm sorry, sir. Truly sorry. And glad, when it came to the nitty-gritty, I failed the test."

"But you *didn't* fail, Chris. If you had we wouldn't be here like this now, would we?"

"Oh, God," he murmured, shuddering in horror of what might have happened.

"It's all right," Jeff comforted him, and for the first time in their life together he felt that it really was all right between them. "Forget it, son. Just forget it."

"Can you forget it?"

"I already have," Jeff assured him, not quite truthfully, for the enormity of the entire situation could not just miraculously disappear without any emotional residue for either of them. But he was confident that it would, eventually.

At that precise moment a wild racket came from the forest, a din such as Christopher had never heard before. Startled, he gazed anxiously at his father.

Certain of the source, Jeff urged, "Come outside, Chris! You'll want to see this!"

"What is it?" he asked excitedly. "Bears?"

"No. A buck fight."

Grabbing rifles, they rushed outside and soon located the arena, a clearing in the brush some fifty yards away. The principals were two white-tail deer, the challenger weighing in at a vigorous two hundred or so pounds, the defender older by several years and heavier by perhaps fifty pounds, a battle-scarred veteran. Both were handsome animals, unquestionably male, with strong, sharp, deadly antlers. They had already engaged in a preliminary bout, each testing the other's mettle and potential and apparently confident that each had the advantage. It was the height of the rutting season, and the prize was five does, the present property of the older stag, all stashed at a safe distance from the battleground.

Now they were measuring each other again, snorting, pawing, bluffing in the hope of avoiding actual physical conflict. Then, evidently convinced there was no alternative and no honor but attack, they retreated some twenty feet and charged head-on. The fierce impact upset the lighter buck's balance momentarily. He wavered precariously. Then, infuriated by the affront to his dignity, he made a swift and agile recovery, asserting his youth and vigor, managing to gore his opponent violently enough to inflict another permanent scar.

Fascinated, eyes riveted on the scene, Christopher asked, "What're they fighting about?"

"What males usually fight about," Jeff replied. "Females. The young one wants the old one's harem, and he obviously isn't ready to surrender it."

The sparring and testing were over. The animals were fighting in earnest now, locked in mortal combat, victory or death. The fury of their clashing antlers rattled and reverberated in the forest, and their rutty odors befouled the air. Wounds opened, blood ran. The does watched passively, fickle creatures chewing their cuds, ready to welcome the winner whichever he might be.

"We could kill them both at this range, sir."

"That wouldn't be cricket, would it? They've got their horns full, literally."

"You're right, sir, and cleverly put. It's a bloody good battle. I'll bet on the young stag."

"I'll take the senior. He has more at stake, more experience, too. That pays off in combat."

The deer were in a savage frenzy, twisting and turning in an effort to free their tangled racks. Finally they succeeded and separated, only to retreat and charge again. The challenger was swifter, sturdier, but being defeated by his eagerness and impatience. The defender, champion by virtue of possession, was cautiously complacent, determined, waiting for the marauder to drop his guard. Inevitably, he did, and the old master moved in for the kill, thrusting the sharpest points of his weapon into the enemy's throat and shoulder, goring for the vital heart. The youngster went down with an anguished cry, hide and flesh torn, hot blood spurting. The victor hovered over him a few triumphant moments, winded, nostrils flaring, eyes blazing, trying to decide whether or not to finish him off completely, granting him conditional reprieve, then moving warily off to join the does and herd them deeper into the woods.

"Whew!" Christopher blew a long, deep sigh. "What a show! You won, sir. The young one was just too anxious, I guess. Think he'll die of his injuries?"

"No, but he'll have learned from them. His pride and maleness are hurt most now. He'll lick his wounds and retire to fight another time . . . and perhaps win."

"Why doesn't he get up?"

"Battle fatigue."

33

The analogy of the atavistic contest between youth and age, maturity and immaturity, wisdom and inexperience, preoccupied Christopher on the silent stroll back to the cabin. He was much like his rambunctious counterpart, reckless and defiant, full of self-importance and ambition, trying the patience and compassion of his elders. Indeed, that wild young buck may have been the son of the older, wiser one! He had to be defeated in his brash challenge, had to be taught some valuable, lasting lessons.

Inside the shelter again, Jeff made more coffee, which Christopher was beginning to like as much as tea, and they relaxed before the hearth, legs stretched out, warmed and braced by the strong black brew. Still excited by the deer fight, the boy was unable to talk or even think much about anything else. At his request, Jeff related other wilderness confrontations he had witnessed: bears, wolves, bobcats, alligators in the Dismal Swamp, whose ferocious roars and tail thrashings could be heard for miles.

Filling the bowl of his favorite briar from a foil pouch of tobacco, he said, "Sometimes they fight over food or territory, but more often over the female of the species, indicating that the mating instinct is greater and more inherent than any other. It's born in the beast, man included—which explains why some of us behave like primitive animals, more or less, on occasion. It's been that way since creation and will go on to eternity. Nature must be served."

"So it seems. What's the bloodiest animal battle you've ever seen? Do they actually kill each other sometimes?"

"Only rarely, when one or the other is too stubborn to surrender or retreat. Most seem to have sense enough to quit before their wounds are fatal—unless they're literally mad. That's where they differ from their human counterparts, who often continue fighting until death, annihilation, utter destruction. Whether it's a domestic quarrel between families, or war between nations, people seem to lack the intelligence or sanity to end it before total disaster. And because they can't keep their wits, they lose their lives, loves, homes, governments, countries."

"Doesn't that make man inferior to animal?"

"Well, it's certainly a grave indictment against so-called superior humanity," Jeff mused, tamping and lighting the pipe. "We're all guilty of gross violations in that respect, and God knows I've committed my share. I just hope to be forgiven for them."

Christopher said nothing, although he understood what his father meant. He was subtly beseeching pardon for his crimes, absolution of his sins both of commission and omission. Was he, the innocent victim, ready, willing yet to forgive the trespasses against his mother and himself?

The lore and excitement of the mountains keyed him for the rest of the day—and disturbed his sleep that evening.

He woke around midnight and checked the other cot, which was visibly empty in the firelight. Probably had to pee, he decided. Or had heard the wounded deer moaning and gone on a mercy killing, though there was hardly enough moonlight to guide him. He peered through the windows to detect a lantern in the shadowy woods, but saw none. Lighting the kerosene lamp, he waited a few minutes before calling, "Dad! Hey, Dad, where are you?"

The door opened on a frigid draft, and Jeff entered with a familiar friend, Jack Daniel's, in hand.

"Did I wake you, Chris?"

"No, sir. I woke myself. What's that for?"

"The whiskey? I couldn't sleep, thought it might help." He paused, opening the bottle. "What did you call me a while ago, Chris?"

He glanced away, lowering his head in embarrassment. "What did it sound like?"

"Like Dad, unless my ears or the wind deceived me."

"They didn't."

"What made you say it, son? You never have before."

Christopher shrugged, uncertain. "I don't know. Never felt like it before, I guess. Felt like it then."

"Thanks," Jeff said, humble gratitude in his voice and expression. "Will you have a drink of bourbon and branch water with me? I think you're old enough. I had my first shot of hard liquor at sixteen, to toast one of my father's successful hunts."

"Was he a great hunter?"

"Rabid. Foxes, red and gray. Chased them in hunts all over Virginia and Maryland. Never killed anything but himself, though. We have something more important to celebrate, Chris. Don't you agree?"

Slight hesitation, then positive assent. "Yes, sir."

While Jeff poured the drinks, Christopher told him he

had once got smashed on cheap gin and ended up in the tenement basement with a cheap girl.

His father nodded understandingly. "Was she a virgin?"

"No, but I was."

"Well, there has to be a first time for everybody, with the possible exception of monks and nuns. Were you in love with her?"

"I thought so, at first. Then I learnt she was servicing every ready prick in the neighborhood, which was how she got so experienced. She knew lots of tricks."

"Whores usually do. Innocent girls have to be taught."

They touched mugs, eyes meeting over the rims, the habitual hostility abated in the boy's. Immensely relieved and gratified, Jeff proposed, "To us, and a new alliance! Cheers!"

"Cheers!" Christopher repeated, swallowed the whiskey, and extended his mug for more. "An encore, sir?"

"Better not, son. I wouldn't want you to develop a taste for this corn nectar of the earthly mortals. It's an ugly, vicious habit."

"Then why do you practice it?"

Setting his mug on the mantelpiece, Jeff bent to stoke the fire, toying with the poker until Christopher probed his conscience. "It's because of Mrs. Courtland, isn't it? You couldn't sleep thinking of her and went after your sourmash sedative because of her."

Striking sparks from the glowing logs with the tool, Jeff pondered the embers and ashes that fell through the grate. No point denying it. "Yes."

"What good does it do? Drinking, I mean. If you want her back, why not do as those stags did? Fight!"

"That's the law of the jungle, Chris. Civilized men no longer live by it. Women choose their mates now, and Mrs. Courtland has chosen Major Lawrence."

"I don't think it was choice by preference, sir. I think she was sort of pushed into it, and I—I helped. Shoved might be more accurate."

"Don't blame yourself, Chris. There are too many guilt complexes in this family already."

"But I *am* guilty, sir. I told her—"

"I know, son. I know what you told her. Unfortunately, she believed it."

"Unfortunately?" The boy gazed at him, puzzled. "Then it wasn't true, what you told me that night?"

"It was, and it wasn't, Chris. That is, I didn't know the truth myself at the time. I cared for your mother and think I would have married her had I been free. But I wasn't free, and I was in love with my wife—does that make any sense to you? I was young and pretty mixed up then. The whole goddamned world was crazy and mixed up then. It still is, I'm afraid. My world, anyway. But I hope not yours—at least not anymore."

"Not so much anymore," Christopher murmured after a few moments of assimilation, for he believed Courtland's confession of his youthful confusion in a confused time and situation. Indeed, his mother had also spoken about the insanity, indiscretion, bewilderment, desperation of that incredible world teetering on the brink of bomb craters, threatening to vanish in flame and smoke.

Jeff poured himself another drink before sitting down on his cot. "I'm glad of that, son. Glad that something good came of this mess."

"Well, sir—what're you going to do about it?"

"About what?"

Christopher squared his shoulders. "The mess, sir. Surely you've given it some thought?"

* * *

Oh, yes! he'd thought about it. On every count and from every angle, drunk and sober, rational and irrational, he'd thought about it, and more than once contemplated the same solution those primitive bucks had. He'd also considered the antidote of other women.

Skeets Martin had introduced him to one of his highly voluptuous babes, and after an evening of booze and banter they'd gone to bed together. Fantastic in the sack, Skeets had described Lorna Patterson, and she was that, all right. Erotically talented, totally uninhibited. Her expertise encompassed all the professional innovations, and her own sexuality seemed insatiable. Lorna knew how to rejuvenate a man in exhaustion, how to kindle a waning fire, how to drive her partner beyond his capacity and endurance.

And it was great and diverting while it lasted. But afterwards Jeff was more than a little disgusted with himself, wondering what he was doing in a stranger's arms. They had nothing in common, and he couldn't expect her to understand or care about his personal problems. There was no point even mentioning them. Lorna just wanted a man, any potent stud, and had probably accommodated Frank Benedict and other lecherous friends of Skeets Martin.

While massaging him with musk oil, she hinted that she knew some prominent politicians intimately, including several senators and congressmen and even a cabinet member, but insisted that she was not a prostitute. Couldn't bring herself to take money for it, she declared modestly, although jewels, furs, cars, clothes, trips, rental fees were acceptable. Scruples. Well, there were many kinds of ethics. And though she invited Jeff to frequent her apartment and he was tempted, he never returned.

If he was going to resort to sexual therapy, it should at least be with a sympathetic friend, someone with whom he could do more than copulate, experience more than release of animal tensions. Conversation was important, too.

Shirley Martin came to mind. She seemed to have a gift for understanding misunderstood husbands, apparently excluding only her own. But in reality he couldn't betray Skeets, although he suspected that every other cocksman in their crowd—with the possible exception of Kenneth Cranshaw—had long ago done so. And he really wasn't interested in playing musical beds, anyway. Promiscuity had never been his bag, and the much-touted sexual revolution gaining strength in the country now did not appeal to him. The "key parties," wife-swapping swingers, orgies, repulsed him, in fact. He wanted, needed a meaningful relationship. A commitment. Even in youth he had functioned best on a committed basis: a steady girl in high school, early marriage, and then the foreign affair with Anne Bentley, cleaving unto one mistress while other guys were breaking records in variety and producing bastards wholesale without a qualm. Whatever Carol thought of his fidelity, morality, and sexuality, he was essentially and inherently monogamous—and he actually had an aversion to whores and pity for their desperate patrons.

It occurred to him that he might communicate by more than memos with his secretary. He invited Doris out to dinner, but it was almost a continuation of their day at the office, about as exciting as working late. She wore the same tailored suit and flat heels, the same familiar essence of ink and carbon paper, and discussed business fervently, as if afraid of discussing anything else. Jeff responded mechanically, like a machine digesting data fed into it. And yet there was something sad and even pathetic about her suppressed intensity. She was probably one of those women whose appearance and manner suggested frigidity but who were actually ice-capped volcanoes ready to erupt at the slightest male advance—and he had no wish to liberate a passion he lacked the desire and possibly even the capacity to appease. He would only lose his self-respect and a damned good secretary. He took Doris home to her efficiency apartment in Georgetown, and left her there, without so much as a touch of hands much less of lips.

On the way to Alexandria, Jeff drove by the Wilton house, intending to stop if a light was on. Margaret would welcome him, he knew. She had made it clear in their telephone conversations that, while she admired and respected Major Lawrence and believed him truly in love with her daughter, she did not believe it was mutual and felt that marriage between them would be a grave and tragic mistake. Her tacit alliance with Jeffrey was one of the curious aspects of the case, for he had not known his mother-in-law was so fond of him. And while he imagined her concern was primarily for the child caught in this marital tug of war, he was nonetheless grateful for her sympathy and support.

His plan, then, was simply to go up to Carol's room, tell her he had changed his mind and there would be no divorce, unless she was willing to fight it out in court. If so, she could expect no quarter from him. It would be a brutal no-holds-barred contest, with Major Lawrence named corespondent and his commission at stake, as well as her reputation; that he would disgrace and scandalize them all, and to hell with honor, chivalry, civility, and the rest of the antiquated armor that characterized the modern cuckold. Maybe the clubbing cavemen had a better idea, after all, or the latter-day duelists, or even the wild animals that used tooth and claw and horns.

But the house on Cameron Street was dark that night, and Jeff drove on to his own residence on the Potomac.

Such boorish conduct, he told himself, was all it would
have taken to convince Carol that he was a real son-of-a-
bitch, if she still had doubts. After putting the car in the
garage, he went inside and phoned Ken to say that he
would sign the papers as soon as he returned from the
mountains.

"Did you have to decide at this crazy goddamn hour?"
Ken asked, yawning.

"Now or maybe never," Jeff replied and hung up.

Now Christopher was questioning his acquiescence. Why?
Was it important to him? Did he miss Carol, too? Want the
three of them together again as a family as much as Jeff
himself did?

"What's on your mind, son?"

"Just thinking, sir. Women are pretty much alike, aren't
they?"

"In some ways, yes. Not easy to understand."

"Definitely not," Christopher agreed, frowning over his
own female enigma and dilemma.

"A universal male complaint, son. But I suspect yours
has to do with a particular girl, right? Miss Cranshaw."

Christopher sighed in assent. "She does some stupid
things and gets miffed over nothing, and I think she'd
drive a chap batty if he gave her half a chance."

"But you want to give her the chance?"

"That's about the size of it, sir."

"Send her a bid to the Hitchfield Cadet Hop," Jeff
suggested. "That used to be reserved for Best Girls Only."

"Still is, and I've thought of it. But we're not on the
best of terms at present. Besides, I don't think her folks
approve of me."

"Where'd you get that idea?"

"They were rather cool to me toward the end of the summer. Perhaps they thought, as you and Mrs. Courtland, that Kay and I were getting involved?"

"Were you getting involved?"

"Sort of," Christopher admitted. "And I suppose we could have got real tangled up, you know? So perhaps they did the right thing separating us. Right for their daughter, anyway, and proper. Kay didn't want to go back to Abbey Hall, and they probably feared we might try to elope or something."

"You care that much for her, Chris?"

"Enough to marry her?" He shrugged. "Shoot, I don't know. We're just kids, and marriage is heavy stuff."

"Real heavy, Chris. Try to remember that if you and Kay get together again. If you just want to play around, there are plenty of willing girls. Like that wench you had in London. You knew she was easy, didn't you?"

But that was a drastic mistake, and Jeff realized and regretted it immediately. His son was quiet and thoughtful, finally posing the dreaded question. "Was my mother easy?"

"No, Christopher, not at all. I knew her several months before we became lovers. We were mature adults, you know, and there were extenuating circumstances. But Anne was a lady in every respect. Only a very fine woman could have raised a child like you, alone. You can be proud of her. Anybody, even a saint, can make a mistake, Chris. I've made plenty. And Anne may have made one with me. But I'm not sorry about it, because I got you. A man would have to be a mighty fool to regret having a son like you."

"Even if he lost his beloved wife in the process?"

Jeff uncorked the bottle again, then hesitated. "That's another matter, Chris. She has found someone else, and I hope she'll be happy with him. We can't have everything, can we?''

Christopher cupped his chin in an attitude of serious meditation. "It seems to me I read somewhere once that twentieth-century gallantry is often masquerade—a social suit of armor to shield gentlemen from their own timidity or cowardice, and the true knights of old would never have employed such subterfuge in personal affairs of the heart. You were brave and bold enough in the war, weren't you? I shouldn't think you could just meekly and mildly surrender your fair lady to that love-warrior now . . .''

"I get your point, son, and I don't believe you read that anywhere. You're just adept at fencing words. And since you don't seem to lack either boldness or courage, why not apply that clever maneuver to yourself by sending Miss Kay Cranshaw that bid?''

"You think she'd accept?''

"It's worth a try, isn't it?''

"I was going to suggest that about Mrs. Courtland.''

"You already did,'' Jeff responded, shunning another drink. "Why don't we go to Alexandria tomorrow?''

"What about our hunting?''

"It's rather served its purpose, hasn't it?''

"Rather,'' Christopher agreed cogently. "Mrs. Wilton will be having Thanksgiving dinner, won't she? Truth is, sir, I'd as soon feast on tame turkey as wild. Reckon she'd invite us?''

The word "reckon,'' not in his vocabulary before his arrival in Virginia, made his father smile. "I'm positive, son. Incidentally, she sent along a gift for you. A nice sweater, made it herself. You don't have to wear it if you don't want to, but thank her for it.''

"Aunt Agatha used to knit things for me,'' he recalled. "I wore them. I'll wear Grand Mam's sweater, too.''

"That would make her very happy, Chris. Especially the Grand Mam."

"Oh, well," he said sheepishly, "that's what she wanted me to call her. I don't know why, but you know how women are. Doesn't hurt to please and humor them, does it?" A thoughtful pause crinkled his brow. "Maybe you should call them first? Say the hunters didn't have any luck and are starving for some home cooking and family atmosphere. That should get their sympathy. And an invitation."

Jeff grinned, rubbing his stubbled chin. "Of course we'll have to spruce up a bit. Shave and scrub ourselves in the rain-barrel. We don't want to go in looking like Crusoe and Friday. You know how ladies are about men's appearance."

"Yeah, Kay just raved about my uniform. As if I were a general or something. And I must admit Hitchfield cadets do look spiffy. All that spit-and-polish, I guess."

"Wait till she sees you in your dress uniform! I trust you can dance well, Cadet Courtland?"

"Well, I don't have two left feet. But maybe I could practice some . . . with Mrs. Courtland. I bet she's a terrific dancer!"

"Yes, she is," Jeff reflected. "She was always the prom queen at Foxcroft School and Sweet Briar College, and the belle of the hunt balls." He stared into the fire a few wistful moments, then said, "We'd better get some rest, Chris. It's a long hard road back."

"But we'll make it, won't we, Dad?"

"We'll make it, son. God willing."

It was the first time Christopher had ever heard his father acknowledge the need of Providence. It was, in fact, the first time Christopher had consciously acknowledged that need himself. God willing, he thought, lying back on the cot and reaching for the U.S. Army blanket.

Highly Acclaimed
Historical Romances From Berkley